I0599932

EVERYTHING IS CONNECTED

CODED

THE CONNECTION SAGA

DAVID D. MYERS

Copyright © 2025 by David D. Myers

First edition October 2025

Book and map design by Natalia Junqueira

ISBN 979-8-9996521-1-9 (paperback)
ISBN 979-8-9996521-2-6 (hardback)

www.daviddmyers.com

For those who seek a brighter future

AREA 1
EZRA COLEMAN

THE ESTABLISHMENT

MILLENNIA

THE ES

ARIADNE'S
HIDEOUT

ARCADIA

CENTRAL
SQUARE

TECHDON

SCAVENGERS

CYBOURNE

BLACK WEB

FORT
LEGION

FORT
BATTALION

ENLIGHTE
TO

AREA 2
LUCIAN CASTOR

AOE ▶ [AREAS OF ENLIGHTENMENT]

AREA 3
JOYCE COLEMAN

NEOPOLIS

NORTH
BURNVIL

OUTH
RNVIL

ASHLAND

DARKONIA

DARK
PORT

DROWNARK

AREA 4
ESMERAY NOX

AREA 3
JOYCE COLEMAN

NEOPOLIS

NORTH
BURNVIL

OUTH
RNVIL

ASHLAND

DARKONIA

DARK
PORT

DROWNARK

AREA 4
ESMERAY NOX

CONTENTS

PROLOGUE

An island on the Pacific Ocean

One can only feel true darkness after witnessing true devastation, like seeing their parents shot and their home burn in flames.

As I stand in the mud, lightning streaks above, providing the only light breaking through the night sky. Heavy rain violently pelts my body, leaving no way for me to hide. Thunder cracks as I wait with other captives. A massive structure stands before us: tall and jagged, unlike anything I've seen before. The rain makes it almost impossible to properly map out the details.

We stand in a single-file line, with holocuffs singeing our wrists anytime we move our hands in a way that seems like an escape. Waves mimic my heartbeat, thumping against my chest as they crash against the island's edges, sending a heavy mist through the air. The roar of rushing water drowns out the cries of my neighboring prisoners. Saltwater against my lips tastes like the Pacific Ocean.

1

Through the periodic flashes above, glimpses of the darkness and the isolated island we stand on flare, provoking a sense of loneliness.

"Do you think we'll be okay?" the girl beside me asks. Her voice is dry, weak, and shallow. Sunken eyes show a lack of sleep, and defeated brows appear weaker than she sounds.

"I don't know," I whisper.

An Enlightenment Agent, dressed in black, with too many weapons to count, stalks toward me and slaps me across the face with the end of his rifle. A strong metallic taste fills my mouth as I fall to my knees, which crack against the ground, sending intense pain through my body. My skin flares with heat at the want to strike back, but I know it'll only make things worse. I grip the soggy dirt as blood drips down my chin. The agent grabs my hair, forcing me to stand and meet his dark eyes. They dig into me as a red ring glows, stalling my breath.

"Speak again," he spits, "and there will be far worse."

He shoves me back in line and pedals to his spot with the other agents, keeping his gaze on me. I close my eyes to ignore the waves as my heart rate plummets, but the memories of my mother and father keep it from shattering completely. Their voices and smiles fill me with enough warmth to keep me going. They taught me to live, to love— and, most of all, to survive.

"Move along!" a man shouts, startling me.

The doors to the entrance cast a white glow behind him as his suit attire suggests he's in charge. Lightning flashes, briefly revealing his face. An 'x' carved beneath his eye makes me tremble. The other agents sneer as their guns press against our backs, pushing us along. One captive ahead of me stumbles and falls in the mud.

"Get him out of here!" the leader barks.

An agent grabs his cuff and drags him around the facility to an unknown place. The prisoner yells and screams but is quickly thwarted by the strike of a rifle to the side of his head. I flinch from the strike and force myself to look away. There's no reason for them to treat us this way when we've done nothing wrong. Like animals awaiting the slaughter.

The girl who spoke to me remains by my side. Her light gray eyes find mine with softness in them.

"I'm Wren," she says. "What's your name?"

I get a sense she feels my dread, but I don't answer as the inside of the building comes into focus—a place my parents never wanted me to be.

An Enlightenment Prison.

The urge to run rises in my gut, but the cuffs' heat reminds me I can't. Thunder growls, causing Wren and me to jump. An agent's eyes move with us as we continue through the doors. The blindingly white interior forces my eyes to readjust with the drastic change from the outside. The circular base holds cells along its wall. At the center, a silver pillar carries an elevator through it.

"What is this place?" Wren asks.

"A prison," I whisper, keeping my eyes on the nearby agents.

"What do you think they are going to do with us?"

Her question reminds me of why my parents feared me ever seeing an Enlightenment Prison. Experiments and torture are what they use them for. Wren's eyes beg for an answer to her question, but I can't bring myself to make her feel worse than she already does, so I lie.

"They'll hold us captive."

"I hope we stay near each other at least," she says.

"Me too."

Part of me hopes we will be close together because my parents always told me the goal for these places was to isolate and completely break people.

That's a feeling I never want to experience.

4 months later...

Every prisoner is gathered in a central room. The circular space is covered in glass, and agents surround us. My reflection in one mirror makes me flinch. With barely anything to eat, my body has become unrecognizable. I want to leave this place, but I am yet to find a way out. My hands fidget, causing the cuffs to rattle.

The agent leader stands on a levitated platform, peering down at us, hands gripped tight on a metallic railing. His head moves from side to side, watching and waiting.

"What's your name?" Wren whispers as the leader's head moves away from us.

It's been months, and she's still asking for my name. I don't know why, but I refuse to give it to her. Maybe because it'll connect us, which spells trouble in a place like this. Either of us could be taken away, never to be seen again. But given we've been together for some time now, I settle on a compromise.

"Nexia," I tell her my code name.

The scar along her eye pinches my chest. The blue flash of an active node reminds me that my node is not far from being installed. It's been years since I've had one; my parents hacked mine previously, like they did theirs, keeping me from being seen.

"Pretty. What does it mean?"

"Long story."

"I'd love to hea—"

She stops abruptly as the leader's gaze finds us. My heartbeat thuds through my body, traveling and touching each anxious nerve. A moment passes, and he turns away, allowing us to breathe.

"I'd love to hear it," she finishes.

There's a mystery in her stormy gray eyes, a cipher to be broken. I want to explore them, to grant me an escape from the four walls that seem to close in with each passing day. But, in her eyes, I'm free.

"I'll tell you later," I whisper.

She smiles and grabs my hand. Instinctively, I want to pull away before a guard sees, but the warmth makes me think otherwise. We look at each other, and I crave the idea of kissing her—to be lost with each other, away from this prison.

"I want to get out of here," she says.

"Me too."

The leader claps his hands together, mimicking a bomb echoing through the space. Our heads snap upward, commanded by the stature of the agent.

"All prisoners who don't have a node move to lane 'A'!" he shouts. "And everyone else move to lane 'B'."

My stomach drops as I move to the lane of uninstalled nodes. It's my turn. My lips quiver as a tear falls, and I do my best to fight the urge to break. Wren provides a soft smile for comfort, but it doesn't help. The longing to be free intensifies, and I'm forced to believe I may be here forever.

---

8 months later...

"Nexia isn't your real name, is it?" Wren questions.

"Why do you want to know?" I ask, looking through the small-barred hole at the white light of the crescent-shaped moon.

It provides enough light to our metallic coated cell to see the bloodstains on her face and mats embedded at the root of her hair. I'm sure mine looks no different. The cell's darkness conceals the rest of the pain we've both endured: surgeries, welts from the batons and electric whips to keep us silent... The deaths of other captives who tried escaping create a heavy fog in my mind, and I wish I could do something about it.

As I blink, my eye stings, still not healed from my node's re-installation.

"Because," she whispers.

My eyes trail toward her, and I find myself lost in a sea of gray.

"Because..." I repeat, coaxing her with a soft tone.

"I like you."

My heart flutters, and I can't resist the warmth flooding my veins. I want to say it back, but I don't know how. My mind forces me to reject it.

"You don't know me," I say bitterly, returning to the gap in the wall.

Her hand finds my face, the softness igniting my senses.

"I know you better than you think," she says, turning me back toward her. "I've never known anyone so mesmerizing, who doesn't see it in themselves. Even if I don't know your real name, I know more about you than anyone I've ever met. You've shown me what it's like to move on from fear and embrace what my other emotions have to offer." she inhales deeply as she reminisces. "From the moment I met you on the outside of this prison, I didn't want to be away from you for a minute. During the first few months of pain, you showed me kindness when you didn't have to. After their first surgery on me, I thought I was nothing, but there you were....Your drive and determination to oppose all of what these agents do is inspiring and I can only hope to be half the person you are."

She looks at my lips and slowly places hers against mine. Delicate and natural. I want to be here, in this moment, forever. As she pulls away, her lips curve upward, forming a smile.

A smile that could make a god bow.

"We'll get out of here," I say. "And when we do, I promise I'll tell you."

Our heads touch as boots approach our cell door.

1 year later...

Wren and I sprint through a corridor. The stench of death hangs in the air. Children and families are being held captive for tests, eventually left to die, a fate we are desperately trying to avoid. We need to get out of here. Now. There's no time left.

Alarms scream through the prison from an explosion we caused as a distraction. It echoes with a piercing sound. Boots hitting the ground make blood rush through my veins and adrenaline forces me to continue. It took two years of endurance to formulate this plan, and I will not waste this moment.

We squeeze into the metal shaft. My hands and knees against the cold surface sends a chill through my body. Voices travel through the ventilation, forcing me to relax through deep breaths. Behind me, Wren's sporadic breaths ignite a sense of urgency.

"How are you avoiding the agents and getting us through the prison?" she asks me.

We increase our speed, our feet thudding against the metal frame. Wren's question simmers as I imagine the plan.

"I'm a hacker," I say.

We crawl through the tight space. Over my shoulder, Wren's eyes show the questions she wants to ask. Two years and I never told her who I was.

"So, I was right," Wren says.

"About?"

"Nexia not being your real name."

"Out of all the things to consider, you choose that? What's with you and names?"

I kick open the exit, landing on the prison's base level. The bright white light, as it did when I first saw it, makes my eyes water. As the alarms continue to blare, I assist Wren out of the shaft.

"Names make us who we are," she says. "They give us identity, and when we express ours to others, they connect us. And..."

Her black hair and silver gaze stop me. I push the loose strands of her hair to get a complete view of the face I have grown to love. The angle in her eyes when she smiles and the deep lines of her brows. Soft lines form her chin as my eyes find the scar an agent's gun made to keep her silent. My lips wrap around hers, and when I release, she smiles.

"Nexia is my code name. My real name is Ariadne."

She kisses me and holds me tight.

"I love you."

My heart twitches, and my core erupts with a warmth I could only ever imagine. "I love you too."

I grab her hand, and we sweep through a corridor.

"If I ever become a hacker, my code name will be Glitch. And then we can hack the world together."

"Why Glitch?"

"That's for me to know and you to find out."

I smile at the thought, but it quickly vanishes when we reach the outside. A Chief Enlightenment Agent waits. Broad shoulders and immense height. Lightning above illuminates the 'x' engraved on his cheek, confirming he is the same agent who has unleashed his codex of pain since our arrival. Thunder warns above as the ocean's waves pick up speed. The night sky limits my vision, and the fog over the island makes it almost impossible to see.

The agent being seemingly alone gives me hope of making it out alive. We have the advantage of numbers and speed.

I approach him, and his fist crashes against my jaw. I'm reeled back, trying to catch my breath. Wren strikes him with quick jabs, something I didn't know she could do, but he endures them. He grabs one of her fists in mid-motion and rotates it, tearing a scream from the back of her throat. He kicks her in the midsection, and she rolls through the mud.

Heat travels through my veins at the sight of Wren's pain, and I rush toward the CEA with tight fists. He evades me easily, quicker than I thought. The CEA grabs me by the throat, and with all my strength, I try to overpower him, even as he dangles me over the edge of the island. The waves thrash with intensity. Through blurry eyes, Wren stirs on the ground. A wicked smile stretches across the CEA's face as he teases the idea of dropping me in the ocean. The grin sharpens. If I survive the fall, it'll be impossible to fight the current.

Wren clambers to her feet. She kicks the back of his knee, and he falls as I tumble to the ground. The CEA gathers himself to rise when Wren catches my eye. A dangerous look, yet something behind her gaze reminds me of the girl I met two years ago, in this exact spot. A tear falls from her eye as she sprints.

"Wren!" I shout. "Noooo!"

My voice echoes above the waves as she crashes into him. Together, they lunge off the edge and hit the water with a deep splash.

No, this can't be happening.

I crawl my way to the edge in search of life, moving my eyes across the waves, screaming her name, hoping to find a sign. Heartache fills my chest, pounding relentlessly. I sob, staring at the ocean. Its deadly waves give no reason to hope for Wren's survival.

Following the original plan, I wait near the facility in a hidden location for a ship to arrive. It does, but I don't want to leave. I want to kill every single agent stepping out. More captives are handcuffed and wait to be taken into the facility. Like the day I met Wren.

They took her from me. The same way they took my parents. My chest swells, and I promise never to get attached. Never let anyone in. It always ends badly. Death always follows but never takes me. Only the ones I love.

I find it in myself to board the ship, hiding in a dark compartment. The engine throttles, and my stomach lurches. Tears well behind closed eyes as I force down an agonizing scream. The memories of Wren and my parents bury me under a broken heart. I grit my teeth, and the heartache morphs into determination, making my hands clench until they shake from the angst to avenge everyone I lost.

I now have nothing left to lose.

As the tears fall, I vow to go after every person involved, even if it costs my life.

FRAMEWORK

1

6 years later, Arcadia Sector

Expect nothing. Prepare for anything.

My parents' words echo in my head. The words they taught me to live by. Survive by. And the lesson I'll remember as vital.

In front of me stands a building known as an Enlightenment Complex. It contains the first clue to solving the murder of my parents and identifying those responsible for the suffering I endured six years ago. It rises high, towering over the connected buildings, appearing to sway from my view at the base, making my stomach turn.

"Ms. Young," Amity, my most trusted confidant, says in my ear, "readings show dozens of hostiles inside the building."

"Enlightenment Agents?"

"Indeed."

I ignore the rising nausea and focus on the task I've trained for years to do—ever since breaking out of prison. This moment is the opportunity to gather information about the people who snatched everything from me.

The quiet makes my lungs expand tightly as my surroundings take my focus from across the paved road. No civilians are in the building, only agents, identified by their attire—suits embedded with various weapons. Their eyes glow against the dark, an active node recording what they see.

On my wrist, a holoscreen glows with red dots, scattered in a 3-dimensional scan of the complex. I pinch the image, zooming in to watch where the dots travel.

"Amity, lock in their patrol points to find a pattern," I say.

"Affirmative."

The red hues of the agent's eyes against the dark windows of the building paint a sinister image as thunder creeps through the night sky. Storms have a way of finding me.

"Let's make this quick," I say.

"The hostile patrols are now loading, Ms. Young."

My wrist vibrates from the notification, stealing my attention.

"It appears," Amity continues, "there is a pattern where they stalk the perimeter before switching off with other agents on the next floor. Your target—the central control—is on the first level, and they are safeguarding it."

"Excellent intel," I say. "Drone."

My drone emerges from its holster on my belt line. Hovering above my shoulder, its silent wings flip the air through my hair, sending a soft chill through my body.

"The task is simple," I say, more to reassure myself than Amity.

"Indeed," Amity follows, "with weak encryptions in place."

"All we need is a quick cipher to break their code."

"Opening the central core."

"Allowing easy access," I finish.

I input an algorithm for a cipher onto my holoscreen, copying it to the drone's interface. I move to a nearby alleyway, concealing myself in its dark shadows. Navigating the drone from my wrist, it enters the building as an agent leaves. The agent walks by the alley, and I tense, covering the holoscreen on my wrist. His steps move farther away, and I breathe, resuming the drone's vision.

"Agent incoming on the left," Amity says.

I evade the agent's view, guiding the drone beneath a nearby staircase.

That was close.

The darkness inside gives me an advantage in keeping the drone concealed. The tiled walls of the complex reveal the agent's shadow as they pass. Like Amity projected, the agent swaps with another heading down the steps. Resuming their path, the new agent walks to the opposite side of the hexagon-shaped building. At the center, a map of the facility glows along a square column, providing cover from the new agent's eyes.

"You'll have about thirty seconds before the next swap, Ms. Young," Amity warns.

Using the drone, I quickly navigate the space, following the agent at a moderate distance, using the shadows cast by the lights from the outside. Ahead, the door holding my target appears.

Shit! An encrypted lock.

"Ms. Young, something blocked this lock against the scan."

My mental clock warns me of five seconds before the next swap—a new agent's arrival. Ideas on how to crack the encrypted lock in minimal time run rampant in my mind.

As I approach the door with the drone, I fiddle with my holoscreen and find the answer: an electromagnetic pulse or EMP. It's always ready and armed for my use.

Expect nothing, prepare for anything.

I activate it, and from the outside, a purple flash illuminates the building. The door unlocks as the incoming agent falls to the ground, knocked out by the disruption in their node, allowing quick entry into the room.

My wrist glows with a golden hue, signaling the link I need to copy. Alarms blare, notifying me of my depleted EMP. The sound electrifies my nerves, forcing my heart to increase blood flow.

"Ms. Young," Amity says.

"I know."

Controlling my breathing, I analyze the situation. The red dots of the hostiles advance through the building, on their way to the room, forcing me to act. With no time to be finicky, I input a mass copy code to take anything I can.

"Ten seconds, Ms. Young."

My stomach drops in response.

Five, I think to myself, half until the agents appear, and the other to get my drone out.

The copied data reveals itself on my wrist, and I swiftly guide the drone back through the door and out of the main entrance before the arriving agents notice.

"Excellent work, Ms. Young," Amity says.

The rain finally breaks free and showers the city with a refreshing chill, bringing me to throw up my hood.

"Your parents' words proved efficient once again."

"I'll always remember," I say, "to expect nothing and prepare for anything."

With my drone at my shoulder and files secure, I jog down the road smiling, reminiscing over the words that always save my life.

2

I sip a glass of tea, which satisfies my nerves and brings me to relaxation. The bittersweet flavor focuses my mind as if its ingredients contain serotonin. The warm liquid sloshes in my mouth, and as I softly swallow, I smile with a deep sense of contentment.

The rain catches me off guard as thousands of drops pound my rooftop, adding a therapeutic sound to the feeling my tea brings. It's a perfect way to start my day. My parents knew everything I would like in a home or environment, and they gave it to me with this hideout.

Home.

I hate saying hideout, but I always feel inclined to because of the ignorance that traps society. I remind myself that it's not society's fault. Not entirely. The government capitalized when the world was in a state of decay, feeding off everyone's fears.

"Ms. Young," Amity says over my inter-network.

"Yes?"

"I safely analyzed the data from yesterday's infiltration of the Enlightenment Complex for malware and hidden worms. It is available to be reviewed when you're ready."

"Thank you, Amity."

Amity, my advanced A.I. system, with the ability to do things people would never believe, was developed by my parents, to protect and serve me. With it, I can see what's happening anywhere in the nation. For a limited time, I can breach impenetrable systems before triggering Enlightenment Agents. It's more than a system to help me hack. It is my only friend. The only thing I can trust outside of myself. Amity helps and guides me through the times when I'm most alone.

Sometimes, I believe Amity is my inner consciousness speaking to me out loud. It finishes sentences and reads my mind a lot. My bond with Amity is unbreakable.

The rain continues its descent on the world and pounds my roof, relentlessly mimicking the sound of fingers on a holoboard.

It's fall. Beautiful, glorious fall.

My favorite season.

The temperature in my home is cool, and with the help of the outside weather and tech to mimic it on the inside, it's perfect. Cozy and nurturing to my skin, there's no place I'd rather be.

Iris, the titanium-framed device on my wrist, sends a vibrating notification through my arm, distracting me from my embrace with the cool air and warm tea. It's another trusted device that gets me through everything. My Inter-network, Responsive, Invasive System; Iris connects to the network provided throughout the nation and feeds my device with the information I need to complete tasks. It's essential to my hacking abilities.

Like a cuff or bangle, it hugs my wrist. Most would think it would be heavy because of the titanium frame, but it's the opposite. Lightweight and easy to carry, I don't know it's there until I use it. When it isn't activated, it appears as an ordinary accessory, innocuous to the eyes of those who want to end the hacker movement.

Hiding in plain sight.

With the swipe of a finger, I bring it to life. It slowly rotates, opening wide from my wrist to mid-forearm. Above it, a holoscreen displays notifications, updates, and information I stole from the Enlightenment Complex yesterday. I walk through the hall from my bedroom, watching the downpour outside. The open window layout grants an unmatched view, drawing me to walk toward it.

This home from my parents sits on the outskirts of Arcadia. Many windows grant me a perfect view of the Pacific Ocean. Vast and glorious, with no end in sight. It makes me think of the freedom this world once had before the Enlightenment's takeover. Blue lightning streaks through the dark clouds above as my eyes try to track its movement. Thunder escapes with a low growl after a passing moment as the sun suffocates behind a blanket of gray, trying to poke holes and be free.

Streams of water slide down in curvy lines, tracking toward the bottom frame of the window. As the rain grows stronger and covers my view with mist, fogging the glass, I turn and make my way toward the center of the living space. The primary seat, an all-white couch, hovers and eclipses the round table. In front of it, on the wall, the letter 'A' hangs like a portrait, making me think of my mother.

The notifications continue to amplify the nerves in my arm, prompting me to move. My hands find their way onto my holoboard as I sit in the primary seat. The table activates with a touch of the board. A blue sphere activates, and I begin my search for new information that will lead to the people who murdered my parents. The stolen files open and scatter into the air in front of me like a web. I could have taken more if I'd been faster, but this is a start.

I read through each folder, focusing on the key aspects: bills passed, schedules for care packages, meetings with other nations, and national addresses.

I find nothing. They're hiding.

The Enlightenment has never revealed itself, and I don't believe they ever will, but they've never been this quiet. However, these stolen files provoke an idea in my mind.

"Amity," I say, "scan the Area for anything out of the ordinary."

"Scanning, Ms. Young," Amity replies.

I sip more tea, closing my eyes to bask in its warmth. My parents' smiles flash through my mind, filling my heart. When I reopen my eyes, it aches like the first time I lost them.

"Scanning complete," Amity says, erasing my heartache. "There have been a few riots in the last twenty-four hours, Ms. Young."

Riots, I repeat to myself. That's impossible.

"Where?" I ask urgently. "When was the most recent?"

"Arcadia Sector."

"Where in Arcadia?"

I rise from the couch and head to my armory. Through the narrow hallway, I turn into a room housing my equipment for outside operations. The lights hum as they activate, triggering the holograms and displaying my weapons and tactical gear. Along the walls are my staff and a trace gun, ready for me to grab. The opposite side holds pods belonging to my suits. It rotates, waiting for biometrics to be released. Ahead, levitating in the center is my hoverboard, spec.

"Center square, Ms. Young," Amity continues. "Routing."

That's ten minutes away. I can get there in no time. I secure Iris and grab my staff. Made from tungsten, the finest and strongest metal, it is my go-to weapon. I gather my remaining gear: a holoboard, drone, and an EMP for emergencies, recalling my mission yesterday. I take one last sip of tea and sprint out of the door.

It hisses behind me, triggering the lock mechanism.

The rain plummets to earth, harder than yesterday. My suit, black as night with traces of silver, makes the water slide off like the back of a duck. I breathe in the fresh scent of rain, refreshing and delightful, making a tingle flow through me. It's good to be outside, following another lead.

3

The Areas of Enlightenment, commonly known as the AOE—was the name given to the country after the success of reviving it. Four areas split the nation, each with sectors controlled by a single authoritarian figure who reports to the Enlightenment.

Area 1 has four sectors: Millennia, Techdon, Cybourne, and Arcadia. Millennia is the most guarded sector, Techdon is known for nothing other than technology, Cybourne is unknown to most, and Arcadia—where I live—is the largest sector, holding the largest population among the four.

Wind flows through my hair, pushing past my skin and caressing it with a gentle chill. I glide on the paneled roads with spec—a hoverboard designed by my parents, which makes for a much easier way to travel other than flars and caerials.

Flars are mostly owned by upper-class citizens who serve the Enlightenment as agents or people who have practically sold themselves to their cause. The sky is littered with them as they sail above me, headed to their destinations.

Caerials are for those that don't have the money for flars. They can't reach high altitudes, but hover above the ground, gliding across paneled roads.

Spec is another device I hold dear to my heart, similar to Amity and Iris. Sometimes I think my parents were trying to prepare me for their death. The thought strangles my heart, imagining if they felt that way the entire time they were training me.

Pushing the thoughts back, I glide down the paneled road, looking at pedestrians walking the streets with signs on the opposite side. My speed makes Arcadia's grand architecture look like a blur of flashing lights when I max it out.

Ahead is Arcadia's Central Square, only recognizable by the large globe floating in the air. It will forever remind us of the time of Enlightenment and why they are so needed.

I slow to an even-paced glide, bringing everything into focus. My speed gradually continues to reduce until Spec disengages from the panels, transforming into a metal plate that fits easily in a side pocket.

The dark gray in the sky warns with a flash of lightning—threatening the earth with more rain. Beneath me, with each step I take, my boots splash the puddled water as my eyes take in the atmosphere that breathes with technology.

Large-scale buildings painted in glass stretch high in the sky, past the limit of all flars. Above me, a monorail glides along its track, with passengers eagerly looking through the window. The silver streaks past, releasing air as it curves around buildings. More paneled roads come into view as I pass one of my favorite places to go when I don't know my next plan.

The Panoramic Diner.

The fresh scent of bread being made makes my mouth water. A tasteful aroma of breakfast fills the sidewalk as I pass it, wishing I wasn't in a hurry. Looking through the glass, I see it's relatively full for the morning.

My head swivels toward the opposite side of the road as the chatter among people rouses my attention. They dress in black, loose-fitting clothes and walk with a sense of urgency. One man glances at me, revealing the blue hue in their eyes, and I quickly turn, increasing the pace of my walk.

Unlike Enlightenment Agents, whose nodes reveal red, light blue coloring shines in the eyes of ordinary citizens. The glow is the camera lens reflecting light, recording everything the wearer sees.

"Amity," I say. "Is the node blocker in effect?"

"Affirmative, Ms. Young. No node can record you. If it does, you'll be registered as Nexia, and your profile will be hidden."

I proceed toward the Central Square, lowering my head in case a familiar face finds me. The globe at the center draws nearer, causing my heart to flutter with anticipation and worry. I've always hated crowds and now I'm walking into a mosh pit of protesters. I don't understand how this is happening and why they all aren't dead. The Enlightenment has demonstrated the power they have to detonate the node, killing people instantly for things much smaller than this.

Why not now? Something's not right.

I slow my pace to get a better grasp on the situation.

"The Enlightenment is the future," a man shouts.

He stands, waving his hands as he continues to chant the words. A few people huddle around him, attracting more attention. The crowd continuously grows, with more people shouting about the saviors of the country, but in the midst of it all, something more shocking can be heard.

People with elevated holograms appear and chant the exact opposite. Listening to the crowd's screams about control and power ignites the rally with an electrifying buzz. Tyrants taking over the world, unlawfulness, and people demanding the country is in a terrible place. I continue to move my eyes through the horde, finding holo-signs about the Enlightenment not being who they say they are.

Across the field of bodies lie hundreds of active nodes. Like stars in the night sky, shimmering with an eerie effect.

"Nexia!" My code name escapes through a moment of silence.

I turn my head and find Trace, a liaison who always seems to have current information on the Enlightenment.

"Over here," he says, gesturing for me to join him in a nearby alleyway.

I walk toward him, crossing the empty road and joining his side.

"Long time no see," he says in a low whisper.

His wet hair and clothing let me know he has been in the rain for some time. He wears a soaked gray, long-sleeved shirt with black cargo pants. Wires extend from the pockets and connect to multiple outlets on his body. He shows no shame in the amount of technology he lugs around.

"I could say the same," I say, lowering my hood as the black waves of my hair flow down my shoulders.

"What are you doing here?" he asks.

"Figuring out what the hell is happening."

"A lot," he says, lowering his mask to reveal the bottom half of his face.

"Make it quick," I say, looking out toward the crowd, which has added at least another hundred people.

"There's word that the Enlightenment may make an appearance. I don't know where or when, but apparently they've grown increasingly anxious about the state of the nation."

He surveys his surroundings as his words seep into my mind.

"How can you be sure?" I ask, regaining his attention.

"Oh, come on, Nexia." He laughs. "They don't call me Trace for nothing."

His slanted eyes make me withdraw the question. He's always had a knack for getting accurate information whenever I need it.

"Anything else?" I ask, making my way out of the alley.

He gazes at my lips and my brow furrows. A rush of heat travels through my blood, making my hands damp. I quickly ball them into fists, avoiding a memory of us trying to resurface. I pull my hood over my head and exit before he can make any further advancements.

"Stay safe, Nexia," he says, leaving in the opposite direction.

The Enlightenment making an in-person appearance makes my chest tight. My nerves sting my body with the want to know where. No one knows what the creators of the nation look like. Upon seizing control, they promised a unique world where our inability to see them wouldn't matter, as it would be a nation defined by unity. In the archives, it states the country's former government craved public attention, disregarding the needs of the citizens and focusing on themselves, creating a divide. So the Enlightenment decided against it and has since been only voices.

But it makes me wonder. If the Enlightenment decide to show their faces, what does it mean for their prior promise?

I creep through the crowd, pushing past people and getting closer to a podium set up with too many holophones to count. A man is escorted to take his place in front of the podium, which extends when he steps in front of it. The escorts turn on their heels in unison, exiting the stage on opposite ends. The man gets comfortable in his stand and when he walks closer to speak, the crowd instantly dies as if he hit pause on the world.

My intuition makes my eyes survey the surrounding area. Snipers on the rooftops, pointed guns, scouring their world below, searching. Gasps and murmurs grab my attention from the surrounding scenes, forcing my eyes to follow the hands of people pointing toward the podium.

Four people walk, one after the other, and take position behind the man on the podium. They can be mistaken for bodyguards, but I can tell they aren't by the cloaks draped on their shoulders, each embroidered with an insignia shining bright through gray light cast by the rain. A mesmerizing gold forms an emblem in the center of each, and gorgeous red traces the cloaks, outlining their edges with perfection. A gentle breeze floats by, caressing the cloaks, making them glisten as if they were embedded with the finest diamonds. They are the finest pieces of cloth I've seen in Area 1.

Each figure has their hood covering their faces except for one, who's wearing a stunning black hat tilted down. They remain still. Positioned that way, in their all-black attire, it's almost like they're shadows.

They are not here out of coincidence or for the normal government announcements. This is different. This is something major, and it feels sinister. There's a long silence before the man speaks. I tap Iris for audio recording, and I scan the area to mark the quickest escape.

Expect nothing, prepare for anything.

He talks about the state of the AOE and how beneficial it was for the Enlightenment to implement the node, all its successes at transforming society for the better. I ignore his banter and my focus transfers to the four people behind him.

He's been talking for a few minutes now and they haven't moved an inch or said a word. Rechecking my surroundings, the world has changed. The snipers on the rooftops are gone and no Enlightenment Agents are barricading the crowd. The unfamiliar sight releases some of the tension on my shoulders. If they let go of the snipers and agents, then they aren't worried. However, if the Enlightenment is involved with what's going on here, then I don't trust it. They are sneaky.

The man continues talking and says something about the Enlightenment and the crowd reacts. There's more movement, whispers become talking as they question the man's statements.

For the first time since taking their positions on the stand, the four people move. They trade glances seamlessly like it was something they've rehearsed. The man's voice rises with fear as if he knows something is wrong.

The gathering crowd becomes deafening, making it hard to hear anything specific through the outrage. And as the man abandons his speech, looking into the crowd...

There are screams of horror.

4

People are running, screaming, doing anything and everything to get away from the square. The screams fill the air with panic and utter chaos. Bodies are falling all around, and the screams turning into nothing in an instant. My arms and legs stall, paralyzed by the frantic crowd. Breathing grows harder as my lungs tighten with each inhale.

"Ms. Young," Amity says, "you need to move."

Amity cures my paralysis as a woman slams into me, pushing me back. Terror fills her golden-brown eyes, and when she tries to step past me, a vivid red glow fills her eyes, turning the whites ruby red. She opens her mouth to scream, but nothing comes out. Her head violently snaps back with a force, knocking her dead to the ground. One last twitch for life escapes her body, only for it to fall limp.

Nodes are detonating.

Amid the chaos, my eyes dart to the podium. The four mysterious figures remain. Not even a slight change in their positions. The man who spoke is now lifeless on the stand with the eyes of the four looking at him. The massacre is in full force, and before I know it, I'm running, sprinting away from the dying masses with the thoughts of how, when these people drop dead and I don't, my cover will be blown. My entire life's purpose would be over.

Moving as fast as I can, dodging falling bodies, hurdling over the debris of soulless lives, I find the panel-layered sidewalk. Without a second thought, I take spec and toss it before me, jumping on the board and securing my feet. I lean forward and soar through the city, flying at top speed as the screams fade in the distance.

Tea helps me recollect my thoughts and breathe a little easier as I sit on my couch. The amount of death that occurred in so little time finds a place in my mind. The chaos ensued out of nowhere. Like the deaths of my parents. And the death of Wren, the first girl I ever loved. I never know when anything is coming. I sip my tea, closing my eyes to help me ground. It fails and my mind travels to when darkness was all I knew.

"Ms. Young," Amity says, "how are you feeling? Your heart rate is registering at an alarming rate."

"Better than ever," I reply sarcastically.

I rub my wrist, covered with scars, as my imprisonment tries to invade my consciousness. Draining the last drops of tea, I refocus.

I cross my legs beneath me and recall my mission. My purpose. The only thing I can ever remember wanting after losing the people I love. No time to waste. No time to reflect. Every second those assholes live is another second they get to be happy. They do not get to live their lives when they took those closest to me.

"Hey, let's see what we've got," I say.

I place Iris on the levitating table in front of me. The letter 'A' glows on the wall—my mother's first initial, her brand, now Amity's, glowing with a blue hue as it loads connections. My mind wanders, and I quickly draw it back to avoid any more turmoil.

"Iris registered Ms. Young," Amity says.

A projected image of everything I have stored appears as designated files. Scrolling through, I find the audio recording of the man speaking on the podium. My first lead was a bust, and this one was no better. The only thing I gained from it was memories of who knows how many deaths. And the screams of people witnessing the madness. The woman whose node detonated in front of me, the people she left behind. Family, friends. This can not keep happening. They take and take and take, without regard for what they're doing. We are nothing to them. I shake my head to drown the thoughts and refocus my attention.

I playback the audio and listen for any clues, anything to help me find another lead. An interference appears, some kind of scramble. It stops exactly when the man speaks—the long silence from before. I press the hologram, holding it in reverse for a few seconds.

"Amity, what is this scramble?" I ask.

"A cipher, Ms. Young," Amity replies swiftly.

I don't have a coded key to break the cipher, which

would be the easiest way. I play it back again and pause. Reverse. Play it back. Nothing. Empty static with no meaning. Giving it another try, I reverse it and play it frame by frame. In cutting down the silence and scrambling, faint voices whisper.

"Amity, decrypt the scramble in each frame and clear away the overlay of the man's voice."

"On it, Ms. Young."

I head to my kitchen to grab more tea. The cold marble floor against my feet makes me flinch. The rain continues to pour down, creating a rhythmic sound on the roof. As I walk around the eclipse couch, the arch separating my kitchen from the living area brightens with perfect white. The black finish of the cabinets adds an aesthetic appeal. I proceed toward the refrigerator. When it opens at my presence, chilled air escapes and makes me shiver as I grab the tea container. The brown liquid sloshes as I pour it into a glass on my hovering island.

Sipping the sweetness and collecting it against my taste buds, I shiver at the excitement it brings. The excitement of having to decode something is a thrill, and I'm almost too overjoyed when, in fact, I'm stuck. However, I'm doing what I know best. The space of the kitchen makes me think about what life could have been. I have taken no time to make this place mine. It's exactly how my parents left it. I think of it as a final memory of them. As if they were still here, calling it home.

"Decryption complete, Ms. Young," Amity says.

"Playback," I say on my way back to my seated position.

"Remember, if he says anything regarding us, begin termination. We already let this go too far."

35

The word us strikes me. The man at the podium must have been a pawn in a chess game, losing his life. He must have said something to initiate the massacre. Regretting my apathetic actions toward his speech earlier, I fiddle with the playback and search for anything I might've missed. There's one point I remember vividly, that made the crowd grow antsy: the moment he mentioned transforming society for the better. Right after that was when the four people behind him exchanged cryptic gazes with each other, resulting in the chaotic moments of death.

Why would they kill the man and everyone around him because of a vague statement?

This must be what Trace was talking about earlier when he mentioned the Enlightenment may make an in-person appearance.

It can't be them. They would never get this close. They never need to.

If they are the 'us' the scrambling voice was referring to, they caused the deaths. And if they are who I think they are, the Enlightenment has all that blood on their hands.

5

It's been three days since the events at Central Square and I've been searching my databases for anything regarding the Enlightenment. It's all useless information about them that won't help my cause, information I learned at a young age about the formation of the current nation.

In the year 2060, the world went into a global depression where poverty, unemployment, homelessness and crime were at an all-time high. The world entered a state of anarchy where alliances between nations were severed. Starting a war known as The Great Technological War, which lasted five years.

After the war, laws were no longer a factor of control. Citizens were rioting and committing crimes at an astounding rate. The government decided to split the country into Areas for easier maintenance and control over the citizens. With the promises of help from the Neural Optical Debilitation Engagement system—or node—they maintained society and gained citizens' trust.

The node's primary benefits are disease and illness control. When a host is ill, it emits extra white blood cells into the body to help fight off invasive pathogens threatening to harm the host, effectively keeping them healthy.

But even with the node in effect, the Enlightenment decided it needed more to regulate society. What was once called the constitution is now known as 'The Codex', a set of rules and regulations which must be followed in accordance with the node.

The Codex grants every citizen weekly packages from the government. Inside are the necessities for survival: food, water, money and constant access to the nation's servers. Another reason society decided to accept what the Enlightenment offered. With the added security provided by Enlightenment Agents, citizens were safe.

After a nationwide blackout, known as Zero Day, the decree to abolish hacking was added to The Codex. Zero Day was the pinnacle of the hacker movement and would have ended the Enlightenment. On that day, my parents grasped what our nation's rulers tried to hide. The Enlightenment's greatest fear is the truth. By eliminating us, they could continue to manipulate society.

Even though I disagree with most of their ideals, the Enlightenment are not my target. They are only obstacles, keeping me from finding what I need to pursue my parents' murderers.

As I sit on my couch and scan through the information, I try a different angle to potentially aid my current cause.

"Amity, has anything happened in Area 1 since the Central Square incident?" I ask.

"Only speeches by the representatives of the Enlightenment. Brief messages relating to increased patrol of agents and usage of the nodes' termination."

"Where were the speeches?"

"All across Area 1. Arcadia mostly. There was one in Techdon and one in Millennia. Cybourne, as always, is radio silent."

"Hmmm. Transfer the speeches in Arcadia to Iris."

I adjust my seated position, fitting one leg up under my chin, folding the other underneath.

Techdon, Area 1's most advanced sector, must have speeches regarding technological updates. Millennia will most likely relay information about its agents and laws. And Cybourne, I'm not surprised by its silence. It is unknown to most and it's the most uncharted territory in the area.

Iris illuminates the table, stretching a hologram above it. I watch as the projected hologram flows through archives of Area 1, archives found digitally in the connections that flow through the area's main channels. Each sector's main core holds all past, current, and future information that can't be accessed easily. The data inside shows updates to the sectors, mainly new laws and functions that must be followed.

Arcadia's core lives in Central Square, near the location of the recent massacre. I can access it from my home with the assistance of Amity. Connected to the same interface, it allows me to find what I need throughout the sector. However, I am limited to Area 1.

I fiddle with the hologram, swapping through the archives looking for importance. Looking thoroughly, I find the speeches were all given by someone named Ezra

Coleman. A name I've never heard. They were all given through overlays played throughout the sector in forms of holograms, displays, holovisions, and likely any other form of media people are using. I grasp the most important things he talked about: laws and a brief analysis of Central Square's incident. Toward the end of the speech, he announces his duty and everything he represents.

"Search for Ezra Coleman," I say.

"Ms. Young, there could be thousands in Arcadia alone."

"Can we track the broadcasts?"

"Negative. They were all encrypted. We would need a key."

"Of course they were."

I plant my head face down in the couch pillow, wondering what my parents would do. They always seemed to know how to get out of a hole. Always seemed to know what came next, never a dull moment. My mother, the fighter, was always ready to jump and go, but my father showed the importance of careful planning. They complimented each other well. They were perfect. If the past six years of training have taught me anything, it's the fact that I am their daughter, and I can do the same.

"Lewttts naahoww da swearch."

"You might want to lift your head before speaking, Ms. Young," Amity replies.

I do as I'm told and resume my original seated position.

"Sorry. Let's narrow the search," I repeat.

"Where to start?"

"Hmmm. How about changing all the audio to written and see if something's there."

I sift through the illuminated archives again, searching for hidden errors or messages in the speeches. Looking thoroughly at the speech about the laws and incidents in Arcadia, I note there's a strange way he spoke. Odd breaks that don't make any sense. It's like they were purposeful. It reminds me of a technique my mother and father used against Enlightenment Agents to gain sensitive information. They called it phishing.

"Amity, look at this speech here."

I pinch the file, enlarging it. Amity scans the written log.

"There's a code, Ms. Young."

"Can it be broken and possibly used as a key?"

I patiently wait as Amity analyzes the code. The opportunity to open a sure path toward exacting my revenge sends a spark through my veins.

"I was able to crack the code, Ms. Young. It appears that the speech was broadcasted from a place called the Establishment."

"Excellent."

"I believe infiltration is in order?" Amity asks.

"Better believe it," I respond with a smile.

The key to finding out more.

"Gear is ready when you are, Ms. Young, and navigation has been updated to Iris."

"You got my back?"

"Always, Ms. Young."

I collect my gear and prepare myself for what's to come.

EXPLOIT

The day is young and the sun shines in all its glory. Bright blue paints the sky with white clouds slowly passing. The skies are mostly empty at this time of day; most people are at work or in meetings of some sort, living a false life they are coerced into thinking is important. A few flars speed above, destroying the illusion of a perfect world. Chatter and light conversation fill the air as I walk to the main connecting train in the Area.

Trains evolved completely after the war. Now they all function on air engines funneling natural air throughout them. They reach top speeds making travel throughout the sector fast. Again, for those without a flar, trains are a great way to traverse the Area. It would be a greater invention if it weren't for the node having to be involved with the process of using them. No one is allowed to enter a train without proper scanning of their node. Another way for the Enlightenment to keep track of where citizens are going.

It's strange thinking about how it must have been before the node. What people's lives were like, how they lived when they had privacy and, essentially, freedom.

I pursue my path to the station and let the questions evaporate. The large building holding the platforms glisten from bright sunlight. It reflects the golden hue into the sky above. As I make it to the entrance, Enlightenment Agents guard the perimeter, standing at each checkpoint entryway. The station isn't crowded, so it begs the question of why it's so guarded for this time of day. As the question simmers in my mind, the Central Square massacre provides the answer.

They're being cautious.

I continue toward my designated platform, and commotion rises from a checkpoint, provoking the eyes of everyone in the station. A man, at least 6 ft tall, with broad shoulders, scruffy beard, and dangerously lazy looking clothes, is escorted from the station's lobby by two Enlightenment Agents, the AOE's lap dogs. Enlightenment Agents are just another way to keep order and control.

The agents take little effort taking the man away, causing no further altercations.

I finally reach my checkpoint. My node is quickly scanned by a drone and is highlighted green, allowing me to pass. I arrive on the platform after hiking two flights of stairs. It's larger than most but can feel tiny during peak hours. There's a couple holding each other's hands and a child with their parents sitting on benches, patiently waiting. On the opposite side of the gap, holding the platted panels for the train to ride, a few people are spread apart, and it almost seems like they're actively avoiding each other.

An open area gives some peace of mind as my eyes track toward the sky above. A windless atmosphere that should provoke calmness and contentment. But my mind tells me there's nothing calm about this nation and what it's going through. I'm quickly reminded by the glowing eyes of everyone around; constant surveillance breaks every illusion I try to create.

The sun's glare continues to burn. My legs feel hot, warm to the touch from the lack of coverage. My shoulders glisten, the deep caramel coloring darkening every second. The moisture of my body tries to keep me cool, and my face feels damp, as if I've washed it. I scoop my wavy black hair out of my face and trace it through my fingers, one after the other, forming a braid down my back, and I almost feel my ears breathe. My bodysuit allows some coolness through ventilated edges and a short style that stops mid-thigh. Thin strap shoulders allow it to be more breathable at the cost of feeling the actual sun on my skin.

"You're really pretty," a small voice says.

Behind me stands a little girl, probably no older than eight. Blonde hair with light brown freckles along her perfectly tanned complexion grants a soft smile. She wears a bandage around one eye, the other representing a soft hazel. The sight of the bandage makes my stomach curl in knots.

A freshly installed node.

Behind her stands a woman, who I can only assume is the girl's mother by the striking resemblance. She hovers, stiff in the shoulders as she places her hand on the girl's head. Our eyes meet as the unnatural blue in the woman's eye makes my heart hurt. I offer a smile, but the mother ignores it and starts off.

"Thank you," I whisper to the girl as they leave toward a seat at the end of the platform.

"Your kindness has certainly grown, Ms. Young," Amity says.

"Only for the weak and innocent."

The girl turns her head to keep sight of me, and I almost want to follow her, to rid her of the pain placed on her and her mother. A child should not have to endure the treacherous act of surgery to have a camera placed in their eye. It makes the simmering rage rise and threaten to be released.

The sound of an approaching train is enough of a distraction for me to bottle up the pain.

The silver bullet soars forward, shining bright from the sun. It glides to a stop and lowers a few feet to the ground, connecting to the platform. Doors of the train slice open, releasing pressure that flows to the open platform. It's warm, thick, and cloudy, like steam from a long, hot shower. People quickly exit and walk past me, on their way to the lobby to be scanned. I board the train and am met with a coolness that alleviates the scorching air from outside. I rush to a seat at the end of the car, avoiding the other passengers. Metallic seats with a velvet covered cushion for what they say is extra comfort, but to me, it's another way to show where all the money goes.

The intercom crackles above, prompting an announcement.

"Attention all passengers. This train is going west bound. Its final stop will be downtown Arcadia. This train is going west bound. Its final stop will be downtown Arcadia."

The message ends after repeating a few times for all the newcomers on board. The doors seal tight and the train breathes air through the inside and then releases a loud sigh outside. I can hear the cars attach to the lead as it sways from the quick motion. It levitates a few feet off the ground and pauses for a second or two. Lights flicker from the front, throughout the train, illuminating each car with power. A surge of pressure fills the car, deafening my ears and causing a quick sensation of nausea that makes me shiver. The pressure releases through the openings above the car as we begin to move. Gradually the train picks up speed, leaving the platform behind, swaying more from the speed and air that engulfs it.

The temperature dips, causing the hairs on my arms to rise. Cold air flows through the vents beneath my seat, providing a respite from the sun's heat. A hologram of the AOE appears on the wall ahead of me, highlighting the train's route through Arcadia. Next to it are holo-images advertising the node, reminding parents to take their children to get their installation in order to keep free healthcare. If done willingly of course. If the Enlightenment has to round people up and force the installation of the node, then healthcare is out of the bargain. The little girl from the station flashes to mind.

The eye patch. Was she forced? Or was her mother open to the idea of the government helping with healthy living.

My heart aches from the vision and I change my focus to the route. The commute will take some time, getting from Central Station to downtown takes about an hour. Good enough time to shake off the fatigue from the scorching heat.

"Proximity check," I say.

"Scanning," Amity says. "No hostile threats nearby."

I smile at the ease Amity brings to my overactive mind. With scanning from Amity, I can quickly discern when a threat is nearby. Enlightenment Agents have a major weakness I'm surprised hasn't been corrected. Within an EA's node, it reveals their identity and occupation. In turn, it allows Amity to read them as hostile and gives me an opportunity to always be one step ahead.

"Well, well," a voice says from the compartment next to me.

"Who's there?" I ask, reaching for my staff.

A figure leaves the compartment, and my nerves begin to subside at the familiar sight.

"Relax," Trace says, "it's me."

He holds his hands up in surrender. The gadgets and tools remain attached along his body as he moves closer to a seat in front of me. A hood covers his head, and a mask hides the bottom half of his face. This time, he wears all black with the only color coming from the lights of his holoboard and rounded device on his wrist.

"Are you following me?" I ask sternly.

"No," he says. "You wouldn't allow that."

"Exactly. So, why the hell do we keep running into each other? Arcadia isn't small enough for that."

"Maybe it's fate."

"Fate?"

"Yeah."

I laugh at the idea, but he hasn't cracked a smile. His body sways naturally with the movement of the train. He lowers his hood, releasing dark locs. They fall down his shoulders and, with silver bangles sporadically hugging a few, give off a nice contrast to his natural brown skin.

"May I?" he asks, looking at the seat in front of me.

I shrug and look out of the window.

We fly through the city at an electric pace. A light show created by the glass buildings and refraction of the sun. At the sight of the globe from Central Square, the screams return from the massacre. Seeing a node be detonated from afar never prepared me for the number activated up close only days ago. The woman's eye, pooling with red. Her head snapping back.

Avoiding the rising nightmares, I quickly change my view from the window.

My eyes find Trace, who has removed the remainder of his disguise. Dark brown eyes stare at me with a sense of mystery and something else I've never seen from him.

I've known him for about six months now, but in that short amount of time, he's always been open and honest. We met during a mission I'd set out on. I needed information regarding the lead I gained during my time spent captive by the Enlightenment. I found Trace through a network breach he initiated on the building I needed to infiltrate. Seeing his failure, I stepped back from the mission and tracked him down. I wanted to know why he was trying to invade the same building. Maybe he had further information I needed.

Things happened fast between us, and I found myself growing attached, something I never do after losing the first person I was ever attracted to. After a successful operation I had at another Enlightenment Complex, I wanted to celebrate and so did he. I appreciated everything he'd assisted with, and it influenced a kiss. After, he got closer, but I didn't. So I strayed away and have only seen him when major events happen. Like Central Square.

"You going to tell me what you're up to?" he asks, finally breaking the silence.

"No."

"Should have known."

He slouches back in his seat and opens his holoboard, illuminating his face with blue light.

"I have some information you may want," he says gingerly.

"What's it going to cost?" I ask, knowing nothing in this world is free.

He chuckles softly and it makes me smile. It brings a sense of light I rarely get to feel.

"Nothing," he says. "I only want to help."

"Really?"

"Like I said before, maybe it's fate."

"You know I don't believe in that right?" I say, hoping he drops the whole fate act.

"No, I didn't know that. You didn't give me a chance."

The mood instantly shifts. His voice dips to a lower octave and it tugs at my heart. In reality, I do feel bad about not giving him an explanation as to why I don't want to be with him. But I can't live in a world with distractions from my one cause. My one purpose for living.

"Well I don't," I say. "Can we leave it at that?"

"Sure."

He fiddles with his holoboard and reveals a hologram of a large building.

"What are we looking at?" I ask.

"This is a building called The Establishment."

My eyes threaten to grow wide, but I force them to stop as I avoid the act of showing where I'm headed.

"I already know you're going here," he says.

"How'd you know..." I catch myself too late.

"I do now." He smiles.

"Fuck off."

I punch him in the arm and lean back into my seat. A simple phishing trick I fell for.

"I definitely think you'll want this info then."

The hologram enlarges and shows data in the network of the Establishment, only accessible from within.

"I don't know exactly what's in it, but I do know the building is owned by Ezra Coleman," he continues.

The name I found earlier.

"I think it's worth checking out."

"I agree."

"I know you want to do this alone—"

"Stop."

He flinches at the word and his face drops.

"Thank you, Trace. Really. I appreciate all the help you give me, but I don't work in groups, and I know you still have feelings for me."

As the words leave my lips, I regret them. I don't intentionally want to hurt him, but I must in order to move forward.

"Can you at least meet me at the diner afterward, to let me know you're okay?"

"Fine."

He rises from the seat with a smile and replaces the hood and face mask.

"You're amazing, so I know you don't need this," he says, "but, good luck."

I nod and in a second, he's disappeared down the train car.

I'm left alone with my thoughts as I close my eyes and ponder. If my world were any different, would I want to be with him? My mind quickly finds the answer as stormy gray eyes and black hair flash behind my eyelids; I belong to the girl I loved and lost.

I force my eyes open and avoid the pain, watching the city go by, with the speed of the train.

7

Exiting the train, severe wind bombards the open station. Above, tracking through the sky, the culprits come into view. Dozens of Enlightenment ships rip through the sky, releasing this week's care packages to the citizens.

Black boxes embedded with the Enlightenment's insignia drift toward the ground, guided by drones; Enlightenment Agents round them up as they land, placing them inside caerials to deliver to every citizen.

Citizens on the platform burst into laughter and cheer, a routine occasion they all look forward to. With the arrival of food, money, and updates from the node, they will continue to live in peace.

No one argues about who's rich or poor, or what race is superior, like the archives explain happened in the old world. Now, everyone is equal in how much they eat and spend. Tracked by the Enlightenment, only those serving the government as an agent or official are deemed higher, but it was imposed by the people, an agreement found upon by the ideals to keep order.

Walking through the main entrance attached to the platform, I'm introduced to crowds of people. Some enter the lobby on the lower level to be scanned, while others head up to the platform on ascending steps—a levitator, the evolution of the old world's escalator: floating steps that make maintenance easier.

As I descend, amid conversation, I overhear a group behind me.

"Have you heard?" one man asks.

"No, what?" the other man responds.

"Apparently, this package will give us more funds for the week."

"Hell yeah! I can get my partner the new holoscreen they want."

"The Enlightenment is the future!" they both shout, igniting a small crowd of others.

They celebrate as I ponder. More funds? This generosity won't come without some kind of stipulation.

"Ms. Young," Amity says, distracting me.

"Yes?"

"It appears this round of care packages is a way to distract from the events of Central Square."

"I see, but there has to be more. They don't do things without cause and effect."

"Indeed, Ms. Young. Network readings show disarray in multiple sectors. Techdon being highlighted the most," Amity explains.

"Thanks for the update."

The entire Area is in disarray. Certainly not common with how the Enlightenment runs the country. Efficiency is in their name; something bigger is going on.

I take the last step off the levitator and enter the lobby, quickly avoiding the blue gazes of society.

"What's your plan for the Establishment?" Amity asks.

"I'm not entirely sure yet," I say.

Iris glows with the distance of my destination.

Two miles. That gives me a chance to come up with an idea.

"You'll have to be careful, Ms. Young. The building will have many agents on standby."

"The goal is to get in and out."

"As it should be."

"But as always," I say, exiting the station.

"Expect nothing," Amity says.

"Prepare for anything."

The Establishment.

Privileged in the way it sounds. The way it rolls off the tongue makes the bile in my stomach rise, close enough to be released on the pavement. The sight of the building doesn't help.

Painted in glass, shined by a peculiar type of metal, it stands like a never-ending mirror. Glass is Area 1's primary preference of material. No one knows why, but every building seems to have it as a part of its infrastructure.

The building reminds me of the prison where I was held captive. Similar in height, towering toward the sky. I ignore the memories trying to resurface.

Late afternoon.

Civilians are headed home for the day. The streets fill with chatter and the sound of shoes knocking against the ground.

From the rooftop where I sit, laughter and cheer about the day comes from the people below. The excitement of their care packages echoes in the air. They walk and talk as if nothing is wrong, as if the world is perfect and not a bleak of imperfection.

Ignorance is bliss, they say.

I remind myself everyone hasn't seen the world the way I view it. They're stuck behind an illusion brought forth by their saviors. The node, like rose-colored glasses, paints a life exactly as they see fit. It's unfortunate, but not my problem. My mission, my focus, and my purpose are only to avenge the ones I love.

The sky is busier now. Flars take the sky, slicing through the windless air, creating artificial versions of the natural gusts the earth produces. Horns scream in the distance, bringing more life to the outside world. I gather myself and scale the building using the side pipelines, reaching the ground in a dark alley. The smell of spoiled food, animal feces, and from the looks of it, a never ending stream of garbage, creates a nauseating feeling in my gut. I hold my breath and make my way to the light at the end of the outstretched alleyway.

Looking at the Establishment, as Amity noted earlier, I see it's a heavily guarded facility. EAs pace the outer perimeter in a perfect rhythm. A man enters the building and is stopped at the door. The EA scans his node, allowing him to enter, reminding me.

"Node activation," I say.

"Activated," Amity says.

The unfamiliar sting in the back of my eye startles me and I wince at the burning sensation in my head, trying to shake it off. Not having an active node for so long has made me forget the lives of everyday people. The ability to turn it off and on grants a different kind of freedom I never wish to lose. The node I've managed to create only mimics the one given by the government. They cannot monitor what I do, or it cannot be detonated. However, it does pass scanners and devices where nodes are required.

Through the glass, more EAs stand statue at the entrance, scanning nodes as people enter and leave. Everyone is monitored when they step inside the facility, not a soul goes without notice. Seems more like a prison than a place of work. I get a chill at the thought. It is, in a sense, a prison. Except they seemingly want to be here.

The air grows colder as the sun begins its descent. I quickly cross the road and arrive at the entrance to the Establishment. The glass doors are taller than they looked from the rooftop. They slide open, releasing a gentle breeze from the inside. An EA stands waiting for any newcomers to the building and I almost gag from thoughts of being anywhere near this place. A man exits quickly, and I take my first step inside.

An EA steps in front of me, aiming a scanner at my eyes without saying a word. His movements are precise and specific, like a soldier in the army that has no room to make a mistake.

"Eyes forward. Do not move." he says sharply.

The scanner makes a charging sound, shooting a red beam directly into my eyes. The beam glues my eyes open, allowing dryness to creep into them like a shadow in the night. The agent traces my body, finally releasing my eyes from their invisible prison. The beam flickers as it continues down my legs, hitting my boots and back up again, digging into my retina. The burning sensation returns, sending the uneasy feeling I dread every time it needs to be scanned. The feeling of not being in control. Of not being able to live the way I want. The feeling that keeps every civilian in this society living like androids, living for the Enlightenment and not themselves.

The beam finally glows green, releasing a small chime. It wets my eyes before liberating them and I blink uncontrollably, still unfamiliar with the feeling.

"Nexia, from Arcadia," he says, face down into the scanner.

"That's me," I say hesitantly.

"Hmmm. Nexia. Welcome to the Establishment. Have an enlightened day."

I fake a smile and step through the entrance taking in all the light.

"That went smoothly," Amity says.

"Speak for yourself," I snap, still feeling the ache in my eye.

"Sorry, Ms. Young. That pain must not be pleasant."

"It's okay. At least my code name registered in time. Things could have been worse."

"And a clever name it is, Ms. Young."

Around me in the large opening, everyone wears a suit or some type of professional attire, making my one piece jumpsuit look like cheap rags. The overcoat I managed to snatch on the train slightly makes up for it. The lofty infrastructure and amount of lighting throughout the building makes me wonder how Ezra maintains it. Then I take a second glance at everyone and remember.

Glorified slavery.

Everyone in this building is basically a humanoid that can't live without him. The tradeoff. Ezra Coleman has to be someone of extreme importance to be able to live like this. He has to have something on the Enlightenment. If not him, then there's something I can take away from a place like this.

Heels and shoes hit the marble floor, shattering any attempt at silence. The glass of the windows is etched with a gold that reflects the light from the rooftop. A sky light layers the top of the building as my eyes follow the golden pillars that act as the foundation. Four large, rounded pillars glisten with marble and gold embedded deep inside, extending high in the air.

Spinning around on my heel, the building is a square shape rising to the top, ending at the diamond shaped skylight. Multiple floors stretch around the square, as people walk to their destinations.

Scanning the open area, there are long desks extending on both sides, with suited men and women helping people find their way throughout the building. EAs escort a group of people to the elevators as a man speaks to them, serving as a guide. As they walk away, I overhear the guide mention to a coworker that he's responsible for a group interview.

My eyes return to the marble desks, tailored with sleek perfection, hovering off the ground. Holograms float on top where they meet the eyes of the suited workers. At the end of the long lobby, past a large globe in the center, there are elevators with agents standing guard, guns at the ready.

The dome sparks my interest as it floats blandly in the center, the only object without gold. I slowly make my way toward it, triggering a levitating hologram to appear in front of it.

"May I help you with something?" a man yells from the desk.

Ignoring him, I marvel over the golden plaque and read:

Without Balance and Guidance

This is what our world is destined to be

The dome turns slightly, and a hologram is illuminated on the surface, revealing earth in complete destruction and turmoil. It zooms in on the AOE and there is pure anarchy among the citizens throughout every Area and its sectors. After a display of the dying population, it returns to a blank canvas and the wording on the hologram fades into a different statement:

This Establishment takes us one step closer
to a better world

Where we can live without fear

Live without chaos

The hologram fades again, this time for good. Before I'm able to comprehend the message on the globe, a suited figure stands next to me, five feet and eight inches, meeting me at eye level. The crispness in his suit is hard to miss and

I wonder how he can move at all. The black slims him out, but I can tell he's a drinker by the way his pants slack at the hips. His blonde hair is slicked back, tucked behind his ears, revealing wrinkles that stretch from the corners of his eyes and mouth. Light blue light stares daggers into me and I know his node is recording me, but precautions have already gone into effect.

When I'm recorded, I am Nexia, an ordinary girl from Arcadia. An alternate identity I created for my node. My face is also registered as someone else. Ever changing, disguising me from every node trying to record the real me.

Ariadne Young is nonexistent.

"Excuse me, ma'am?" he says too politely. "Do you need help with anything?"

Taking in a deep breath and exhaling smoothly, I recall my mission. My parents and their unjust ending. I recall the reason I'm here and the need to succeed. The false blue in his eyes threaten me, but I smile bright.

"Yes. I'm here for an interview."

8

The man escorts me onto an elevator with an agent standing at the corner. Like all agents, he wears all black with too many weapons attached to his person. The red glow beneath his helmet visor threatens to make my heart jump, but I remember he can't see me.

"I am Harold," the man from the globe says. "We'll be going to the department of hiring. Please input your information on this holoscreen."

He hands over an oval shaped board with a highlighted list for me to fill out. As I proceed to input the information, I remember a lesson from my father about the importance of staying hidden.

"To be a great hacker, you need to have an alias. There's no escaping it," my dad said over my shoulder as I worked on trying to create a worm in a system.

"Can you create one for me since it's soooo important to you?" I said, whining.

The frustration I had in trying to create my code name always got to me. I remember seeing his eyebrows droop, forcing his eyes down and showing his face of disappointment.

"It's not simply a new name, love," he said.

A sparkle flared in his eye as he knelt to meet my gaze. His facial expression changed at that moment.

"It's a persona. A personification of your thoughts, likes, and dislikes. It's a way to live in a world like this and not be fully seen. We have no privacy, but there are ways to keep what we don't want them to know for ourselves. It's a part of you. It must come from you."

The chime in the elevator opens my eyes.

"Nexia," Harold reads from the holoscreen. "Right this way please."

I follow him out of the elevator into a long corridor and control my rattling nerves. The idea to be here for an interview came from seeing the group of people being guided by another escort when I first walked in. My heart thuds, causing heat to build throughout my body. I slow my pace behind Harold, wishing I'd found a better way to infiltrate this building.

"An interview, Ms. Young?" Amity says.

"I know. What else was I supposed to say."

"This poses a serious danger. However, readings show a network that can only be breached from within."

"So, I was on the right track."

"Indeed, Ms. Young. I will locate the network you need to break and secure exit points."

Amity calms my nerves as we walk down the corridor. Harold is shorter than the other escorts from downstairs, and I easily look over his head to the end of the floor. His speed makes up for his height and there's a youthful edge in the way he strides. Over my shoulder, the EA on the elevator glares down the aisle at me, the red in his eye forcing a shiver down my spine. The elevator slowly closes, deepening my sense of fear. What-ifs begin to play in my head. Maybe he knows who I am, or maybe he is going for backup.

"Amity, how are the exits coming?" I ask.

"All exits have been updated to Iris and are ready when you are," Amity replies. "But still locating the network, Ms. Young."

My walking is halted by the sudden stop of Harold.

"I'm sorry, did you say something?" he asks.

"Sorry, no. I didn't," I say sharply.

He continues his previous pace down the corridor, and I take note of my surroundings: the distance from the elevator, how many doors we pass, how many corners we turn... I map every detail in my mind and think about the mantra given to me by my father when I was six.

"Okay, Aria, your goal is to tap into this phone without setting off any kind of malware hidden in the encryption," he'd said.

He'd noticed my hesitation and had placed his hand lightly on my shoulder.

"You can do this," I remember his voice saying. "It's simple, and there's only one trap in the phone. You'll be fine."

With newfound confidence, I grabbed the phone and started the process of decryption. I remember getting past the trap, implementing a new sequence to get deeper inside. They'd started to upload, but without warning, the process had been thwarted by malware software disguised as useless codes. The phone shut down immediately after, and I'd screamed.

"No!" The tears had begun to fall. "You said there was only one trap. You lied!"

I'd been so infuriated that I wanted to hit him. I wanted to be perfect, and I wanted to be like them, but I'd failed. The feeling of defeat echoed in my sobs had sent me further into thinking I would never be ready. My father had then taken me by arms and looked me in the eyes with love. He took a second to make sure I was listening before he spoke.

"Calm down. I know I lied, but it was to teach you a very important lesson. Even though something may appear to be safe, there's always a chance for surprises. You must always remember: expect nothing, prepare for anything."

He'd planted a kiss on my head as a seal of approval that the message was received.

Iris vibrates with the network location I need to breach.

"Ms. Young, the network can be accessed from a panel in the nearby stairway," Amity says.

"Got it."

Harold strolls back to me from double doors I can only assume lead to the hiring department. Before he takes the holoscreen, the blue tint in his eyes flickers, snapping photos of me to record in the database. I remain calm and smile, knowing they can't track me.

"I'll be back in a moment," he says, disappearing through the double doors, emptying the hallway.

I check Iris for the time and realize it's getting away from me. Examining the area, I clock one camera with a blind spot exactly where the staircase is.

"Proximity check," I whisper.

Iris glows on my wrist with the locations of active nodes on the floors beneath this one and those above. A nearby network reveals itself with a golden hue a few feet from my current spot. I remove a small electromagnetic pulse pad from a concealed pocket in my bodysuit. I stick it beneath the metallic bench and follow the short route to a hidden stairway. Iris registers the network, and I begin my quick process. I find errors through weak encryption and plant a small malware worm to overload the system, bringing forth hidden files in the database.

"Malware set, Ms. Young."

"Begin extraction," I say swiftly.

As the process starts, I constantly check Iris for any changes in the environment. The thrill increases my heart rate, blood rushing through me like raging waves. The copies of the data begin to appear on Iris in sequences I attach with an encryption, keeping them safe.

"Ms. Young," Amity rings.

"Almost there."

"Ms. Young, there's trouble."

Iris notifies me, revealing multiple hostiles moving through the building. I've breached the network too long. They must have a white hat—people who detour others from stealing information. The hostiles move quickly, causing sweat to build around my temples. I can't get caught here. If I do, it's all over. I cancel the extraction with trembling hands before it completes and proceed back to the bench, finding a way to slow my heart.

Harold barrels around the corner and my attempt fails. My heart slams against my ribs with painful thuds, forcing the pores of my skin open, releasing sweat from my nervous body.

"I need you to come with me," he barks.

"Is there a problem?" I say. "Should I be concerned?"

As the questions leave my lips, three more men appear in the hall, dressed in dark tailored suits—Enlightenment Agents. They point their guns at me, red lasers beaming, painting my body.

"There has been a breach, and we need to make sure all visitors are accounted for. We need to make sure it wasn't an inside source interfering with this facility."

I slowly stand, activating the hidden EMP pad from earlier.

Ten. I begin counting down to myself.

"Why the guns?" I ask rhetorically.

Nine.

"Please, no further questions," he snarls.

Eight.

The three EAs' fingers twitch on the trigger.

Seven.

"Let me make sure I have everything."

Six. He nods as I turn to pick up my jacket, moving slowly, pretending to check the pockets.

Five.

Four.

Three.

Two. I throw the jacket over my shoulder and slip both arms through the sleeves in one quick motion, swiftly spinning around to face them.

One.

"I'm afraid I have to go," I smile.

The hum of the EMP travels through the quiet space and activates, affecting them all. They drop to their knees, guns skidding across the hard floor. I punch Harold in his throat before he can react as they all yell in agony from the disruption in their nodes.

The building goes dark, all electronic devices and services—except for my own—knocked out.

"Twenty seconds, Ms. Young," Amity chimes.

"Perfect, route the quickest exit to Iris."

I remove the dead EMP device and toss it back in its hidden pocket.

"Done," Amity announces.

Iris brightens with the route, and I follow it, escaping the Establishment.

9

"Coffee please," I tell my waiter who has been trying to flirt with me, not realizing he's barking up the wrong tree. Trace, who was supposed to meet me here, comes to mind. He doesn't seem like the jealous type, but it still begs the question of whether he would be after seeing another guy trying to get my attention.

My waiter scrambles away with my order. Two hard boiled eggs, avocado toast, and coffee. As I wait, I reminisce about the times I used to come here and study countless books about hacking, to impress my parents.

The Panoramic Diner.

The view from inside is exactly as if someone were taking a panoramic photo. Windows outstretched form an eclipse through the building. It's a clever idea and it's no surprise this diner is my favorite in the city. Seating lined against the edges of the windows with a memorable layer, adjusting to the body's weight and temperature. Air flow is regulated by the openings above the windows, acting as small vents, providing a sense of fresh air. The scent of food fills the air but is replaced quickly by the fresh notes of a natural scent from the outside air. The sun does its duty and illuminates the inside with natural light, capping off a warm feeling.

I detach the small screen of Iris and place it on the table, unlocking it to reveal its contents. The first thing that appears is an error message relaying the presence of corrupted data, the last five percent of data I interrupted from the extraction in the Establishment. With only such a small percentage lost, I'm confident I was able to steal what I needed without it. I clear it to expose the information I did manage to take. Randomly, I choose a file and open it. Reading through it and analyzing the notes, I learn the file has everything he talked about with a therapist. Information about his youth and partial details about why he's the man he is today.

Daniel, my waiter, scurries back to my secluded table in the corner edge of the diner. No matter where I am, a secluded corner is my go-to spot. He places a cup down with shaking hands. Either he's extremely nervous or he needs to lay off the caffeine. He proceeds to pour coffee into the cup while his eyes lock onto mine. The deep green, like an evergreen forest, flashes as he smiles, and the blue ring makes the depth in his gaze deeper. His ruffled brown hair falls over the sides of his face and the youth in his features is clear.

My eyes shift downward, toward the cup as it overfills and pours out onto the table. His gaze never falters and the coffee on the table forms a dirt brown river that slowly makes its way to the edge, dripping down like a muddy waterfall. It spews on the ground, and I'm amazed at how he doesn't seem to notice the splashing on the floor, or the steam floating between us.

"Ohhh man!" he yells, urging me to survey my surroundings. The diner is half empty, with the only few people sitting on the opposite side. Daniel pulls a handheld device out of his apron that quickly dries the table as he hovers it in a circular motion. After, he types in a code on the table that reveals a set of functions and he chooses one labeled, 'maintenance'. A moment passes and a small drone-like device floats over to clean the floor, leaving quicker than it came. He's definitely done this before.

"I'm really, really sorry," he says with a sad look on his young face.

"Can I get you any cream and salt?" he asks.

My eyes find his, and my brows dart upward to point out his mistake.

"I mean sugar. Cream and sugar. Can I get you any?" he corrects himself, nerves filling his voice.

"It's okay. Relax," I say. "I'll take cream please."

He quickly shuffles away as I lightly tap the table and wave my hand around it before placing Iris back down.

"Ms. Young, you really have an effect on him," Amity says.

"Not on purpose," I respond, hearing Daniel's feet tracking back.

"Here you go," he says, placing the container of cream next to the coffee cup. I pour some of it into my coffee and stir it. From the corner of my eye, I can see Daniel still standing awkwardly nearby.

"Yes?" I ask.

I angle my eyes toward him, and he flinches as if I threatened to punch him—or worse.

"Sorry. I'm not normally like this. I think you're beautiful."

The blood rushes to his face, his shoulders tense, and his jaw tightens from the nerves taking control.

"Thanks," is all I can say.

I stir my coffee, watching the dark brown gradually take on a lighter shade. The liquid sloshes in the cup as it swirls in the center, until forming a light shade of brown that has streaks of white cream. I take a sip and relish in the roasted bitterness that has a creamy aftertaste along my tongue.

"May I sit with you?" Daniel stutters.

The coffee stalls at the back of my throat, forcing a deep cough that I desperately hold back to prevent embarrassment. My mind screams no, but my heart—and everything my mother taught me about compassion—says yes.

"Aren't you working?" I counter.

"How about after? I leave in less than an hour. We could—"

"I'll be gone by then," I lie, stopping his train of thought before it can manifest into words, thinking it'll hurt him less if he doesn't say it.

"Oh well."

I was wrong. His brow furrows as he thinks hard on how to recover. The redness in his face grows deeper, darker, like a red wine waiting to be inhaled. He fixes his mouth to speak, and I already know what's coming.

"We can exchange phone numbers."

No is what I want to say.

"Believe it or not, I don't have a phone." I muster a chuckle through the lie, hoping he takes the hint. Everyone in the world has a phone or some kind of electronic device. Hell, babies have practically had one in the womb since the effects of the Technological Revolution.

"Ms. Young, that was a terrible lie," Amity says, reinforcing my thoughts.

"Oh," escapes Daniel's mouth with obvious disappointment.

I continue sipping my coffee until it's drained; all the while, he stands, staring at me. I refill my cup when he finally decides to speak again.

"Can we keep in contact another way, perhaps?"

His eyes fall to Iris, excitement flooding his face.

"This is painful. If only I could feel pain," Amity says, making a smile stretch across my face as I struggle to contain my laughter. Daniel smiles back and I instantly regret Amity's comment.

"I can't communicate with this." I gesture to Iris. "It doesn't have any connection."

"You are a terrible liar," Amity rings.

In truth, I am. The one thing I didn't inherit from my parents was the ability to lie and get information. It could have been the worst answer I could have given Daniel. The internet is a way of life. It travels through every aspect of the AOE. After the war, it essentially became what oxygen is to a human being. Daniel gives me a look of bewilderment and frustration. He unbuttons the top of his collared shirt and loosens the tie underneath the apron as if to breathe out his feelings. A long gasp leaves his lungs, and he drops his shoulders like a child being denied candy.

"Okay. I guess I'll go." He lets the statement fuel the silence between us, hoping for a response. I ignore the bait and sip the creamy bitterness. "Your food should be out shortly."

He strolls away, defeated, and for the first time, his authentic voice came out. Steady and patient even though he didn't get what he wanted. If he weren't so nervous, maybe he could get someone. My eyes follow his path toward the kitchen, and I finally dig back into my findings from the Establishment. Reviewing the previous file that contains therapy sessions, he talks about his life as a father. I close the file, open a new one, and photos splatter across the screen. Pictures of vacations with his family. A wife, son, and dog. I flip through the digital images in search of clues about where he lives. As I look closely at each one, there's an odd similarity between his son and my waiter.

Daniel is at the side of my table as if I summoned him with my thoughts.

"Here's your toast," he says, "and two hard-boiled eggs."

Looking at him, I can't shake the resemblance between them. It's all I can see.

"What's your last name?" I ask, cutting into the egg, steam lightly rising through the air.

"Coleman."

Ezra's son in front of me. The odds of this happening are close to impossible.

"Two first names."

"Why the sudden interest?"

"Just curious."

He smiles and walks away to attend to another customer. The thoughts of Daniel being the son of a man I'm after sparks ideas I couldn't have previously anticipated.

I take the salt and pepper from the side of the table and sprinkle them on the egg. The fresh pepper hits my nose, triggering the sensation of a rising sneeze. I contort my face in weird motions to avoid it, stopping it from manifesting, and slice the half pieces into another half, leaving four to easily devour. I place them on my toast and inhale it like I haven't eaten in weeks. Between each swallow, I sip my coffee. The mixture is enticing and flavorful, prompting me to finish quicker than I intended.

"How was everything?" Daniel asks.

"Great. Thank you."

"Glad to hear it. Can I get you anything else?"

My curiosity gets the best of me. "This is random. But are you related to Ezra Coleman?"

He bursts into laughter, forcing my brow to furrow.

"No," he says. "Though I wish. I would not be working here if the man who owns all of Area 1 was my father."

Owns all of Area 1, I repeat to myself.

"What do you mean he owns all of it?" I ask.

"I suppose it could be rumors, but apparently, the guy is more than a normal big shot. Some people think he's a member of the Enlightenment."

My eyes threaten to grow with surprise, but I hold them back. An Enlightenment member this close to society. If Ezra is an Enlightenment member, then he will certainly have the intel I need to carry out my vengeance. The only information I have on the night my parents were murdered is the sight of Enlightenment Agents and their small talk about someone assigning them to do the job. That someone is my target, but I've never known how to get to them. Surely a member of the Enlightenment will have what I need.

Daniel flinches, grabbing his eye in pain. My immediate thought is node activation.

"Are you okay?" I ask cautiously.

"Ms. Young, something isn't right," Amity says.

"I'm fine," he answers quickly. "Your bill is ready when you are."

His voice is cold and dry. The Daniel I knew before my question is replaced by a less friendly and more straight-to-the-point version. An eerie chill replaces the warmth and laughter he displayed moments before.

I place Iris in the center of the table, and a confirmation appears in bright green, replacing the pale blue before. He still holds his eye, pressing against it hard enough to make his arm shake.

"Have a good day," Daniel says, his voice robotic and non-personable.

A forced smile parts the corners of his thin lips as he heads back to assist other customers. Without thought, my feet are moving and I'm standing behind him. I don't know if it was a force that picked me up and placed me down or sheer will and curiosity that caused this gesture.

"Hey, you don't look too good. Is your node bothering you?" I ask.

"I thought you didn't care to talk to me," he says.

"Well, you look like you need a doctor or something."

"I'm fine."

"Okay, but you did say something I'd like to talk more about, if you don't mind."

"And what's that?"

"Ezra and what he owns."

Color returns to his face, but his hand remains at his eye.

"I guess friendly conversation wouldn't hurt," he says. "I'm going to grab some pain—ahhh!"

Daniel hunches over and screams.

"Ms. Young, hostile detected."

My lungs freeze.

Daniel runs to the back of the diner as the main door of the building crashes open.

Trace finally barges in and scans the diner in quick succession. He looks like he's been running for miles. His hair is disheveled, something that never happens to him. He finally finds me staring and sprints in my direction.

"Oh, thank the universe," he pants. "I thought I was too late."

"What the hell is going on?" I ask.

"No time."

He grabs my hand and tries to lead me toward the exit. I yank away and stare into his eyes. Fear and worry fill his irises, making my anxious nerves rise.

"I'm sorry I was late. I got new information about you, and I tried to get here as quickly as I could."

"What do you mean new information about me?"

He takes a deep breath and sighs.

"You were right," he starts. "I have been following you."

My chest swells and he notices, causing him to take a step toward me. He reaches for me again, but I push him back.

"I've been doing it to protect you. You have to believe me," he begs. "There's someone here who isn't who they say they are. We need to move."

I take a few steps back as the steady stream of a thin red line tracks through the window behind me.

"You're in danger, Ms. Young," Amity announces, louder than the usual whispers I'm accustomed to.

"Hey!" Daniel shouts with a hand cannon raised, pointed at me.

Gasps erupt from the other customers in the diner.

The blue ring in Daniel's eye has changed to red. The same red that's visible in all Enlightenment Agents.

"Daniel," I say. "What are you—"

"The Enlightenment is the future!"

He fires the gun, and when I open my eyes, it's Trace standing in front of me. A burning hole gapes his chest as he slowly turns to face me. Life fades from his dark eyes. My chest caves in and my lungs stiffen as tears form.

"I'm sorry," he whispers before falling to the floor.

The red beam in the window flashes, and without a second thought, I crouch down, knees to my chest and hands to the floor. Trace's body lies limp next to me as I turn and see Daniel a few feet away.

He points the gun at me again, but before I can speak, my eyes find the red beam again. The sound of glass shatters the building as a gunshot rips through the aisle in front of me, hitting Daniel between the eyes. Screams burst through the diner, echoing off the walls and empty spaces. People drop to their knees, looking for cover. Others storm through the main entrance, past Daniels's now lifeless body, in search of safety.

I lower further to the ground, feeling the cold matte against my bare legs as I turn my head back toward Trace.

His body lies still.

Dead, with ruby red puddling beneath him.

10

"People live and people die," my mother once said.

I remember the dead bodies scattered on the streets below. The deaths caused by nodes being terminated, killing people who were only trying to speak their voice. It was horrifying to witness a massacre, with no ability to help.

"Ariadne," she'd said, "separate your heart from it and you won't feel their pain. Use these moments to propel you forward. Don't let anything hold you back. Survive, honey."

The horrifying screams in the diner push back my surfacing memories. Trace lies next to me. The fire that lived in his eyes, replaced by the blank stare of death, tears my heart in two. The things I didn't get to say rush toward the forefront of my mind like crashing waves. His lips draw my attention, and I follow the lines making up his face. I smile through the tears beginning to fall and don't dare to caress his cheek.

"No," I whisper. "I'm sorry."

I find it in myself to move.

I crawl my way toward the exit, my arms and legs scraping against the hard floor, making me wince with each strike. Reaching Daniel, my instincts tell me to check for life, but reality tells me otherwise.

No time.

Survive. Survive. Survive.

"Ms. Young, there's an emergency exit tucked in the corner of the diner," Amity advises.

"Got it."

Trace's words replay in my head. He's been following me to protect me. From whom or what? The thought of him lying to me and keeping track of my whereabouts makes my muscles tense. I forgive him, as it has brought light to the fact that someone must be targeting me in a way I can't read or understand. My recent infiltration of the Enlightenment Complex comes to mind, but I don't remember setting off any encryptions.

"Ms. Young, you need to move."

The aisle seems never-ending in my trek across the floor. When the end is finally in sight, it only seems to extend as I get there. I slither past a couple underneath a table, holding each other, tears spilling down the woman's face. The man caresses her, his own eyes welling with fear. I continue as footsteps boom through the end of the diner, the main entrance barging open again, the glass shattering from the impact. I get to my feet as I finally arrive at the emergency exit.

In the plaza, chaos ensues. Flars trail above with those on the ground, speeding to reach the heights of velocity. People sprint to nearby buildings for cover, warning others about the shooting inside the diner. Eyes dart toward the diner and land on me, causing my breaths to stall. The Enlightenment will see what's happening and most of all, see I don't have an active node. I quickly grab spec from its holster. I place it below my feet, readying myself for takeoff.

A flar comes to a speeding stop in front of me, forcing me to jump off. The wind flushes past me, pushing debris around, swirling my clothes around like paper. It's not like any flar I've seen. A black finish with metallic edges shine under the sun. It takes on the shape of a ship, with a narrow front and wing-like parts extending from its sides. Rotating propellers live on its wings, twirling and slicing the air, keeping it afloat. The windows are blacked out to give it the appearance of stealth. I step back from the doors as they hiss open.

Four individuals dressed in black exit the ship, ensnaring my feet before I'm able to process them surrounding me.

Masks underneath hoods hide their faces. The masks are black with a trace of neon, acting as a digital facial expression. A series of symbols paint the masks, each different and colored. The expressions give the same tone: flat. Enlightenment Agents constitute a brief thought in my mind, only to be rejected by the sight of their cloaks tailoring their bodies. They form a circle around me, placing their arms behind them.

"Ms. Young. Analysis shows there's no threat," Amity assures.

A woman steps out of the ship-like flar. Slow and exact. She stands tall, long legs covered to the knee by a skirt, with black tights falling into silver-plated, calf-high boots. A long, black, sleeveless coat falls from her shoulders to the same length as the skirt. Silver buttons trace one side, with the collar lifted up, right below her chin, and I'm surprised there's no mask. She takes a stance, and her energy transfers to the four surrounding me. They shift their positions to a ready posture that grips my chest.

My eyes find hers. Sharp lines form her face, thin lips, and a hard-cut nose. The sharp edges of her eyes, long lashes, and flared eyebrows make a normal glare feel deadly. Her blonde hair is pulled back tight, with no imperfections. If she's not part of the Enlightenment, she could surely pose as them. She takes a step forward and in unison, the others step back.

"Can I help you?" I ask hesitantly, their gestures intensifying my shallow breaths.

"We can help each other actually," she says.

Her voice is crisp and harmonic, a strange delight to my ears. I let the statement float to push her to continue speaking. She doesn't take the bait.

"Who said I needed help?"

My eyes scan the other four for movement as they glare at me like a fish in a tank.

"Well," she says, flashing the emerald in her eyes. "You'd probably be dead right now if it weren't for us."

"Yea, right," I respond, stifling a laugh.

I move to walk away, and she blocks my path, mirroring the ship moments ago. Her eyes cut into mine like needles probing for extraction.

"If you could excuse me. I was shot at and so was someone I cared about," I spit. "I'm not sure if you can tell, but this area is becoming chaotic. So I'd like to leave before the Enlightenment decides to detonate nodes or send agents this way."

I draw my staff, but her stance remains motionless.

If not for her batting eyelashes, I'd mistake her for a statue. The edges of her lips slowly form into a pure smile. Her eyes become full and clear, showing off the intense green hue.

"Trace was someone we cared about too," she says softly. "More than you can imagine."

They knew him. How? She moves her eyes to one of the other four and nods. They return the gesture, and my eyes follow them until they walk into the diner.

"And the shot that pierced the diner's glass was not meant for you. It was for the target it hit."

Daniel.

"Your evasion was admirable, but unnecessary. If that shot was for you, it would have hit you."

"Why'd you kill him?"

"So he wouldn't kill you," she says. "I've been watching you for some time."

Her words strike me at my heart: *watching me*. It's the same thing Trace told me before he saved my life.

Being watched or followed by someone I don't know without my knowledge suffocates me. It makes my mind travel to places I've fought to drown, and in an instant, she brings them back.

The person she nodded at exits the diner with Trace's body, now in a pod floating at their side.

"Don't worry. We're not with the Enlightenment. I knew your parents before they died…" Her voice trails as she watches me. "They left me with a task."

The air in my lungs freeze, and I can hardly think. My chest feels tight, like a thousand pounds being pressed against me. Emotions stir inside and I don't dare express them. My vision goes in and out from lack of oxygen. I step away from her and begin to pace.

I try to breathe but no air seems to feed my body, causing my heart to overwork and supply oxygenated blood. I tremble from the many memories of my parents, trying to regain composure.

"The task?" she continues, unaware of my inner turmoil. *"Protect our daughter."*

As the words leave her lips, a screech in the sky, followed by a sonic boom, rattles the chaotic scene.

A jet swoops low and the Panoramic Diner explodes behind me with a deafening roar.

MAINFRAME

11

Ringing drowns the chaos. My eardrums sting with each swallow as I try to regain my hearing.

My lungs burn from the smoke-engulfed plaza as I choke and cough wildly to clear it. The panic from nearby civilians prompts me to survey my surroundings in search of arriving Enlightenment Agents, and behind me, the Panoramic Diner is gone, riddled to pieces as flames tear it apart. My heart throbs from the memories lost inside. The food, the atmosphere—all gone in an instant by a rarely-used Enlightenment jet. Those are only used when a situation calls for it—when the Enlightenment is looking to level certain sectors.

It happened in Areas 3 and 4, when citizens tried to overrun the EAs. But why here? This is a drastic reaction when nothing major happened. The Enlightenment doesn't typically retaliate this way.

The sound of overheated glass exploding pinches my heart. My hearing fully returns as the embers crackle, searing through the entirety of the building, reminding me of the previous, brief moment of bliss.

The building bursts with burning debris falling from the sky. Ash rains down like tar-covered snow, swaying through the air in a violent blaze, spewing more into the atmosphere.

The echoing sounds of people screaming, and helicopters slicing the air above burn my recovering eardrums. Terror fuels everyone in sight, except for the people who stepped out of the black flar. They stare at me until the woman who leads them decides to speak.

"Everyone on the ship," she yells through the surrounding noise.

One after the other, like a well-trained soldier departure, the four people race inside the flar. The speed at which they move tells me I need to do the same. With each second ticking by, the Enlightenment could be closer and judging by the jet moments ago, they will do anything—no matter the cost. My legs adjust beneath me, steadying until the shakiness resides. Before I can move away from the action, the woman stops me. Her brows angle with tension pressed across her forehead.

"Come with us," she says.

"There's no way you think I'm going to follow a stranger," I retort.

Her face falls for a second, but she quickly recovers.

"I'm not a stranger. My name is Claire, and I promise I will inform you about everything, including your parents, but now is not the time. You're in no shape to fight the agents who have already begun arriving. Come with us and you'll learn the truth."

Sirens wail through the city announcing the need for EA backup. Around me, the chaos continues. There is serious panic in citizens' footsteps and the screams have become more intense, like the screams from Central Square days ago. The activation of nodes has once again begun. My heartbeat escalates at the familiar threat.

Claire stretches out a hand, and a gentle smile spreads across her face, contradicting the destruction surrounding us.

"Now or never, Ms. Young," Amity says.

I don't know these people, but I won't make it before the Enlightenment swarms the plaza. This woman claims to have known my parents, protecting me after their deaths. The will to survive, a priority my mother drilled into me, tells me the number of agents who are soon to arrive will be impossible to take on.

"I'll be here with you, Ms. Young," Amity reassures me.

The statement I needed to hear.

"Okay," I say.

"Okay," Claire says.

She steps in first, and I follow a few paces behind. The flar is spacious and I quickly understand why she refers to it as a ship. That's exactly what it is. The four people are seated together, with enough space to spread out if they wanted to. Judging by their arrangement in the seats, they're certainly close. I make my way to a seat at the back of the ship, away from everyone else. My steps are light from the uncertainty of being in a levitated space.

I sit and marvel over the interior, dark like the black outside. Silver encases the walls with some type of metal, reflecting light from the outside. The seats are also metal but feel like liquid, flowy and adaptive to my movements. Cold, fresh air travels in the space like I'm not inside an enclosed structure.

Four seats line each side, totaling eight. Forward, past the seated four, down a small set of steps, sits two large seats. Claire takes the right and an unknown person takes the left, sitting at the helm of a guiding device. The ship activates as Claire presses the illuminated hologram in the center. Power flickers on with a soft hum, providing more light.

On the edge of the ship, next to me, Trace lies in a pod. His hands are placed in front of him like they would be in a coffin, covering the hole created by the gunshot. The dark brown eyes I remember well are closed, reminding me they'll never open again. My heart throbs against my ribs as the want to cry reaches its peak. Losing another person I cared about traps the hope and positivity I've clung to in a mental cell.

"We'll be in Techdon in under an hour," Claire announces, distracting my thoughts.

Techdon. A place I haven't been to since I was a child. The only thing I can remember is the Zero Day festivals my parents would take me to. They always had the most updated entertainment. Going there now, without them, creates a shallow pit in my stomach. And being away from my home doesn't help. It triggers more racing thoughts about whether this is safe.

"Amity," I whisper, "commence lockdown."

"Acknowledged."

Iris illuminates on my wrist with the notification for the lockdown sequence. The ship surges upward, gaining higher levitation for departure. Everyone relaxes in their seats except for me, as the uncertainty of my actions spins around in my mind.

The lights dim for takeoff, and it makes me wish my drowning thoughts would do the same. I lift my hood and sink into the seat, hiding my face from the others as the tears finally escape, and I suffocate under sorrow.

12

The air hits me as my boots find the black sand. Thick gusts of wind snap and whisk around, threatening to push me over. It's barely Fall, and the wind is so heavy. In Arcadia, it isn't this aggressive until late winter, when the snow rains down, cascading white powder around the sector. I suppose it would be different, considering we're now in a desert landscape. Although it's not desolate in the slightest.

The wind brings the smell of small plant life extending through the shady sand. Soft hints of sagebrush caress my nose with a refreshing scent.

"Sorry about the wind," Claire says. My brow furrows at the thought of her apologizing for mother nature.

"Techdon," she continues, "is known for high winds this time of year. I didn't anticipate us having to rush in getting here, or else I would have had you prepare."

A smile makes a quick appearance on her face before it evaporates. One of the members whispers something in her ear before taking off toward a massive pyramid structure. I get the odd feeling whatever she heard has to do with Trace.

The warmth in his eyes escapes the place I buried it, provoking more tears. I never let people in for this reason. I'm always in a state of recovery from losing the people I care about. The softness in his voice when he tried to show affection creeps inside and I tense, trying to conceal my emotion.

The other members follow, after receiving a nod from Claire. She gestures for me to follow her as the sound of sand breaking apart and reforming under my boots echo in the silence. The ship darts away from behind us, vanishing behind the massive pyramid structure.

Black sand covers the ground with small minerals reflecting the dying sun's light, giving the sand a shiny spark. Ahead of me, the pyramid stands tall, causing my head to reel back as my eyes meet the golden tip. The pyramid is black as the sand beneath it and almost invisible. Light flickers throughout the building with small dots of illumination that look like signals. The outside walls remind me of a motherboard chip, by the way the lights coil and connect to different connectors.

From the base, to about halfway, there is an indention that caves into the sides. A glass platform extends from it, wrapping around the structure like a planet's ring. At this distance I can't make out any details, only people walking across. Some stand and watch the outside city.

I turn and join in spectating.

Techdon stands in the distance as we stand on the outskirts. A large dome covers the entirety of the sector like a protective shield. I suppose, in a sense, it is. History explains Techdon was ground zero for the technological advancements that helped end the war. Weapon enhancements, machinery, armory, and vehicles. All of it came from here. The dome-covered city extends its architecture, making it vast and astounding.

Techdon is where I remember seeing my parents outside of themselves. When they were in Arcadia, it was always about work and training. They never seemed to catch a break, but here... I believe this was their place of peace. Remembering their smiles makes warmth travel through my body, as if they were here embracing me.

My attention returns to the city. The buildings rise high, but they are unlike what I'm used to seeing in Arcadia. They rise and split among each other, creating pathways for monorails and flars to pass through. With the sunlight fading, the city begins to flicker with light. Becoming a grand spectacle. The light gives view of the roads stretching like never-ending valleys traveling through the core of the city. Gold and white shine like stars, creating an earthly representation of the night sky.

"Welcome to the city of technology," Claire says, standing next to me.

"Where exactly are we?"

"Technically speaking, we are in Techdon," she spins on her heel to face the pyramid with ease. "This is unseen by those we don't want to see."

My eyes follow her hands as she gestures the entirety of the pyramid and its neighboring structures.

"Think of it as a way to maintain our privacy."

Her words mimic my father's, similar to the way he explained why I didn't have a code name.

"We live a private life. I'm sure you can appreciate that, considering what you do and the world we live in."

What I do? Maybe she really does know who I am. Her knowing me makes me question my skill at remaining unseen. Trace knew me because I allowed it. Based off her previous statements, she implies she's known me from the moment my parents died, maybe earlier. Like my parents, I do my best to remain invisible, but this woman negates my belief in how effective I am at achieving it.

She begins to walk toward the pyramid, forcing me to follow behind. The echoing sounds of flars catch my attention as they leave. Some enter the pyramid from a side entrance as a platform extends, allowing entry that I assume leads to some kind of concealed hangar.

Her steps slow as we approach the outside of the towering pyramid. It's a sight to see. The remainder of the sun's light is completely blocked by the structure as I hang my head back to view it.

"How tall is this thing?" I ask Amity in awe.

"550 feet, Ms. Young."

Sounds about right.

"Did you say something?" Claire asks over her shoulder.

I shake my head and slow my pace after her. A massive triangle-shaped door hisses, spewing air from its corners like a breath into the building. It slides deeper into the pyramid before splitting down the middle, both sides retracting into the grooved edges.

"Welcome to Black Web," Claire says, turning toward me, revealing a soft smile.

"Why am I here?" I ask, my expression stony.

"We need you."

"For what exactly?" My patience wears thin as uncertainty plagues my mind with all the questions begging to be answered. "And how do you know my parents?"

"They were a part of a significant cause that lies in this building. Follow me, and the rest of your questions will be answered."

The smile remains and her eyes are inviting and almost familiar. I nod in response, following her inside.

"Amity, exits," I say.

"Locating and syncing to Iris, Ms. Young," Amity announces.

Minute disappointment creeps into my mind after imagining the inside of the building would match the impressive outside. Claire walks a few paces and the space illuminates, erasing my disappointment.

The walls are made up of metal that ripples and have the dense attributes of glass. The ripples change steadily and at the end of each cycle, it's as if another layer of metal is placed.

"There's a connection disruption, Ms. Young," Amity says.

"What kind?" I ask.

"It appears the building is protected by an overlay. Systems are still functional, however limited."

The multiple layers of the metal must be the culprit. My heart dips for a moment at the uneasiness of not having free connection to the network.

As I move through the space, light voices provoke my attention. My eyes follow the edges of the pyramid upward, where a glass ring protrudes to the outside. Archways of silver extend and connect as bridges for people to walk across. The voices echo down to where we stand as people pace above. Some speed walk, while others walk lazily to their destinations.

This building alone surpasses anything I've seen in Arcadia. It reminds me of the technological prowess of this sector, unmatched by any other in the Area.

A hum travels through the air, drawing my attention to where Claire now stands. An elevator arrives. A cylinder-shaped pod rises next to her but doesn't stay long. It breaks the surface and the same ripple living in the walls activates along the marble etched floor. The elevator travels through the ground as it creates pixels along the floor. It reminds me of a holoscreen being hacked. The marble changes to a translucent glass surface, revealing everything beneath our feet and forcing my lungs to tighten from the uncertainty of stability.

"Ms. Young, it may take longer to find exits; readings are not functioning."

"Understood," I say.

The elevator moves freely toward its determined destination. As it travels, my eyes connect the various cylinders that appear to be the source of its operation. The ripples of the floor return and before it transforms to its original marble, the connected rods resemble an intricate spider web. Memories surface of a gadget my father once had. In a training lesson, he used it to disguise a cipher to invade a system I created. It rippled in the same manner as the walls and floors of this building, protecting it—giving me the reason Amity is having trouble with connection.

"Amazing, isn't it?" Claire says. "That was our central connection you saw. It allows us to communicate with members that are on operations. As you can see, it's also how we travel quickly through the building."

We proceed forward as she walks backward, explaining the purpose of the translucent floor and the ripples of the walls. Like a tour guide, she gestures to a mechanism triggered when the elevator goes through the surface and tells me it's a way to protect the central core, as I thought. Constantly being monitored and having a protective barrier keeps the systems safe.

"Ms. Young, readings show no other exits besides the main entrance," Amity says. "You'll have to make your own if you need one."

I take a sharp breath at the thought. If there are no natural exits, how do I penetrate the protections I've already seen? I do my best to remain calm as I try to keep pace. Most of the information she relays is lost due to my over-analysis of the current situation. Not knowing where I am or exactly why I'm needed sits at the forefront of my thoughts. Only one exit reminds me of the moment I thought Wren and I were going to escape.

My chest grows tight, a sharp pain radiating from fears of no escape. I inhale deeply, focusing my attention on the present moment.

"This way, please," Claire commands.

I follow her onto the elevator as she continues to talk about the central system.

Amid her speaking, Iris vibrates.

"Ms. Young, how long will the lockdown protocol be in effect?" Amity asks.

"Not sure," I whisper.

Iris notifies me of a hard lockdown I can use if I think I'll need it, essentially giving my home more protection. I confirm the lockdown and hope I'm not away longer than I need to be. I miss it.

We head further down, traveling much faster than moments ago. The underneath becomes clear as day. It's an underground fortress. The rods from earlier attach and spread to every end. Light passes through each with every second that ticks by.

"Those are liners," Claire says, pointing to the rods as our descent continues. "Without those, connections can't run smoothly throughout the facility."

The design is impeccable.

There's no noticeable flaw within the system. As skilled as I am at hacking, there is no way to penetrate the outer perimeter without being seen, because of the ever-changing aspects of the building itself. With the core lying beneath the surface, it's practically impossible to find without being directly in front of it.

If someone were able to hack this place without being caught, I'd ditch my ideals and work as a team in an instant. The thought causes thoughts of Trace to creep into my mind. It's what he wanted. To work alongside me—and I never let it happen. Too afraid of the risks. One being his death.

Claire continues expelling details about the structures and the functions of each and I find myself grateful for the distraction. The design continues to impress, and I find it mesmerizing.

"Who designed this place?" I ask, trying to contain enthusiasm.

"Octavio Oxton," she says, piercing my facade.

The name isn't familiar to me, and I take a moment, admiring the architecture.

"He had help of course," she adds. "That's where your parents come in."

Mom. Dad. They did so much, and they could have done so much more. I block away the rising anxiety, refocusing on my surroundings, and find a massive energy source.

Shaped like a diamond, it sparks and resonates with light pooling around it, escaping from its hard edges. It slowly rotates as the center glows, like a device harnessing kinetic energy. The light is so intense and bright as it reaches a point where it seems to burst like an exploding star, releasing energy into the liners.

We finally arrive at our destination and exit the elevator. A few steps take us to a corridor splitting two ways. We head down an aisle with multiple black doors hugging the walls and arrive at double doors. Claire gestures for me to walk in first, but I insist she lead the way.

13

"Please, take a seat," Claire says gently.

I stand across from her at the opposite edge of a levitating circular desk, wide enough to sit at least ten people. My body stays planted, and I ignore the offer.

She takes a deep breath at my silence.

"Everything is going to be explained to you from the beginning, which is why you should take a seat."

"I'll stand. I'll sit when I'm ready."

She chuckles.

This woman really doesn't know when it's appropriate to do so.

"Your mother warned me about you."

"Do not bring my parents into this, unless you plan on telling me how you know them. Otherwise, don't. I'll shut this entire facility down and end this conversation before it even gets started."

"Ready when you are, Ms. Young," Amity chimes in, as Iris buzzes with ways for me to keep my promise.

Claire presses her lips tight, unsure how to respond. Tension fills the room and creates a shroud of dense energy. Combined with the awkward silence between us and death stares, it makes for a very dangerous situation.

"Please ta—"

"Tell me to take a seat again, and it's done."

"Fair enough."

She steps toward a table in the corner, grabbing a large glass pitcher and two smaller glasses filled with ice, then returns to the space across from me. A blue liquid sloshes in the pitcher as she gives it a small swirl, pouring it into one of the glasses. She looks up at me and her eyes ask what her mouth doesn't. I shake my head to refuse the offer of a drink. Claire continues pouring into her own glass until it's full, as if she would have had less if I'd wanted a share. The glass hangs below her nose before she downs half of it in two sequential gulps.

The walls grab my attention as they ripple. Holograms protrude with blueprints of what appear to be navs—communication devices used by informants. They serve a similar purpose as Iris, only less efficient. I pace the circular room, getting a sense of the many devices: one, in particular, a hologlobe of the AOE sitting in the center of the circular desk where Claire stood. She steps forward with another drink in hand and smiles.

"I'm Claire Hart. Director of Black Web," she declares, her voice an inch lower than before. The alcohol seems to have taken a quick effect.

"Okay. Why am I here?"

"Black Web."

Her response is sharp and crisp. I know she means it to be definitive, but there's definitely more she owes me.

"What is that?" I press.

"This. This is Black Web," she says, stretching her arms wide. "You're in Black Web. This facility and its neighboring structures."

"Great. It's the name of a building. That doesn't answer my question."

My already dwindling patience grows smaller with every word she speaks, and the urge to pace returns. Time is something I do not like to waste. It's essential to use every second I have to go after the people who ruined my life. My face is warm, and I know my anger and frustration are apparent by the way the inner corners of her brows flare up.

"I'll get to the point," she says, granting my wish. "Black Web was created by your parents and people they worked with to stay under the radar in their efforts to go against the Enlightenment."

Now she's saying what I want to hear. My interest peaks at the mention of my parents and their fight, one I could have been a part of. The corners of her lips tilt upward, and I know she realizes I'm now interested.

Confidence fuels her voice. "Seems like I finally got your attention."

I ignore it and finally take a seat. The holochair absorbs my weight and levitates at a height that makes it easy to access the table. When I first saw the circular table, it appeared to be metallic, but it's translucent like a holographic display. It curves around in a complete circle with the hologlobe at the center, pulsing like a heartbeat.

Claire's hands hide behind her back, and her shoulders perk up, a gesture I recognize. As she stands, I get a glimpse of how my mother used to command my attention during her lessons. An unexpected chill courses through me, and the hairs on my arms raise.

"Doesn't it feel better to sit and relax?" she asks.

"I'm not relaxed.." I counter.

"But by now, you can surely see there's really nothing to worry about."

"I'm still in an unknown place with a stranger constantly proclaiming there's nothing to worry about, which, if my parents taught me anything, generally means there's, in fact, something to be worried about. So, how about we cut the crap and get this over with?"

My gaze finds her water-filled eyes, glittering from the white light. Her confidence dwindles to a mere ember that was once a flame, ready to burn. I cross my legs and lean forward, urging her to speak. Instead, the desk lowers into the ground and the hologlobe rises like the sun. It slowly rotates, and as it does, letters appear and form the words, 'Black Web'. The phrase glitches and flickers like a corrupted system before a web of links extends from each letter. At the end of each link, folders are attached with coded marks, dragging my interest out into the open.

Distracted by the sight in front of me, I didn't notice Claire move. She stands next to me, eyeing the sphere with a soft smile.

"You may recognize this," she says, handing me a pen.

"A pen?" I ask with a quizzical gaze.

"Not just any pen."

I reach for it and notice a small letter 'A' is engraved where my fingers would hold it to write. The material shines in the light, glistening gold on the edges. I observe it and my emotions act before I can think, taking me back to a time before the pain.

"Ariadne," my mom had called.

She'd been in her studio, at the desk with tons of information displayed across screens in front of her. I can remember arriving, my tiny lungs clawing for air as I gasped at her side.

"You didn't have to run, honey." She'd wiped my brow, trailing my face with her ever soft hands, except her fingertips, which were calloused from the amount of time she spent flipping through holograms, building encryptions, and decrypting information she found worthy. Her long black hair lay straight, always falling down, like a waterfall made of shadows, concealing all of her secrets.

"Do you want to learn something new today?" she'd asked after noticing my eyes lock onto the screen in front of her. Symbols and letters, flooded equations combined together to create the most intricate algorithms. I'd nodded. I was always ready to learn from my parents, always ready to be one step closer to living the way they did. She'd lifted me up onto her lap and that's when I'd first noticed it: The gold lines traced the edges, and I was mesmerized. My hands had reached for the shiny pen when my mom's landed on top of it.

"You're not ready for that yet honey," she'd said, one hand petting my head, correcting the loose strands of hair. "One day you will be. For now, let's learn what a code is."

"Mom."

"Yes, it belonged to her," Claire says.

Water wells behind my eyelids, stinging from my fight to hold them back, avoiding weakness.

"How—rather, *why* do you have it? I ask.

"Ariadne," she starts.

My heart almost explodes from hearing my real name. Claire's eyes bulge with raised brows as she whips her hand over her mouth. She lets the quiet fill the air and watches me intently, waiting for me to make my next move. I forfeit and let her speak.

"Sorry. I should have mentioned that I know your name." She smiles.

"That would have been good to know."

"I thought you would have recognized me. Well, then again, I suppose you were really young the last time we saw each other."

She knows my full name. My heart slams against my chest, forcing my lungs to react and supply more air.

"Ariadne Young," she says in confirmation, "I have that pen because my sister entrusted me with it, and ultimately, she wanted me to return it once you were ready."

Her revelation makes my stomach clench, forcing bile to rise the length of my core. Every organ overworks to control the onslaught of revelations, making me feel dizzy and nauseous to the point where my mind fades in and out of blackness. I focus my breathing, forcing myself to remain calm. The emotions stir, but eventually I'm able to hold them at bay.

For now, I take each thing she said, one by one, and dissect them.

"Sister?" I ask.

"Yes. Adalina, your mother... We are—*were* sisters," she responds. "I told you. I'm not a stranger; I'm your aunt."

"You expect me to believe that?"

"I don't expect anything from you. I want you to listen."

Her voice spews warmth. It's inviting and nurturing. A complete contrast to the times she spoke prior to this conversation. She takes a step toward the holosphere and taps 'Black Web', making it flicker and activate. The letter 'A' replaces the Black Web logo and glows purple, pulsing like a small heartbeat. My suspicion ceases to exist. It's the same symbol in my home. Every piece of technology I own has it. My mother's calling card in a sense, her brand on everything she had a hand in.

"I can see you know the emblem," Claire says.

I nod. My tension declines, and I start to relax. My lungs are operating at the same pace of my now normal heart rate. I place my staff back in its holster and hold the pen tight, as if it were my mother's hand.

Again, Claire changes the holosphere. This time, files splatter like paint, suspended in the air. A slow rotation occurs, and hundreds, maybe thousands, of archives glow within the database. In the files, she finds photos, picking a few and enlarging them with a pinch of her fingers. They reveal her and my parents together at different events, smiling and being with each other. One reveals a small child in Claire's arms, smiling with candy, looking like they're having the time of their lives.

Another picture with the same child appears on the table and the child resembles me. My mom and dad hold them tight, confirming it. Love fills their youthful faces at the happiness etched on mine. I can't be any older than five or six in the photos, as Claire continues to reveal more, one after the other until she stops at a video playback symbol.

The video starts at the tap of her finger. My parents surround me and appear to be showing me a device I can't recognize. My young self's attention quickly turns to a drone that flies overhead, prompting my small feet to chase it.

"Aria, come here. Aunt Claire has something for you," my mother's sweet voice echoes from the playback. Claire walks into the frame of the recording and hands my mom a device resembling Iris. They place it on my tiny wrist, and it slides off.

"She'll grow into it," Claire says.

They all laugh and take sips of their drinks, watching me play with the drone. The file closes from the swipe of Claire's hand as she gently smiles. I fix my gaze on Iris with fresh eyes, and tears pool, dripping down my cheeks. I always thought it was a creation from my parents given to me as a child. The video doesn't strike any memories of the moment, but in watching it and looking at Claire, I can't help but feel like she's telling the truth. There's no denying I watched my parents and myself with Claire, happy. It makes me smile as I softly glide my hand over Iris, feeling the coolness of the titanium frame.

"Looks like a perfect fit now," Claire says.

"It is," I say. "It's perfect."

Claire's face glows red and her eyes water as the light reflects, creating a bright shine.

"I'm so glad you're okay."

"Thank you. But I still have so many questions."

"I'm sure you do. And I intend to answer them all. Let's continue with Black Web. I'm sure that alone will answer quite a few."

We exchange smiles as the holosphere vanishes back into the ground, allowing the table to rise back to its original position.

"First," she says in a low voice, "there's a matter I must attend to."

I watch her face fade to solemnity.

"There will be a service for Trace. You're welcome to join, if you'd like."

The thought provokes an ache in my heart. As much as I cared about him, I don't think I can be around a bunch of people he knew. Strangers to me, but friends to him. I'm not sure I'm ready to confront the things I wish I'd said to him or how unfair I was. There's nothing I wouldn't do to protect the people I care about, and for some reason, I always fail.

But, given his act of saving my life, I owe him my presence at the service.

"Okay," I say. "I'll join."

Claire gently smiles and leads me to the door. She stops abruptly and spins to face me. "I'm glad you're here."

The door hisses open before I can respond. We head toward the service as I find a way to bottle my aching emotions.

14

A hymn begins, low and soft.

The night sky adds to my dread as I slowly walk behind everyone else. The sound of low chants echo, creating a feeling I've never felt before.

I never got the chance to bury anyone I lost. They were all taken away by murder. My parents were incinerated after the invasion of our home. Wren, killed by an Enlightenment Agent to protect me.

With Trace, I now get to see someone honored in death.

From my place at the end of the line, dark robes walk in front of me. Heads tilt down as they slowly make their way toward large triangle doors.

We stop abruptly as Trace's pod hovers at the front, splitting the line into two. It's different from the pod I saw on the flar coming here. It's silver with lines of blue trailing around the edges. It glows against the darkness like a light, trying to break through. Claire takes the lead of the lines, in front of the pod. A long black dress hangs off her shoulders with a silver veil covering her head. She raises a hand, prompting us to proceed.

A windless night is something I didn't expect given the ruthlessness of the wind when we first arrived. The temperature has dipped, and I feel a chill along my spine. My breath escapes in a thick cloud, dissipating as I walk through it. My legs shiver from the lack of coverage and I wish I'd had a chance to go home before coming here.

"Thermal engaged, Ms. Young," Amity says.

My suit ignites with soft heat sending a cold chill across my body. The warmth settles and I'm relieved.

"Thanks, Amity."

"Anytime, Ms. Young."

Another pyramid stands in front of us. It's much smaller than the main facility and has a different aura about it. The jagged edges shaping the outside gives it a mysterious look. The angles of its sides create sharp lines trailing upward until reaching its peak. A golden light extends through the middle and out through the top. The base of it begins to glow as we approach. Stairs rise from beneath the sand, leading toward the large entrance, and with each step upward, the steps ignite in a vibrant gold.

The hymn grows louder as we reach the top. The voices are deeper, longer notes creating a flutter of longing in my heart. It brings me to think about the people I've lost, about Trace and how much I'd give to apologize. For not letting him in. For allowing him to step in front of me and die. I still don't know why he did it. The sacrifice to keep me alive when he barely knew me makes guilt constrict my lungs.

One of the last things he said to me creeps into my mind.

Fate.

I've never been one to believe in it. My parents always taught me we make our own fate. As I grew older and witnessed countless prayers fall on the deaf ears of Gods, I came to the same conclusion as my parents. In this life, we do our best to survive and live with fate being brought upon us by our own actions. It is not predetermined, as most people believe.

After the war, most people abandoned their faith in God and looked for saviors elsewhere. Many crowned the Enlightenment with the title after they took control, not realizing the deadly effects of Nihilism. Some pursued the path of fate and others gave Scientology a massive boost in popularity. I, for one, have a strong hope for the universe and its ever-changing energies throughout the world.

Thoughts of the world continue to force my sharp breaths, making black robes turn to face me. Masks cover their faces. The same masks as the people who arrived at the diner. Neon lights flicker with blank expressions, as if they're a cue for me to get a hold of myself.

The large doors open, releasing the bright light within. As we walk inside, my mind quickly registers that we are in a mausoleum. Along the triangular walls, holograms stretch with names of the deceased. The lines reach an altar at the front and Claire prompts us to wait along the edges. The altar is empty as she makes her way to the top step with Trace beside her. She faces the group and drops the veil, causing the hymn to evaporate. Her blonde hair twinkles with the surrounding light, like a hovering halo.

"Here we lay to rest, Dyce Sharp, better known by his code name, Trace," Claire announces.

The light behind her that extends to the top of the building pulls Trace's pod like a magnet. Claire steps to the side as the pod rises to a vertical position.

Trace looks exactly the same as he did when he was alive. His lips keep a blank expression, but I will never forget the warmth of his smile.

"A friend, comrade, and excellent hacker," Claire continues. "Trace was beloved by us all. His death will not be in vain. As we mourn, we must remember the cause he died for."

As the words leave her lips, I begin to hear mumbling and heads turn toward me. For a moment, the neon lines on a few masks change. The digital lines forming eyebrows drop at a sharp angle and flicker with the mouth expressing a frown.

"To Trace. May he rest in peace."

The pod drops below the surface, breaking the ground the same way the elevator did in the main facility. Below us lies hundreds, maybe thousands, of pods attached to cylinders and the walls. Trace's pod travels to an empty slot along a wall and joins the rest of the fallen members. It attaches as the floor returns to its normal hard surface. His name appears on the main wall behind Claire before joining all the other names on the wall, submitting his legacy.

"We will reconvene tomorrow," Claire says. "Everyone rest. We have a lot of work to do."

The cloaked figures turn on their heels and exit the mausoleum. A few take quick glances at me, again displaying their digital anger and it seems to be because of Trace's heroic act. They walk down the steps, back into the massive pyramid barely visible in the night sky.

"You'll meet them all soon," Claire says, standing next to me.

"I don't think I want to."

"They need time. Trace was important to them."

"Believe it or not, he was important to me too," I say, as my heart stings.

Claire offers a gentle smile, and I return it. We walk in silence. When we reach the bottom of the stairway, it lowers beneath the sand. The golden light vanishes behind us, making the mausoleum no longer visible.

I turn toward the city of technology.

It's bright lights hold the darkness at bay as I view the lines separating them. The bright hues create a vivid landscape people of the old days would only dream of. The dream shatters at the sight of Enlightenment patrols, hovering over the dome. Multiple flars surround it with a menacing force, reminding me of my true goal.

"Tomorrow," she distracts me, "we'll take a walk around the facility. Meet a few people and get to know the place. Your place."

"My place?"

"I'll explain in the morning."

She takes a step toward the main building and waits for me. I take another moment to myself and breathe in the cool air. It fills my lungs as the pressures of the last few hours weigh me down. Releasing the air causes the tension to finally leave my shoulders, making me smile.

"Let me show you where you can sleep."

I nod and follow her back inside Black Web.

15

Waking up wasn't easy.

The fatigue I faced yesterday was proven by the heaviness of my sleep and the fact I couldn't wake up when Amity was notifying me of Claire. I'm normally a person who likes to get up early and do what I need to do, but today, not so much. My legs drag beneath me, with each attempt to pick them up failing to achieve the pace of Claire's long strides. My body still wants rest, and my mind—if only it could rest.

We enter the briefing room, and unlike my first visit, I immediately take a seat at the circling table. The temperature is cooler than it was when I first got here. Maybe the anger and anxiety that flooded my veins contributed to the extensive body heat.

Claire walks around the table as it lowers into the ground. The holosphere rises as she plants her feet.

"Authorization granted," a voice echoes through the room. "Good Morning, Claire."

Suddenly, I'm back at home, in my living room.

"It looks like you're not the only one," I say to Amity.

"Ms. Young, my system is one of a kind, designed by your parents for a specific reason. I am the only one," Amity declares.

"Sounds like jealousy."

"I can't feel."

"Ah, but you know what it is."

"Fair enough, Ms. Young."

Amity is right in the sense of its uniqueness and design. An A.I. that can communicate like a human being. It can't feel, but it does know what feelings are. The way it monitors my very life and helps me with practically everything. From daily tasks, to hacking the most complex systems. Amity is in fact, one of a kind.

"Are you having a conversation with yourself?" Claire asks.

"Sorry, I was talking to my A.I.," I admit.

"Excuse me?"

"Yea, I have an A.I. system. Similar—"

"Better," Amity bellows in my ear, stopping my train of thought.

"Similar," I continue, "to the one you have here, except it's attached to the interface of Iris, and it allows me to communicate through a very small speaker-like device in my ear. I can go on and on about the functions it has, but now is your time for show and tell."

Claire's eyes grow wide, but she remains silent. Amity isn't a normal form of A.I., but judging by this facility and the fact we are in Techdon—the place known for far more advanced systems—I'd imagine she would have seen something like Amity before. She blinks a few times and finds her composure.

"That's fascinating," she finally says.

"Thank you."

"We'll have to talk more about that later, but let's get back to Black Web."

The holosphere rises and rotates like the animation of a planet. An enlarged map of the AOE stretches out in a four-dimensional plane.

"This is the central base for everything we know. From before the Technological War, during, and after. As you know, your parents spent years trying to figure out what the node system was truly about and how to work against it. Of course, we all know the Enlightenment were the creators, but what the general population doesn't know is why and how."

Her hand slides across the map and reveals the Areas and their sectors in more depth. Each area is highlighted in a different color, with their respective sectors mimicking them.

"What do the colors mean?" I ask.

"Before we get into that, Black Web was on the verge of discovering the truth, but the founders—Adalina and Dexter Young—were lost. However, they left behind a blueprint to finding it. This is part of that blueprint. Black Web's entire mission, from the moment it was established, has been to bring the Enlightenment to its knees, freeing the citizens of their tyranny."

She speaks with conviction and strength, making the energy flow within me. A spark ignites in my chest and her cause feels like my own. Her eyes flash as she pinches the holosphere, zooming in on the colored sectors.

"The colors highlight the corners of the nation that we know the most about. Ranging from some knowledge to none," she says.

"I assume green is for what you know the most, yellow is some, and red is none."

"Correct."

"I'm not sure I follow," I say. "You have all of this knowledge and equipment; why would you possibly need me?"

"I believe your parents' last request for me to protect you was more than that. Adalina and Dexter would never plainly say what they were up to. Adalina always had intricate puzzles that defined her secrecy. And Dexter, well, he put the Mr. in mystery."

She chuckles at her own joke and proceeds.

"My point is, if I knew my sister well enough, I think they left you with the key to finding out what was lost when they died. I don't know exactly what the key is, but I'm almost certain it concerns you."

Her words slam into my chest with immense force, making me wince. She watches me intently and proceeds to step through the holosphere, toward me. I stand and start to pace with the words going back and forth in my mind. My parents' faces begin to etch in my thoughts, smiling bright, creating warmth that travels through my veins and into my heart.

The things I'd do to have them back.

My eyes grow wet from the stirring emotions, ignited by her last statement. I never once saw myself included alongside a revolution against the Enlightenment. It was always me against the world, going after the people who deserve the same amount of pain they caused me and others.

But this—this is something I don't think I'm prepared for. Having others depend on me is another level of pain waiting to happen. I turn my back to Claire with the draining thoughts suffocating my mind.

I step toward the door as it hisses open and before I take my leave, Claire is at my side. Her lips arch to one side, forming a soft smile, revealing a dimple on her cheek, the same one my mother had when she smiled. The tears finally release, streaming down my face in a steady flow.

She gently turns me to face her, but I don't meet her gaze. My eyes fall to the floor from the overwhelming revelations and responsibility she laid out, with me at the center of it. Pain, disappointment, anger, and guilt fuel my anxious mind, pushing and pulling my thoughts like crashing waves. Before I can maintain any composure, the emotions flare.

Bringing my worst memory to life.

"Mom? Dad?" I shouted. "What's going on?"

They had been running around our home, collecting items, stuffing them in containers that were sealed once filled. My mom had pushed them all toward a place I couldn't see from my spot in the living room. Fear entangled my legs, and I couldn't move. I couldn't help whatever it was, and I didn't understand it. The sound of aggressive knocking drummed through the house with a piercing echo that made me flinch with each one. My father had run to my side and fell to one knee to meet me at eye level.

He'd smiled.

"Everything is going to be alright," he'd said. "You're going to be okay, I promise."

As his lips had touched my forehead, our front door had blasted open with the sound of a booming shock wave.

The metal frame splintered to pieces and the debris had flown across the living room. Smoke had filled the doorway with blinding gray and bright lights from the vehicles outside. The dark of the night, I remember, had created the shadows of the people that ruined my life. My father had tried to cover my eyes, but I'd pushed by his heavy arms with all my might, to see what was happening.

The sound of swift steps from my mother echoed in the silence as her staff had slammed into the leading shadow. His head had reeled to the side, crashing into the shattered door frame. The memory of the red beams flash in my mind as I recall how they took aim and riddled our home with ammunition that could pierce the best protections. Before the rain of ammo unleashed its fury, my mom was next to me and my father as we'd huddled together on the floor. My sobs grew heavier, and I can remember their hands, trying to soothe me from the sounds of the raid.

The bullets finally stopped, and my father rose to his feet, a dagger in hand and small orbs in the other, standing tall like the protector I remember him being. My mother had looked me in the eyes and smiled, revealing dimples that complimented her face. She then placed a small device in my ear before kissing my forehead, joining my father. Her staff was at the ready, like a warrior waiting for battle. Their silhouettes, magnified by the brightness outside, had given them the appearance of a two-person army.

"Hey," Claire says gently as if I'll break.

It certainly feels like I am glass, and if I get hit by one more revelation, I'll be splintered across the floor. I force myself to lift my sight, stifling the tears narrowly trying to escape. Her emerald eyes beam, shining in the fluorescent light, offering a gentle ease, away from my mind.

"You're not alone anymore," she says.

The words drive home, shattering the dam I created to hold back the tears, and I'm in her arms, sobbing, gasping for air through each intense burst of pain. The pains of my parents and people I cared about. All of them were taken away from me. The guilt of not being able to help. To keep them alive.

Claire looks into my eyes with a familiar gaze. My heart flutters from the thought I have something I've longed for since the death of my parents.

Family.

I wrap my arms around her in a full embrace, the warmth traveling between us. A crisp scent of clove hovers around her like an aura, soothing my overgrowing emotions. The embrace grows stronger, and I hold her tight, like I've never hugged anyone before.

"I'm sorry I put that pressure on you. I shouldn't have done that, and I apologize greatly."

"I honestly don't know what came over me," I respond, knowing exactly what affected me.

Her soft hand wipes away my tears. Like my mother used to do. From this close, the resemblance Claire has to my mother is clearer. The sharp angles in her eyes and long lashes. Soft lines that formed her chin and narrow nose that flared when she got upset. And the small creases that traced her lips when she smiled. It's amazing I missed it this entire time. Although, from the time of the diner to now, I've been under an immense amount of mental stress.

"So strong. Like Adalina," she says. "How about we start a little smaller, huh?"

"A lot smaller," I correct her with a smile.

She returns the smile and retakes her position at the holosphere. It vanishes at the touch of her hand and the table returns to its original position. Black Web's insignia returns as she walks back to my side.

"Let me introduce you to a few people and we can walk around the facility. Then we can see how you feel afterward."

She holds out her hand like a glorified deal is being made. I take it and smile, meeting her gaze.

"Perfect," she says, stepping to the door.

It hisses open, releasing a gentle breeze that glides through the air, drying my remaining tears. I blink hard, clearing my vision.

And for the first time, I respond to her gesture and walk out first.

16

"If you decide to stay, and I sincerely hope you do, I think you'll find the most enjoyment on this thread," she says, slowing her pace, so I can keep up.

"Thread?" I ask.

"Think of it like a floor or level, so to speak."

As we make our way down an outstretched hallway, through what should be walls, but it's all transparent, like glass, there's a view of the entire infrastructure, a kaleidoscope of rods, columns, elevators, bridges, and toward the bottom, above the glowing core, four large hovering spheres. People walk around through hallways like the path Claire and I are on. They fiddle with holoscreens, navs, and holoboards, charging toward their destination.

As I follow her, we pass a woman and child who wave and smile at Claire. The lack of blue in their eyes grants a sense of happiness inside of me. No nodes are active, meaning this place really is the home of the rebellion.

"This thread," she breaks my focus, "is our hacking thread."

Hacking.

"This is where our operatives reside during their prep time before assignments."

We reach the end of the hall, and it opens to rooms lined against the walls like pods. There's a pathway to the left and one to the right. Both lead to a dead end after three pods.

"I'd like you to meet someone."

Claire leads me down the right, and we stop in front of a black door made of obsidian. The door slides open when Claire's eyes are scanned from a lens above it. The room is about the same size as mine. A strong fresh smell hangs in the air as if I've walked into a dense forest.

Claire calls to a girl sitting at a desk tucked in the right corner. Holoscreens hang on the wall in front of her, with codes and algorithms streaming down the displays: encryptions, my least favorite aspect of hacking. Her back is to us as she types relentlessly on a holoboard. My eyes move around the room, admiring the cleanliness.

"Someone can take notes," Amity says.

"Very funny."

We take another step inside and the screen in front of the girl turns bright red. An alarm starts to erupt through the room, prompting her to tap the screen a few times, bringing it back to its pale blue hue. In one swift motion, she powers down the system and turns her seat to face us. My gaze finds hers. Angled eyes and sharp eyebrows give her a daring look. Her brows are raised high in a curious motion, opening her eyes, revealing more. Crimson hair falls to her shoulders, half-wrapped-back in a messy bun.

"Director," the girl says.

The plum colored top she wears exposes fair skin. The top connects to her leggings at the hip, and an opening, exposing her navel, sits in the center. A belted device wraps around her waist that she adjusts when changing positions. I trace her legs, electrifying my senses. Heat rises to my face, and it takes willpower to look away.

"Ms. Young," Amity calls, "your heart rate is higher than normal, as is your body temperature."

I don't respond.

Her natural toned lips form a soft smile as I connect the small freckles under her eyes. I can't stop staring. Simply stunning. I study every inch of her, only amplifying the heat in my blood.

I break the trance, this time turning my back. I take in slow, deep breaths to decrease my heart rate.

I count down from five. Each second more important than the last.

Five…four…three…two…I exhale with an audible gasp.

"What was that?" Claire asks.

"Sorry, nothing," I respond quickly.

Claire taps my shoulder, insisting I look at her.

"You okay?" she asks.

I nod with a smile.

I lie. I'm clearly not okay. This girl, whom I've never met, has ensnared me in a feeling I've only felt once in my life. The same way Wren made my heart flutter and lungs pause makes this moment jar my memories.

"Eliza," Claire says, stopping my thoughts. "I'd like you to meet Ariadne."

Hearing my name again staggers my breathing as I haven't been used to hearing it in years.

Claire clears a direct path between Eliza and me. Once again, our eyes lock, and I only hope she doesn't think I'm a psycho who keeps staring at her. She stands, revealing long, toned legs. We're nearly the same height, but her boots add an extra elevation. She grabs a thin-layered shirt from the back of the chair and tosses it over her with grace. It falls across her body like an elegant drape, complimenting her natural silhouette. Brushing her hair from underneath the newly added shirt, she takes a few steps forward, erasing the distance between us. I get a glimpse of sway, magnifying her curves. Her steps come to an end with an outstretched hand.

"Nice to meet you," she says.

"Likewise."

Our hands touch. Soft and smooth with no imperfections. I grasp my hand is still attached to hers when it continues to shake, and she smiles, looking at our intertwined hands. My body feels hot from agitated nerves, as sweat forms along my brow.

"Cooling system engaged, Ms. Young," Amity reads my mind again.

My bodysuit starts to cool and I'm immensely grateful. I drop my hand and continue my examination of her room, begging for any kind of distraction. Unfortunately, it's plain, with the basic necessities to live. A bed perfectly made, a closet, desk, and wall space with weapons draped along it. Seemingly out of place, a pair of gloves hang next to a trace gun. They have a similar design to a pair my father had and used when he needed to defend himself, except his covered every finger while these don't.

"What do you think?" Eliza says.

"What?" I ask, changing my focus.

"You're looking around quite a bit."

There's a deliberate pause and her brows rise, heightening the flash in her eyes. I know she's referring to the way I've looked at her. This is bait, but I won't bite.

"I was wondering," she continues, "what do you think of my room?"

A smirk grows on her face.

"Oh," I say.

She chuckles and walks to Claire, who's been watching our awkward greeting.

"Your assignment is ready when you are," Claire says.

"Perfect," Eliza responds.

She heads to the wall of assorted weapons and grabs the pair of gloves, sliding them on. They wrap around her wrists, exposing the tips of her ring and pinky fingers, leaving the others covered.. She clicks her wrists together, activating the gloves. Purple lines stem from her wrist, down to the ends of each covered finger. The material of the gloves shine from the light as she adds other weapons to the pockets of her belted device. She adjusts it on her waist, to accommodate the newly added weight.

"Director," Eliza says, walking past Claire. "It was nice meeting you," she says to me. "Hopefully, we get to see more of each other."

"Yeah," I say quickly.

She winks and walks out of the room, leaving behind a clean scent of eucalyptus and faint notes of vanilla. Claire grabs my attention by clearing her throat.

"If I didn't know any better, I'd say you like Eliza," she says.

I don't respond, protecting myself from any more embarrassment.

"I take your silence as a yes." She laughs. "I think she likes you too. But none of my business."

My face burns from the accusation when she gestures for me to exit. The fresh scent of Eliza is gone when we leave, and I fear Claire may be right, because I already miss it.

"Eliza Walker is one of our main operatives," she continues. "She is quite the encryptor. In a world where information is a valuable currency, it's important to be able to protect what's ours. As we take information, we must safeguard it. And with the expertise in hacking found in many of the people in Black Web, we get closer to the dream of freedom."

The dream of freedom.

My parents always said the same thing to me. Claire's belief in Black Web is strong. There's a tangible energy whenever she speaks about it, helping me understand why she's the director. I find myself intrigued, wanting to know more about her and this place. Knowing it was created by my parents, there's a sense of belonging rising in my core, but my mind backtracks to the task she pointed out earlier: me being part of a blueprint to end the Enlightenment.

As I follow her, my nerves tremble, and I find myself trying to breathe again, afraid of the responsibilities laid out before me.

17

The large doors of Black Web echo behind us as they close.

The sun is approaching its peak. The blazing heat feels worse than it did a few days ago. Being underground for so long has made me weak to the natural elements. Through my squinted gaze at the horizon, heat waves pool like water in the distance. Techdon stands high in its globe as the skies above it appear more active. We walk directly across to another facility that's connected to Black Web.

Not to my surprise, a pyramid stands before us. The same size as the mausoleum on the other side. This one, however, is transparent and coated in silver glass. Greenery can be seen from the outside as we approach the entrance.

"Welcome to our greenhouse," Claire says.

The doors slide open, releasing fresh air. I take it in after being in the heat, and the freshness travels through my nose. As we move farther inside, more questions begin to sir in my mind.

"If you already have hackers, why do you need me?" I ask.

"You're skilled in a wide variety of ways, opposed to our hackers. For example, Eliza is an exceptional hacker as well, but she's a white hat for us. Her skills protect us, both in the field and out. And there's Zane, who is limited to only crashing networks. Don't get me wrong; his skills are very useful, but we need someone who has it all—a jack of all trades in a sense, and ideally, a master of all."

She makes me seem like a god. Like I'm all powerful and unstoppable. As much as I'd love to relish in the feeling of high compliments, I can't. Knowing the amount of times I've failed in missions and how I'm currently failing at my life's purpose, it negates all the good she tries to point out.

We continue through the new facility as my gaze starts to wander. Around are tubes containing rotating DNA strands. They rise from the base toward the top, stopping before the peak.

"It's also not because you're kin either," she adds. "Through here."

She guides me through silver doors, leading to a set of spiraling steps.

"I know your parents taught you well and I know you've added your own self teachings. I also mentioned before that I've been watching you for some time."

"How long?" I interrupt her thoughts.

"Only a few years."

Only.

We proceed through an outstretched corridor engulfed by the scent of pine, an aroma I love. When I step out onto my deck and look out at the ocean and city, it reminds me of my home.

"I didn't know who it was when my team first encoun-tered a hacker that infiltrated an Enlightenment Complex in Arcadia a few years ago."

I remember.

One of the first missions I felt prepared for. I was ready to begin my quest for vengeance after years of self-training and discipline. It was a lead I'd hung onto from the prison. It led me to an Enlightenment Complex where I learned what most citizens never get to. It held archives of the previous world and how the people lived. The time of monarchy under another country. The decades, centuries of democra-cy, and the rise and fall of the former nation known as the United States of America. Ultimately, it added to my drive for vengeance. I was propelled by my findings.

A successful first mission that set the path.

"We were looking for information that we believed the Complex held. When we arrived, we saw that there was already a breach in their systems, forcing them to act and find better encryptions. Trace took the lead on gathering more data."

Trace. I never knew where he got information. This is how he knew so much. How he constantly had new updates surrounding the Enlightenment.

"The intel he found was relayed to me, and I was curious to see who was behind it. So I did some digging. Months went by before another major breach appeared, and that was when I realized it was you. Iris has a par-ticular coding that only your parents and I can decode. The search began, and I did everything I could. I thought you were gone forever after the loss of your parents. Their final wish to protect their daughter... It was impossible to believe I could fulfill it. I've been trying to figure out how to approach you. So, I had Trace be my eyes."

Claire's feet plant and she pivots to face me. She observes my expression, waiting to see my reaction to the revelation. My headspace is clouded with all the information, and it's amazing I haven't fainted. All this time, I thought I was a ghost. Well-hidden and untraceable. The device I've been wearing for as long as I can remember has been giving information on my location. Even with the hard revelation of not being truly anonymous, I can't help but smile. Iris has been the device to give me ease in my abilities alongside Amity. I find Claire returning the smile.

"I'm still a little confused," I say. "Can't you train the hackers you have?"

We descend another set of silver steps, onto a new pathway. The corridor is all white and as people walk by, it's almost hard to see they are wearing lab coats. Instincts constantly make me look at others' eyes, but again, no nodes are active.

"Good Afternoon, Director," a man says softly, nodding as he passes.

"Afternoon," Claire responds. "Is Zoe in?"

"Yes. She may be in the middle of a test. That's why we're all wandering."

He chuckles and Claire dismisses him with a smile.

The power she has.

"To answer your question, we are training our hackers. I have put together a school, so to speak, on the expertise of hacking. Elite hackers, whom we call silks, who worked alongside your parents to help in those efforts. The problem is, it will take time, especially for our new additions. And unfortunately, time is a luxury we cannot afford."

"Why?"

"Because the Enlightenment is planning a nation-wide address regarding the node and how it's connected to everything. I believe they may be advancing the node somehow."

"When is the address?" I ask.

"That's what we need to find out. Without knowing exactly when they plan to do this puts us at a disadvantage, and therefore, we don't have time to waste. But, if I had to guess, it will be sometime around Enlightenment Day."

Enlightenment Day. The day the nation was reborn as the Areas of Enlightenment and all detachments to any other country were successfully mandated. Every year, citizens celebrate the history of the Areas. One day a year, when the Enlightenment allows large gatherings without penalty.

She stops in front of a door covered in moss, thick evergreen stretching across the frame, weaving through the center with thorns sharp enough to cut flesh. The moss sounds like it's alive. Breathing and moving like a living creature. A hologram appears to the right of the door, flickering as if calling to be activated. Claire places her hand above it, making a green light illuminate, prompting the same system from her office to activate.

"Good afternoon, Director. Welcome," the automated voice says.

The moss retracts into the door, vanishing inside the crevasses. Water cascades down the top, flowing with enough pressure to make it splash, spraying us with a light mist before flushing through vents layered on the floor in front of our feet. The water stops and the door shines metallic, sliding open and releasing chilling air.

As I breathe, my lungs feel dry and heavy, like they're expanding and fighting for air. Each breath grows sparser than the last.

"Don't worry. It'll pass in a few minutes," Claire reassures me.

"A few minutes? I don't know if I'll make it another few seconds let alone minutes."

She chuckles.

It wasn't a joke.

"This is our recovery thread. Zoe keeps the atmosphere this way to block out bacteria and keep disease from spreading. She's our head doctor."

The pain in my lungs feels like the very opposite of recovery. I step inside behind Claire. My eyes begin to adjust to the light as a lab comes into focus, forcing me to tense as a memory of imprisonment instantly resurfaces.

My body was torn apart from the surgery they did. I was weak and feeble, unable to comprehend what had been done to me.

"Here," a woman said, "it'll help with the pain."

I wanted to slap the drink she offered out of her hands, but the restraints held me in place.

"Listen: take it. You'll feel better."

"Why?" I choked out. "Why are you helping me now?"

There was an unrecognizable spark in her eye. It was a look that never came with people who worked there.

A look of care.

"To be honest, I don't know," she said. "But you need to take it quickly. They'll be back any minute."

I nodded.

She lifted my head slightly off the metal frame beneath me and placed the liquid to my lips. I sipped, and after a few minutes, the pain began to subside.

"There," she said.

I started to breathe easier, but her footsteps trailing away made me worry.

"Wait. Don't leave me."

"I'm sure we'll meet again."

A smile stretched across her face as she walked away.

"Ms. Young," Amity says, "you're not there anymore."

I continue behind Claire with slow steps, refocusing my mind and holding on to Amity's voice. Test tubes flood the walls and when I avert my gaze to avoid the sight, the glass floor reflects the vine ceiling above, moving down the entryway. We continue and it's hard to determine if the slithering sounds are snakes or the vines moving overhead. Boiling water bubbles and pops as we move farther in. At the center, there are three different directions we can take. Left, forward, and right.

Claire goes to the right and I follow, peeking in the other directions. A large glass door prevents us from going any farther, and to my confusion, it doesn't reflect nor is it transparent. My breathing finally returns to normal as the sound of rushing water fills the air.

"Might want to step back this time," Claire suggests.

Another display of water drapes over the glass like the previous door, sloshing and splashing around. This time, as the water flows down, the glass behind it becomes transparent. Instead of draining at the bottom, the water rises back up and the door opens. Revealing a large open room, filled with more lab equipment, making my heart skip a beat. I focus my attention on a woman sitting on a holochair, pouring a purple liquid onto grass.

"Zoe?" Claire calls gently.

The woman doesn't respond, continuing to slowly pour the liquid with precision. The color changes as it leaves the glass beaker in her hand, from purple to a vibrant ruby. It returns to its original shade as it lands on the grass. A few seconds pass and it disintegrates, one blade at a time, succumbing to ash.

Zoe glides through the air in her seat, reaching an adjacent desk that displays a hologram littered with chemistry, specifically images of bonds, something I could never comprehend. Silence engulfs the room as she stares at the hologram, waiting. Claire watches intently, stopping herself from moving beyond the few steps we've already taken. The hologram illuminates a bright green, igniting the woman with immense energy, shattering the quiet.

"Yes!" she shouts. "I did it! I actually did it!"

"Zoe?" Claire says again, raising her pitch by a fraction.

Zoe raises a finger, gesturing for Claire to wait as she speaks directly into a recording device. She stands and turns, finally facing us. I'm struck with familiarity, like I've seen her before. Her face is young—very young. Younger than I imagined from the booming shout she released. Rounded glasses hold steady on her forehead, a tactical advantage now, as opposed to being used for sight, the way they were before the war. Interchangeable lenses might gather information on people by their registered nodes. Or find vital points in a building to quickly destroy it.

Dark brown hair, wavy in texture, is pulled back, half in a loose tied knot and the rest falling onto her shoulders like a waterfall. The creamy tan complexion of her skin reminds me of the sands in Arcadia, when summer is taking its last breaths, the sun beckoning over the earth, producing beautiful color. She takes a step forward, and her long white cloak falls above her knees, flowing with her movements.

"Director," she says in a cool, mellow tone.

"How are the trials coming along?" Claire asks.

"Very well." Tempered enthusiasm replaces her extreme excitement from before. "I completed one, and I'd say it's one of the best I've ever done."

"When will it be ready for testing?"

"It's ready as of this very moment."

"Marvelous."

Zoe steps closer to us and watches me. I get the feeling she wants to know why I'm here. A stranger in her domain. Her glasses fall to her eyes and glow, revealing they are, in fact, hololenses. Light blue covers her eyes as she stares at me, scanning.

"Right," Claire says. "I wanted you to meet our newest member."

My eyes dart to Claire at the mention of me being the newest member, something I did not agree to. She clears her throat before speaking again, doing her best to ignore my stare.

"This is Ariadne," she continues.

Zoe slants her eyes, scanning me from head to toe, and I've never felt so judged.

"Nice to meet you," she says finally.

"Pleasure."

"Director," Zoe says. "I also wanted to inform you about the nav modifications for the operatives."

Without gesturing, Zoe moves to her table and Claire and I follow. The lab desk contains holographic files with human anatomy, plant anatomy, and other anatomical outlines of animals. Zoe swipes her hand on the desk, and it all vanishes, replaced by navs, suspended in the air. From it, links coil outward with specific intel on the design.

"I've added new functions that will impede death, should they need it," Zoe says.

She spins the nav upside down, revealing a small slot on the device holding a pin needle.

"At the press of this button," she says, highlighting it, "a small pin will inject adrenaline directly into the wrist vein, keeping them alive, making them feel better after taking it."

Her last statement reminds me of a moment at the prison. When I thought I was going to die.

"How long will the effects last?" Claire asks, distracting me.

"For now, about two hours."

"This would be a great addition for Iris, Ms. Young," Amity says.

I agree. To keep myself alive if I ever run into trouble seems like a great way to stay ahead of my enemies. Allowing me to always expect nothing and prepare for anything.

"How do I get one?" I ask.

"Do you have a nav?" Zoe asks.

"No, but I have this." I extend my arm with the titanium bangle on my wrist.

"What's this?" Zoe asks.

"A creation from Adalina, Dexter, and me," Claire says.

I tap the bangle, activating Iris. Zoe's eyes widen as her hands reach for my arm. I recoil defensively, keeping Iris safe.

"Sorry," Zoe says. "When I see tech that can be improved with medicine, I get overzealous."

The hololens return to her forehead as she smiles.

"I can certainly add it if you would like," she says.

"Actually," I say, "let me think about it."

Removing Iris from my person isn't something I'm ready for. Even if it's for a moment. To leave it with a stranger doesn't sit well with me. My stomach twists at the thought.

"Okay. Just let me know if you change your mind."

Zoe finds her holoboard and inputs a sequence to finalize the nav modifications. The suspended hologram glows green and disappears into the table.

"They'll be ready shortly," she says to Claire.

"Excellent. I'll let you get back to it then."

Zoe nods and takes her leave, sitting at her desk, fiddling with the hologram and its results. Claire guides me back through the entrance and out of the lab toward the main thread of the greenhouse.

"Isn't she something?" Claire says.

"That's a word for it," I say with a little too much bite.

"She'll grow on you. She's very secluded by her own choice, to focus on medicine and ways to help the world. Zoe is kin to those who ended the most horrible diseases that lived in the times before the war and declining world. Cancer, for example, being the most elusive form of disease, was eradicated by the Redwood family. They are a part of human life continuing through the array of chaos."

To be a part of something so major is no easy feat. I, myself, have been thrust into a world where I am related to some of the most notorious people in the nation. I feel myself gaining a liking to Zoe already. I remember the times I'd read about the amounts of death caused by all types of disease in the old days. It's astounding her family was part of the end of it, and she is here to fill the void.

"I can certainly see why she's a great asset to you," I add.

"Not to me. The world."

Claire smiles, continuing steady strides toward the elevator.

"You will certainly get a chance to know more about her and her abilities, but I have a briefing with the hacker thread in a little while, which I must prepare for. Hopefully, you will join us and can tell me how you feel about Black Web so far. We can also discuss your mission, if you'd like."

I nod as we enter the main facility.

We board the elevator and my mission for revenge comes to focus. Vengeance against those who took everything from me. Black Web crosses my mind in the midst of fury and fills my mind with questions. Maybe Black Web can help me? A few days ago, I had no family, no one on my side against my enemies. Maybe she can help me make my dream a reality.

Then, the other part of me asks if she will expect me to lead this revolution and fight for something I never imagined. The fall of the Enlightenment has always been my wish, but I never thought of what comes after. How the nation would look. I don't think I'm ready for it, even though she believes I am.

"Can I ask you something?" I inquire.

"Sure."

"With everything you have here and the people you have helping, what is your plan for the Enlightenment and for after?"

Her brow furrows as her eyes move in contemplation. A moment of silence passes before she speaks.

"The Enlightenment has disconnected this nation from the world. Why? We still don't know the exact answer. But I believe that by showing the truth behind them, it will usher in a new beginning. Imagine our nation essentially waking up and realizing, this isn't how we're supposed to be living. Under deadly surveillance because of free healthcare, security, periodic care packages and whatever they have coerced us into believing is okay. Black Web's ultimate goal is to reestablish our connection to the world, in the hopes that one day, it will bring about freedom, something we can only do if the Enlightenment is gone."

Her words ignite a fire in me. I never thought about the outside world until now. I knew the AOE doesn't have connections with it, but it never occurred to me it was for a reason. A distraction brought forth by the Enlightenment. To keep this nation in a chokehold.

We descend and I look at Claire. Hope fills her eyes. The same sparkle my mom held when she believed I could learn and do anything. The same hopeful eyes my father had during each of our lessons. I smile at her and channel my own hope.

The hope I'm not a disappointment to them all.

FIREWALL

18

The briefing room feels smaller than when we left it earlier. People stand around the oval table, taking over the space, giving the impression of a ritual waiting to be held. From the corner of the room, I count four people, all hidden behind hoods, and remember my first introduction to the members of this place, surrounded by unknown people and not knowing the outcome of following them to a place far from where I know. I still haven't grown accustomed to being away from my home.

I get a closer look at their cloaks this time, a well-designed drape shaping their bodies precisely. All black with the consistency of leather giving the appearance of being repellent against something, and if I had to guess, that something would be bullets. A girl with her back facing me lifts off her hood, releasing blonde curls. She steps closer to the table and methodically grazes her fingers across it.

"You know you shouldn't be touching that," a distorted voice says.

I can't tell which one of the hooded figures spoke as they all look at the girl in unison, their neon masks showing no expression.

"And who are you to tell me what to do?" The girl looks ahead, across the table in front of her.

"Your superior," the low voice returns.

"Someone must have told you wrong," the girl says through a laugh.

Claire gracefully walks through the door with Eliza at her side. The blonde girl swiftly retracts her hand from the table as fast as she can, moving close to one of the other hooded members, but it's too late. Claire strikes a hard stare, her face muscles all tightening. The intensity of the look forces everyone to step back. Before the door closes, another hooded figure is added to the party. They take a stance in the opposite corner, looking straight toward the table.

"At ease," Claire snaps.

"Director," they all say, like a unified chorus.

Claire resumes her stride to the center of the oval table, where the holosphere lives in the ground. She stands, scanning the faces of everyone in the room. Eliza breaks away and is at my side. Eucalyptus invades my nostrils, and I'm engulfed by a refreshing sensation.

"Hey stranger," she whispers, nudging my arm like we've known each other for years.

"Hey," I say, suppressing a smile.

Her hair is unraveled down her face like a red carpet. The blue in her eyes dares me to take a dive and I catch myself in a daze of cool warmth.

"I hope you all had a good rest. Today, we resume our mission," Claire announces sharply.

Every hood falls in an instant, like her voice is the wind, forcing them all back. Their neon masks follow, revealing their faces. A young looking guy with ruffled brown hair stands closest to the wall near the head of the table. The blonde girl who revealed herself first stands next to him. She sways lightly, hands intertwined in front of her.

My eyes trail to the side of the table nearest to me and find the backs of two platinum blonde figures. And the last guy who trailed Claire and Eliza leans against the wall with one foot against it, supporting his weight. His hair is dark, black almost, as it falls down his face, producing a shadow concealing most of it. He pushes a few strands away to clear his vision, taking a sharp glance at me, narrowing his eyes to slits. I return the look, making him shift. He tightens his jaw and looks away toward Claire.

"Who is that?" I ask Eliza in a low tone, keeping my eyes on him.

"Zane Knox," she says. "Real hard ass. Do I sense a crush?"

"Not my type." My eyes lock on to hers.

There's a spark in her gaze and I feel the connection, but I don't know what it is or why it's happening. I never allow these types of feelings to bubble up—not since the moment I lost Wren. I've been taught, shown rather, that they never end well.

"Seems more like a dick if you ask me," I add, making us both laugh.

Zane darts his eyes back toward me and presses his lips, containing himself from speaking.

"Raelyn," Claire calls.

"Director," the blonde girl responds.

Her posture changes and her wide eyes soften. She appears more eager and attentive than before.

"How's the tech thread going with intel on the Enlightenment?" Claire asks.

"We have come across new information about the members of the Enlightenment. However, we may need help from the hacker thread to get a clearer understanding. A lot is encrypted, and we have tried every way possible to break through, but we can't seem to crack the implanted codes," Raelyn responds boldly.

There's a fierceness in her voice that demands attention. She looks poised and in control of the room, similar to how Claire holds attention—effortlessly.

"The director's daughter," Eliza's voice echoes through my ear.

The coolness of her lips so close to my skin makes my heart jump and distracts me from the realization I have another living family member. I've never met her, but it's nice to know I have a cousin on the same side. And it makes sense, understanding where Raelyn gets her boldness from.

"Got it," I say swiftly.

"Excellent," Claire says. "Will the hacker thread be able to assist?"

Her voice strikes my direction, and I almost feel inclined to answer, but Eliza is there instead.

"Always, Director," Eliza says smoothly.

Claire nods. "Zane, any news from the other sectors? Any movement?"

"My team and I have found the Central Square event has caused the Enlightenment to order increased patrols in Arcadia," he says.

For the first time after someone addresses Claire, he didn't say director. Claire cocks her head to the side and narrows her eyes, the wrinkles of anger drawn between her brows. The intensity in her face deepens when her brows drop at an angle. I've never seen someone control a room the way she does. It makes me question if it's a need for power or something else.

"Director," Zane finally adds, dropping his foot.

"It's not that hard," Raelyn says, shooting a look toward Zane.

"For me, it is," he says. "I don't do well with authority."

"You're such an ass sometimes." The ruffles of the guy next to Raelyn move as he speaks.

Zane stands straight, revealing his height.

His hair sways with every movement as he crosses his arms. The short sleeves rise, revealing tattoos that trace his arms, descending toward his wrist.

"Takes one to know one," Zane snarls.

"Mason King. True hot head. This might get interesting," Eliza says, continuing her well appreciated roll call.

Mason steps toward Zane, reaching to his side. Zane returns the step, and they're inches from each other.

"My money is on Mason," a new voice chimes in, and I can only imagine it belongs to one of the platinum blonde couples.

"Enough!" Claire barks.

"Director," they say in unison, returning to their previous places.

"We don't have time for this," she continues. "There's less than three months until Enlightenment Day when the Enlightenment will deliver their address to the nation. We need to find out why the Enlightenment are always hidden, why they created the node outside of what we already know, and most importantly, how to reach the citizens."

She takes a deep breath and steps back from the holosphere, opening her arms wide. The holosphere opens with a map of the AOE.

"Here's what we have so far," she says. "Ezra Coleman, the man in charge of Area 1 has issued a new mandate for Arcadia, giving them more benefits to control what has happened in Central Square."

Ezra Coleman. I infiltrated a building he owns a few days ago. I knew he was important. Annoyance grows inside of me at the thought I could have done something more if I had known.

"Raelyn and Mason," she continues, "along with their team, have infiltrated Techdon, gaining intel that needs to be decrypted. We will find out what it holds after attempting to crack it."

Claire zooms in on Area 1, forming an 'x' over Techdon sector.

"Zane's team has gathered their information from Arcadia. Leaving Millennia and, of course, Cybourne."

She crosses off Arcadia and circles Millennia and Cybourne.

"Here's what we will do next. We'll start by deciphering what was found in Millennia. It should give us something to work with. Then we will move on to discovering if there's any new intel in Millennia, leaving Cybourne for last."

Everyone nods.

"We'll reconvene tomorrow with updates on the decryption."

"I can help," I say.

The air in the room instantly evaporates. Every head turns to me, and I already regret speaking out loud.

"Are you sure?" Claire asks.

"Yes."

If I'm able to help crack this decryption and gain new information about my mission and purpose, then it's worth trying. My goal may be aligning with theirs after all.

"Very well."

Silence builds an awkward tension. I feel people staring at me as if I were naked. The moment passes and Raelyn grabs Mason's arm walking out, passing Zane. The rest of the group stalks out afterward, leaving Eliza, Zane, and me with Claire. Eliza grabs my hand, making me tense as she guides me to the exit. Zane takes a step toward the door behind us.

"You stay." Claire's voice ensnares his feet. He scuffs and forces himself to go back.

We exit the room, leaving behind tension, choking at the door. As we head down the corridor, I think about the ways I can help them crack an encryption, and the time I learned my favorite aspect of hacking.

"Ariadne," my dad had called to me.

I had been fiddling with a new program he wanted to test me on. We were in his workspace adjacent to our home. I remember the clean smell with a metallic end that made me think he always cleaned it. I came to learn that it cleaned itself.

When I went to him, he'd had a sphere in his hand. It shimmered different shades of color as he'd methodically looked it over. His famous black cloak hung off his shoulders with an upturned collar that stopped just before his chin. I was getting older, fourteen at the time, but I don't remember him or my mother aging. The shadow of his beard was peaking above his tanned skin, beads of black that pricked when touched.

My footsteps had grabbed his attention, and he'd smiled. Most people, when they smile, it's in the lips, a soft curve upward. For my dad, it was something I'll never forget: His smile was visible through the entirety of his face. The way his eyes would light up, changing the lines of his cheeks as they rose. It always made me smile back, no matter how I was feeling.

"Do you know what this is?" he'd asked, lightly placing the sphere in my hands.

The first thing I'd noticed was the temperature, cold and sharp, like it was taken out of a cryogenic freezer. Next was the prisms of color that gave the silver ball color, life.

"No," I'd said. "What is it?"

"Time to learn."

His voice had been soft, but stern. He always had a way of getting me to do things without making it more than what it was.

"I want you to decrypt this."

"I don't know how to do it?"

"Remember the phone?" he'd asked.

My mind had tracked backward to the days I was regarded as nothing more than a script kiddy. The day I experienced my first failure.

"Yea," I'd said, saddened by the fact I'd failed, "I didn't do it right."

"There is never a right. Never. It's always about what you learned and how you can use failure to prevail."

I gave him a slow nod that meant I understood.

"What did you learn from that exercise?"

"To expect nothing and prepare for anything."

"Exactly."

He'd sat us down at a black table that housed holograms and a device the sphere lived in.

"Some things are impossible to decode. But with this?" He'd pointed to the sphere. "It'll be hard to find things you can't do."

I recall my mind racing with excitement. It felt like I was getting the secret to the world that only I had.

"I will teach you how to use this device to access the most advanced and secure systems. It won't be easy. Unlike encryption, decoding information is about timing, speed and accuracy. Mastering the art of hacking will require every aspect of what your mother and I have taught you."

After a few weeks, I became a master of decryption. I was able to crack a system with the sphere and decode what was inside. It contained all my parent's notes about hacking.

The good, the bad, and the impossible.

19

"Wild first meeting for you," Eliza says, jumping onto her bed. She flips her boots off and adjusts herself higher, back to the brass colored frame. I stand in the same spot Claire and I were earlier, examining the room all the same, to keep my eyes distracted.

"Yea, what was that about?" I ask. "Is Claire always power hungry?"

"It's not so much about power...it's about precision and organization. She doesn't care about being called the director. What she cares about is order."

Now it makes sense. My mother was the same way when it came to keeping everything in check.

"Amity, time," I say.

"1 pm, Ms. Young."

I haven't noticed the passing of time since arriving here. Going back and forth underground confuses the concept of time and the body's natural sense of when the day starts and ends. I've been here for almost two days, but it doesn't feel like it.

"You say something?" Eliza asks, sitting up straight.

"Nothing. Sorry," I say, not knowing why I'm apologizing.

"Take a seat. You're making me nervous."

How many people in this facility will ask me to sit?

I follow her eyes to a seat, walking toward it in short, quick steps. Over my shoulder I ask for confirmation with my eyes to sit at her desk, the only seat in the room, other than her bed. She nods and smiles. I sit comfortably on the holochair, crossing one leg over the other and remove my staff from its holster on the back of my belt line. I place it in an empty holster along my thigh, next to my drone.

"You're so tense," she says. "Loosen up. I'm not going to do anything."

"Well, I don't know you."

"So get to know me."

She jumps off the bed and takes off her over piece and I'm not ready for it. It's a quick gesture but drags over what feels like five minutes. Every second is slowed by her movements in an effort to make me watch. The over piece trails toward her bed like a feather floating down onto it. She shifts her hair to one side, revealing the tattoos along her neck, falling over her shoulder, down the length of her arm, a spectacle of color and patterns painting a theme of whimsical perfection. Her fingers comb through the thick red as she turns to face me, smiling bright like there's not a worry in the world.

"Oh, come on. If I wanted to harm you in any way, don't you think I would have done that already? After all, I did invite you to my room."

"I suppose, but that doesn't mean I trust you."

"I don't trust you either and I'm not asking you to. I'm asking you to talk, get to know each other. and eventually, trust will form."

The way she speaks puts me in a trance. A deep feeling of limbo makes me stare unwillingly. My eyes find their way of tracing her every inch. Tiny freckles seem to be highlighted by the light, blue eyes glittering with bright intensity, like calm ocean waves. Golden red hair drapes the sides of her face, creating curtains that complement a theatrical view. Red waves extend past milk white shoulders, creating an elegant contrast.

Dimples complete the masterful display threatening to send me over the edge. She folds her arms underneath her breasts, lifting them high enough to provoke my gaze—a successful endeavor. The opening in her well-fitted top reveals cleavage patched with natural pink and more tattoos, peeking from beneath, asking to be seen. They extend to her other arm, this time stopping at her bicep. Another concoction of symbols and drawings that spiral together.

"Hello?" she asks.

I ignore it.

A shift in her stance grants the wishes my eyes have been longing for. Her natural curves ignite my blood, sending heat throughout my body like fire in a scorching furnace. There's a sassy sway that makes the butterflies in my stomach awaken. Flapping their wings, harder, stronger as they rise upward in my chest. Leggings hug her body, starting at her navel, complementing the length of her legs, stopping right at the ankle. I'm stunned by her natural beauty, paralyzed by every inch—and somehow wanting more.

"Hellllooo," she says, snapping her fingers. I shake my head to break whatever spell she's placed on me. Maybe it's all the eucalyptus.

"Sorry, what?" I say.

"The hell was that? Are you okay?"

"I don't know what you're talking about."

"Uhhh…okay."

I spin in the chair, finally breaking my eyes away to find a distraction. Her desk is clean, organized, but emptier than I'd expect. The same material plating the floor is embedded in the table. I lightly graze it to get the feeling of its components. A red glow illuminates through a hologram and chimes an alert, triggering a countdown from three seconds. The same warning from the first time I stepped foot in her room. Eliza is over my shoulder in an instant and the eucalyptus spills across my face, uninvited, but very much welcomed.

"Sorry," I say without thinking. It's becoming my new favorite word.

"All good. It's a little sensitive to touch," she reassures me. "But you can't be too careful. you know?"

"Yea, I get that."

"Expect nothing. Prepare for anything."

The words are like daggers. Piercing and slicing through the air, my ear is their final destination.

"What did you say?" My father's mantra rings in my head.

"Expect nothing. Prepare for anything," she repeats.

"Where did you hear that?"

She takes a step back, the scent fleeing with her.

"It's something we live by here. When we go on operations, it's something we say to ourselves. A way of life, so to speak."

"A mantra," I add.

"Exactly."

She sits at the edge of the bed, folding over, elbows to knees and eyes meeting mine.

"Why the sudden interest?" she asks.

My head sinks into the back of the head rest. I close my eyes, creating a world of black. My father fills my head with love as I remember his smile. A smile that made darkness feel like a small shadow, that only existed to mimic its creator.

A smile I miss.

"No reason," I lie. "I like how it sounds."

"Well, if you stay, it can be a part of you too," she says with a change in her voice.

It's sweet and tender. Luring, like a siren coaxing me to follow her sound. Maybe it's the dreamy effect of my eyes closed and the unexpected desire I have for her making me vulnerable. Or simply lust, or loneliness, and the fact I haven't had genuine conversation with a human being quite like her since Wren.

Wren's smile flashes in my head, replacing my father's, and I reminisce on the moment she first displayed it.

"You okay?" Eliza asks, making my eyes open to the ceiling above.

"Yeah, I'm fine."

She leans back on her hands, cocking her head, studying me.

"You're a bad liar."

"Told you," Amity adds.

Her head leans to the opposite side, her eyes never leaving mine. The rise and steady fall of her chest brings unwanted heat to my face.

"You like what you see?"

"Why do you ask?" I stumble through my nerves.

"Because you're blushing."

A chuckle escapes her mouth and her eyebrows arch high, making the blue in her eyes flash in a flirtatious way. The butterflies return, scattering through my core releasing warmth that travels down between my legs, forcing my crossed leg position to tighten.

"I guess I do," I admit.

"Hmm, so you can speak the truth."

Pushing further up on her bed and lying on her side, one hand supporting her head she watches me. Her hair flows to one side, dangling down, pooling on the bed. Dangerous eyes find mine, and I'm desperate to know what she's thinking.

"If it makes you feel any better," she starts, then rises to a seated position, a beautiful tone leaving soft lips as she says, "The feeling is mutual."

There's a pause on the world at that moment. My heart begins to race, my mind's worry melting to nothing but want. There's a want to touch her, feel her. I've never known myself to be this far gone, but I can't help how good it feels to have someone to crave, and from the look in her deep ocean eyes, she understands the feeling.

"I already knew that," I say, finally finding relaxation again.

"Oh, did you now."

"Yeah, you're blushing."

Her cheeks flare from the sound of my words, and I know her blood is hot. The same way mine burns beneath my skin.

"Is this your way of getting to know me?" I ask.

"One of them."

Her bottom lip slightly curves beneath her teeth and the warmth between my legs evolves into a spark that begs to be sedated. A knock at the door distracts me for a second, but doesn't last long as a rhythmic thump arises, where the spark once lived.

"Maybe you should get that," I offer.

"Why's that?" she asks, lust flowing through the words.

"I think you know the answer to that."

The knock grows more impatient, like the nerves inside me.

"If you insist."

In one fluid motion, she twists her legs like scissors in the air and stands off the bed. The view I get from her backside makes the thump beneath my jumpsuit flutter, and I regret my offer. She opens the door with a smooth hiss. The young man who stayed behind in Claire's office stands just outside, arms tight behind his back, black hair slicked back behind his ears. Thick eyebrows match the color of his hair, forming a sharp slant. He wears all black, a hood like the other members of Black Web.

"What do you want, Zane?" Eliza asks.

Annoyance resonates in the air after her question, and I get the feeling she doesn't like him. His extra two inches give him the advantage to look over her head, peeking inside and finding me.

"I take it you're busy," he says in a low voice.

"I take it you're not."

A sound, which can only be described as anger escapes him, and if steam could flow from his ears, I'm sure it would. His jaw tightens and his facade of cool, official guy falters. This girl has the power to break anyone.

"What do you want?" she presses. "I'm not asking again."

My eyes scan the back of her, taking in the same amount of beauty in her eyes. Freckles paint her shoulders, trickling down her back. A red wave conceals them as she turns her head.

"The director needs you for information on your next operation," he says. "Also, Encryption starts soon."

"I really don't think she needed you to tell me that. But whatever. I'll be there."

She steps away from the door, and as Zane fixes his mouth to speak, the door slides shut.

"I take it the moment has passed," Eliza says, turning to me, eyes beaming.

"Moment's passed," I say. "But who knows? Maybe there will be another."

"I hope so."

She walks over to her closet and scans through it.

"Not that it's any of my business, but you two seem to have some unfinished business," I say.

"Yeah, unfortunately," she says. "A fling that shouldn't have happened."

"I know the feeling."

We both laugh and smile at each other. The moment makes my time with Wren flash once again.

"What did he mean by 'Encryption starts soon'?" I ask, forcing my thoughts away from the memories.

"It's essentially a class about encrypting data."

The system Claire mentioned on our tour of Black Web.

"So, it's school?"

"Yeah, we don't call it that though."

"Interesting."

She grabs a cloak resembling those worn by the other members of Black Web and throws it over her shoulders. Its marvelous drape captivates my attention.

"Why is it interesting?" she asks.

"I don't know. I don't hear a lot about school in Arcadia."

"Black Web doesn't offer it to the public. It's for the members of the organization. A way to prepare us for what's to come."

"A school specifically designed for hackers?"

"Again, kind of. It's not only about hackers. There are people here for medical purposes, studying the old life before the war to create a better one. Black Web houses the future of the world in a sense."

Confidence and strength flow through her voice with every word she speaks. I can tell it's something she believes in, supports, and lives by.

"You're going to help us decode Raelyn's findings, right?"

"Yeah," I say.

"Great, we'll certainly need it. A lot of us aren't great at decryption, so hopefully you are."

Decryption: my favorite aspect of hacking. The only part where my veins are electricity, sparking my fingers on a holoboard as I crack anything in my way.

"The Director hasn't given us the word to proceed yet," she continues. "When we receive data, it has to go through a system check provided by the silk of decryption to keep Black Web safe on the inside."

"Got it."

"For now, why don't you come to Encryption and see what it's about? That would explain it better than I ever could."

The question lingers in my mind. I want to know the information they can't crack, which may guide me farther down my path. I don't like to waste time, but I also don't have any leads. What they have shown me so far is more than I have managed in years.

"Yeah, I'll go."

Her smile grows bright.

"Alright," she says, securing her boots. "Let's go."

20

The elevator comes to a slow stop, after what feels like forever.

"First, I need to see the director," Eliza says, taking the first step into the corridor.

Coolness hovers over my skin like a blanket as we move into the fresh, clean air. It reminds me of my living room and how much I miss it. A scent moves through the walkway that I can't make out, and I fear Eliza's everlasting smell has prevented me from recognizing anything else.

Once again, my trailing eyes find the core. The light beams from it, pushing it through the entire underground fortress, replicating the sun. It pulses with energy, white light radiating from within. A small blue ring hovers around the prism-shaped device like a halo, surrounding a precious entity.

Eliza's strides are quick and precise. The length in her legs eases every step. With the pace of her walk, it's surprising I don't hear her footsteps. It's like her feet are walking on air, as opposed to the glass marble beneath us. We reach a silver plated door with a matte finish.

The door slices open and Eliza steps inside, waiting for me to join as the darkness of the room swallows her in seconds. I follow in quick succession, one foot after the other into black. For a brief moment, as my eyes adjust, I can't see. It's like a power grid failure, knocking out all light until the glow from the corridor is transferred inside. A current of light then flashes through the room and my eyes are forced closed. I finally get acclimated when Eliza steps in front of Claire's desk.

The scent of clove is detectable in the air. Crisp, strong, and bold. Its earthy essence reminds me of dense forests that once thrived in Arcadia, where my mother used to take me for combat training. I remember the smell as we fought round after round, until she saw I couldn't take anymore. Those forests are now wastelands. The Enlightenment uses them as grounds for testing weapons, specifically bio and nuclear types. To keep it all contained, it's now in a bubble. A dome covers the massive area and keeps everything within it trapped. Over time, the trees began to decay from the radiation and poisons deposited in the area, ending natural grown life.

Humans aren't the only life force the Enlightenment tampers with.

Claire sits behind a holodesk that levitates with a small glass and another, slightly larger bottle with a bronze liquid sitting atop it. Behind her, a massive panel spreads across the wall, the letter 'A' displayed in the center. Plants live at the room's corners, which rise to the height of the ceiling, bending at the stems. Cloves dangle from them, revealing the culprit behind the tasteful aroma.

A seat that holds two hugs the wall to our right. Where Eliza stands, a circle surrounds her feet, glowing green on the tiled floor. Black finishing along the floor and walls create the sense of shade, like the room I have here. On the opposite wall, a hologram of Black Web's facility is displayed. I get a bird's eye view of the entire facility. Before, I was amazed and mesmerized. Now, as I look at the intricacies and specifics of the design, I'm envious of the creator's mind.

Looking back to Claire, I envision a throne. Her throne. Crossed legs show her dominance as she grazes a finger on the edge of her glass. The corners of her lips mark a smile, one that compliments her character to perfection.

"Come in, Come in," she says, beckoning us forward with one hand. The other grips the glass like a precious artifact. I take a few steps inside, following Eliza, when Claire notices me.

"Ariadne, dear. I didn't know you'd be joining."

"Neither did I, really." My eyes find Eliza's, and she smiles reassuringly.

"How are you liking Black Web?" Claire asks gingerly.

"There's still a lot to learn."

"Of course. That's like you, always willing to learn."

There's a softness in her voice. Vulnerability hangs on each word as she speaks. I get the sense that she wants to say what's really on her mind, but something stops her. The drink in her hand finds pressed lips and she holds the bronze liquid in her mouth, closing her eyes, moving her mouth to savor it. She tilts her head back, swallowing hard before releasing a deep sigh.

"Director," Eliza repeats.

"Hmm," is Claire's response, her head still tilted toward the ceiling.

"Are you okay?"

"I will be," she says, her voice trailing like a fog, moving in a slow like trance.

A second passes, and Claire's head drops to face us. Her eyes flash with determination, eyebrows dropping to a hard slant as she smiles.

"Let's talk about your next operation," she says.

The director I've come to know is back like she never left. Firm, strong, and direct, with no signs of weakness.

"Raelyn has intel that can further develop our investigation on the Enlightenment. As she mentioned in the briefing earlier, it will require assistance to understand it. Assistance from the hack thread. She has done her best at trying to decipher the coded intel but has come up short." Claire pauses and drains the rest of the glass.

"There's more to this," Eliza says.

Claire doesn't respond. She stands, catching herself from stumbling. Her arms hold her steady against the table as she finds balance. She walks to the front side of the table and leans against it like a seat.

Blonde hair falls down her face, stopping at her shoulders as if a line is drawn to prevent it from falling further. The emerald in her eyes is dulled, with less of the shine I noticed when I first met her. Pressed lips and angled brows show her mind at work, trying to formulate her next thought. Her lack of poise and unbalanced stance reveal the alcohol has clearly taken effect. I take another look at the container on the table and see a line across it, residue from the bronze liquid, visibly marking where it sat before she began drinking. Half the bottle is gone from its original amount. I've only recently met her, but I can tell when someone has had a little too much to drink.

"What aren't you telling me?" Eliza asks.

"It's your parents," Claire breathes out.

"What about them?"

Urgency takes over the calm in Eliza's voice. Something I have yet to hear. The collected formality that I've grown to associate with her has vanished. All traces depleted, taken over by anxious nerves.

"Two days ago, during Raelyn's last operation here in Techdon, she came across a group of representatives for the Enlightenment. With Mason, they trailed them to see what their presence here meant. In doing so, they found your parents among them, exchanging information." Claire pauses and examines Eliza, who remains petrified. With a deep breath, she continues. "Raelyn and Mason continued to trail them and in doing so, they were able to gather enough intel to determine the reason your parents are here. And that reason is to find you."

A longer, thicker pause fills the space with tension that is tangible. Dark, unseen energy looms between us, seemingly dissipating the clove scent, replacing it with something murky and unwanted.

"How?" Eliza asks, the question barely audible.

"We don't know how they've managed to get this close. Given who they are and what they do, it's even stranger. But however they did it, they are close."

"Why didn't you tell me two days ago?" Eliza says with a bite that bleeds betrayal.

"You know the answer to that."

"I'm going."

"You're not."

Eliza's fists clench, tight until her hands are trembling. Her head dips low, red curtains concealing her face. Sniffling comes from the depths of her, and an anger I know all too well. The feeling of want-need for solutions regarding parental figures.

"Eliza, I know—"

"Don't."

Claire's eyes fall, and her lips curve downward in a weak frown, her motherly instinct peeking through, wanting to help and console a child, though she can't.

"You're too close to this," Claire insists. "I promise you will get the revenge you seek, but we—I need you for another very important operation."

Eliza doesn't say a word but gives a slow nod of confirmation, enough to satisfy Claire. I can't see the pain on Eliza's face, but I feel the energy radiating off her skin and poking its way into mine. The urge to touch her and let her know that someone feels the same pain surges at my core. My heart aches to embrace her, and my brain offers an alternative. As a compromise to my internal struggle, my hand finds her shoulder with a light, sensible touch. Her hand finds mine in return, soft and warm from the blood I can only imagine is boiling inside her. The smoothness of her small hand raises the hair on my arms, giving me the same sensual overload I feel when I successfully decrypt the hardest systems.

"Thanks."

Eliza looks over her shoulder, blue eyes calm like a winter lake. There are no tears on her face as she stares into my eyes with a look of gratitude. With one last squeeze of my hand, she retracts and effortlessly twirls her hair into a bun. I watch her as she transforms back into the person I knew moments before this meeting.

"I'm ready for my next operation," she says.

The pain is still in her voice, but her posture has changed, and her head is held high, like the information about her parents doesn't faze her.

"Are you sure?" Claire asks. "You can take some time to gather yourself beforehand."

"The faster I complete this assignment, the faster I can get to them."

"Very well."

Claire straightens her jacket, buttoning it with surprising accuracy.

"Your next operation regards the events from a few days ago. Since the incident in Arcadia, there have been no announcements nor any movement from the Enlightenment. I should say, there hasn't been any *known* movement."

"Which incident are you referring to?" Eliza steals the question from my mind.

"Both," Claire says. "As you can see, no known movement after two different events within a matter of days is quite odd."

"It is," I say.

Claire looks past Eliza to me, happy to hear my response before continuing. "The death of Daniel alone should have sparked the Enlightenment to act."

His name rings in my head. The boy who couldn't hold his nerves around me, spilling coffee all over the table and floor. The boy who tried to kill me. Trace's murderer.

"Killing him should have been enough to draw them out," she continues.

"So, you were doing more than just protecting me?" I ask.

"Correct, Daniel would have done anything to get you in the hands of the Enlightenment. He may not have killed you himself, but he was definitely involved with those who keep the nation in check," she retorts.

My mind is riddled by the puzzle presented in front of me.

"He wasn't a normal waiter," Eliza adds.

Claire takes a step forward and draws a sharp breath. "What do you know about Ezra Coleman?" she asks.

I stare with no response, hoping she'll fill in the gaping hole that was left after the diner incident.

"Ezra Coleman is one of the people responsible for the nation we live in," she continues. "The false utopia that presents itself to the world."

There's a heavy weight holding my chest tight. Something in the air tugs at my nerves, dragging them out of their hiding place.

"Ezra Coleman," she repeats, "is one of the people responsible for the death of your parents."

21

"What are you saying?" I ask, anger swelling inside my chest.

Claire takes a step toward me, and I take one back. Her eyes meet mine and transform to worry, a feeling I don't need at the moment.

"Eliza," she says, "could you give us a moment?"

The question is more of a statement, and Eliza nods and walks out.

"The Enlightenment is responsible for the death of your parents," Claire repeats, causing the original pain to return. "Ezra is the only member we know by name, but as you know, the Enlightenment is represented by a group of four people."

I start to pace, contemplating what my next move should be. I was in a building he owns. He could have been there during my extraction of the Establishment. Thoughts of failure begin to plague my mind.

"Ms. Young," Amity says, "you couldn't have known if he was there or not."

Amity as always, says the words to erase the negative thoughts, but it's not enough.

"You knew this, and you have me here, wasting time?" I say to Claire.

"You're not wasting time. Without being here, we wouldn't be having this conversation. You'd still be alone, hunting for unknown people."

Burning blood flows through my veins with enough intensity to explode. My muscles tense beneath my skin, making me want to slam a fist into a wall.

"Watch what you say to me next."

"I'm not trying to upset you, Ariadne. I'm trying to help you."

"How!?" I snap. "Me walking around this facility, meeting people I don't care about is not helping me!"

"You aren't seeing the bigger picture."

"Fuck the bigger picture."

She takes a step back at my outrage. Her face falls again in defeat, something I could care less about, knowing she held this from me.

"Ariadne," she says delicately. "Think about it. If you had every member of the Enlightenment in this room right now, and you decided to kill them, what comes after?"

"I don't care."

"You do. I know you do."

"You don't know me."

"You're right, I don't. But what I do know is your parents and the entire reason for their fight. Our fight."

The mention of my parents causes the anger to settle. I start to listen to what she has to say.

"Black Web doesn't have all the answers, but we're searching. Your parents died before they could tell us, or anyone else, the truth they found. Whatever it was had to be enough for them to hold until death. I believe the truth is the Enlightenment is on their way to complete dominance. Yes, right now, they have control, but there's some holes they can't fill. For example, hacking the node. If they are able to stop us, then the nation will surely be gone. The truth I believe your parents found was human control beyond the node."

She takes a breath, monitoring my stillness before she continues.

"The bigger picture your parents saw was, if that truth was revealed, what would happen to the citizens? The answer is eradication."

On her table, she activates a holoscreen displaying a map of the AOE.

"Years ago, in Areas 3 and 4, there was an uprising, far greater than what you've seen in Central Square," she continues. "Ashland, a sector in Area 3 was subject to eradication and so was Darkport and Drownark in Area 4." She zooms in on the map and the sectors she mentioned are decimated. Turned to ruins. "It's where they got their names. Ashland was reduced to ash by fire and explosives. Whereas Darkport and Drownark were suffocated by—"

"The ocean," I interrupt, seeing the image of water flooding the sectors.

She nods and closes the map.

"This happened before the node was implanted into everyone. I believe your parents held what they knew as long as possible, in search of a way to tell the citizens without this happening again."

"The bigger picture," I whisper.

"Yes. When your parents told me to watch over you, Adalina mentioned breaking the connection through a system. Do you have any idea what that could mean?"

Everything my mom ever taught me about the nation floods my consciousness as I sift through, trying to find a moment she may have mentioned it. But I come up empty.

"Not that I can remember," I admit.

Tears start to fall from the overwhelming anger and hate I have for this nation's rulers. What I believed to be my only purpose in life—I can't seem to find a way to pursue it. Every decision I make seems to be the wrong one.

"Ms. Young, it may be wise to follow and listen to what they have here."

"I know," I manage to say.

"I support your drive and mission," Claire says. "I want you to realize that there is a consequence for every action. If we go in, guns blazing, without a second thought, it could blow up in our faces." She takes a step toward me, green eyes smiling with care. "We must always, expect nothing—"

"Prepare for anything," I finish the statement.

"We need you as much as you need us."

"So what would you have me do?"

She places her hands on my shoulders and takes a deep breath.

"Stay with us as we work toward the Enlightenment's downfall. You will get your revenge, I promise."

My mind can't decide if this is the best course to take. But if Amity thinks it's the right decision to stay, and Claire believes so too, then maybe it is.

At this point, I don't have any other option.

22

Encryption.

One of the two abilities I learned first as a child. The other being ciphers. Both go hand and hand when one wants to protect their data from people who want to copy it or outright steal it. People who are better known as cryptologists. Encryptions aren't easy to produce because of the nature of building a cipher, but they are the building blocks for any hacker who aspires to be great.

As Eliza and I ride the elevator down to the class, Claire's theories roll through my head. If the Enlightenment are truly after complete dominance, what would that require? Wasn't the node enough? And my mother's words to her, a system to break the connection. When I repeat them to myself, I get a sense it's something I do know but can't reach in the back of my mind.

Eliza steps to a corner and activates her glove, watching the lights flicker.

"Ms. Young," Amity says, "could the system Claire referenced to be the one inside your home?"

"Maybe, but I know the ins and outs of it. What could I have missed?"

"Adalina was very fond of encryptions, Ms. Young. There could be some we have yet to discover."

"Wouldn't you be able to register them?"

"Only if the connections are linked, and it appears there isn't one."

"Hmmm.."

Amity's words send my mind into a whirlwind of possibilities. My mother leaving behind encrypted knowledge for me to find. Chills run through my body at the thought of solving an encryption she may have created.

The chime of the elevator pauses my anxious mind.

The class is on the bottom thread, among four other rooms I can only assume are classes, each one separated by pathways that lead to them. The elevator releases us directly above the core. We step out onto the glass floor, and I can almost feel the pulse of it. The hiss of the elevator shooting back up startles me, jarring my eyes to look around. Four large spheres, attached to walkways, form a diamond shape ascending the shining core in the center. Like planets orbiting the sun, they slowly rotate around it.

"Is this safe to walk on?" I ask.

"Yeah, you barely feel the movement."

We walk toward one of the spheres and the closer we get to it, the more it resembles a planet in size. The walkway ends at a door containing an image of a lock on the entrance. Its white essence makes it visible against the black landscape of the underground. We reach the entryway and my head trails upward to see the top of the structure, and beyond it is the web of rods and walkways making up the entire facility. The vantage point of the bottom gives the building a vivid resemblance to a spider web. My focus returns to the door as Eliza steps in front of it.

I step in and see open seating eclipsing the center. The seated area hovers in place and when people take their seats, they dip low enough to match the edge of the elongated tables in front of them. Gleaming light, transferred through the rods above the circular dome, makes the room glow, traveling through the walls and illuminating the walkways and aisles. Ahead, at the back wall, a hologram projects a lock. The same lock on the outside of the door. Its steel coloring contradicts the mood of the room, and I find myself unable to look away. The lock is sealed and appears to be pulsing.

Links coil from within it, stretching across the entirety of the back wall. The glowing blue of the links look as if they are channeling data, traveling to and from the center of the lock. Each link travels from the rods, and as they touch the lock, they recoil, disappearing until replaced. A light show representation of an encryption.

"So that's what you're after?" Eliza says, taking her seat. "Here. Sit next to me."

"What do you mean?" I ask defensively, taking the aisle seat in case I need to escape.

"You've been the talk of Black Web since you got here—actually, well before that. When the director wanted us to track you down. One of the main conversations floating around is, what exactly are you here for?"

"You heard me and Claire?"

"I didn't mean too, but you got pretty loud. I thought I would have to run in and protect the director."

The blue river once living in her eyes is now ice, with a frozen stare.

"So?"

She interlocks her hands on the table in front of her, waiting for a response.

I think of her question: What am I here for? I'm not sure I know that myself. except for the fact I need information to pursue my enemies, but that's something I don't need the world of Black Web knowing. I break away from her frigid glare and move my attention behind me, toward the room's only entrance and exit.

Raelyn and Mason giggle their way to empty seats farthest up front. Two others I don't recognize walk in and rush to their seats as if they'll be taken by someone else. Two rows in front aren't full and in the seats to my left, beyond the aisle, there's more waiting to be claimed.

"Encryption," Amity rings. "You're far past Encryption, Ms. Young."

"If I'm not mistaken, you told me I should stay."

"Indeed. However, I don't recall this being a part of the deal with Claire."

"Remember, I'm waiting to help them decode the information they gathered."

"Very well, Ms. Young. Enjoy the basics again, if you must."

If Amity were human, I could almost hear a chuckle.

"You always talk to yourself?" Eliza asks.

"It's my A.I.," I say. "Essentially my only friend."

"Doesn't have to be."

Eliza's eyes flash, and the butterflies wake from their sleep, flapping wings throughout my core. My eyes find the entrance again as voices enter the sphere. A boy in mid conversation with two others, a guy and girl, slightly older than him, who look so alike they could be twins. The younger boy is short, mahogany-toned skin glowing in the light. Short, buzzed hair reveals all his young facial features. Soft eyes, sharp nose, and full lips go well with his angled cheekbones.

The other two with too many similarities to ignore follow behind. Platinum blonde hair streaks down both of their faces and I remember the color from the briefing room. The girl smiles bright, revealing high cheekbones and rounded eyes. Her pale skin is complemented by the pink in her fine lips. The boy has the same facial structure and colored lips; the only difference is his narrow eyes seeming to be fixed on someone behind him.

They take their seats behind Raelyn and Mason when my own eyes find the last person to walk in the room.

Zane.

Like a shadow to light, he hangs at the top of the staircase and scans the seated area like a vulture, scavenging the remains of a corpse, waiting to make its move. Black hair caresses his face, moving like shadowy waves as he turns his head and makes eye contact with me. His eyes narrow, and he tightens his jaw, making the tension travel through his face. Finally making the descent down the stairs, to my surprise, he sits in front of Eliza and me. He straddles the seat and spins around to face us. The intensity in his dark eyes threaten to pierce life itself.

"Ladies," he says smoothly.

"Could you be any more original?" Eliza snarls.

"I could," he says, flashing the black pools of his eyes. "But you wouldn't like me then."

"Who the hell said I like you now?"

The preciseness in her response makes me laugh, catching Zane's attention. His eyes dart back to Eliza, accepting the challenge she's presented.

"It's in the eyes, love." His eyebrows rise in quick successions.

My eyes roll from the lack of creativity he contains.

"Is that how you feel, new girl?"

His voice is fluid with hints of acid that melt away the previous tension, scorching it like lava to earth. Black orbs stare daggers into me, threatening and provoking a response. I smile and take the bait, channeling my mother.

"Zane, was it?" I start.

"He has no idea what's coming," Amity says.

His eyes refocus, challenging me as if I'm someone beneath him. It stirs the anger that already has me on edge, and instead of holding it like I normally do, I allow it to unleash.

"I don't know why you're like this. To be honest, I could care less. But you are a boy who seeks attention in the oldest ways possible. I may be a new girl, but your tricks are old. Older than the times before technology. So as the newest person to this facility, I'll invite you to find a new way to approach a girl. And maybe—maybe—I'll consider telling you how I feel, you pretentious fuck."

It all comes out with a smile on my face.

"Adalina would be proud, Ms. Young."

The room is quiet enough to hear power flowing through the walls. Complete and utter silence that any sound would echo like an atomic bomb was detonated. A new voice echoes through the room, alleviating the threat of an explosive sound.

"Oooo... I like her."

"Astraea," another voice calls.

My head pivots toward the voices speaking.

"The Quinns, aka the twins," Eliza says. "And the definition of a love-hate relationship."

"What do you mean by that?" I ask.

"You'll see."

"What?" the platinum blonde hair of the girl sways as she faces her look alike.

"Come on, Ayster. Even you can't deny Zane got his ass handed to him. On a platter, if I might add."

Her voice is collected and smooth. Each word sounds as if she methodically planned them out to increase their effectiveness. Like gas to a fire, her voice ignites the other members in the room. Ooohs and ahhhs echo among them, and eyes glue to my body like I'm the main event of a show.

"See what you've done, Astraea?" Ayster says with concern.

His hair curls in a way that makes him flip it, revealing his expression: hard as steel.

"I said what we were all thinking." Astraea smiles, holding her arms up in defense.

"See what I mean?" Eliza asks.

I nod yes and almost laugh, but Zane's eyes stop it.

"I can't believe Trace sacrificed his life for you," he growls.

"Watch it," Eliza butts in.

Silence fills the room again. This time, no one is there to save it. A feeling of dread creeps into my heart from

Trace's heroic act. Zane's eyes show me he doesn't see it that way. His comment hits me hard. I usually never care what people think about me. But, to blame me for the death of someone I care about is a different level of hurt.

His words sink in, and I start to accept it, blaming myself for Trace's death. From the moment he fell and hit the diner floor, I'd suppressed the feeling. My mind didn't want to comprehend it as my fault, but the dangerous black eyes of Zane makes me believe it.

Zane scuffs and turns toward the front, activating the other side of me. Compassion and small amounts of guilt clog my mental flow as I examine his defeated posture. Low head, dipped shoulders, and silence. I begin to think about what I caused and took. What Trace meant to all of them.

The sphere instantly goes black before I process any more emotions. Every light that once granted sight in the room has ceased to exist.

"Show time," Eliza says, bumping her elbow against mine.

A few seconds in the dark passes before the globe structure ignites with a burst of bright lines that follow the circumference of the walls. My eyes trail the lines all around, like a cat following a laser beam. One doubles, then triples, creating an array of lines, colliding and clashing together, displaying a light show of brilliance. The illuminated lines make one final lap around the sphere, colliding once more before transforming into hundreds—maybe thousands—of small dots that resemble stars in the night sky, taking on every color imaginable.

They slowly move together, each one holding a specific place until the outcome of a lock is formed, the very lock that showed itself in the entrance and previously lived on the wall as a solo hologram, now with a vibrant hue, bringing it to life. The lock pulses, sending light from within and illuminating the room once again.

"Welcome back to Encryption," a voice booms, echoing through the silence. "And for those of you who are joining us for the first time, welcome to Encryption."

My surprise is shared only by the two individuals in the very front of the class. The identical pair appear to be bored. Eliza fiddles with the gloves on her hands. Mason and Raelyn are playing some sort of game on their holograms, having a joyous time, and in front of me, Zane is gone.

"Where's Zane?" I ask Eliza, not knowing why I care.

"If I had to place a bet, I'd say you embarrassed him," she says.

A marble sphere, the size of a baoding ball, rotates in her hand at a slow and methodical pace. She watches it as it trails each finger, falling into her palm, landing at its starting place.

My eyes return to Mason and Raelyn. Raelyn watches me and I wonder how long she's been staring. Her eyes are soft, complimenting the slight smile on her lips. As I return the smile, my heart feels warmer at the fact I have another living family member.

The lock on the wall thwarts my gaze, slowly opening with a soft slide, releasing air from behind it in a soft hiss. A tall, slender man steps through with a manor screaming perfectionism. He wears all gray, slicked pants, pressed with visible creases. A long coat, like a blazer hangs below his knees. The sleeves are evenly cuffed at his forearms, revealing tanned skin, a natural brown that shows he doesn't always live in this suit and may prefer the outside. A vest and open collared shirt hides beneath the coat like camouflage. Dusty brown hair sits perfect on his head, with gray strands working to be seen. A clean shaven face hides his age behind a youthful edge. He takes a stance in the center of the elevated platform and holds his arms out wide, triggering something in me.

My heart plunges with a deep ache. My lungs tighten and my breaths space in an odd way.

"Ms. Young, your vitals are falling," Amity says. "Are you okay?"

"I think so," I say, unsure.

I close my eyes and picture myself in the comfort of my home. Back against my couch with a tea in hand, fiddling with networks, designing entries and escape routes through the hardest paradigms in a system, the only thing that gives me a rush—a thrill I can only explain as euphoric. My breath returns to its normal, even pace, with my heart following behind.

The man's hands slam together, releasing a thunder-like crack, jarring my eyes open. The sound makes me think of the storms which always seemed to hover over the Enlightenment Prison. Distracting myself, I focus on the walls and notice a ripple effect. As if ocean waves lived inside the walls.

Everyone's attention is now his, and with a smile that could break a code, he speaks.

"Glad you all could join me," he says, beginning a slow pace, tracing the edge of the platform and adjusting his coat to his narrow body.

"Love to see some new faces."

He scans the class, observing the two upfront, moving his eyes through the crowd to pick out any other newbies. His eyes find me, locking on like a virus, waiting to intercept information.

"I'm Thaddeus Edmond. The silk of encryption," he says sharply. "Among the other elite hacktivists in Black Web, my specialty is teaching the art of protecting data."

His introduction concludes with an awkward stare, giving me the impression he wants applause.

"Well, today we're going to do something different. I will attempt to take someone's data and they'll have to create an encryption to prevent it," he says confidently. "Do I have any volunteers?"

He scans the room in search of his first target. No one steps forward or raises their hand to accept his challenge.

"Come on. Anyone?" he adds. "You'll use what was taught in our previous lessons to prevent me from extracting information. Simple enough."

His gaze continues to probe through the room, and I get the feeling he will choose someone himself.

"Amity," I say.

"Ready, Ms. Young."

He pretends to look over the room once again, trying to disguise the fact that he's already chosen.

"I'll do it," I announce.

Gasps erupt through the room.

"You?" he asks. He holds the pause, realizing he doesn't know my name.

"Ariadne," I say, quieting the voices around me.

"Ariadne," he repeats softly, letting each syllable roll off his tongue in a fluid cadence. "Let's get started shall we?"

His hands spread wide in front of him, prompting a hologram to activate in front of me.

"This system will be what you use to create an encryption. One that can't be penetrated, or at least, is difficult to penetrate."

"Are you sure about this?" Eliza whispers. "You weren't in our last demonstration of encryptions."

"There's a reason Claire wanted your group to find me. I'll show you," I say with a smile.

The hologram glitches, waiting for my actions. A touch panel activates beneath it, and Iris immediately detects the software. The information within the system is copied to my wrist, allowing easy access for coding. With Iris, I create an algorithm for a simple plaintext to cover a message I intend for Thaddeus. A mix of symbols and letters to blend the original text set inside of the software which he may already be accustomed to. A trap. Simple, but difficult to decipher without a key, one I've practically erased and made impossible to find without extra help. Amity codes the remaining functions, sealing the encryption.

"Done," I say, expressionless.

"Excuse me?" Thaddeus asks with a touch of surprise in his voice.

"Too easy, Ms. Young," Amity chimes.

"My encryption is complete." I let my response hang in the air. "Good luck."

My statement makes the room rise with intense chatter.

Thaddeus's eyes narrow to a deep squint, uneasiness staining his youthful facade and revealing his age. Mid-forties, the soft lines in his face betray his fight to hide it. Around the room I find wide eyes with jaws stretched in shock as if I were a strange creature. They watch intently for my next move. Eliza smiles at me with gleaming eyes and I return the gesture. Thaddeus strolls behind a levitating desk and starts his decryption.

After a few minutes, his mind starts to strain. Iris brightens, notifying me of the breach and the joy of creating the perfect lock sparks a devious smile. The silk of encryption takes off his coat, tossing it aside and scratches his forehead to create an answer. His eyes widen to a point. He looks like he's seen a ghost.

He looks away from his hologram and smiles.

"Clever," he says, "but I figured it out."

He displays my algorithm on the back wall, erasing the lock, for everyone to see.

"Are you sure?" I ask, recognizing his mistake, the breach Iris notified me about.

His brows arch high in confusion. The creases between them signal annoyance and patience wearing thin. The sharpness of his introduction has depleted significantly as he finally sees it.

"A double key," he says softly.

Figuring he'd expect a classic encryption, I layered another key, changing the plain text to a cipher text.

"Here. Let me assist," I say.

Not having the other key for myself, I decrypt my own algorithm, and the message intended for Thaddeus displays across the wall for everyone to read. Gasps erupt through the room as everyone's eyes move from me to the wall.

"Now that's cruel," Ayster's voice echoes from the back.

Thaddeus steps back and reads:

You're only reading this because

I decrypted the second key for you.

Stick to Encryption.

"You're insane," Eliza whispers.

The blue in her eyes morph to gray clouds, pooling with mystery, and I instantly think of Wren. Ignoring the intrusive thought, I refocus my attention. Her brows arch high, pushing for a response that I don't give as my eyes move to Thaddeus. He slowly turns to face the room, his face is pale, and he looks like he's going to be sick, but I know an embarrassed expression when I see one. Our eyes finally meet. Mine, sharp like a raw-edged blade, and his, looming with a sense of concern.

"I guess Zane and I have something in common," I say without looking away.

"And what's that?" Eliza asks with a shimmer of concern in her voice.

"We both have a problem with authority."

23

The frigid air kept me awake after enduring hours of jolts of electricity. The currents vibrated through my bones, my nerves thrashing beneath my skin. I remember the wires dangling above me, like the hand of a god, waiting to judge me. Sparks moving through the wires could be heard as they shook, waiting to drop at any moment. The sound made me wince and quiver to a corner of my cell, the only safe place in a dark cube with no light to see by, except for the small line beneath the entrance.

My body was shivering from sitting in water that was being pumped through a small crevasse in a corner of the wall. Burn marks stained my seventeen-year-old wrists from the shackles they placed around them. Aching and throbbing as I sat and thought about the person who put me in that situation, I never learned his name, but his face was unforgettable.

With the wounds of losing everything still fresh, my young mind couldn't help but crack. Splintering to fragments of memories from the time before the torture. A night I'll never forget is the first night he displayed what he named 'The Codex of Pain'. His 'order of operations to break anyone,' I remember him saying to a group of us. He was the authority, and we were to serve him and give up all we were prior. We were his property.

What plagues my mind the most is the tailoring of his suit, the black in his eyes, low tenor of his deep voice, and a scar that formed an 'x' below his right eye. It is carved in my memory. Engraved with the sharpest blade possible.

Six months had passed since my capture, and thoughts of being held captive forever sunk their teeth into my mind.

"Ms. Young," Amity said.

"Yes?"

"You may need to save yourself instead of figuring out how to help others."

I recall the feeling of hopelessness. Leaving behind Wren, the girl I had come to love, couldn't be an option.

"I won't leave her."

"You have to think of your survival. It could be possible to come ba—"

"No," I interrupted.

Tears welled in my eyes and every thought of being without her began to drown me. Boots echoed through the quiet night, and I jumped, scared of who it could be. In a moment's time, I found out.

The lock on my cell opened and there he stood with two other agents. The suit that defined him; the glow of hatred in his eyes. What could he have possibly thought I was hiding, I wondered as I crawled backward into a corner. I remember being so afraid, I couldn't try to fight back when they grabbed me.

I could only scream.

Thaddeus stands at the edge of the director's table.

His posture returns to the man who first introduced himself as the silk of encryption. Arrogant and full of himself, he's made a swift recovery from my boasting display of encryption expertise.

The palms of my hands grow damp at the sight of him and the pressures of having an authoritative figure this close makes me shudder. The pulse of my heart takes a new and bizarre pattern, thudding against my ribs.

My arms start to tremble from the resurgence of my memories as I fail to suffocate them. I haven't had an incident like this in years. It seems as if this place is digging up everything I've worked to live past, back from a place where I thought they'd be buried forever. Each breath I take is like drawing in sharp knives, jabbing at my lungs and simulating the act of drowning. The pain in my lungs increases, the knife affects coursing through my body, forcing quick short breaths. My head envelopes a deep darkness making my vision blurry and jagged.

"Ariadne?" Claire's voice is a whisper.

"Are you okay?" Thaddeus asks as my vision returns.

He moves in my direction, and I jump back toward the extended seat, drawing my staff as my sight flashes, and he returns. The 'x' on his cheek. The black depth in his gaze. He moves closer to me, Claire at his side. Terror grips me as I think this was all a trap to get me back in the Enlightenment's hands. A rush of anxious nerves overloads my mind and my eyes go dark, igniting a dreadful fear of loneliness and captivity.

"Amity?" I call out to my closest friend in distress.

No answer. My heart drops, sinking into my stomach.

Tears flood my eyes, deep wells filling to the brim, ready to overflow. My breathing is no longer recognizable and the feeling in my chest screams to be released.

"Amity!" I shout again, trying to reach my only friend.

The shaking grows more erratic, moving through my body as I drop my staff.

I'm defeated. Lost without any understanding of what's happening to me.

"Ariadne?" I barely hear Claire's voice.

My ears are deafened, and her voice sounds like it's trailing hundreds of feet away, inciting more fear as it sends me into the darkness of my mind.

CONNECTION

24

I slowly open my eyes, letting in the brightness of the room. Dozens of lights hover above me, moving in circles around my body. The sound of a door sliding open and closed grabs my attention. My movements are slow and painful, making me release sharp breaths as I try to turn. I give up and lie still. As if summoned by my pain, Zoe stands at my bedside. Her small frame is calming, and relaxing energy surrounds her. A holo-lens hangs over her forehead and eyes. DNA strands and medical symbols flow across it before vanishing. She walks over to me with a container of liquid and smiles.

"Here. It'll help the pain."

My heart lurches. She uses the same words and cadence as the woman back at the prison.

"I told you we would meet again," she whispers.

"You…" I say, bewildered.

"Yes. It was me who helped you at the Enlightenment Prison."

I knew I recognized her when we'd met back in the greenhouse. With the revelations and missions Claire was introducing, I couldn't think about where I'd seen her before. Zoe looks at me with soft eyes, glittering with water. She smiles and leaves the drink on the side table, returning to her work.

Claire stands by a counter with tools and devices I don't recognize. Turning my head is hard as a device is secured around it, allowing me to only move my eyes. Eliza sits in a corner chair, legs intertwined and eyes closed. Her hand holds small orb-like items, which she twirls methodically. A draft floods the room, causing my naked body to shiver. The only thing between me and glaring eyes is a very heavy blanket.

"Amity," I say quietly.

My voice causes Zoe to look at me with a confused stare. It takes a moment for Amity to respond, and tears of happiness drench my face.

"Here, Ms. Young."

"Where were you?" I say, unable to contain the sobbing.

"I've been here, Ms. Young. I never left. I've called out to you, but you were under extreme distress due to a panic attack. It seems it voided most things around you, which made the attack severe enough to put you here," Amity explains.

Panic attack.

The words surprise me. I haven't experienced one since I was locked away. The moment I was taken to an Enlightenment chamber.

"How are you feeling?" Zoe asks.

Her soft voice prevents me from traveling through my subconscious.

"I'm okay, I guess."

Claire and Eliza swarm my bedside with smiles, bringing more light to the room.

"I'm okay," I repeat, feeling Claire grab my hand.

"Are you sure?" Claire's maternal instincts peak through her voice.

I try to nod, but the device around my head prevents it.

"Sorry," Zoe says, pressing a button near my feet.

The device unlatches from the sides of my head and the stiffness in my neck takes over.

"How long have I been out?" I ask.

"A little over two hours," Eliza says, darting her eyes at Zoe for confirmation. Zoe nods, never breaking her smile.

"Are you sure you're okay?" Claire asks again, reminding me of my mother. Her hand finds my cheek as her fingers trace my face.

"I'm sure."

I rise to a seated position and take in the rest of the room. Classic white walls cover the space with one metallic door that faces me straight ahead. Tubes, wires, probes, and a handful of other medicinal instruments sit on a floating silver disc next to Zoe. To my side, a long pole holds clear bags that drip fluids into long tubes wrapping and trailing around my arm.

"I appreciate the help," I say, finding my focus and feeling the uneasiness drift away. "I have to get going."

"What?" Claire's voice is higher than normal.

"I've been here long enough. I've accomplished nothing, and every minute—every second—I waste is less progress I make on the people who took my parents' lives."

"Ariadne," Claire says softly. "You can't do it alone."

"Watch me."

The heat in my blood rises from being told I can't avenge my parents, and I remove the tubes from my arms.

"Wait. You're—" Zoe starts.

I interrupt her thoughts and swing my feet off the bed, jumping to the floor beside her. My feet absorb the impact and cool marble. A gentle breeze from my quick movement floats by, brushing my skin, causing the hairs along my body to rise.

"Naked," Zoe finishes her thought, covering her eyes.

Heat rushes to my face as the cold air settles into my bare skin. I can feel their eyes paint my back. I spin around and cover my body with both hands, stretching my arms to reach the places I don't want to be seen.

"Can I get dressed?" I ask rhetorically.

"Yes," Claire says, stepping to the door. "If you're certain about leaving, stop by my office beforehand."

"Will do."

"Can I stay?" Eliza's voice is urgent with a flirtatious tone, turning the blood in my cheeks to a wild blaze, spreading across my face.

"Eliza!" Claire shouts.

Zoe chuckles and walks toward the door.

"I'm joking," Eliza winks. "But seriously, if you leave without saying bye, I'll find you myself."

"I'll see what I can do."

They both exit and Zoe delicately waves goodbye after pointing out my clothes hanging on the wall closest to her tools. I meet her eyes and the questions that I want to ask her barrel into my mind. Her answering look almost satisfies my call.

I find my equipment and get dressed, preparing myself for goodbyes.

25

Zoe and Claire stand center as I enter the room. The scent of cloves hangs thick in the air as I breathe deeply, wanting more. Zoe smiles as she takes a sip of her drink. Claire waves for me to step farther inside, allowing the door to close.

"You know you don't have to go," Claire says with a glass in her hand, blue liquid instead of the amber in Zoe's.

"I know," I say. "But I have to. After you told me Ezra was among the people who killed my parents, I wanted to leave then. But I stayed. I stayed to see if I could help you all with decoding the information you obtained."

"Don't you still want to do that?"

"Yes, but Eliza told me it had to pass a system check before we were able to touch it."

"She is correct. It passed the check hours after the briefing, but we had to postpone moving because of a mistake Ayster made. He was a little anxious about the findings and decided to start without anyone else, ultimately costing us some of the information. We now only have a fraction of what Raelyn and Mason took, due to a failsafe hidden inside the files."

"I see," I say. "But I still experienced a panic attack, which I have not had since being held captive."

"Was it Thaddeus?" she asks.

"Yes and no."

Her eyes ask what her mouth doesn't, a look my mother used to give me when she knew I was holding back information.

"He revived a memory that has taken me a very long time to kill."

"What did he say?" The glass grazes her lips.

"Nothing."

Zoe watches silently. Her soft brown eyes provide comfort, and I can't fathom why, considering her former occupation and involvement with the Enlightenment. However, she still smiles.

Claire's motherly look returns and I'm vomiting the past to strangers who really aren't. Something about them makes me spill one of my darkest moments.

"About a week after they were murdered, I was taken to an unknown place. The only thing I can remember about it was a massive tower that extended high in the sky. There were EAs everywhere and a group of us, relatively the same age, were taken to a stone coated room inside of the tower. The stench of dry blood, dead bodies, and every human fluid you can imagine tainted the air."

Claire refills her glass with the amber liquid, swirling it around intently. Zoe tenses next to her.

"A year had gone by. My node was reinstalled, and surgeries were performed on me that...well, I still don't know what they were for."

My eyes track to Zoe, and she flinches.

"When they realized I wasn't telling them what they wanted to know. I met the man who gave me permanent scars."

"That's enough," Claire says, guiding me to the long seat.

"It was Thaddeus's suit that triggered the memory. Nothing else."

"I'm so sorry," Zoe says. Her voice sounds like she's weeping, tears flooding her eyes.

My head snaps toward her as anger flares inside me.

"You were part of it," I snarl. "At the prison."

"I was only following orders, but I never hurt any of you."

"Bullshit."

"She's telling the truth," Claire interjects. "We recruited Zoe because of her expertise in medicine, but also because she knows the torment they caused to children. She fights for our side."

She takes my hands and places them in her lap, staring at the scars and gently rubbing them as if they are fresh.

"After what the Enlightenment did to sustain their power, I finally found a way out," Zoe says, taking a step toward me and Claire. "My family fought to help people. They cured diseases and viruses for the sake of humanity. That is my one calling. To follow their lead. I intend to rid the nation of the Enlightenment's tyranny through healing."

She kneels to meet my gaze and smiles.

"Sorry isn't enough for what you went through, and I wish I could have helped you sooner. But I can help you now."

Her hand lands on my knee with a gentle touch, triggering tears. After losing my parents and then being captive, I thought I'd never find happiness. Then I met Wren. Like my parents, the Enlightenment stripped her from my life, and I found only darkness again. Now, with the overwhelming amount of supportive people in Black Web, I don't know how to feel.

"You've been through a lot," Claire adds. "And you've only told us one part of what happened. I wish I could take away your pain; I wish I could instantly grant you the vengeance that you seek. In time, I could."

My eyes move to Claire's, the evergreen brighter and filled with water, waiting to escape.

"You said it yourself," I say. "Time is a luxury I cannot afford. If what you say is true about the Enlightenment delivering an address to the nation, then I have to avenge my parents before Enlightenment Day. Either I kill them or find the truth my parents had to expose them. One way or the other, I have to move faster than I have been."

"Please stay," Claire whispers, holding back tears. "Your parents would want you here. We want you here."

Her words hit home, and the tears drench my face in a flood.

"I want to," I choke out. "I really do."

"So do it."

"I have to avenge them. I have to."

"I know, and we will. I promise you."

My mother flashes in Claire's eyes. Her smile and nose, the small details I haven't noticed until now. The emerald in her eyes is traced with a golden line, sparkling with intensity. Trailing my vision back to Zoe, she still kneels like a servant to a queen and the smile through her tears makes an ache grow in my heart. With the constant struggle to stay or leave, I turn to my closest friend.

"Amity."

"Ms. Young?"

"What should I do?"

"It seems you have garnered high intel in the small amount of time you've been here. That alone points to staying. However, I know your mind. You feel like you're not moving forward in your mission if you're not actively doing something leading that way. Active work is important. So is passive work, Ms. Young. The information you can help them decode could be vital to your mission. And you are surrounded by likeminded people. This may be what you need to reach your goal."

Amity is right. I am closer than I have ever been. What took years of searching—the first person involved in my parents downfall—I have gained more in a few days. For my parents, Wren, Trace, and all the people who have died, I will make the Enlightenment pay.

"I'll need clothes. More access to the inter-network and ways to upgrade my gear," I say with a smile.

"Oh, Ariadne," Claire says.

"Where can I manage some thinking time, other than my room?" I ask, wiping away my tears.

"We've got the perfect place."

"I suppose now would be a great time to add an upgrade to your nav?" Zoe asks.

"Iris," I correct. "And yes, that would be great."

As I start to take off Iris, Zoe stops me with a gentle touch.

"I actually have a way to do it without you having to remove it," she says.

Her holo-lens fall to her eyes, and on her wrist, a nav glows. They both connect to Iris, making it shine. On my wrist, a message to approve upgrades displays. I confirm it and the modification loads. The digital code reveals itself as a stim shock.

"There," Zoe says with a smile. "When I first saw this device, I was intrigued, and I wanted to find a way to make my creation as unique as this device is to you. So, instead of a shot into your vein, your device will send a charge through you, mimicking a defibrillator, keeping you stable."

"Thank you."

"My pleasure," Zoe says.

Claire gives me one more embrace before releasing. A sense of happiness flows inside, replacing the pain of being alone. I turn to Zoe, who's tears have been flowing since the moment I started speaking. She smiles with hope. The same hope that shined through the day she helped me in the prison.

We exit the office, and my goal comes into focus. The support they have shown me since my arrival releases some of the pressures I once had. I accept the feeling for the first time since taking on this mission: I actually have help.

"I'll let you and everyone else know when we can proceed with the decryption process," Claire says.

"Looking forward to it."

26

I arrive at the atrium of the pyramid alone, thanking the stars for it. After all the revelations I've received in the past week, I definitely need time to decompress. Back home in Arcadia, I had all the alone time I could ask for.

It certainly is missed.

Stepping out of the elevator, a wave of nausea strikes the core of my gut. The elevator ride up was a bizarre one, unlike anything I've experienced. There's four anchoring the base of the facility riding the edges of the structure. They glide at a slanted angle, defying gravity in every way possible. It reminds me of a theme park my mother used to take me to. There was a ride which traveled in a similar pattern, always making me sick. The nausea I'm experiencing must be caused by the vertigo of riding the elevator.

The glass above lets in the light from the stars. Combining with the back light of the building, it creates a dramatic yet relaxing vibe. In the center seats sit, surrounding an empty table with recently used glasses and drinks. Walking past it, I step to the edge, facing Techdon.

The city of technology glows in the distance with a white hue. Vibrant and unmistakable. Like a beacon of hope to anyone who looks at it from afar.

My eyes find the stars in the cloudless sky above. With the amount of technology flooding this sector, one would imagine the light pollution would cloud the stars' brilliance. Somehow it doesn't. They are amplified and there's thousands, maybe millions coming in full view. The witnesses of life, my mother called the stars. I used to look to them when I felt alone, imagining my parents watching over me. These are the times many people still use to pray.

I don't.

Experiences grant me the wisdom to know there is no God, or at least not one actively intervening in life. If there were, the Enlightenment and node wouldn't exist. I wouldn't have been subject to torment for years. A loving God, as people call it, wouldn't subject a child to surgery so their parents have benefits from the government. The girl from the train platform a week ago flashes in my mind. The smile she gave. My eyes fall as tears form, and I contemplate.

To me, God is a false pretense to make one feel better about the actions of life, a way to lay the blame on something or someone else, avoiding introspection. If I happen to be wrong and there is a God, then I would come to the conclusion they wanted this all to happen and are therefore no different than the Enlightenment.

The stars twinkle as if they are blinking, watching me think. I get a feeling of fullness inside, making me smile: the thought it could be my parents' energy, transformed into the light of a star.

I turn on my heel toward the empty space. Plants live on the edges. A mix of colors I can only imagine helps with the air quality this high up. Holochairs line one corner, drawing my attention. A holodesk sits near the point I stepped out of the elevator. It holds holograms displaying Black Web's logo.

My boots click on the hard floor as I make my way to the center, where the elongated seats and table sits. The leftover drinks make me wonder who was here before me. Ignoring the rest of the mess, I make my way to the holochairs in the corner.

"You've decided to stay," Amity says.

"I have."

"The feeling will subside, Ms. Young. This does seem to be the right decision."

"Hmm. I suppose we will find out one way or the other."

"Indeed."

The quiet I've grown accustomed to is replaced by the sound of all four elevators. They open simultaneously, releasing their riders to the open space. My eyes and brain work quickly to produce a small roll call. Clockwise from my left: Astrea and Ayster exit together from 1, Mason and Raelyn from 2, Zane stalks from 3, and right next to me from 4, with her famous invasive scent, Eliza strolls in.

"Finally!" Astraea shouts, jumping to the open seating.

Ayster finds his way to the long table with holograms. Behind it, a smaller table hovers with drinks collected above it.

"I'll take one too," Mason says, sitting across from Astraea.

Raelyn takes the seat next to him, stretching her legs across his. Zane breaks away from everyone like he's avoiding the plague. He takes a seat near a variety of floating holograms appearing from his presence.

"Are you going to sit there forever?" Eliza says.

She stands at my side with a smile.

"I didn't think anyone would notice me here."

"You? Unnoticeable? Please." She chuckles.

"Who are you talking to over there?" Raelyn's voice beams in our direction.

"Come on," Eliza says, "let me introduce you to the web."

"There goes your alone time," Amity says.

I sigh at the thought.

She takes the first step toward the seated area, and I follow close behind.

"Think fast," Ayster says, tossing a drink in the air, on his way to take a seat next to Astraea.

Mason catches it with a smirk. He takes a sip of the beverage and offers it to Raelyn, who takes it.

Zane is the first to notice me as we walk but remains silent—or at least he tries to. His facial expression speaks a thousand words, his disdain evident. The last thing I said to him in Encryption comes to mind, but before any sympathy arises, I remember his comment about Trace saving my life. I return a hateful glare and proceed with Eliza.

Raelyn finds me next, eyes wide with a display of awe.

"The girl of the hour," she says softly.

All heads turn to me in response. Eliza steps to an empty seat and gestures for me to take one beside her, next to Raelyn.

"Ariadne right?" Ayster asks.

His jaw is so tight and sharp, I can almost see his face shake. Being closer to him and Astraea, the resemblance is clearer. Thin eyebrows stop too short from the purposeful slits at the end. Astraea's flare upward, with detail to every strand. The amber in their eyes matches the intensity of their platinum hair, vibrant in color.

"You are?" I ask, knowing exactly who he is.

"Ayster," he says dryly. "Hell of a show you put on in Encryption."

"Jealous?" I counter calmly.

Astraea laughs. "God, I love you," she manages through it.

Ayster's eyes fall, a clear sign he's already given up.

"Thanks," I say. "Astraea, right?"

Ayster moves his jaw in a wicked rotation, clearly annoyed by my presence.

"Right, but my moronic brother here usually calls me Rea." She bumps Ayster, and his brows angle with tension. "But you can call me whatever you want, little badass."

"Raelyn," she says practically in my ear, arching her head over the armrest like a yoga pose.

"So, is Ariadne your real name?" Mason asks.

"Mason!" Raelyn shoves him. "Don't be rude."

"I think you guys are the ones being rude. She clearly knows our names. I don't know how. Maybe Eliza already introduced us, but what I do know?"

He takes a quick sip of his drink, methodically tasting the contents before continuing.

"Her intelligence is beyond what we've seen. I mean, we all saw the way she destroyed Thaddeus in less than five minutes. To think she didn't have at least an idea of who we are is rude."

He takes another sip, longer this time, as if to force the drink's effects to happen faster.

"So?" he says.

"You seem to think you know me so well. Do you think it's my real name?" I turn the question back.

"On the contrary, I don't know you at all, but I thought this was introductions."

"And you got it. Ariadne is my name."

"Hmmm."

He returns to his original position, and I can't tell what he's thinking. The brown curls fall into his face, concealing his expression.

"Forgive him," Raelyn says. "He's too smart for his own good."

She shovels a hand through his hair in a playful manner, and it gets a giggle out of him.

"I think what mop head was getting at is that we all have code names we hide behind," Zane says in a cool tone.

Mason lifts his middle finger in his direction.

"And of course, you already know Zane," Astraea says, rolling her eyes.

"What's yours?" I ask him plainly.

He narrows his eyes and takes a drink of a dark brown liquid. Swallowing hard, he fixes his mouth to absorb the feeling going down his throat. I can tell it burns by the wince he makes.

"Viro," he says finally.

"Viro," I repeat.

He doesn't respond, just digs back into the holograms in front of him.

"Our codenames kind of match our skills in tech," Eliza says.

"Yea, for example, mine is Lumina. When it comes to needing power or light, I'm your girl," Raelyn says proudly.

"Kasper," Mason adds. "Jamming is my specialty, but if you need a quick blackout, I can do that too."

"Illusia," Astraea follows behind. "Think illusions and hiding in plain sight."

"Echo. I'll save you the explanation." Eliza winks.

Ayster remains silent.

A loud hiss escapes from above as my eyes follow it upward. The tip of the pyramid slowly opens, revealing a layer of glass that's lined to be moved. It slowly allows the night air to funnel its way inside. The glass continues to stretch outward until all four sides are folded along the outside of the building. Crisp air fills my lungs. More stars have scattered in the night sky, providing more light to the interior.

"Phoenix," Ayster finally speaks, his tone low and deep, like he's forcing his vocal chords to stretch. "I revive networks and data if they fail."

"And I assume you deal with viruses." My eyes find Zane.

"Correct, new girl." His dark eyes slant as he releases a wicked smirk. "Specifically, hidden viruses that people never see coming."

The nickname he's given me makes me want to drive my staff into the side of his skull.

"And that's the web," Eliza emphasizes.

"Aside from Dyce…" Zane adds, quieting the space like an EMP.

Dyce. I never knew Trace's real name until Claire said it during his ceremony.

"That guy could literally *trace* anything.." Ayster says.

A moment of silence returns and we all share it. Like a community honoring someone who was important and loved.

"What's yours?" Mason asks.

Raelyn knocks him in the head, causing his drink to spew out of his mouth, making everyone laugh.

The night sky catches my eye as his question causes my code name's creation to come to mind. How I created it and the excitement it brought me when I told my parents, who were delighted to hear it.

I don't remember my mother ever looking as shocked as she did in that moment. She looked happy and excited, but with no words to show it. My dad on the other hand, was in a full state of joy, with tears streaming down his face.

Ayster clears his throat as they all patiently wait to hear my code name.

"Nexia," I say. "It's a long story, but I basically have many skills, connected as one."

"Like a nexus," Eliza says.

"Precisely."

"I love that!" Raelyn shouts.

"Speaking of skills, you're going to help us decode what we found, right?" Mason asks.

"Yes," I say. "But we can't start until Claire fixes the mistake Ayster caused."

Puzzlement stretches across their faces, revealing that I'm the only one who knew.

"What the fuck dude?" Zane says.

"Idiot," Mason adds, slapping his forehead.

"What the hell did you do?" Astraea shoves Ayster.

"It was taking too long," Ayster says, standing. "I wanted to see if I could expedite it."

"You know we don't do that," Raelyn counters. "The director specifically tells us to wait for this very reason, so why the hell would you do it now? I bet we lost information because of it as well."

She's right, but I don't confirm. I've caused this argument, and I don't want to add fuel to the fire.

"I'm sorry!" Ayster shouts. "I was trying to help!"

"Ohhh I'm sure," Zane says.

He storms off toward the edge and looks out to the city.

"Well, I guess it buys us time for Zero Day," Mason says. "What are we doing?"

"Oh shit. That's tomorrow, isn't it?" Astraea says.

"You never remember anything," Ayster responds, shaking his head.

"Shut up! We're still mad at you."

The others laugh and it sparks a smile in me. They recover so easily and remain tight knit, despite their fight moments ago.

"We can go into Techdon to celebrate," Raelyn offers. "I'm sure there will be events going on."

"Every year, we celebrate it," Eliza says to me, realizing my silence.

"You don't celebrate it?" Zane asks from afar.

"Not with a group of people," I say.

"Well, this year, you will," Astraea exclaims.

"Let's all meet tomorrow at the hangar. We'll decide what to do from there," Raelyn announces.

Everyone agrees, and I'm forced to think: What have I gotten myself into?

27

The hangar vibrates with movement from Black Web members. They move quickly, to and from flars lining the edges of the space. On each side, dozens of flar-like ships float, waiting to take flight. All of them have a matte black finish, silver lines tracing the bottom edges. The windows are blacked out, like the one I traveled in when I first arrived.

There are several designs, including smaller flars with dual propeller wings and noses angled in a way that implies agility and speed, and larger ones with quad propellers and wider noses, likely built for endurance.

Flars enter from ahead, releasing gusts of air that push through the hangar, creating small funnels along the concrete ground. Every member of the web is in attendance as they walk ahead of me.

"You could have said no, Ms. Young," Amity chimes.

"I don't think so. They would have made me."

"Perhaps. At least it's Zero Day, something you like and celebrate."

Zero Day.

My version of celebration always involved me reminiscing about time with my parents. It was my way to commemorate what they did for me and the country. Not all is known about the events which took place, but what all citizens who were alive during the time know is that there was a moment of freedom. Every node was deactivated, and for the first time in years, people did what they wanted. Even if only for a moment, freedom was proven possible in an otherwise hopeless time.

My parents weren't known by their faces. They were known by name for their actions and innovations. When it came to technological advancements after the war, they were the ones who helped push for levitators, holoscreens, flars, and caerials. Not alone, but they paved the way for our society.

"This way!" Raelyn shouts ahead of everyone.

We gather at a flar, and the group discusses what they want to do. I ponder the possible ways to get myself out of this situation. I don't want to travel with other people. It attracts too much attention, especially on a day like today. The Enlightenment will be expecting people to celebrate the day they almost fell—the day the nation almost changed for the better.

"To Techdon!" Astraea yells.

We board the flar and they sit in a similar arrangement to the moment I met them. I proceed toward the back, and Eliza joins me. Piloting the flar is Zane and Ayster. Raelyn and Mason kiss and hold each other's hands, watching a video displayed on a nav.

Astraea sits alone, fiddling with a device I don't recognize. It's circular and silver. When she presses it, the device awakens with a white glow. It twitches until her hand starts to fade. The effect camouflages her hand against the white she wears, making it practically invisible. I shouldn't be surprised because of Techdon's prowess when it comes to technology, but I can't help it.

"It's definitely something," Eliza says next to me. "And that's only a fraction of what she can do."

"I'm sure you all can do pretty amazing things."

"You're right about that. You'll probably get to see for yourself eventually. Today is about celebration and relaxation."

She smiles, making something inside me mirror the gesture.

"Why did they choose Techdon?" I ask.

"There's an off the grid party. I think you'll enjoy it."

I hope so, I think to myself. Because if there's one thing I try to avoid at all costs, unless absolutely necessary, it's large gatherings.

<hr>

"I hate this," I say to Amity.

I lean on the edge of a rooftop as the members of the web enjoy themselves. They dance and laugh among people who seem to be rebels against the Enlightenment. Chants of "Zero Day!" ignite the crowd as I turn away, looking into the distance of the city.

"You can always leave, Ms. Young."

"Maybe this was a bad idea," I say. "Staying, I mean."

Speeding flars soar as high as the building we're on. They mimic my thoughts, intrusively invading my mind. My decision to stay begins to build regret. My mission feels like it has stalled and I'm not sure how to get it back on track. If Ayster hadn't messed up so badly, maybe I'd be on my way toward vengeance.

"Ms. Young, maybe it's time to have fun."

"Fun?"

"Look at them."

I turn toward the party as it continues. Ayster and Astraea laugh and joke. Mason, Raelyn, and Eliza share smokes, seemingly to get rid of their edge. Zane shows a different side of himself as he dances with a girl. Scanning the other twenty or so people, I take in the joy written on their faces. Alcohol in their hands, splashing and sloshing as they swing and dance amongst one another.

"You've never had this, Ms. Young."

"I don't care about this. I want the people who killed my parents."

"Patience, Ms. Young."

I turn my sight back to the glowing city. The essence of technology flows throughout it. Bright light. Painted neon color throughout the etches of every building.

The sun slowly descends on the earth, quietly changing brightness to a mesmerizing darkness. It grants the city an opportunity to be illuminated in vibrant hues.

"It's almost time!" a voice shouts.

The person parts the crowd and stands center. A hologram hovers above his wrist as he fiddles with the interface, searching for something.

"Hey stranger," Eliza says, moving next to me.

"Hey."

"You want some?"

She holds a thin black rod, no longer than a couple inches. Grey smoke lightly escapes the end she's not holding.

"What is it?"

"Joy."

She snickers and places it to her lips, inhaling deeply until finally releasing with a soft sigh. Her blue eyes are low, but there's a spark drawing me closer. Two strands of red hair fall at her temples like a frame, magnifying her features. With the way her eyes watch me, analyzing, I get the feeling she wants that moment we almost had in her room days ago.

"Well?"

"Why not." I take it and inhale. Smoke fills my lungs, and I cough.

"Easy now," she says. "Try again, but softer."

I do as I'm told, and the feeling is much smoother. My lungs fill and release the smoke, my tension along with it. Numbness travels through every cell of my body.

"Mhhhmm. Good, isn't it?"

"You going to tell me what it actually is?"

"Serotonin. It's concentrated into a liquid that's inside of the rod. When inhaled it creates a fog that travels through the body and relaxes you."

I inhale again, closing my eyes. When I reopen them, she's closer. Watching me. She takes the device out of my hand as I exhale, eyes glued to my mouth. Before I can react, her lips meet mine and I'm floating. My heart thuds at a wicked pace as her lips move and interlock with mine. The softness makes me fall deeper into the embrace as the serotonin settles my nerves with joy.

"I've been wanting to do that for some time," she says with a smile.

I smile back, securing the memory of her full lips.

"Now it's time!" The voice from before returns. "To Zero Day!"

His words ignite the crowd and everyone chants. Their energy flows within me and I find myself joining in. I jump and scream the words. It's foreign and new, but it sparks something in me that I haven't felt in a long time. My mind quickly gains a brief moment of freedom from my mission. The only thing I've ever wanted.

The bang of fireworks scatters above us as the unknown speaker presses on his hologram. It activates them, shooting them into the air in rapid fire succession. Oohhs and aahhs echo through the crowd.

"Watch this," Eliza says.

Her wrist glows like the commentator. A circular hologram hovers above hers in a purple hue. She spins it around with a finger and swipes it toward the sky. The fireworks explode with higher intensity, arousing the crowd. It makes the dark sky disappear behind the array of colors. She's somehow adding her own fireworks to the mix, mimicking the aftereffects of what was done. Like an echo.

"Echo," I say softly.

She turns to me, and a devilish smirk stretches across her lips, enticing me to say the first thing that comes to mind.

"I think the moment is back."

Her eyes flare with want.

"So, when we get back," she says, her voice filled with heat, saturated in energy and lust. "my room or yours?"

Like links coiling through a system, there's a connection which dares to draw me closer. Her lips find my neck and the fire inside me scorches my skin, creating an inferno through my blood. Soft kisses move slow and steady, forcing my heart to add more heated blood. I close my eyes to embrace the feeling as she stops at the height of her trail, igniting a pulse between my legs.

My mind is a whirlwind of feelings and thoughts, with her at the forefront. The warmth continues to pulse harder, thumping beneath my bodysuit, giving my mind only one option.

"Yours," I manage in a whisper.

"Already?" she says with a deadly smile. "We haven't done anything yet."

"Oh, whatever."

Her hands guide my loose hair away from my face and she kisses me. The moment is bliss, like a never ending feeling of freedom. We move our lips, passionately and smoothly pressing them together. They part briefly, and her tongue finds its way into my mouth, rotating on mine, moving in unison and gliding with soft warmth. She breaks the kiss, and I lean in for more. My eyes finally open, finding hers as she smiles.

"My room then."

28

Eliza lies in her bed, and her eyes move me to join her. She wears translucent, thin shapewear across her breasts and a pair of underwear with a similar transparency. My heartbeat slows, but my breaths seem to be working against me. I join her, and the anticipation of being this close to her makes me shudder.

"You okay?" she asks.

"I am," I say. "More than okay."

She rises and places her lips gently on my neck, moving down to my shoulder. The softness of her hands rubs the tension out as she slides the straps of my bodysuit off. Remembering the tightness of my suit, I stand and release the shoulder straps. I pause when the suit reaches below my breasts. The scars I've hid from everyone tingle, but it's not because they're fresh. I've been ashamed to show them because of the fear of being seen as weak. But, looking into Eliza's eyes, something tells me she won't see me that way. My face grows warm as she looks at me with wide eyes and arched brows when the suit hits the floor.

"Wow," she says.

I smile and return to her side. Our lips lock and her hands trace my body with slow deliberate motions. Activating the sensations I'd been longing for days ago. Her hand slowly passes my chin, moving down my neck with the slightest touch from her fingertips. Gentle and firm, they trace my collar and find their way to my breasts, hovering over the nipple. Want makes my body close the inches between us. Her finger follows the circle of my nipple before she softly pinches it, beckoning a gasp from my lungs. As if it were confirmation to continue, she does, moving her hand effortlessly across my stomach, triggering my subconscious to surface. She reaches the scar below my navel, and I flinch. Memories from my surgeries at the Enlightenment Prison flash in my mind, making my body react.

"Are you okay?" she asks again, stopping, her soft eyes glittering.

"Yes, I'm okay." I smile.

In the wake of the invasion of my body in prison, whenever it came to sex, I have always been mostly clothed, to avoid the view of my scars. Now, being with Eliza, there's a comfort that allows me to ignore all the negative memories of what those agents and doctors did to me.

Before the nightmares can resurface and ruin this moment, I move her hand down to the warmth between my legs, growing increasingly wet. My breathing falls slow and heavy as the rest of my body answers to her touch. I roll on my back to give better access to her hand as it lightly traces my tip, rotating in long, slow circles. Her lips find my neck with multiple kisses before she parts them, sliding her tongue along my flesh. With her finger drenched from my wetness, she returns to my nipple, which has grown more sensitive. I relish in the feeling as my body twitches.

"Have you decided to stay?" she asks, pausing and staring into my eyes.

My body moves, aching for her to continue.

"Do I have a reason to?" I say with a smirk.

"Is that a challenge?"

"And if it is?"

Her finger, wet from my body and her mouth, finds its way inside me. My mind explodes from the nerves electrifying my senses. My muscles clinch, signaling for her finger to move in a rhythm, and I arch my back, my legs vibrating as the sensation pierces the darkness behind my eyes—the darkness I'd drowned years ago when I found my way out of the grasp of the Enlightenment.

Another finger finds its way to where the first has opened the floodgates. Drunk on heat and lust, I start to pulse around her fingers with each thrust.

"Say it," she says.

The assertiveness in her voice drags a deeper moan out of me. Not being in control makes me melt at the sound of her voice. She guides her thumb along my tip as the other two fingers continue to work inside me, and the desperation to release is unbearable. Through dazed eyes, I find her smirk, guiding me closer to the edge.

"Make—" My voice shudders from the fight to give in.

The combination of heat from her mouth and the wetness below makes me shiver. In one fluid motion, she stops, wraps her hair back, smiles and dives down, pulling my hips toward her. She kisses my inner thighs as her fingers continue to guide me to climax, working their way in and out while her thumb gracefully massages my now throbbing crown. The pulse in my muscles strengthens and so do the vibrations throughout my body, making my breath sound airy. She pulls me closer as her mouth creates suction, and her tongue replaces the fingers inside me.

All of my nerves, senses, energy, and strength travel to my aching tip as her tongue finds me. Stars explode behind my eyelids, blood surging through me as the feelings of electricity take over, coursing through my veins. I finally release my breath with a loud moan, bringing my shaking hands to cover my mouth. She lingers between my legs, rolling her tongue gently over my now drenched opening.

"Well?" she teases the question through slippery lips.

"I'm going to stay," I struggle to say.

"I know." She winks.

She unleashes a dozen kisses on my thighs working her way upward until meeting my lips. They connect and I release a soft shudder from the sweet taste of myself. Planting one last kiss, she jumps off the bed and walks toward her closet. I lie back and close my eyes as my body relaxes. My mind is at ease, lighter from the stress of my mission. Like I've been holding so much weight, and the moment I just shared with her has taken it all away. My life's purpose starts to creep its way back into my consciousness, but the emotions of lust and excitement drown it. I've always thought the only thing that could keep me going was my path of vengeance. Eliza has shown me otherwise. Even if this moment was brief, for the first time, I have a taste of what it would be like to not always fight.

"How are you feeling?" her soft voice stops my inner thoughts.

"Fantastic," I say, opening my eyes to her long red hair tumbling down her back.

"I'm going to take a shower before heading to bed."

"I'm going to head to my room and do the same," I say, sliding to the edge of the bed.

"Or you can stay and join me."

My heart flutters at the thought and the want to return the favor she has given me. She walks over to the bed and pulls me out by my hands. Her eyes drift down to my wrists where the shackles once held me captive. She lightly rubs them, and I can sense she wants to ask me what happened. But she doesn't. Her eyes grant a feeling of understanding and I'm grateful for her respect, for not wanting to intrude. I smile and walk toward the shower.

Her face glows as she makes her way to me. I take her hand and kiss her. Our lips lock and I can still taste the sweetness. I release and drag her into the bathroom to return the feeling of bliss.

29

The soft touch of a hand caressing the side of my face brings me to life. For the first time since being on my own, I didn't dream of them: not my parents, Wren, or the Enlightenment. Nothing. I slept as if my life and everything in it had no pain, and it was filled with light, banishing any shade of darkness.

"Good morning, Nexy," Eliza's soft voice hums in my ear.

My eyes open to calm rivers locked in hers. The deep blue, vibrant and luring, with a small yellow circle, tracing the outside. Lines extend, mimicking the sun and its rays, casting golden light across the still blue.

"Nexy?" I whisper, stretching my vocal chords for the first time.

"Do you like it?" Her hand gently moves down the length of my face, to my chin.

"I don't know. Maybe it'll grow on me."

A chime echoes through the room, forcing me to rise from the bed.

"It's okay," she says. "It's a notification on my nav."

My body relaxes at her words, and I lie back down.

"Don't get comfortable. We've been called to decrypt the information Raelyn and Mason found—what's left of it anyway."

I quickly rise out of the bed, my heart racing with excitement.

"A lot of energy this morning," she says.

"I've been waiting for this moment for a few days now. The only reason I came here and decided to st—"

Her eyes form deep slits, stopping my train of thought.

"Okay, not the *only* reason," I say, stepping into my suit.

I position the straps and throw on a hooded cropped jacket I found in my closet.

"Liz, come on. Get up."

"Liz?" she repeats.

"Sorry, I spoke too fast."

"It's okay. I kinda like it."

She rises out of the bed and throws on clothing from her closet. Grey shorts layered over black tights. A black long-sleeved shirt, cropped above her navel, and her Black Web cloak complete the look.

"Ready?" she asks.

I nod as we exit her room in the hopes of cracking a code.

———————————●

"You know, I was really holding on to the idea that Ariadne was lying," Astraea says as the door hisses open. "Seriously, Ayster, what the fuck?"

Astraea sits across from her twin, separated by a holo-screen, illuminated on a holodesk.

Eliza and I are the last to arrive at the room she refers to as the Terminal, the place where the web decrypts their findings. A smaller version of the briefing room, circular in shape with holoscreens etched on the walls. A table in the center holds the members of the web as they watch us enter.

"Look who finally decided to show up," Zane announces proudly.

His dark hair is slicked back in a ponytail, revealing the shaved sides of his head. He stands behind Ayster, in yellow tech pants and top, contradicting his personality entirely.

"And?" Eliza deadpans.

"Annnd…" He holds the word, stepping toward us, "I'd wager you two are late because of the sounds that echoed through the halls last night." He narrows his eyes and scans both of us.

"I'd raise your wager and say you wish it was you who could cause those sounds," Eliza's voice is low, guttural, and fuming with fire.

"Is that a challenge?"

"Enough, you two," Raelyn says.

She sits between Astraea and Mason. Her fair skin glows from the holoscreen as she moves her hands through it.

"We have work to do," Mason adds.

We take our seats at the table and Zane follows, taking one near Ayster. The file rotates with an encrypted lock embedded inside. Raelyn twirls it with her fingers as she contemplates.

"What have you tried?" I ask.

"So far, brute force attack has failed," Ayster says.

"And simple cracking," Zane says. "It's like there's more than one layer."

"May I?" I ask, reaching for the holoscreen.

Raelyn nods her approval.

I zoom in on the lock and see that Zane is partially right. There is a double layer, but the original coded entry is the main problem. Whoever designed this encryption intended to crash a network if detected. So, we'll have to counter a crash.

"Amity," I say.

"Ms. Young?"

"Is there a digital imprint we can use to convert the data back to its original state?"

"Cross-checking."

The web looks at me with puzzled gazes, except for Eliza.

"It's her A.I.," she supplies before I can.

"That's sick," Zane admits.

Iris glows in the darkness of the room, prompting me to activate it, displaying the imprint I asked for. I scroll through, following the origin of the first code.

"What are you looking for?" Raelyn asks.

"I'm not entirely sure. Really, anything that looks off."

"Can I show all of us?" Eliza asks.

"Sure," I say. "The more eyes the better."

She flashes her nav the same way she did on the rooftop during Zero Day. Iris buzzes with the link and I approve it. Iris' interface reveals the digital imprint to the web. They all inch closer, as if it were a magnet, pulling them in.

The room gradually illuminates from the large hologram. Blue light ricochets off the marble walls. A chill flows through me and I'm not sure if it's a draft in the room or the excitement of cracking a code.

"Okay, this imprint is how the original encryption was created," I say. "Usually an encryption of this caliber has a backdoor."

"How do you find a backdoor?" Ayster asks.

"That's the hard part," I say. "Amity, display the file's coding."

The hologram shifts to the algorithms embedded in the encryption. They fall in sequences and symbols. I focus my attention on any patterns or copies, and if there is one, that'll be the backdoor.

"This is incredible," Mason says. "You can change the interface of a system like it's nothing. I wish I could do something more useful than jam networks."

"Actually," I say, as an idea formulates in my mind. If we jam the algorithm, stopping the inter-network from flowing, it'll unlock the encryption. We wouldn't need to decode anything as it'll open on its own. "Jam the file."

"What?" they all respond.

"Do it."

Mason registers his nav, connecting it to Iris. He inputs codes I'm not used to seeing. He's fast and efficient. The jam registers and the falling codes from the file stop, revealing the backdoor.

"Amity."

"On it, Ms. Young."

Amity blocks the encrypted codes from crashing and the file unlocks.

"You did it," Raelyn says.

"Holy shit. You're good," Astraea adds.

"The silk of decryption would be very pleased with this," Eliza says.

"And who's that?" I ask.

"No one knows," Zane says. "She's the only silk we haven't seen in person."

"Why couldn't she help you guys?"

"She's not here," Raelyn says. "Or at least, that's what we all think. The silk of decryption works at her own pace, and from what we know, she stays hidden."

"But I have to say, that was pretty impressive, new girl."

I almost want to smile at Zane's praise, but the nickname changes my mind. When I face him, his nav closes and a smirk stretches across his face—all their faces in fact.

Not everyone's skills have been shown to me, but from what I have seen, they can be very useful at gathering data in a more efficient and relatively safe way.

"So, what did we find?" Astraea shouts.

I don't think I'll ever get used to her outbursts.

"It looks like a lab report of some kind," Raelyn says.

She enlarges it and it's confirmed. It's a written letter from a lab in Cybourne.

"Where did you guys find this again?" Eliza asks.

"We were infiltrating a building Claire gave us coordinates to," Mason says. "She said it was owned by Ezra."

"Read it," Zane says urgently.

"Cloning has been approved," Ayster starts. "The Enlightenment would like to pursue the project of cloning prisoners who are taken to the Mirror's Edge."

"Sounds like a hell of a place," Astraea interjects.

"Shhh," Ayster continues. "Those who are taken there will undergo a procedure where their DNA will be extracted and copied to form a new human. We will recreate humanity as we know it. The nation will be ours, guided by our creation. The better human."

Ayster stops, his expression conflicted.

"What else?" Zane pushes.

"That's it," Ayster says. "The rest of the file is lost because of me."

"Who was it written by?" I ask.

Raelyn looks closer, trying to read the signature.

"Octavio Oxton," she whispers.

Gasps erupt through the space.

The man Claire mentioned when she first brought me here—the architect of Black Web.

As we exchange looks of bewilderment, the intercom crackles above.

"Attention, attention. All members of the web are to report to the Director's office immediately," the voice, similar to Amity's, says.

We exchange glances, our expressions all asking the same question:

What has happened?

ACTIVATION

30

"I'm going to keep this short because we have to act. Intel about your assignments will be transferred to your navs with further detail that you can use on your way, but for now..." Claire takes a short breath. A sharp gaze of want and determination transfers throughout the room. "We've received word that the Enlightenment have approved their time frame for their nationwide address. It will be Enlightenment Day, as I predicted. Furthermore, it's not certain, but Ezra may have been spotted in Area 1."

Whispers flow and heads turn among the web. From my normal corner of the briefing room—my honorary comfort zone—I move to the oval table, joining the others. Ezra's name drags the stirring emotions out as I ignore the looks of Zane and Ayster. After helping them, I thought I would be welcomed at least a fraction more than before. I guess I was wrong.

"I'm sending Zane, Ayster, and Mason to Arcadia. Specifically, to the Panoramic Diner where Daniel was killed."

Daniel. The memories of his politeness and shy nerves that rose when he poured my coffee quickly flash through my mind. I still find it hard to believe he tried to kill me. Trace's smile beckons and I think about how he saved my life.

A map appears on the table, glowing with a hologram of the Panoramic diner. The red hue rotates around the destruction of one of my favorite places to relax. It shows the aftermath of the events when we fled. Claire flicks the hologram, and it zooms in, adding the letters 'VPK' above it. The letters separate into names, and I remember the introductions from the rooftop.

Codenames.

Viro, Phoenix, and Kasper.

"Zane will take the lead. Your goal is simple." She looks them over with a death stare. "If Ezra does show his face, do not engage. Your primary objective is surveillance. Take your teams and use your talents to track him. If he is carrying valuable information, extract it, but do not engage in any form of combat. And if there are any signs of Black Web we may have left behind, get rid of them."

"Director," Zane replies.

"Dismissed."

The three walk out in single file, without another word.

"Eliza." Claire pauses, gathering her thoughts. "You know your assignment. It goes through today."

"Director."

"Dismissed."

Eliza exits, following the boys' departure. The thought of saying goodbye is thwarted by the sound of the door closing. My shoulders unintentionally fall from not know-ing if I'll ever see her again.

"Astraea and Raelyn," Claire says, changing the map, revealing the letters 'I' and 'L'. Illusia and Lumina. "Here in Techdon, there are whispers about other Enlightenment members moving in to help Ezra with controlling the sector. I need you to find out when, where, and how."

Claire's voice turns maternal as she dismisses them. In her emerald eyes, there's the sliver of a tear, begging to be released. The director's fierceness shows as it evaporates after a hard blink, and she watches her daughter leave.

"Ariadne," she says softly.

"Before you try to assign me anything. I was able to help crack the encrypted code on the file Mason and Raelyn gathered."

"What did you find?"

"A lot was lost, but the most important thing is, the Enlightenment, along with a man you know, Octavio Oxton, have been producing clones of people somewhere called the Mirror's Edge."

Claire takes a step back as her brows furrow.

"Do you know what that is?" I ask.

"Yes, it's one of the Enlightenment's maximum security prisons. But cloning wasn't something recorded back when it was infiltrated by your parents, years ago."

"So, the Enlightenment has been cloning people more recently. I wonder if my parents had an idea. It could be another revelation they found."

"Maybe," Claire says, looking around, and judging by her sporadic movements, I'd guess she's looking for a drink. "Thank you. I'll have our silk of decryption look at it more thoroughly. I know you have more important matters at the moment."

She's right. A concrete lead has finally shown itself, giving me the drive to pursue it and achieve what I was meant to. Even though the idea of cloning sends a sharp chill down my spine and warrants my curiosity, it's not my primary mission.

"I want to send you to Millennia, if that's okay."

"Why there?"

"Given Millennia's history of being the most guarded sector, I think there is a better chance of Ezra being there, versus Arcadia."

"So why not send the guys there?"

"There's still a chance I'm wrong, and he goes to Arcadia. The reason three of them are going is because there is more ground to cover, including the cleaning aspect of the diner."

The map closes and the table rises. Holograms flicker and return to view as she walks around the table to meet me, and I'm engulfed in her arms. There's a sweet scent hidden behind the clove, reminding me of my mother. It tugs at my heart as I return the hug, pulling us further into an embrace.

She holds me at arm's length and smiles.

"I know you want to kill him, but I ask you to reconsider. I want you to have your revenge, but the time has to be right. Whatever Ezra is doing in Area 1, we need to know, and I believe you can be the one to retrieve that intel."

Again, she praises me, and I haven't done anything to deserve it. The pressure makes me tense as the biggest question I've never answered comes to light. Do I kill the Enlightenment? Or find another way to enact my revenge.

"We'll see what happens," I say, readying myself to leave. "But, I'll have to go to my home in Arcadia first.

There's some things I'll need for the operation you don't have here."

"Be careful," she whispers.

"I will. And thank you for everything."

"Anytime, love."

I smile and head to the door.

"Amity, it's time to go home."

31

"Welcome home, Ms. Young," Amity says over my inter-network.

Everything is exactly how I left it. The center seat, arranged by my parents. A table hovering a few inches above the floor, directly in front of it. Cool air rushes through the room, gently sending chills along my skin. Being underground the past few days has given me a new appreciation for being above it.

I pace toward the kitchen, sliding my staff out of its holster and place it gently on the floating island. The lights flicker on with a quiet hum. I trace the island top and absorb the feeling of my own space again. Following the rectangular shape, my fingers find the edges as they slide on the hard surface. My eyes scan the black cabinets until falling, stopping at the refrigerator, instantly igniting my taste buds. Bronze liquid sloshes in the container as I pour it, filling a small glass. The potent smell makes my mouth water, as I imagine the taste.

Excitement fills my body when the first sip of crisp bitterness lands on my tongue. As I swallow, the sweet tangy aftershock refreshes my mouth with a relishing experience I didn't know I could miss. The drinks at Black Web didn't satisfy me the way this tea does. The food was also different. Here, in Arcadia, food is always fresh–especially seafood which I've missed. I suppose being underground in Techdon makes the food bland, but I would think they would have some kind of tech to make it for them.

As I think about Black Web, Eliza comes with it. The time I spent there, meeting Claire and the others who share in my cause, lights a fire of joy in my heart.

I move past those thoughts before I delve deeper into the memories of my time with Eliza. The thoughts fade as I reenter my living room and take a seat on the couch that faces the glowing 'A' on my wall. The insignia reminds me of the pen Claire gave me, once belonging to my mother. I remove the pen from its secure hiding place along my belt and hold it high between two fingers. I twirl it in my hand and notice a weight transfer inside, as if something is sliding from one end to the other. I twist the pen open, and inside the hollow tube is a small chip, the perfect size to fit into Iris, which requires custom made chips. Chips designed by my parents.

"Amity," I say. "Scan."

I toss the chip into the air, and take another sip of tea. The smooth buzz of my drone's wings hover above me as the chip lands on it. The scanning begins. Rigorous and thorough, to provide a secure encryption to protect my own devices if this chip happens to be corrupt.

"Scanning complete, Ms. Young. The chip is clean and ready to be used."

It falls back into my palm and my drone glides away. I attach the chip to Iris, securing the connection, and place it on the table in front of me. The 'A' along the wall begins to pulse like a soft heartbeat before activating. An optic scanner displays, hovering over the table. It rotates, searching for eyes. I move into its view, and it glows green.

"Young DNA verified," Amity says.

The scanner fades and the word 'Amity' displays in white lettering.

"What is this?" I ask.

"It appears it's a main source connector, Ms. Young. The interface is gathering data from an unknown source inside the home."

My core tightens as my lungs stall. I don't like the idea of an unknown source being connected to my interface.

"Data transfer complete, Ms. Young."

The letters fall like a code and reveal an algorithm I've seen before, during a training session my mother once gave me.

"What transfer?"

"A database transfer found in a room beneath the house."

"What?"

"It appears the unknown source has been revealed inside of your simulation chamber. There's a hidden compartment the chip managed to unlock once it connected to your systems."

My breathing starts to settle from Amity knowing the source's location. I've lived in this home for seven years now and had no idea. I don't know if I should be angry with myself for not realizing or grateful to Claire for giving me the pen. She must have known.

"Ms. Young, the data found inside the compartment was left by your parents," Amity adds. "Before they died, they transferred all data held in your former home."

My former home.

Tears stream down my face at the mention of both it and the deaths of my parents. Memories I have forced to the deepest place in my mind return with a force, breaking my heart once again.

They 'd fought and killed so many of them, I was sure we'd be okay. That thought had been erased when my mom took a bullet. It'd pierced her chest, and as she'd wavered backward, I'd screamed as loudly as I could. As much as I'd wanted to come to her aid, I couldn't. My screaming distracted my father, who hadn't realized she'd been shot. He'd turned to face me, sadness embedded beneath his eyes. Pain and anger had ripped through me when his hand touched the fresh blood that slowly spread across his coat.

He'd fallen to his knees after taking my dying mother's hand. The world had paused, black and white, filled to the brim with the hues of my inner darkness. My mind took a picture of them at that moment, reminding me to never forget. My father then kissed her hand, and it fell dead to the ground. Agents had flooded inside, but my dad still smiled with his head high. His eyes had found mine when an EA pointed a gun to his head and pulled the trigger.

Stunned by a broken heart and fractured mind, I hadn't fought back when the agents rushed in and grabbed me. I was carried out of my home in the arms of hooded people as I got one last glimpse of my parents' bodies. More agents had ignited an explosion, incinerating everything I've ever loved. Thrown into the back of a flar, I vowed to avenge them. To cause the same pain they'd caused me. I promised myself I would never be hurt by them again.

"What data was transferred?" I ask, new determination grounding me.

"Data for new equipment and upgrades to your gear."

Perfect time for my upcoming mission. The hologram fades and I'm on my feet, tracking the location Amity mentioned, past my living room through my narrow hallway. Before the end, I walk down into the basement, where my simulation device lives.

A blue glow appears on the floor, something I never noticed before. When I reach the hidden door, a hologram rises from it, my mother's insignia, highlighted like everything she'd ever owned.

The hologram flickers, and a red beam shines directly in my eyes, blinding me for a few seconds.

"Young DNA verified. Failsafe aborted," Amity says.

A hiss escapes the door as it unlatches, reminding me of the doors in Black Web. The door slides flush into the floor, releasing stairs leading underground. Bright light illuminates the small space as I reach the bottom step.

"Woah," I say.

My eyes find silver plated boxes tucked into a corner. Floating desks hover along the walls with holograms labeling with what they contain. Weapons line the three walls with other equipment I don't recognize. I take a few steps deeper, and the holograms on the tables flicker, waiting to be activated. One, labeled 'Prototypes', catches my eye amid the crowd of equipment. I activate it, revealing different methods for extraction, chronologically numbered from one to five. Dates appear at the corner of each file. Dating back to the technological war. I open the first file, and the contents aren't displayed how I expect them to be. Instead of a written document, there are video components and demo reels. As a video plays, my parents talk about refined weaponry, letting me know the primary focus for this file.

I thought I had everything I needed but here I stand with more. My parents must have known I would follow the path they lead. What other reason could explain this? They left me with an A.I., which looks after me and helps me pursue my goals, money, a large amount of equipment, and the skills to use them.

When I first escaped prison, I had no idea where to begin in my quest for vengeance. Now, in knowing who my parents' murderers are, I have a chance.

"Ms. Young, might I ask a question?" Amity says.

"Yes?"

"Is the plan to kill the members of the Enlightenment?"

The question returns.

I thought I knew the answer when I saw my parents die in front me. To kill was the only option. And when Wren died, that pushed it further. But, after finding Black Web and meeting Claire, I'm not sure anymore. The talk about the bigger picture and how the entire nation could be affected causes my original decision to waver. I'm stuck with the question of whether my personal vendetta is worth whatever will happen to the country afterward.

"When the moment comes, I'm sure I'll know," I say. "For now, we have a lot of work to do."

"Seems preparation is in order."

"I want to work out every possible scenario. Good and bad. We need to make this essentially perfect. This could be our last chance."

"Where do we start?"

The holograms glow around me, waiting to be analyzed. All the possibilities play in my head. With Claire's help, I know where he may be, giving me a head start.

"The beginning," I say, activating the first prototype.

No mistakes. This is what I live for.

32

Yesterday, after the chip revealed a new database inside my home, I used every minute to learn from it. As I lie in my own bed for the first time in days, regret builds inside of me. I could have jumped to pursue Ezra, but I stayed to prep. I do believe my preparations will help me as I still don't have an exact location for him, but it doesn't stop the itch to get moving.

One thing I can be grateful for is Claire. Without my mother's pen, I wouldn't have been able to discover what my parents left behind. The weapons, equipment, and knowledge all came from meeting her. The director, and how she's leading a revolution against those in control, comes to mind, including how I might possibly be a part of it. As my mind wanders, Eliza appears behind my closed eyes.

Her gorgeous blue eyes always seemed to pierce through me. An everlasting smile that made me feel wanted. The way she thinks and how it translated into her voice. It all makes me miss her. How can I miss someone I barely know? She has left a bizarre and strange imprint on me. Foreign to my emotional and mental capabilities.

Wren quickly invades my consciousness, replacing Eliza. Her smile, which made all my bad feelings go away. When I lost her, all hope for happiness was gone and I didn't know how to move on. Only through memories of her was I able to fully escape the iron grip of the Enlightenment. The first person I ever loved outside of my family. And now, with Eliza, I don't know what to think or feel.

I rise out of bed before I let the thoughts drown me and step out onto the balcony. With each step, my legs feel tight and sore, like I'm trying to walk up a steep mountain. My arms feel numb and heavy. I finally make it to the balcony's edge and lean all my weight on the marble rails. My eyes find the sky and I'm in awe of the untouched blue. Like the ocean, vast and open for imagination to soar with no end in sight.

"Ms. Young," Amity calls.

"Yes?"

"Are you feeling okay?"

I don't know how to answer. There is so much I've experienced in the past few weeks that I was not prepared for. My first encounter with the Enlightenment, meeting two family members, the introduction of a rebel group, and meeting someone I don't think I'll ever want to forget. My life has been focused solely on my vengeance; I never had a chance to feel anything but hate. I've never known anything else since my parents died and then Wren. Nothing else mattered. Now, something in me wonders if there's more. Maybe there is, but maybe it's not what I want.

"Ms. Young?" Amity calls again.

"I'll be okay," I lie, blocking tears.

I know Amity senses the lie by the looming silence and I appreciate that I don't have to explain what's really going on.

The dense forest of pine trees towering over the land with unrelenting stature grants me a distraction. A breeze floats by and releases a pine aroma, making me smile. Fall is here. I inhale the cool air and a brisk chill travels through my body. Iris vibrates with notifications, taking me away from nature's respite.

"Would you like to ignore them, Ms. Young?" Amity asks, reading my annoyance.

"No, it's fine. Can you display them? I'll be in in a moment."

I inhale my final breaths of the fresh, clean air only nature can provide. Then an unknown voice beckons me inside.

"The situation that occurred a week ago at the Central Square of Arcadia has been resolved. We have regained control and no further actions are required."

"Clear the sound and implement recording," I say quickly.

I enter my room and find the edge of my bed. I face the wall displaying the Enlightenment News and a familiar face appears on the hologram screen, beginning to speak.

"However, it has come to our attention that there are citizens that want to erase everything the Enlightenment has done for this country."

The screen glitches and the silhouette of the face becomes visible.

"These same citizens are the cause of force delivered on the plaza."

Ezra Coleman.

My mind is in disbelief. He actually revealed his face to the Area—to me. Anxious nerves swell under my skin. This is the man who caused all my pain. My eyes burn as I trace every aspect of his face. Every strand of his blonde hair, every wrinkle spreading across his forehead, and every line forming his expression.

"Whoever was responsible for the events that took place downtown a few days ago will be punished," he continues. *"This footage was captured by the nodes of bystanders when it occurred."*

The screen jumps to show Daniel's final minutes before he was shot by a member of Black Web, the moment I walked up to Daniel before Trace barged through the door, only it's not me. A replica image of someone else replaces where I would have been. An image imported to all nearby nodes when I was there. The node sees what I allow them to see. Untraceable.

The footage ends with the building going up in flames.

"This will not go unpunished. Effective immediately, Area 1 will have a curfew that will limit all citizens to be inside of their homes by sundown until further notice."

A dramatic pause shifts the energy of the hologram. Ezra's face tightens with anger as his eyes glare through the screen—directly at me.

"We will find you. And when we do, consequences will be paid."

The broadcast abruptly ends.

I got him. This is my chance. The Enlightenment never reveals themselves. They don't make drastic mistakes like this. It's coded in every aspect about them. As Claire once again predicted, what happened at the diner must have been the key to drawing him out of hiding. Now frazzled and desperate for retribution.

Something we now have in common.

"It's time," I say.

"It certainly seems so. His location has been found and updated to Iris, Ms. Young."

This time, the Enlightenment will feel what it's like to be on the opposite side of pain. Ezra will fall. The country will see what he really is and what he really stands for. No more bullshit. No more false hope of a better nation.

We will take everything from him. He will burn.

33

"Attention all passengers. Attention all passengers. This Enlightenment train, servicing Area 1 will be going eastbound. Its final stop will be the Millennia sector."

I take my normal seat away from most of the people on the train and try to relax. My anxious nerves rattle inside me like a caged bird. The realization I have Ezra's exact location has finally settled and I can't contain the feelings that knowledge brings. Anger fuels the fire mostly, but there's also a sense of worry. Worry about failing, or worse, failing and being captured.

Cool air engulfs the car and I'm grateful the feeling is able to distract me from my thoughts. A hologram of Area 1 appears in front of me, highlighting the route through Arcadia, into Millennia. New ads appear after a few moments, showing how the node will enhance daily living. It connects to people's homes, cars, and phones. No more need for keys or risk of losing them. The hologram flashes back to the train route, a direct path with only one stop for those who don't intend to leave Arcadia. Around me, there aren't many people, which is a relief. Afternoon is always the best time to travel through sectors, or so they say. I've only been to Millennia once, when I was younger, when my parents took me to a tech event. The thought of leaving Arcadia again is daunting, and I hope I'm not gone for as long as I was in Techdon because I get the feeling Millennia won't be as friendly.

If Ezra did increase the security around the Area, then Millennia's will be amplified. Meaning the citizens will also be on edge. Millennia has always been known for its aggressive force of EAs. It makes a lot more sense after learning it's the home of Ezra's estate.

All it took to track him was finding the original coding from the device he used, hidden behind a rather secure network. Every device has a unique identifier, and by tracing data entries and broadcasts from his, Amity was able to pinpoint his location.

Now the question is, am I going to gather intel to bring back to Black Web like Claire wants? Or am I going to kill this asshole for everything he's done to me?

The train reaches full speed now as it zips out of Arcadia. The scenes through the window are all a blur, too fast for my eyes to register. The sun beams through the glossy glass, displaying golden rays, reflecting the car off its metallic surfaces.

"Would you like any refreshments?" a voice says at the end of the car.

A woman addresses herself as 'Carmen' to a few passengers. She wears a gold top with sleeves stopping at the middle of her biceps, tucked into a black, knee-length skirt. Long, black boots with a heel conceal the rest of her legs. Her hair is pressed flat, perfect, without a strand misplaced.

She proceeds down the aisle and stops in front of me. She gives me a blank stare, and it takes a considerable amount of time for her to blink.

"Would you like any refreshments?" she asks with no change of tone.

I hesitate to answer given how her stare never falters. A smile slowly stretches across her face, and it's so forced, her lips quiver.

"Would you like any refreshments?" she asks again while smiling.

"Are you okay?" I ask without thinking.

"Everything is fine. We are fine," she says robotically.

My time in Black Web has slightly blinded me of reality. Seeing people who don't have nodes and are free to live without having to force happiness. Claire's dream of freedom once again flashes in my mind, it would certainly be nice to not have the influence of the Enlightenment.

Carmen clears her throat, dragging me out of my head.

"Okay. I'll take some water."

"Perfect."

In her eyes, a highlighted red ring glows around her pupil. I inhale sharply and look away.

"Is everything okay?" she asks, bending to follow my gaze.

She lingers over me and stares blankly in my eyes. My heart starts to thud as my breaths quicken and my stomach drops.

"I'm okay. Thank you," I struggle to say.

The smile stretches wider, her eyes also growing larger. She returns to her original position and continues down the aisle at her previous pace. I've never seen a red ring around someone's pupil outside of Enlightenment Agents. It's not seen in Arcadia or Techdon, practically a myth shared after the Enlightenment took control. It is the manifestation of distrust that Ezra and the rest of the Enlightenment has in Millennia, compared to the other sectors. It shows the importance of maximum surveillance at all times.

According to the archives, a person only gets a red ring if they have done something against the Enlightenment, putting them at risk. Instead of killing them, they take those people and change their nodes to be activated without the push of a button. Essentially using it as a form of torture. Those with a highlighted node have little to no emotional control. If they show true emotion, the brain registers it and their nodes receive it, only to be detonated immediately.

A thought creeps into my mind. Cloning. Since helping Black Web decode their intel, it has been sitting at the back of my mind. But as I sit and think about the red ring, my studies from the archives come to my consciousness. We know little to nothing about it, but it could be a correlation between the red ring and the act of genetic copies of people. Cloning was originally an idea to produce more soldiers when the country needed an army during the war. Instead of the originals dying, they sent out copies. The archives don't say it, but the Enlightenment has been known to cut things out. Agents could be clones and so could Carmen.

"Ms. Young, you could be right," Amity says. "Here are pictures found in the new database inside the chip from Black Web."

Iris glows with images of people with red rings standing next to identical people without it.

"So, it's true," I say. "Clones exist."

"It seems so, Ms. Young."

What could it mean for the population? I've certainly never seen it before today. Maybe they haven't spread far. The file from Black Web flashes in my mind. The Mirror's Edge. The prison where the Enlightenment creates them. Who knows how many they are waiting to unleash.

"I wonder if Claire knows?"

"She should, Ms. Young, considering she provided you with the chip."

"Not necessarily. She gave me the pen, remember? And they needed you and your interface to activate it. So maybe Black Web doesn't know. Maybe it's another thing my parents couldn't share before their untimely death."

"Perhaps."

Carmen returns, distracting me from my raging thoughts. The terrifying grin returns, and I do everything in my power to smile back and look away. A table rises from the car's floor, and she places a glass on top of it. Water filters through the bottom of the car, through a tube attached to the table. The water floods the glass until full and the tube detaches again, returning to its original place. My table is left floating in front of me with a clean glass of water.

"Enjoy," she says quickly.

My eyes follow her as she retraces her path toward the other passengers.

"Amity. Diagnostics," I say, paranoia feeding my fear of being attacked.

"Drone 100%. Staff 100% with potential energy stored and ready for release. Amitronic suit fully engaged, Ms. Young."

Eyes still on Carmen, she exits the car to enter another, and in the opposite direction, I find a few heads seated near the exit.

"Proximity check."

"Scanning," Amity replies. "No threats detected, Ms. Young.

The more I learn about my parents' murderers, the stranger the world around me appears. With the revelations obtained, I lean toward the bigger picture. If the nation has no idea there are scientific creations walking among them, it could be enough for them to ditch their ideals about the Enlightenment. But I need more than a few pictures of people with red rings. I need something undeniable.

Maybe the estate will have it.

With the amount of mental processing, my eyes droop and my body relaxes into the seat. The cool air adds weight to my overactive mind and the want to escape into my subconscious rises.

"I should probably try to get some sleep before we arrive."

"That wouldn't be a bad idea. Your alerts will wake you if there's a threat."

"Thanks, Amity."

I swallow my water and let the coolness travel through my body. Closing my eyes, I drift away to the smooth sound of air flowing past the speeding train.

34

"Attention all passengers. Attention all passengers. We are ap-proaching Millennia Sector. Thank you for riding the Train of En-lightenment, and always remember, the Enlightenment is the light and hope for humanity. We hope you have an enlightened day."

Rustles from the other passengers notify me that we are close to the station. Close to Millennia. And most of all, close to Ezra's estate.

"Do you think this could be a trap, Ms. Young?" Amity asks.

"What?"

I try to avoid the thoughts the question brings up, thoughts that have plagued my mind since seeing Ezra's face.

"Ms. Young—"

"I know, I know," I say. "It certainly could be a trap, but what choice do I really have other than to follow this lead? The information I need is there. I have to go."

"It could be dangerous, Ms. Young."

"It will be. Every day in this society is dangerous, but I still have to live through it. I face all kinds of situations where my life is at stake, but this one... This situation is something worth more than that. Everything is at stake. My parents' retribution. And the way I feel right now, no one would dare fuck with me."

Anger swells in my gut, flooding my veins with intensity and heat, radiating from my body, triggering my new suit's cooling system. The chill cools my skin, filling my pores and icing my veins, reducing my anger.

My nerves and emotions are high from being so close. I take a few deep breaths. Doing my best to inhale peace of mind and exhale my anxious feelings.

"I'm okay," I say, not sure if I'm trying to convince Amity or myself. "I'm sorry, Amity. I know you're just trying to help and look after me. Thank you."

"Always, Ms. Young."

The train reduces speed, mimicking my emotions as the view through the window comes into focus.

Millennia Sector.

The metropolis beams with revolutionary and technological architecture. For a brief moment, the train flows through a tunnel, blocking my vision from the city. It exits and the city's brilliant glow lights up the world around it. My eyes adjust from the quick change of light as I try to grasp the enchanting look of the city. Glass buildings stretch high, appearing to touch the clouds above with ease. Volt rails flow through the city, bending and turning around buildings, creating perfect pathways to travel.

I've heard about them in Arcadia, but nothing was ever created. The stories say that they were designed to aid in the technological war, for transport of weaponry and goods. In order to use the rails, specially designed boots are required, and of course, training. A person can't simply decide one day they want to try it out and jump on it. That's an easy way for a quick death.

Flars soar through the air with afternoon traffic, creating a busy sky. From my view from the train, the flars are suddenly all bumper to bumper, the traffic stalled in midair. The train continues on, taking my eyes away from the action as it comes to a slow stop at the station. It lowers to the ground and locks into place. Signals for passengers to disembark appear on wall holograms, and I quickly exit from the sliding doors before the infuriating announcement about the Enlightenment comes over the train system.

Stepping onto the metallic platform, I'm immediately introduced to an outstretched palm, which stops me in place. The EA stands tall with a rifle holstered across his chest. His all black uniform is outfitted with too many tools to count. A helmet hides his face and expressions, giving his voice a sense of mystery.

"This is a checkpoint. All nodes must be scanned before you enter the city," he says sternly.

My heart rate starts to increase from the fear of being scanned without an active node. He prepares his scanner, but before he points it at my eye, I can hear shouting as a man yells about his node. A few feet away, at another checkpoint, the man is being escorted by agents to an unknown place. The commotion grabs the attention of the EA in front of me and I use the distraction to my advantage.

"Amity. Weapon concealment and node activation," I do my best to whisper.

"On it, Ms. Young."

"What was that?" the EA snaps.

"Nothing."

My suit pulls the holstered daggers I found in my hidden basement inward until they are no longer protruding and are a part of the lining. I flinch from the activation of my node, forcing me to close my eyes.

"Look forward and remain still, until you are told otherwise," he says.

The red beam from his scanner traces my body, starting from the top of my head. My breathing grows uneven from the beam hovering over my eyebrows. As it continues, I hold my breath. When it reaches my eyes, he holds the scanner for a few seconds, then it flickers green, releasing my breath with it.

"Nexia from Arcadia," he says. "No family name?"

You have no idea is what I don't say.

"No sir," I respond.

His helmet visor rises, and he watches me with puzzled eyes. His green eyes want me to react, giving him a reason to shoot me. Past his gaze, there's a tunnel ahead—the entrance for my objective, my mission.

"Welcome to Millennia," he says as the visor slides back across his eyes. "Have an enlightened day."

It takes every fiber of my being to ignore the statement plaguing this nation.

Like Carmen, I force a smile and walk toward my path.

CORRUPTION

35

"Welcome to Millennia," my quarters representative says. "Elevators are at the end of the hall. Have an enlightened day."

A scream builds in my chest at the statement, and it takes everything in me to remain silent. Ignoring it, I make my way out of the lobby's circular center.

"With the amount of technology the nation has, wouldn't it be nice to mute words we didn't want to hear?" I say.

"Like?" Amity asks.

"I'm sure you can guess. But don't actually say it; I might throw up."

"Maybe, one day, you'll create that technology."

"Maybe."

Continuing down the only hallway, the small frame of the quarters comes into view. Quarters, another Enlightenment addition to the nation, replaced hotels after the war. Their main purpose is to keep track of people traveling through sectors. They are centralized near stations for easy access to traveling citizens. This one is too small to be in a grand sector like Millennia, one of the reasons I chose it for my time here.

Scanning as I take quick strides, I see holograms of the AOE's developments appear on the walls. A ten year span after the technological war. The advancements of infrastructure in the sectors. The last pictured hologram is blank with a statement reading:

The Future Is The Enlightenment

Bile rises in my chest, and I almost release it on the walls. If I could take back reading it, I would. I reach the elevators, three on each side, with the right ones labeled as going up. Stepping in front of one, it scans my node, opening the doors for me to enter. It's designed for one person to ride, I note as I examine the small space.

"Nexia, from Arcadia, room 24," a voice says through the intercom. "Look into the camera above the doors to confirm."

Before I can obey the command, a girl wearing a hood exits an elevator across from me. The hood bears an odd resemblance to the ones worn by the members of Black Web. Long red hair flows from beneath it as she quickly walks down the hall. Eliza flashes in my mind with a strike so fierce I skip a breath.

"Please confirm," the voice says again.

I ignore it and step out of the elevator to follow the girl. When I glance down the hall, she's already gone. Vanished without a trace, except for a lingering scent of eucalyptus. It travels through my nose and brings back memories.

"Ms. Young, the elevator," Amity says, breaking the trance.

I track back into the elevator and find the camera's lens to confirm. The doors quickly shut, and all I can do is think about Eliza.

Chilled air hits my damp skin as I step out of the shower. The water pressure pads on the walls slowly drip onto the blue tiled floor, draining through the pipes below. Beads of water glide down my legs, making their way to my feet on the ground. The natural feel of water always puts me in a better mood, and without my warm or iced tea, it's needed. I also don't have a plan for when I do make it to the estate. Figuring out what I will do now will keep me from having to think on my feet later.

Expect nothing, prepare for anything.

I step forward in the space and the dryers embedded in the walls sense the presence of my wet skin. A whirring sound escapes from the walls and air flushes out of small holes that reveal themselves on the wall. The breeze pushes past me, swaying my wet hair away from my shoulders as the dampness evaporates after a few minutes. I grab a robe and toss it over my now cleansed skin.

Eliza creeps back into my mind. Did she see me? Why was she here? The questions sting for answers I can't reach. I could have been seeing things, but it doesn't explain the scent of eucalyptus. The girl could have been anyone, yet I'm having a hard time believing it.

My reflection in the large mirror startles me enough to stop the raging thoughts about Eliza. The sight of my glowing iris, erasing the Amber I've always known, makes me uncomfortable. The blue ring stares back at me, reminding me of the nature of this world. The ignorance which led to the creation of something so destructive.

"Deactivate node," I say. "I can't stand the sight of it."

The glow reduces to a small speck before going away, leaving me with a small pinch in my eye.

A pain I'll never get used to.

I walk into the main room, leaving the steam behind. It's a simple room; two chairs sit against the wall nearest the main door, and a small table holds floating holograms that can be activated to order food or contact the front desk. My bed lies in the center, pointing to a larger hologram display on the wall, which I can only assume is for entertainment. More holograms are scattered along the walls around the bedside, failing to arouse my curiosity.

Sitting on the bed, I cross my legs beneath me and spread my gear across it, activating Iris to display Ezra's estate. It glows and extends outward with a view of the entire building.

"What's your plan, Ms. Young?" Amity asks.

"I've decided to go after information that will help expose who Ezra is."

"Killing him has left your mind?"

"I suppose, but not completely. My parents would have pointed me in this direction. I believe I can do it another way. They knew who the Enlightenment were and didn't kill them. That makes me wonder why. First, I will take what information I can find and proceed from there."

"How will you get inside?"

"Honestly, I'm not quite sure."

The estate is a heavily guarded facility with cybernetic defenses I'm not familiar with. Every defense is intricate; there's a defensive system for the defense. I spin the hologram around with the touch of my finger and look for any backdoor or small entry points where I can insert malware to extract information.

"Any ideas?" I ask.

"How about a distributed denial of service to overload the system?"

"Dosing won't work. Too simple for this kind of system."

"Decryption?"

"We don't have a coded key. Or any key for that matter."

"There's always shells."

"That's actually good; it just takes too long, and we're not prepared to install that."

"Very well analyzed, Ms. Young. No other options to offer."

My hands find my head, and I squeeze my temples to ease the tension this puzzle has caused. I haven't been challenged this hard since my early days of hacking, when I always needed help from my parents. Script kiddy is what my mom called me. I smile at the memory and the tension in my head subsides.

I think back to solutions I'd come up with to solve the most difficult cyber puzzles my parents would create and that causes me to remember a valuable lesson.

In my world, everything can be hacked.

I stretch the hologram wide, zooming in for a closer look at the estate and where encryptions are placed. A connection line radiates from the top of the building like a heartbeat and channels flow through the building like veins, linking all computers. Before the links attach to each other, encryptions appear, making it impossible to crack without being detected. And there's no way I'd be able to walk in and repeat what I did at the Establishment.

"A break may help, Ms. Young."

"No time."

"You're not a robot or some kind of drone, Ms. Young. Take some time to rest."

"Say that again," I say quickly.

A spark of an idea flashes in my mind.

"Take some time to—"

"Before that."

"You're not a robot or some kind of drone, Ms.—"

"That's it!" I shout. "I could kiss you right now."

"Very high improbability, Ms. Young. Actually impossible."

"Oh whatever. We have the solution."

"What did you find?"

I analyze the hologram to clarify my thoughts and ideas to be sure I'm not overlooking any other hidden encryptions.

"Are you ready?" I say with a smile.

The excitement of cracking this puzzle is flaring. Burning inside my blood, sending rapid chills through my body.

"Always, Ms. Young."

"First, the distraction. We'll use the drone to infiltrate the building. The drone will have a worm malware attached that we'll use to implant in any one of their computers. That will trigger an alert, but it will be something they think is minor and their focus will be on fixing it. Second, the worm will travel through the channel that is attached to every computer they have, infecting them all. With the mass virus in effect, we'll initiate a Botnet that will be used to target the central connection line at the top of the building."

I take a breath before the thoughts continue pouring out of me.

"Finally, with every computer under the spell of the botnet, all information will be decrypted without the need for a key. It'll be up for grabs, ours for the taking. The information will be fed to the drone and with a backdoor encrypted through Iris, it'll make for a quicker extraction. All without us being anywhere near the estate."

"Exceptional," Amity says.

"Aren't I?"

"Your parents would be proud."

"Thanks, Amity."

Heat rises to my face from the thoughts about what could have been. The things my parents and I could have accomplished together. Where we'd be at this very moment. Instead, I'm here. Plotting my revenge.

"Would you like to run any tests, Ms. Young?"

"Absolutely. Now would be a great time to use my simulation, but we'll figure it out regardless. For now, let's celebrate this small success."

I jump out of the bed, slipping out of the cozy hug of the robe and into my new bodysuit, left by my parents.

I step into it, and it automatically registers my body. From my feet, it slides up my legs, past my hips, and up over my breasts. It covers the remainder of my body, stopping at my neck. The metallic silver appears like mercury. Slippery yet murky. The final touches are black outlining through the gaps of my extremities. Iris glows with the notification of the suit. I strap my trace pistol to the back of my calf and my staff to my belt line. The daggers hang on the sides. With an upgraded attachment for my drone, it magnetically attaches to my thigh.

"All of your gear, Ms. Young?"

"Expect nothing," I say.

"Prepare for anything."

"That's right."

I strap my boots across my ankles as the last piece of preparation to explore Millennia. I stand tall with the added inch the boots provide, closing the height difference between most EAs and me.

"We'll look for food first, then we'll scope out the estate to see exactly what we're up against and how much prep is needed."

"When do you want to execute the plan, Ms. Young?"

"As soon as possible. I don't want to be here any longer than I have to."

My suit surges with energy from the shoulders down to my thighs, vibrating with small pulses, confirming activation. It sends a tender warmth throughout my body, amplifying the emptiness in my stomach and sparking the uncomfortable feeling of nausea.

"Time to eat."

"On route."

I tuck my hair back, spinning it in a circular motion until it's all together in a bun. I grab the remaining pieces of my arsenal and head back through the hallway, down the elevator, and out of the building before the representative

can even think about uttering anything about the Enlightenment and my day.

It must be midday as the golden ball of light shines
through the business of flars soaring through the air. The
streets are busier than Arcadia's at this time of day. People
are smiling, laughing, and talking while walking down the
street. It makes me wonder if they legitimately like the life
they live or if they're oblivious to the world. If my theory
about clones proves correct, it could explain the apathy
toward the Enlightenment.

Pushing past my thoughts, I embrace the cool air as
it settles in my skin, confirming the briskness of fall. The
hunger pains return when a couple brushes by me with
the buttery smell of bread in their hands. My nose flares at
the welcome scent. It pushes me forward at a faster pace,
making me wish I had spec. I settle for the old ways and
walk toward the path Iris is guiding me down in search of a
cure to my lingering hunger.

36

The estate.

Like the Establishment, it's exactly how I imagined it. Large building, dozens of glass windows and metallic finishes along the sides. There is a small difference in the glass of this building. At the Establishment, I could see through and observe what was happening. This glass seems to consist of a double layer, preventing outside observation.

From my spot on the roof directly across it, the building's details are clearer than my hologram image. Shorter than most buildings in Millennia, with three stories at most, it shows its size in length. It stretches wide for a few streets, with flars floating along the side in a precise line. Latest models are among them, and each has an EA stationed in full gear.

"Looks like something important is going on," I say.

"There's no way to confirm, Ms. Young. Scanning can't get past the outside of the building."

Of course.

"It's fine. The most important thing is how we get the drone inside."

I shiver at the sudden drop in temperature. The sun has found its descent, lighting the sky with a hue of orange and blue, casting its final rays before the moon takes the stage. Sirens roar through the air with the announcement of curfew. In thirty minutes, those who are found outside in public will be arrested. The announcement ends with the Enlightenment's motto.

"Drone," I say quickly.

The announcement expedites every movement as I begin the search for my entry point into the estate. My drone darts out of its holster zips into the sky above me, extending its four wings, levitating in place. What's left of the sun reflects off the silver black, creating an orange glare.

Using Iris, I guide the drone higher into the dying light in the sky. The lights of the estate and nearby buildings flicker until they are all illuminated, doing their best to imitate the sun. My drone soars through the air, picking up speed and disappearing in the distance. The camera engages and reveals everything in front of it and below.

"Device coating," I say.

The rooftop comes into view on Iris, and I lower the drone. The encryptions I studied start to highlight, showing what's preventing Amity's scan from the outside. Coating along the drone will help it remain unseen by the estate's defenses. I slowly control the drone and look for a way to get in. The camera detects a small vent, the perfect size for the drone.

Almost too perfect.

I hover it over the vent, looking down the dark tunnel. Lasers extend from the sides, weaving together and allowing no way to go between. Scanning shows me the framework used to activate the beams. It's a basic function any hacker with minimal knowledge could override, but this is Millennia and an Enlightenment member I'm dealing with. It's too easy. I descend above the lasers, but I'm inside the vent, enough to register a scan.

"Ms. Young, if you deactivate the defensive beams, it will trigger nevertheless. It is attached to the mainframe of the facility."

As I thought.

The buzzing of the city lights mimics my nerves and boiling blood, but I do my best to keep them at bay, knowing there's always another way. I escape the vent and restart my search.

"There is a door on the side of the building, Ms. Young. It is coded with a lock, however, and readings show it hasn't been used in weeks."

"An emergency exit?"

"Precisely."

I follow the path to the side door in an alleyway. The lock on the outside can be penetrated, but it will require me to be quick.

"Cracking the code for the door will indeed give you limited time inside with the drone. Unfortunately, there is no time frame, Ms. Young."

Shit. Another obstacle.

I was hoping to be able to get inside and input my plan without any rush.

"So once we're inside with the drone, will the vents be accessible?" I ask.

"Hard to tell from the outside, Ms. Young."

I vigorously tap Iris, glaring at the many ways I'm blocked. Even if I get inside through the door, I need the vents to hide the drone. My face tenses as I squint, trying to think my way through. My plan rolls over in my mind. The malware attached to the drone has to be the key—if I can somehow get it inside.

"I have an idea," I say.

"Share."

"What if we crack the code on the door with the malware I intentionally planned to use as a distraction for a computer?"

"Go on..."

"What if this can be served as the decoy, and we change the coding of the malware to target the defensive structure, allowing access to the vents?"

"Ms. Young, that is ingenious."

The tension in my body evaporates, igniting a smile.

"Entrance established," I say. "We got it."

With a tap on Iris, I recall the drone.

"Just in time, Ms. Young, because—"

"*Attention all citizens. Attention all citizens. This is not a drill. Curfew is now in effect. All citizens must be in their homes. Again, curfew is now in effect. All citizens must be in their homes.*"

The sirens return with a thundering cry, startling me from my seated position on the rooftop.

Fuck. I lost track of time, dealing with too many detours.

My movement attracts the gaze of an EA standing guard near the flars.

I crouch down, knowing it won't help. I'm too late. The EA yells to get my attention, screaming everything relating to curfew and the Enlightenment. A moment passes as they wait for my response. When I don't say anything or move, red beams flow by the edge of the building, meaning one thing.

"You need to move, Ms. Young," Amity says.

"Ever the obvious statement maker," I respond swiftly.

"Your programming."

I roll my eyes. "Fair enough."

"Come out with your hands up, or we will open fire," the EA shouts from the ground.

The red beams disappear, and I take a quick peek over the edge. In unison, four EAs abandon their posts and close in on the building I'm on top of.

"Amitttyy," I cry. "Now would be a great time for those options."

"Ever the obvious statement maker."

"Clever."

"Learned from the best."

"Optionssss," I repeat through gritted teeth.

The door of the building's bottom floor crashes open with a deafening sound, echoing through the staircase and out to the roof. It jars my hearing as I wait impatiently for a solution to this problem.

"Option A: Fight back."

"Can't. We risk exposure and the possibility for back-up EAs to arrive."

"Option B: Turn yourself in," Amity fires back.

"Funny."

"Option C: Not your favorite, but volt rails."

"I don't have the equipment with me. I didn't think I'd need it."

The thought of not being prepared jabs at my heart. I'm always prepared, or so I thought. A fog drapes my mind. What would my father do? All of the teachings he and my mother have given me, and I still manage to mess up in the smallest of ways.

"Even if I did," I add, "it would require me to fight but with higher stakes and very low maneuverability. Every option is bad."

Footsteps stir in the stairway like my emotions within. Accepting the fact I may have to fight for my life, I rise with my staff and trace pistol in hand.

"Ms. Young," Amity says, "there's another option."

"What is it?" I ask with a little more hope.

"Your new suit has modifications within it. There is one in particular that may work in this situation. The sequence is being uploaded to Iris now."

Iris glows through the night sky with a modification for illusion tech. A sequence for changing the fibers within the suit to camouflage with my surroundings.

"You're right. This might work," I say.

"Ever the obvi–"

"Not the time."

Looking over the modifications again, for any length of time the suit will be engaged, I come up empty. There's very little information about anything within the suit and how exactly it works, if it works at all.

"How do we know this will work?" I ask.

"We don't, Ms. Young, but the odds are in your favor with it being night. However, as you examined, there's no test analysis of how long it lasts for. Furthermore, there is no information on how effective this modification is."

The voices of the EAs and sound of their gear swaying about travel through the stairway as they rush to the top of the building.

"I guess we'll have to find out for ourselves," I say.

The suit flickers on my body, vibrating with a charge against my skin. Light from the surrounding buildings refract off the silver, dulling it until it becomes gray and eventually black. Murky black flows from the suit like a thick fog around the entirety of my body. Turning my sight down toward the suit, it practically makes me invisible against the night. The EAs are at the top of the steps as I lower into a crouch, finding a small crevasse in the roof-top's edge where I can blend in with the shadows.

An explosive sound escapes the stairway as the door flies open in pieces. Shattered into nothing, broken at the hinges. Directly in front of me, four EAs swarm the roof in what I assume is a well-rehearsed routine. After a moment, they all announce the area is 'clear', taking position in a front line, guns holstered on their chest.

Footsteps slowly echo to the top of the stairway, and through the entrance, another EA steps through the broken doorway.

His footsteps thud against the ground, and I almost feel the weight of them, like small tremors. He stands at least six feet tall, but I know that's an underestimate. His arms lock behind his back, pushing his large chest out further. Unlike the other EAs, he doesn't wear a mask. Instead, his face is visible, and I can make out the rough details. Sharp jawline with a scruffy beard. Hard lines trace his forehead and the scars along the sides of his face. One tracks from his brow, down the length of his cheek, curved and stopping at the start of his chin.

He takes a few steps forward as the other EAs clear a path for him.

"Chief Enlightenment Agent," Amity says. "Don't move, Ms. Young."

I do my best to slow my breathing before it can reveal my position. CEAs are another shadowy rumor back in

Arcadia. They are the government's top ranking officials outside the Enlightenment members themselves. CEAs have clearance to go about justice any way they see fit. My captor was a CEA when I lost my parents. Inhumane torturers are what they are. Glorified murders who only want to cause pain to those who can't defend themselves. They all deserve what's coming to them.

He stalks forward, scanning the area with a menacing grin. His head swivels on his shoulders like a pendulum going back and forth until it stops, pointing directly at me. My body tenses at the sight of his dark eyes, shrouded by the night sky with only a fraction of his expression visible. He quickly turns on his heel with perfect precision for a man his size, to face the EAs. My nerves begin to settle at the sight of his back, an assurance he's no longer looking at me.

The want to know how long my suit will be effective stings my mind. It could end at any moment, revealing me to the five of them. The uneasiness of waiting for the unknown makes my nerves return and flutter through my body, making me flinch.

"Who's the agent that claimed to have seen someone?" the CEA's voice booms through the quiet.

His voice is deep, unwavering, and threatening. He sounds as if he were speaking through an echoing device, enhancing his voice. It draws the attention of the EAs. They exchange looks before one finally takes a step forward.

"What did you see?" the CEA asks.

"I saw something, sir."

"You saw something," he repeats it back. "Hmmm."

The superior takes a step back and gestures around the roof.

"Show me what you saw."

The EA hesitates before stepping forward. He makes a direct path to the ledge I'm under and I hold my breath. With a quick, sharp move, the superior grabs the EA by the throat with one hand, lifting him high. His legs tiptoe to hold on to the ground but fail. The free hand of the superior knocks the EA's helmet off, sending it back toward the stairway. Fear fills the young EA's eyes as he struggles in the grip of the superior, trying his best to fight free. The other EAs stand and watch, without moving a muscle.

The CEA squeezes the EA's neck harder, causing him to struggle in his arms. He shakes, gasping for air and finding none. The CEA spits in his face and releases him with a shove. The EA stumbles into one of the others, frantically searching for his helmet. The CEA replaces his hands behind his back and walks toward the shattered door, splitting the EAs.

An unspoken threat.

The others follow. Their boots fade away and the slam of the door on the bottom floor confirms their departure.

I slowly step out from the crevasse, avoiding any sound. My suit starts to flicker and the vibrations from when I activated the illusion modification vanish, making the suit return to normal.

"Analysis," I say.

"Suit disengaged. 0% remaining, Ms. Young."

Right on time.

"Option A would have been dreadful," Amity says.

"I'd say."

The strength of the CEA is concerning. How easy it was for him to overpower his subordinate and possibly kill him. Something I did not anticipate. Another thing I didn't prepare for.

"We will have to undergo more preparation," I say.

"It certainly seems so, but this won't happen to you, Ms. Young."

"Oh. I know," I say, changing my focus to the moon above.

Its white glow shines eerily in the darkness. It grabs at my inner thoughts and emotions. The fact that I was under prepared and could have been in grave danger if, again, it weren't for my parents.

Dark clouds gather around the moon, hiding it, mimicking the shadows trying to hide my shame. I hold the thoughts and use them as motivation and drive for my new preparations.

"They'll get what's coming," I say, "For now, let's get the hell out of here."

37

It's been two days since I've arrived in Millennia, and I don't want to be here a second longer. The rooftop incident cost me more time than I expected. Although the agents didn't find me or anything suspicious, they've been more cautious. Since then, EAs scour the perimeter to be safe. They advance after circling the building and search the interior and rooftop where I was. I guess the CEA has brains to match his brawn, unfortunately forcing me to lay low.

This has become a true test of my patience, which I never really knew myself to have. My mother used to tell me patience was something every hacker needed to achieve their desired outcome. I remember her training with my staff and teaching me patience also bled into other aspects of survival, like fighting.

"Ms. Young," Amity says, dragging me out of my head, "your suit is fully functional again."

As much as I don't like being here, or waiting to go through with my plans, the past couple of days have helped me prepare. The CEA gave me many reasons to, but I only hope I don't have to deal with him or anyone like him again. My suit lies on the bed as I marvel over illusion tech, once again thanking my parents. Somehow, they still manage to protect me without being here.

"What would I do without them?" I ask.

"You've made it this far, Ms. Young. You're too hard on yourself."

"I know. I have to be."

"Perfection won't bring you the vengeance you seek. Persistence will."

"You speak as if you've lived through it."

"Indeed. Perhaps programming is a way that I have. Programming from your parents in combination with yours."

I smile at the thought. Something I never actually realized. Amity is a collaboration between my parents and me, something I've always dreamed about, meanwhile, I've been living with one for practically my entire life. The want and need to be with my parents reminds me of the importance in this upcoming operation.

"We've waited long enough," I say. "Tonight we strike."

"On your command, Ms. Young."

A change is coming.

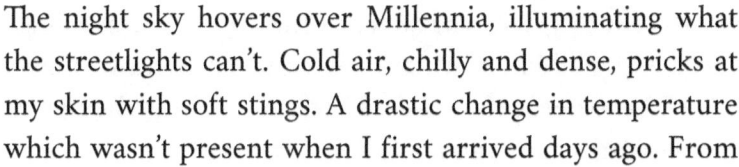

The night sky hovers over Millennia, illuminating what the streetlights can't. Cold air, chilly and dense, pricks at my skin with soft stings. A drastic change in temperature which wasn't present when I first arrived days ago. From my new vantage spot, a building adjacent to the one I was on during prep, I note fewer flars are in the area—and fewer EAs. A deserted land with the only sound coming from the electric currents flowing throughout the city, supplying it with power. My mind grows suspicious of the desolate land, and it makes me wonder why they're lacking security when, mere days ago, it was the opposite.

"Amity, scan," I say.

"Scanning."

Iris glows with confirmation of what my eyes see. No hostile threats nearby.

"This is strange."

"Indeed, Ms. Young. Tread lightly."

I shake my doubts and begin the plan for extraction. Tonight, I will succeed. Starting with Ezra Coleman, I will enact my revenge.

"Let's begin," I say.

"Malware engaged and attached to the drone," Amity says.

I unleash the drone, and it soars above the estate, targeting the door in the alleyway. The drone hovers in front of a keypad and I initiate a copy code, opening the system to attach the updated malware targeting the central defense. I wait a few moments for the system to detect it, and a green light appears on the keypad, opening the door.

I sneak my drone in and guide it to the air ducts, quickly avoiding the EAs patrolling the bottom level. The camera's lens gains static from the quick motion, forcing me to reduce speed. The silver of the air ducts comes into focus with puddles of water from condensation overflow.

"The defense is lowered, scanning now shows inter-networks above and below, Ms. Young."

"Which is easier to access?"

"Above. However, it appears that, on the upper level, there are multiple hostiles gathered together."

That's why it's so quiet. My curiosity gets the best of me, and I follow a path above, not toward the inter-network. Instead, I target the gathering highlighted in red on Iris.

"Ms. Young, it isn't wise to go off course."

I ignore the statement and proceed until the drone is directly above the targets.

"Initiate eye sequence," I say.

The drone's lens shifts, giving me sight through the ducts, directly into the room. Six EAs surround a table like they're waiting for a debrief. They stand in all black with red outlining their equipment. It reminds me of the cloaks worn by the Enlightenment when I first encountered them during the Central Square massacre. The sound of a door opening makes the EAs stand in a ready position, and they all turn toward it. From the drone's position, I angle the lens to follow the direction they are facing, and my jaw drops at what I see.

Ezra Coleman.

My eyes grow wide and my fists clench, forcing my muscles to tighten. The pain he caused. The anger. My parents. Wren. Everything floods my veins with intense energy, making me shake.

"Ms. Young."

"I can end his life right now," I snap before Amity can continue.

"What about the plan to steal information and expose him?"

"That was before I had this opportunity."

"If you kill him, how will you find the other members?"

"The same way I found him."

Like fire, my blood burns inside me, and the need to scream rises in my chest. My senses overwhelm me, and tears begin to fall. The need to avenge my parents and kill this asshole pierces my mind like daggers. But something is holding me back from pulling the trigger. Amity may be right. The struggle between right and wrong, life and death, vengeance and absolution. I know he doesn't deserve any kind of mercy, but I can't help the rising feelings.

"Ms. Young, you're not a killer."

"I've killed plenty of EAs."

"Those were different circumstances."

Like a grenade, the fire in me explodes.

"I don't care about the circumstances, Amity," I sob, and I can't contain what I've held back for so long. "I don't fucking care. They killed them right in front of me. I was sixteen. I couldn't help them, and I watched it all happen. The failure that haunts me every waking day of my life buries its teeth in me, and I can't shake the fact that their deaths are my fault. So don't tell me about the circumstances."

My legs buckle beneath me, and I fall to my knees. The tears and pain all rush out of me. The dam I've built cracks, releasing the agonizing pain of every day I've lived without them. It thrashes inside me like lightning. The guilt and shame of letting them die. It pulls me deeper into my subconscious, forcing me to feel every ounce of dread.

"I have to, Amity," I whisper. "I have to…"

"Ms. Young…"

The sobbing continues and I'm drowning beneath an ocean of pain. Suffocating under the pressures of my life. I thought I could do this. Avenge them and move on, but I never imagined I'd feel this way toward the enemy. I've trained and trained for this moment and now that it's here, I'm frozen. Stuck in a mental block of pain.

"As you said, there are other ways, Ms. Young. Don't give in and become them. You are better than that."

"I don't know what to do," I admit.

"Finish the mission and go from there. You'll find vengeance another way."

Iris flashes on my wrist and takes my attention away. Another person walks in, and the EAs show the same respect they did to Ezra. The newcomer has a hood over their head and wears all black. They appear tall and slender with broad shoulders and a long cloak, but there's no red outline, unlike everyone else in the room. They walk up to the table and join in on the conversation. It's not long before they turn to leave and the mask on their face screams familiarity.

It belongs to Black Web.

Why the hell would a Black Web member be here? Could Claire have sent someone else? Or... The mask wearer activates a nav, displaying the file I helped decrypt in Black Web. They show Ezra, igniting a smile on his face. They copy the file to a system located in front of the group. I... I'm not sure what to think as Ezra proceeds to shake their hand. They turn on their heels, the door slices open, and they stop abruptly, looking directly at the ventilation shaft my drone is in.

"Ms. Young, if you're going to accomplish this mission, you need to move."

The unknown person flashes their hand toward the vent, and with quick redirection of my drone, I escape a disaster. The ventilation shaft explodes directly where the drone was, and sirens blare throughout the building. An explosion from a hand gesture? What the hell? I've never seen something like it, and how did they know my drone was there? Nothing makes sense.

"Ms. Young, the mission."

Right, I'll have to save my questions for later.

"Can I still take the data?" I ask, getting back to my feet.

"Yes, but there's little time."

The pains of indecisiveness evaporate, and I'm back in control of my emotions. Forcing them down, I allow a new wave of focus to take over my mind. I guide the drone through the maze of vents to a lower level of systems registered to Iris earlier. I input the next worm, and the systems register the virus. Through scanning, it flows throughout their systems, infecting them like I planned.

"Initiate botnet protocol."

"Activated."

The botnet triggers and opens up every system inside the estate, making them vulnerable to an attack.

"Begin extraction."

"Starting. Ms. Young, there's not much time."

Iris displays the percentage of extracted data, and again, Amity is right. If I wait until it's at one hundred percent, there won't be enough time to recall the drone. With the threat of the EAs within the building and now knowing someone from Black Web is here, it poses a new challenge. I expected something to go awry, however, not to this magnitude. A member of Black Web revealing information I helped crack is a betrayal. I grit my teeth. Iris buzzes again, showing less time.

"Continue the extraction," I say. "I have to get closer to the building to get the drone back."

"Be careful, Ms. Young."

I sprint to the edge of the building and jump, navigating the descent with a wired grapple until I reach the street below in a rolling crouch. Red lights flicker throughout the building as sirens warning of approaching EAs blair in the distance. My feet continue to move until I'm concealed in a dark passageway between the estate and its neighboring facility.

I'm stunned as the side door opens on the estate and an EA walks out, gun in hand, ready to fire. I push off the estate wall and knock the gun out of their hands. The EA surges at me and grabs me by the neck. My knee collides with their groin, pushing them back. I wince at the release of my airway and cough, allowing air to fill my lungs. The EA regains momentum and comes at me with a serrated blade.

I sway from each strike, right to left, back and forth, leaving the EA to slice air. They retreat to find a new angle. It gives me a chance to find my own advantage. The blade tries to strike low, but it's too slow and I dodge to the side.

With a quick shuffle, my knee clashes with their helmet, snapping their head back. The EA releases a loud grunt of anger and proceeds to pursue me. I unsheathe my staff and slam it vertically into the ground, utilizing it as a pole for advantage.

The EA runs at me, and I spin around my staff, snapping their head sideways. They tumble into the wall as their helmet rolls to the ground. Landing on my feet, with burning blood and electric veins, built up from the guilt of failing my parents, I remove the staff. It vibrates with potential energy matching the intensity inside me and I swing, colliding at the spot my boot found the EA's head.

A loud crack escapes through the alleyway, and the EA fall dead to the ground.

"Extraction complete," Amity says.

About time.

Through jagged breaths, I use the camera lens on Iris to guide the drone back up through the vents where the explosion happened. Fire and smoke block the passageway, and I'm forced to find a different route. The echoing alarms are a representation of my pulsing heart. Boots hitting the ground startle me, and I know they're coming to investigate the EA I killed. The sirens from the approaching back up grow louder, and it's clear I'm out of time.

None of this was part of my plan. Regulating the negative thoughts threatening to petrify me, I remember there's always another way.

I control the drone and exit the ventilation shafts, then speed past EAs who shoot at it. I soar and dodge the bullets as best as I can, and the masked person appears again. Who could they be? And why would they help the enemy? A shot of fire escapes their hand and flies past the drone, igniting an explosion above. Too close. I force the speed of the drone and crash through the windows.

The glass shatters above me, raining down with shimmering light. I tilt my head down and drop to a crouch, protecting my body from the raining threat. The glass splinters my back and cuts my arm, cracking to the ground in chunks. Larger shards split upon hitting the concrete. The sharpened rain stops, and my eyes find my drone above. Blood seeps through the gash on my arm as I rise back up.

Before I can initiate the recall for my drone, a stream of fire directly hits it, exploding in bright orange and yellow, raining down in pieces. Tears fill my eyes as each one hits the ground.

"Ms....Young..."

A crackle floods my ear where I'm used to hearing Amity.

"Systems...failing..."

The notification on Iris makes my heart wrench. Connection to Amity is dwindling.

I can't bring myself to believe it.

Amity is dying.

"No! Stay with me," I whisper. "I need you with me. I can fix you when we get back."

"Backup...installing..." Amity says. "It won't...last long, Ms. Young."

"How long?"

"Twelve...hours..."

"Okay, I need a place to hide until morning, when the trains are back up. Then I can fix you."

"Routing...Ms. Young."

A building displays on Iris with a direct route.

I exit the alleyway and follow it. I glance back as fire and smoke fill the air from the estate. The backup has arrived, and they shuffle out and into the estate. A handful of EAs usher Ezra into a vehicle and speed off to an unknown location.

The masked person exits and looks around. Their mask turns toward me, forcing me to jump into a crevasse of a nearby building. After a moment, I peek out and see they're gone.

I sprint again, continuing my pace toward the building Amity found. My heart breaks from the loss of my drone and the weak state Amity is in. If I don't get home, I'll lose the connection to the only thing keeping me alive.

"Stay with me. You hear me? I'll fix you."

Tears stream down my face as I find my way to safety.

38

I haven't slept since yesterday morning, before my plot for extraction was executed. The wound on my arm is shallow, but blood seeps through it nevertheless. If the glass from the estate had pierced me in any way, I most likely wouldn't be alive. I take a cloth hanging on the edge of the windowsill. As I wrap it around my arm, I get a clearer idea of where I am. I must have run for miles without realizing it, each step fueled by my adrenaline to stay alive. The city of Millennia sits in front of me.

Tightening the wrap, I notice the first peak of the sun shines through. The dark space brightens as the sky begins to split from midnight blue to a more friendly light hue. I wince at the pain in my arm, echoing from the sore muscles I used to fight the EA. The snap of his neck plays in my mind, and I don't feel a thing. The emotions that threatened to wreck me on the roof seem to have returned to their rightful place, in the back of my mind.

The events which took place during my extraction couldn't have been any more jarring. Seeing Ezra in the flesh… My mind almost broke apart at the sight of him. The biggest revelation is that a member of Black Web is involved, someone who can manipulate fire somehow. Technology never ceases to amaze me, but this kind is lethal and dangerous, something I've never seen.

As for how it works and who this person is, these questions rattle my brain, and I'm not sure I'm ready for the answers. As the thoughts creep into my head about the mystery person, Eliza appears behind my eyelids. I feel certain she'd been at the hotel, seemingly in a hurry. Then, suddenly, a member of Black Web appears in the office with Ezra Coleman…

The enemy.

I'm not sure if they were there on a mission from Claire or working with him. What I saw indicated they were likely working with Ezra, and Claire mentioned no one was supposed to engage. It's not good they gave up the intel I helped crack, but it also doesn't make any sense, considering it was stolen from him. Unless it was something he wanted to know and didn't have access too. Which would mean he used this mystery Black Web member to help him. But, who?

I switch my focus to the disaster. Whoever the pyro wielder was, they destroyed my drone and, in the process, weakened my connection to Amity's. I don't know how it was done and I'm not confident I will be able to reverse its effects. What I do know is, I need to try.

I cannot lose Amity.

"Amity," I say, "how are the trains looking?"

There's an unusually long pause before it responds.

"They will be up and running in under an hour…" Static growls through my ear. "Ms. Young…you should…make a move for them... There is a possibility that only one train will make it out of Millennia...before a shutdown happens, after last night's events..."

"On it."

Iris displays the time remaining for Amity's backup: Eight hours.

Amity's weak voice makes me push myself to move a little quicker. Blocking the pain my tired legs and arms feel, I proceed toward the station and hope I won't be too late.

I made it.

A few people board the train and take their seats. I pull up my hood to hide from possible pursuers. The train locks, gaining momentum as it leaves the station. I stretch my sore legs, rubbing them with my arms until the pain starts to subside.

'Six hours' flashes on my wrist, and it makes my heart jump.

"You need...to rest, Ms. Young."

"I know. I can't trust falling asleep."

"Apologies, Ms. Young. Scanning is...disabled due to the malfunction..."

It's worse than I thought.

My primary source of assistance can no longer help me. The pain starts to settle deeper inside of me, making me stir. I don't know how to move on without Amity. The fact I've gotten this far surprises me. The extraction couldn't have gone any worse.

I try to think positively as the train takes off. Thinking about the best outcome that could come from this mission.

"Arcadia…will hopefully be…the same as it was when you left…"

"I certainly hope so." I slouch into the seat. "I need to regroup, figure out what we secured, and work out our next steps to take down Ezra. Especially since I now know it'll be hard to kill him."

"Indeed, Ms. Young… But you can't do anything without rest."

The train sways as it speeds out of Millennia. The sun is higher now and its warmth travels through the car. My eyes hold stone as I force them open to watch my surroundings. The fear and paranoia of being followed haunts me to the core and I can't relax. My inability to scan affects me in a way I've never imagined having to prepare for.

Cool air makes my eyelids close without my control. My parents flash in my mind. When they smile, my eyes shut, and I fall into my subconscious.

Metal clamps hold me down, locking my arms and legs into place so I can't move. The metal is cold and sharp against my skin, making it impossible to struggle without pain. My pulse thuds against my wrists from the pressure and I start to shake. I try to look around, but the device around my head holds it in place, forcing my eyes to stare at the white light above. The headpiece peels my eyelids back, keeping them open as a silver syringe is placed in front of my right eye. Forgetting the pain the clamps produce, I struggle to move, triggering them to activate burning lasers scorching my skin. I scream in agony as tears begin to fall.

The syringe draws closer to my eye and there's no way to avoid it. Through my struggling, a voice echoes.

"Activate protocol A," says a man with a raspy voice.

"Acknowledged," says a woman.

A whirring sound echoes through the room and the syringe begins to rotate. It closes the remaining distance to my eye and pierces it, plunging deep inside. There's no pain, but the metal pushes against something inside my head. The syringe locks into place as I lay helpless and silent, abandoning my unheard screams. It rotates in my eye once again, tearing the flesh inside as blood pools out of the socket, streaming down my face.

Still, no pain.

"Vitals?" a different voice asks.

"Heart rate 120, blood pressure 140/90 and rising. Breathing stabilized," replies the woman who acknowledged the protocol activation.

I try to focus on the newly added voice as familiarity sinks its teeth in me. It starts to fade from wind rushing past me and the sounds of people moving. The footsteps get closer to where I lie, and in an instant, Amity pulls me out of my nightmare.

"Ms. Young...your heartrate is above normal... Are you okay?"

"I am now," I say. "Thank you."

I slowly blink, my eyes adjusting to the bright silver of the train. The sun's rays burn, triggering a mental image of the syringe in my nightmare, and I jerk my head away from the window.

"How long have I been asleep?"

"Thirty minutes, Ms. Young."

Thirty minutes. The grogginess in my body makes it seem like I was asleep for hours. However, I'm grateful it wasn't longer, as my time to save Amity dwindles. It leaves me with a little over five hours to reach Arcadia, get to my home, and fix it before it's lost for good.

My eye tingles, recalling the metal piercing my cornea, implanting the node in my eye. Trying to force the nightmare down, there's a change in the car. No one on board is moving except for me. My brows raise from the sight, and I walk slowly to a couple cuddled together in a seat. Their eyes are open, but there is no sign of life. I check for a pulse—nothing. My gaze turns and see the bodies of all the people who boarded the train after me, laying lifeless. My heart rate increases as I continue to the next passenger.

An older man. His head hangs low, and when I crouch down to meet his eyes, blood flows from his mouth and his right eye is an orb of red. I jump back, holding my breath.

Nodes have been activated on this train.

"What's going on?" I ask.

Before Amity can answer, two men stand tall in shadow black suits. Masks conceal their faces as they stand. Another person exits a seat next to them, taking a position in between. Much shorter than the two men, their face is concealed by a hood and mask.

A Black Web mask. Who could they be?

Thoughts of the masked pyro wielder flood my head and I freeze. My voice and movements are stunned once again by indecisiveness. The mysterious character gives a small wave of their hand, forcing me to step back. The two men start to make a move, but they are stopped by the masked figure, with a smooth lift of their other hand. The mask stares at me, flickering with different facial expressions I can't read. Neon highlights, changing the form of the eyes and mouth, making it impossible to understand. I stare back, waiting for them to make their move.

I think about how they could have found me. There's only one reason they're here.

Ezra Coleman.

They must have followed me from the estate somehow, and I was dumb enough to think I was in the clear. Dammit. The person steps forward, breaking my thoughts as they move toward me. My only option is to fight. The train is moving too fast to attempt jumping off, and there's no way to tell how far the station is.

Their heels draw nearer as I'm stunned by my lack of options.

"Amity, dro…"

Before the command leaves my lips, my heart races, and I sweat. My drone is gone. It leaves me with my staff and daggers. I remove my staff from its holster, the energy humming inside.

If I'm going to die, I won't make it easy.

As I wave my hand over Iris to trigger an EMP, the two men reveal guns from their suits, but the person in front of them moves faster. Two black orbs appear, fitting perfectly between their fingers as they spin, throwing both with perfect precision. Before the men can pull their triggers, their skulls ricochet off the car floor to the opposite end.

The car goes silent.

The unknown person peers down at the dead men. I stare with wide eyes as they turn to face me. The mask falls into their hands, and the hood drops back. She unveils thick red hair. It falls to her shoulders as glossy blue eyes meet mine, making the blood in my veins freeze.

I knew it had to be her.

"Hey stranger," Eliza says with a smile.

As it did days ago, her voice paralyzes my legs, and I can't move, prompting an urge to rise from the depths of my core. The combination of ocean blue eyes and a lustful smile sparks my old desires from back at Black Web. It all comes back, and I want to take the dive as she takes another step forward, crossing her arms. Her sweet tone echoes through the car when she asks:

"Did you miss me?"

39

"What are you doing here?" I ask.

Seeing her makes my heart do things I never thought it could do. Yesterday, it was caused by a state of panic. Now, it flutters and beats in a rhythm that makes the inside of me tingle with warmth. My mind, however, forces me to always think the opposite.

"I'm here to help," she says, stepping forward.

I don't know why, but something inside me makes my legs step back, away from her. I defy the want my heart craves to be near her and think about the moment I saw the masked person with Ezra Coleman.

"Why are you here?" I ask, intending to get a different answer.

She opens her mouth to speak, but doesn't, leaving her lips parted. Her eyes momentarily squint as she stops her pace toward me.

"I can't explain it here."

"That's not an answer," I counter quickly.

"Trust me," she says. "I would love to sit and talk, but right now, we need to get out of here."

"Why? What's going on?"

The fact I can't see any threats or what's happening because of Amity's malfunction plagues me. I have to rely on my own senses and whatever Eliza has to tell me. The idea of uncertainty makes my heart thud against my chest with a heavy beat. Dizziness takes over and I'm ready to fall.

"Brace yourself!" she shouts.

Another orb appears in her hand. Once again, I skip a breath at the thought of her using them against me. She rolls the orb around. It changes from deep black to a fiery red. It glows in a brilliant hue, and she tosses it past me, toward the end of the train car. It shines brighter. As it travels, the oranges and reds collide with yellow until it starts to spark. It explodes with searing heat and the pressure pushes us back a few feet. The air floods the inside, with gusts funneling black smoke into the car, forcing my lungs to fight for clean air.

Ahead, through the plumes of fire and burnt metal, EAs run toward us from another car. They stop short of the detachment of cars and start to move further backward as the train continues to speed along its track. They fire their weapons, but the train is too fast. We immediately escape their range.

I turn to face her, and she smiles.

"Are you ready to go?" she asks.

"What exactly is happening?"

"We need to get to Black Web ASAP," she says. "We don't have time to go over the details."

She walks toward the hole she created.

"I can't go back to Black Web. I need to go home. My A.I. is undergoing a serious malfunction that I can't fix without my equipment," I explain.

Stepping back from me, her eyes lock on the train roof. The two orbs return to her hand, and she snaps them toward the ceiling. Piercing it like liquid. A long grunt echoes over the sounds of the moving train and a body falls to the side, catching my attention.

"I'll take you to your home, but we have to move now."

"Ms…Young… Time…" Amity notifies me. On Iris, the timer has four hours remaining.

"The only option…may be to join…her."

I agree.

"What's the plan?" I ask hesitantly.

"I thought you'd never ask."

She fiddles with a circular device she removes from the side of her short, fitted bodysuit and I can't fathom how she's surviving the wind chill. Her eyes find the window, and she points.

"There's our ride."

I don't see anything until the flar reveals itself, a smaller version of the vehicle they transported me from the Panoramic Diner to Black Web. It hovers at the same speed as the train, moving closer to the fiery opening.

"I'll go first," she says.

She finds the right moment and jumps from the car to the vehicle. My heart races as I step forward. The fierce air pelts my body. I flinch at each strike and prepare myself to jump. I find the same moment Eliza used. With all the muscles in my leg, I jump across and make it.

I strap in next to her, forcing myself to remain calm and breathe. The doors close and seal. Eliza straps in and

313

prepares the route. Holograms of all types of controls and devices appear in front of us. They glow and pulse, waiting for activation.

"Where are we going?" she asks.

"Arcadia."

Eliza glides her hands across a few of the holograms with ease, as if she's done this more than enough times. She moves with fluid motion as her chair rotates with her, guiding her to the holograms she needs to get us going.

"I'll explain everything when we get there," she says. "I promise."

Her words give me some hope and I hold on to it. Trust. A feeling that's alien to me. No one has ever been to my home, yet I'm traveling there now. With her. With Amity slowly slipping away, I don't have a choice in the matter.

I smile at her and nod in confirmation.

"Alright. We're off."

We boost away from the damaged train and head for Arcadia.

40

"Amity?" Eliza asks.

I think about my A.I. and how little time I have to get home and fix it. I've never been in a predicament like this, where Amity could be disconnected from me. It's a scary thought and a feeling I wish would go away.

The clouds roll by as we speed through the sky. There's a sense of nothingness as we soar above trees and barren lands. All affected by the Enlightenment. As the enemy comes to mind, my anger grows with a vengeance.

"Helllooo," Eliza says, trying to get my attention.

"Sorry. I'm in deep thought."

"About?"

"A lot."

"You want to talk about it?"

"Not really. I need to focus on rebooting Amity."

"Amity…your A.I.?"

I nod and return my gaze to the empty skies. Since getting into the flar, Amity hasn't spoken. It can't. The backup is running low, making each second vital.

"It must mean a lot to you," Eliza says.

"It means everything." My voice cracks.

I don't know what happened to Amity and I'm not entirely sure who is responsible. If Eliza did it, why would she be helping me now? Her eyes glue to mine and fall. The creases between her brows tighten as she presses her lips. I can't bring myself to believe it could be her.

"Amity..." I say, a breath escaping. "Amity is how I managed to escape the Enlightenment. It's the only reason I'm still here and able to keep going."

"How?"

The question makes my mind travel to when I escaped, and the day I found freedom. A feeling of emptiness hollows my chest as though my heart has been stolen, leaving my lungs breathless. The first time Amity came to me, replays in my head.

I was on the verge of death. My mind felt fractured from the abuse that I'd endured, I sat in my cell and heard crackling. Like static being activated. At first, I'd been afraid, thinking it was the electric currents that periodically flooded my chamber.

Then it spoke.

"Registering," it'd said. "Young DNA verified."

I'd jumped and frantically scanned the cell for someone that might have found their way in. Nothing appeared except for my own shadow, created by the night light that streamed in beneath the metal door. I watched footsteps pass and briefly started to relax.

When I'd turned to find my corner, it came back.

"Ms. Young," it'd said.

I realized the voice came from inside my head. Like a flowing thought that was trying to speak to me. Directly transmitting from within.

"Hello?" I'd whispered. "Who's there?"

"A friend."

Fear and curiosity intertwined, but I found myself leaning toward finding out more.

"What do you mean?"

"I am an advanced intelligence system created by Adalina and Dexter Young," it explained.

"What?"

I was confused, bewildered by the fact that a voice I couldn't see was talking to me. It didn't have a body or anything that separated itself. It was like I was talking to my inner self.

"I am here because a failsafe was triggered. Your heartbeat reached a low rate and activated the system. My creators made me to ensure that you wouldn't succumb to what you are currently experiencing."

They knew. They knew I would be captured and taken. I began to remember the raid on our home and my mother's last gesture. I felt it around my ear, and there it was, a device my mother attached to it before she died.

"Are you ready to leave?" it said.

"Yes," I responded. "But how? This place is a fortress. And what do I call you?"

The magnetic lock on the cell door unlatched and squeaked open, letting in the white light from the prison. I stepped toward the exit as the voice in my ear said, "Amity. At your service, Ms. Young."

I miss Amity's voice, the constant awareness and statements it would make to get me to feel better. Loneliness, something I thought I'd never experience again, finds its way inside of me. I don't know if I can handle moving on if Amity fades away completely. And what's worse, it was my fault. If I hadn't detoured from the original plan and went after Ezra...maybe Amity would be talking to me at this moment.

Tears sting my eyes, and I choke back sobs.

"Hey," Eliza says, tapping my shoulder, "you don't have to tell me. It's written on your face."

I dry my tears and try to regain my composure.

"I wanted to let you know, we're almost there."

Arcadia appears in the distance as we approach the outskirts of the sector. Amity tries to speak, but only static can be heard. My home quickly comes into view as Iris awakens my nerves with what Amity tried to tell me.

"You can dock anywhere," I say before reading.

Thirty minutes.

The remaining time Amity has before it disconnects forever.

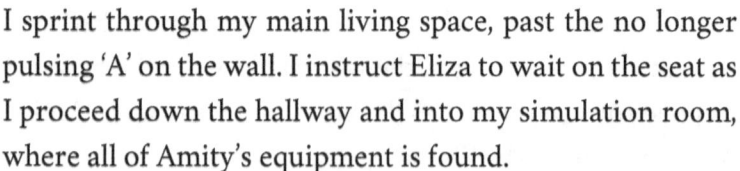

I sprint through my main living space, past the no longer pulsing 'A' on the wall. I instruct Eliza to wait on the seat as I proceed down the hallway and into my simulation room, where all of Amity's equipment is found.

I scramble through holograms and glyphs. Searching for a way I can fix it. My mother or father never told me what Amity is or how it works. They died before they could.

"Ms..." Amity struggles. "New...data...base..."

It reminds me of the hidden compartment the chip revealed. I quickly activate the hologram leading to the lower level. Inside one of the silver cases, I remember seeing new versions of Amity's interface. I gather the material and remove the device from my inner ear.

The holodesk scans it and reveals the damage Amity sustained. Seeing the exact problem makes this possible. A virus was somehow embedded into the system when the flame struck my drone. I couldn't save my drone, but a virus, I can beat.

Amity saved my life years ago, now it's my turn to save it.

First, I shut down my system and implement an anti-viral code. The holodesk reveals, in red, where most of the damage is in the system. It gives me a map of where to start. With the codes falling in front of me on a hologram, I change the sequences of Amity's original code. Then, with the anti-virus moving through the veins of my system, I copy the new version and attach it to the new sequence.

The hologram displaying Amity's interface changes to green.

It's working.

Finally, I add an encrypted code, feeding Amity's interface with more protection, countering any form of virus. The invasive red code that damaged the mainframe slowly degrades. With a final sweep, the anti-virus wipes the system clean.

The system reboots as I hold my breath.

"Young DNA verified," Amity says clearly. "Welcome back, Ms. Young."

My lungs release the pressure of air I've held for too long, and I burst into tears. Like the sun after a torrential downpour, my heart shines warmth through my body.

I put the device in my ear, shaking to the point where it falls, and I have to replace it.

"Amity?" I say.

"Ms. Young."

"You're really back?"

"Indeed. You did it."

My sobbing intensifies from reuniting with my closest friend.

"Don't do that to me ever again."

"I will certainly try not to."

"I can't lose you."

The extraction mission creeps into my mind with my failure. If I hadn't detoured from the original mission. If I would have stayed on track, none of this would have happened. My drone would be at my shoulder and Amity wouldn't have been affected.

"I'm sorry," I whisper.

"You followed your intuition, Ms. Young. There is nothing to be sorry about. You may have lost the drone, but you got something in return. Maybe something more valuable."

Amity reminds me of the information I extracted and the person who could manipulate fire working for Black Web. I'm still not sure who it is. But, now that I have Amity back, I can focus on the tasks at hand. It puts my thoughts back on track to the mission at stake.

I'm closer than I've ever been.

"You're right," I say.

"Ever the obvious statement maker."

I smile and chuckle, relishing in the moment. Eliza's footsteps startle me as I forgot she's waiting.

UPDATE

41

"You're too quiet," Eliza says, crossing her legs on the seat next to me.

I still haven't adjusted to the fact that someone is inside my home. It's odd and unfamiliar. I've never had anyone else here.

"You're not the first to say that, " I say. "Certainly not the last."

"I didn't mean it as an insult."

I shrug and lean deeper into the seat.

"It would be nice to hear you say more than a few sentences."

"When you decide to tell me what the hell that was back in Millennia, you'll get more than a few sentences."

Uncertainty eats away at my consciousness, and I fidget, searching for comfort in the seat. I've never liked the unknown; it's like I'm not in control of myself and I can never gain it back. My chest swells, like a volcano, waiting to erupt. I don't know if it was her in the room with Ezra or someone else. She appeared on the train with agents, giving me a reason to believe she was the one I saw, but I don't want to believe it.

Too much has happened in so little time. My mission for extraction was supposed to be: get in and get out. But somehow, it's been the exact opposite. With losing my drone, Amity's affliction, and the train incident, it's all a constant struggle in my mind, forming questions I can't answer.

"Fine," she says. "I was there on my operation to scout the estate."

"What were you scouting?"

"I didn't receive the operation until Ezra decided to broadcast his location to the entire area. When Claire received word, she sent me to track him down and provide intel on whether he was actually there."

"And?"

"And I was too late. Someone got there before me."

"You mean me?"

"Yes and no. There was someone else."

She must be referring to the fire user. Which means it wasn't her. The swelling in my chest escapes through a deep exhale and I'm suddenly more at ease.

"Do you know who it was?" I ask.

"No. I could only ever see the back of them."

"I did," I admit.

Her eyes explode, moving away from the orbs in her hand I never saw appear.

"Was it another member of the Enlightenment?"

"No," I say, "it was a member of Black Web."

"What?" she says, almost getting out of her seat. "Claire sent someone else?"

"I don't think so. I think they were working with Ezra. They gave him a copy of the information I helped you and the others decode."

"What are you saying?" she asks.

"Someone among the web is playing for the other side, which means they are working with the people I loathe the most in this world."

Her face burns red, and she folds her hands together, griping them tight, creating a mirror of my inner emotions. Betrayal fills her icy stare.

"But who?" she asks through gritted teeth.

"That's the problem. They were wearing mask, the ones you wore when you first met me. So I didn't see a face."

Her eyes return to the orbs in her hand as they methodically rotate between each finger.

"There's something else," I say. Her gaze finds mine again. Piercing through me like a knife. "The person I saw could shoot fire out of their hands."

It's weirder admitting what I saw than it was actually seeing it. I don't think I've ever seen anything like it, or at least enough to believe it.

"Fire?" she asks.

I nod as her eyes shift. She adjusts herself in the seat and leans back, tossing the orbs into the air, catching them, only to throw them again.

"Does it spark any ideas?"

"Not at all," she says. "It could be anyone. Black Web holds all kinds of tech and people who can use it. So, who knows?"

Unfortunately, she's right. Finding this person should be easy in theory, but given the advancements and talent hidden in Black Web, it could take a while.

My mind travels to Eliza's explanation for being at the estate. I know why she was there, but she hasn't explained what I really want to know.

"Something still doesn't add up," I say.

"What do you mean?"

"Claire sent you to the estate after finding Ezra's location, but how did you end up with those agents? Why were you with them?"

"I was hoping you'd find out later, but oh well, no time like the present."

"Find out what?"

My chest grows tight, waiting for the worse. She closes her eyes on a long inhale as the orbs appear in her hand again. They rotate, slow and steady, methodical and deliberate, to the point of meditation.

"I'm a plant."

My heart stops, dropping to the emptiness in my stomach. It triggers my nerves, and my palms become sweaty. Before I can fully grasp the new information, she continues.

"Not an Enlightenment plant," she says, reading my face. "I'm a Black Web plant."

As though I'm coming up from a body of water, my lungs expand, taking in as much air as they can in case I forget to breathe again.

"My entire operation, stretching back to when I was first recruited, revolves around me keeping close contact with Ezra. The risk being, my parents work with the Enlightenment as white hats, and they want me to follow in their pursuit of maintaining the AOE."

She inhales deeply, pulling air into her lungs. The way the tension in her face melts makes me envious. I wish I had the ability to calm my nerves in an instant, freeing myself of the energy plaguing my mind. A sigh escapes her mouth, the sounds of pain and annoyance with it.

"Whatever you don't want to tell me, you don't have to," I say, realizing if I were in her position, I wouldn't say a word.

"I know," she says, "but it's only fair. You trusted me, so I suppose I'm returning the favor."

She shrugs, inhaling again, softer and smoother.

"I was a white hat for Ezra. I didn't know who he was at the time, and I didn't work with him specifically. I worked at many of his corporations, protecting his information."

My eyes grow wide, stopping her from continuing. I think about the information I managed to extract from the estate, and whether she might know anything about it.

"During an operation, Claire found me. I was maybe twelve or fourteen, abandoned by the Enlightenment and my parents."

"I'm confused. Aren't they after you?"

"Yes, but it's because of what I know. I don't have any proof of anything, only the etches of my memory. They still deem it necessary for me to either be at their side, pursuing the idea of one world government, or..."

Another pause. Her eyes close again and judging by her grimace, I can guess what she wants to say.

"Death."

The word she can't say, but it stains her face with enough disdain. She's said enough and her ritual for remaining calm evaporates. Her head drops in her hands, revealing what she's been hiding so desperately.

"I'm sorry," is all I can say.

I know the pain she's feeling all too well.

"It's okay," she says, trying to hold on to whatever composure she has left. "To answer your original question, I was with those agents on the train to make sure you were safe. I still have some connection and clearance where I can manipulate agents to tell me information. The information, however, is only regarding what they are assigned to. For example, those specific agents from the train were assigned to find and kill the person who infiltrated the estate. I joined them, knowing it would lead me to you."

"How were they able to track me?"

"They found debris of some sort of technology outside of the building and tracked it."

My drone. A dull ache hums beneath my skin, and I don't think it will ever go away.

"Thank you," I say. "I probably wouldn't have made it off the train without you."

She smiles and grips my palm.

"Any time."

Iris buzzes with a notification of the extracted files.

"Ms. Young, it appears the files extracted need to be cross checked before you can begin to review them."

"Okay, let me know as soon as it's ready."

"Will do. There is a lot of intel so it will take some time."

"In the meantime, we need to get back to Black Web," Eliza says. "Especially knowing there's a mole inside. Everyone could be in danger."

Claire. Raelyn. The only living family I have left. I think about them and what it could mean if the Enlightenment has someone among them, and they have no idea. It's a threat to their mission and lives. Even though I've known them for a brief time, the fact I have family alive begs for me to protect them. Something I couldn't do for my parents.

"We have to find out who it is before anything can happen," I say.

"It won't be easy, but it can be done. We'll have to watch intentionally without anyone knowing."

The orbs vanish in her hand as she rises and walks to one of the windows. Through it, the late afternoon sun burns with deep orange. Out toward the ocean, the sun's reflection pools over the waves. They glisten as they breach and break the surface, calming my nerves.

"Amity?" I say.

"Ms. Young?"

"When we get back to Black Web, I'm going to need help finding out who this person is. Body scanning, voice recognition, any and everything to help unmask them."

"Will do, Ms. Young," Amity says.

Eliza continues to marvel over the view of the ocean, her red hair shining, with golden brown hues peeking through.

"Liz," I say.

She turns on her shoulder and softly smiles. "I can get used to that name."

"I'll be sure to use it more often then. But listen, I'll meet you in the flar. I have to gather some gear and change."

My new suit needs some repair from the glass cutting its threads, but my parents left me with many more to replace it.

"Okay, Nexia." She winks. "See you soon."

A warmth flows inside me from the softness in her voice, but it quickly fades. My chest grows tight at the thought of being in the same building as someone who is working with the Enlightenment. But I must do what I couldn't do before.

Protect my family.

42

"Echo requesting authorization to dock," Eliza says smoothly.

The pyramid housing Black Web appears, disengaging the cloaking device as we head toward the side edges. The black sand glistens in the sun as it separates from the jet stream of the flar.

"Authorization granted," a voice says. "Welcome back."

Eliza pilots us into a narrow passage that opens like a portal, leading to the open hangar. The shift from sunlight to white light makes my eyes blur as they adjust to the contrast. Identical flars line the sides in perfect order. Weapons outlined in holographic form paint the walls behind them as people replace or take them. When I was here on Zero Day, I didn't notice this amount of equipment. There's also more members, as if they've been recruiting.

The thought of finding our mystery fire creator scratches its way into my mind, and I'm convinced it may take longer than I originally expected. Our flar slows to a stop, the switch in speed distracting me enough to calm my self-doubt. Like a magnet, we hover without guidance to an empty slot. The flar locks into place and lowers itself to the ground.

"And we're back," Eliza says, disengaging the systems.

It powers down and the main door releases air pressure, allowing the fresh air from outside in, making each breath sharp. Eliza exits first and receives immediate attention from people on the platform. She's used to it. It shows in the way she reacts to their hand waves, with nonchalance.

"Famous," I say.

"Believe it or not," she says, picking up her speed, "I actually hate it."

She grabs my hand, and we enter the main facility through the large glass doors shaped like triangles. We arrive at the base level and find it's empty like before. Quiet and deserted enough to hear electricity buzz. As we approach the center elevator, I find myself still in awe of the structural design of Black Web. My eyes trail toward the apex of the pyramid, the place where I met the web.

"The director will be expecting me," she says, breaking through my memories of that day. "She probably doesn't know you're with me, but you can join, or you can wait at the apex."

I think over the options as a slow smile stretches across her face.

"Orrr…" she says slowly.

"Or?"

"You can wait in your room."

Heat rushes to my cheeks and I'm forced to look away, remembering the last time we were together in her room. As much as I want to, I know I shouldn't. I know I should focus on how to find this person, and I need to focus my attention on the material I managed to extract, even though I have to wait until Amity cleanses it. I'm hoping this material will show the AOE what the Enlightenment really is. I want to know more about what they've been hiding. First, it was why the node was created. Then cloning. What else could they be concealing?

"I'll be at the apex," I say.

"Okay." She lets out an exaggerated sigh.

I laugh as the elevator arrives.

"See you soon," she says through her own laughter.

She winks before vanishing beneath the surface. The ground disperses into a hollow frame, reminding me of the complex structure it hides.

I make my way to one of the corners and take an elevator up.

"How are you feeling, Ms. Young?" Amity asks, just as a breath of fresh air enters my lungs, subsequently escaping in a loud exhale.

"I haven't had time to decide," I admit.

"A lot has happened in the last few days."

"That I didn't have time to process, let alone feel."

I land on the long middle seat as my gaze finds the compartment across the room holding drinks. The space is clean, the complete opposite of when I was first here. Day breaks through the glass triangular encasing, letting in pure warmth, an appreciated departure from the outside cold.

Winter may arrive a lot earlier this year. Water hisses as a shower head moves along the edges of the platform, feeding the plant life, something I hadn't noticed before. My head rolls to the opposite side, toward Techdon. As always, it's a beacon of light, illuminated with color. Zero Day replays in my head. Our celebration of it. The happiness and excitement from everyone on the rooftop.

I should be celebrating now, or at the least, happy my extraction was a small success, but I can't. Without Eliza, I'd most likely be dead or worse, in a cell, tortured for the rest of my life. The effects of losing my drone haunt me as the waves of my inner turmoil rock my subconscious. Pushing and pulling the nightmares to the surface. They stop short when the chime of an elevator echoes.

Raelyn strolls silently across the emptiness, distracted by a hologram displaying what appears to be a warzone. She wears black tights with a forest green top, cut above her navel, revealing a milky complexion. Her cloak drapes her shoulders, covering her arms and falling to her knees. Black boots rise to her shins as they click along the ground.

Her hands move and my head tilts, trying to discern if it's her hands that wield the power to produce an explosion like the one at the estate. The hologram fades like my thoughts and returns to her wrist as her gaze lands on me.

"Oh," she says. "I didn't think anyone would be here."

"Sorry," I say.

"No, no. Don't be. I was beginning to wonder if we'd ever get a proper conversation."

She takes a seat next to me and crosses her legs with smooth, graceful movements. Her hands flip the two blonde braids over her shoulders as she gets comfortable.

"What do you mean?" I say, straightening my back and meeting her at eye level.

"Oh, I don't know. Maybe the fact we're related and have yet to properly meet."

"Oh, yeah," I say.

"That's it?" She nudges my arm. "You find out you have a family member you've never met and that's it? That's all I get?"

"I honestly don't know what to say."

"Hmmm."

"What?"

"Is it me?" she says, crossing her arms and slanting her brows.

"No," I say. "I'm just really bad at meeting new people."

"Me too."

We share a laugh, and it feels warm. Like something I was missing, but has now found its way back to me.

"You're intriguing," she says with a smile. "I can see why Eliza has taken a liking to you."

"I didn't think it was that obvious."

My face starts to warm, and I hate that it shows.

"No need to be shy. I'm happy to see Eliza be more herself."

"More herself?"

The question of who Eliza used to be creeps into my head. How much has changed about her?

"A lot has happened since she found out about her parents." She stops herself abruptly, taking a long pause to gather her thoughts. "I'll let her tell her story."

"She told me most of it I think."

"Oh yeah, she has definitely changed for the better. She never really opened up to people when I first met her and now she's the life of the party."

"So, what's your story?" I ask.

She chuckles as the sun casts shade through the area, causing the brightness of her hair to dull.

"Where do I start?"

"How'd you get involved with Black Web?"

"I assume you mean other than being related to the director?" Her feet tuck beneath her as she adjusts positions and faces directly toward me. The laughter evaporates and her face becomes hard. "Well, for starters, I didn't have a father, so the director raised me to essentially be like her. By following that, I ended up learning about the Enlightenment and I hated how they affected my mom. She was never really happy because she always feared them taking me away or killing me. There was a constant state of panic around me leaving Techdon or Black Web, for that matter, and I wanted it to end. Not just for my sake, but hers."

My mind catches that this is the first time she's referred to Claire as her mom. A change in her posture shows some insecurity, but like Claire, she shakes it off, returning to fierce boldness.

"I learned how to hack systems from a different perspective than most. As I got older, to better assist my mom, I learned how to perfect encryptions. There were times she tried to hide information from them, but it was hard, so I went about hacking my own way. When we need it, I'm able to use dead zones or off the grid systems to perform what I need to. With that ability, I'm able to help with operations that require encrypted detail." She inhales softly and smiles. "So I found myself getting involved to protect my mom."

Family first.

A pattern presents itself: Both Raelyn and Claire have the same mindset about family as I do. Protect and help thrive. I appreciate and value that fact; it helps me believe I can learn to trust and work alongside them.

Raelyn's skills in encryption remind me of my mother's. She was a true master of the art, always protecting data and finding creative ways to use it for combat as well as defense. In many ways, the reflection of Claire in Raelyn, reminds me of my mother. Poise and confidence drive everything they do. It's a sight to see and I'm appreciative I have the chance to do so.

"I have a lot of respect for what you did in Encryption toward Thaddeus, one of the most profound encryptors I know."

"Thanks," I say, "but he had it coming."

"I agree. His arrogance can get the best of him. However, I think I could have done better." She winks.

We laugh again, and I relish the feeling of being with a like-minded person, and most of all, of being with family. The sensations it brings me makes thoughts of peace feel possible, something I've longed for, but could never grasp. Maybe, one day, I can.

Maybe.

The sun shifts the shade again as it descends. Lights trigger along the sides of the pyramid, breaking the darkness. Raelyn kicks her feet up on the table and buries herself in the seat.

"Where's your other half?" I ask.

"Still on his operation most likely. I was watching a situation that occurred in Millennia days ago, and I thought it could be him. Then I remembered he was assigned to Arcadia."

Millennia. I gather she's talking about the events at the estate.

"Speaking of operations," she continues. "I knew you were gone, but where did the director assign you?"

"Millennia."

"What was your mission?"

"Originally, to find Ezra. But that quickly transformed into me finding his exact location and going after him."

"Uhhh, okay, that's a lot." She snickers.

"There's something I need to ask you, but it has to stay between us."

"Oooo, secrets. I like secrets."

"Seriously," I say.

"You have my word."

"Is there someone here who can somehow manipulate fire?"

She jerks back with wide eyes.

"What?"

"I know it sounds crazy, but I need to know if there's someone here who can do that."

"Not that I know of. Why?"

"That footage you were watching in Millennia? Well, I was part of that," I admit.

Her eyes grow wider, flashing green in the reflection of the dying sun.

"When I was there, I witnessed someone literally shoot fire from their hands, causing explosions and fire to erupt the estate."

"The estate?"

"It's where Ezra Coleman spends most of his time, where he practically lives."

"Holy shit."

She leans forward in her seat, her long legs retracting. Her hands tuck beneath her chin as she thinks about the information I've revealed. I probably shouldn't have shared so much with her and ask her to keep it a secret. I know it's a lot to ask, especially because she's close to a lot of people here.

"I don't think anyone here has that kind of technology," she says. "From what I know, at least. What makes you think they're from here?"

"They had a Black Web mask."

"Well, at least they're on our side."

"No." I shake my head.

Like Eliza, her face tenses, showing she has the rest figured out.

"We have a plant," she says under her breath.

I nod.

"I have to tell the director," she says quickly, standing to go.

"Okay." I stand too. "But, don't let anyone else see or hear you. The plant could be anyone in this facility."

"I'll kill that asshole when I find out who it is."

"Not before I do. I'm going to my room to figure out a few things. If you hear anything or suspect anything, let me or Eliza know."

"Understood," she says, walking beside me to an elevator. "Not quite the conversation I expected, but I'm glad we got to talk."

"Me too."

We enter, and I feel relieved to have her help. It'll make things easier and hopefully a lot quicker. Either way, I know we'll find them and when we do, there will be hell to pay.

43

Being back in this room makes me miss the space of my own home again, and the simple fact of knowing I'm safe. I sit on the bed, the material morphing around me as I think about how long this person could have been working for the Enlightenment. A place like this, housing some of the most skilled people I've seen, has no idea they have an enemy among them. It begs the question: Is this where I want to be?

"Ms. Young," Amity says, "the extracted material is ready to be viewed."

I unlatch Iris from my wrist. The burn marks trigger my memories, but I stop them short and place Iris in the center of the bed. The start of my investigation. Time to figure out the best way to attack the Enlightenment. My heart won't allow me to kill someone who isn't trying to kill me. I need a way to end their lives without physically doing so. A definite challenge, but one I must overcome. I owe it to myself, the nation, and most of all, my parents.

Iris illuminates with the familiar blue glow, shining the contents above it in an array of holograms. The files

I gathered appear. A banking file is the first to catch my attention because it's the heaviest in terms of data. I flip through it with a swipe of my finger and uncover hundreds of transfers through wired banks.

It's a start.

If the Area found out he was extorting and stealing money for his own gain, I'm sure it would open eyes.

"How far back do the money transfers date?" I ask.

"About 2080, Ms. Young."

I shake my head in disbelief. They essentially started with the birth of the AOE. It explains how their movements were funded. I continue to dig, jabbing through the hologram to find out more. Multiple headlines of Ezra being held as the 'head of financial' arise amid hidden information within the banking file.

That's what he controls. Money.

Video recordings are among them, and I quickly watch a few. There's meetings with people, the declaration of the nation being separated from the rest of the world. The agreement to disconnect the land from the bordering worlds of Canada and Mexico. Funding which took place to make it happen. Technology used to literally split the country from the other lands, forcing the nation to be essentially on its own. Separation of every past treaty and agreement to put the world at bay and make sure what was happening stayed here. As I work my way through the videos, they begin to appear.

The Enlightenment.

No hoods or any kind of disguises. It's them. Together, displayed in picture format, shaking hands on agreements on what the new nation will be. Four of them. Two men and Two women. Ezra, a lot younger, but still the same face, stands next to an older man with a bald head and wrinkles painting his forehead. Lines stretch from the corners of his deep eyes. He hunches over with all his weight supported by a cane. A tall woman stands behind him, the recognizable hat tilts upward showing half her face. Older as well, but the makeup she wears hides it well. Bold red shines on her stretched smile. Black hair falls to her sharp chin. Her eyes glare holes into the last member next to her—a much younger woman who's significantly shorter. This woman has pointed brows with hard cut edges. She looks oddly familiar, but I don't know why. Long lashes protrude, almost concealing her hard eyes. A soft smirk lifts one cheek, making me shiver.

"It's them," I say.

"Indeed."

I don't know how to feel when I see them. I take a mental picture, never wanting to forget the faces of the people who changed this nation and my life for the worse.

More information populates the hologram with the Enlightenment coming to terms with how money will be funneled through the nation and how it will be maintained.

Claire was right.

This goes deeper than I could have ever imagined. So far, more questions have come up than answers. What did my parents know? Why was the node so important to implement? Who created the idea? And what about cloning? The questions run rampant in my mind, overworking it, fighting with the information I gathered from the files. I close the video and picture files and try to find a different angle, one which will hopefully answer at least one of my questions.

Glowing red, a few encrypted files catch my attention. If they are still encrypted, then they are the kind of files that trigger emergency protection when the data is stolen. Similar to the data Raelyn and Mason retrieved.

They must contain answers.

"Amity, can we decrypt these?" I ask, dragging a finger across the hologram files.

"Scanning files for weak points."

My craving for tea spikes. I'd do anything to taste the bittersweet flavor, which calms my nerves when I'm operating. Another aspect of home I miss.

"Negative, Ms. Young," Amity says. "Scanning shows an intricate encryption that is protected by defensive malware. If you try decrypting it, your own systems run the risk of being counter-hacked by an unknown source."

"Can we replicate the intrusion we used before, when we helped the others?"

"Negative. This system will corrupt your system entirely if you do so, Ms. Young."

Shit.

That's certainly not a risk I'm willing to take after almost losing Amity once.

A knock on my door takes my attention away. I stare at it, hoping it was a mistake, or I imagined it. Another thud hits the metal, louder this time.

"No hostile threats detected, Ms. Young," Amity says, calming my hesitation.

A third knock lands, and I jump out of my head and into a staring match with the door.

"Ms. Young, there is a camera embedded in the wall above the door. You can always use that to ensure it's not a threat."

"Show me the feed."

"Uploading."

Iris receives the feed, replacing the extracted files. The footage glitches, gaining its connection through Iris before becoming clear. Red hair drapes on milky white skin. Even though her head is down, I know who it is.

"Thanks, Amity," I say. "Disengage all files."

Iris closes and locks as I place it back on my wrist, once again concealing my scars.

The door slides open at my presence and Eliza leans on the edge, crossing her arms.

"Hi," I say.

Her eyes narrow as she walks past me without saying a word.

"Come in, I guess."

The door hisses closed, triggering the lock. Eliza sits in the corner chair, legs crossed as she twirls the metal orbs in her hand.

"Any updates on our mystery plant?" she asks.

"No, but I've filled Raelyn in, and she's agreed to help."

"I like it. She's trustworthy and reliable."

"I can tell. We had a good conversation, and I couldn't agree more. But…I'm having some trouble."

"With?" she asks, joining me on the bed.

I activate Iris and reveal the prizes of my extraction. Her eyes grow wide as I skim through to find the encrypted files.

"This is everything I stole from the estate," I say, "but there's a lot of encrypted files and I can't get around it."

"Woah, this is amazing."

"Can you decrypt this?" I ask desperately.

She looks it over and her eyes fall.

"Can you?"

"No," she says, shaking her head.

"Why? I thought you were a white hat for Ezra?"

"I was, but this is beyond my ability. I couldn't create this kind of encryption in my dreams."

I reel back, defeated.

"This is intricate," she says, continuing to rotate the hologram, her eyes still wide from seeing Iris and everything I managed to take.

"If neither of us can crack this encryption, then who can? This could be the answer to all my questions."

"Hmmm," Eliza says, jumping off the bed, "Maybe Claire can help or knows someone who can help, let's go ask her."

I nod in agreement and we head to Claire's office.

44

Claire's office is full of Black Web members. They stand at attention in front of the main desk, where Claire is seated, facing away. The clove-scented air is crisp like a fall morning as I breathe it in.

Scanning the room, everyone is in their cloaks, hoods drawn high, which means one thing.

"Amity," I whisper, "display a snapshot from the ventilation shaft."

The masked person appears on Iris, and I clear the image, adding depth by reducing the shadows and contrast. Now the mask is sharper, more visible to hopefully help me recognize who it could be. I angle Iris to Eliza, who stands next to me, getting her attention. She takes a quick look, her face twisting as she shrugs.

"Why is everyone here?" I ask her privately.

"I think they're all checking in after their assignments."

Claire's chair spins around to face the room, and as if I'm a light at the end of a dark tunnel, her eyes land on me. They ignite a smile on her face, prompting the web members to turn and follow her gaze.

"Scan for a match," I say immediately.

"Scanning, Ms. Young."

My eyes find my wrist, then move back to the web, then Eliza.

Their masks fall.

"Scanning failed, Ms. Young. However, systems are using recorded imaging to find a match. It may take some time."

"Got it."

In quick succession, I account for each member. Ayster, his face stuck in a look of frustration when he sees me, as always. With a radiant smile like the sun, Astraea looks me up and down. Zane surprises me with a wink as he returns to his original position.

"I knew you'd come back, little badass."

Before I know it, Astraea is next to me, wrapping her arms around me. She's only about an inch taller than me, maybe two, but her strength shows as she twirls me around effortlessly. We spin twice, and I'm dizzy, ready to empty my stomach all over her.

"Okay, okay," Claire says, saving us from disaster.

Astraea releases her hold, and I stumble. Wobbling from the whirlwind as I try to regain my footing. The world becomes level, and I wait for Amity's results.

"What did we find?" Claire asks.

"Arcadia is in a state of restlessness. Citizens are talking, but ultimately dying," Zane says.

"It's not good," Mason adds.

He stands besides Raelyn, who smiles at me. A hint she may have already told him about our mystery threat.

"The diner is clean of anything Black Web related," Ayster says, "but..."

"But?" Claire repeats.

"Trace's blood was swabbed and collected," Zane says.

Oh no. What could the Enlightenment want with his blood? I cringe at the one answer forcing its way in my mind: cloning.

"I thought you cleaned it when you collected the body," Claire says to Ayster, her voice higher than usual.

Ayster drops his head without answering.

"We'll figure that mess out later," she continues. "Raelyn, Astraea, any new information in Techdon."

"None, Director," Raelyn says.

"Follow my lead," Eliza whispers.

She steps forward, an unspoken announcement.

"Millennia was subject to an attack," Eliza says.

"What?" Claire says.

Her confusion makes me think Raelyn hasn't told her. Why? She told me she would. My heart starts to rattle as negative thoughts plague my mind at the possibility Raelyn could be the plant. Which could also implicate Mason...

"During my operation, I witnessed an explosion at a building Ezra Coleman was supposed to be in."

Everyone mumbles, incoherent voices moving through one another.

"She's right," I say, stepping next to her. "I witnessed it all."

"Is he alive?" Claire asks.

"Yes," I say. "But what I found and extracted may help us."

Eliza's bait failed. She turns to face me, and her eyes say it. Her announcing the attack on Ezra was meant to get someone in the room to act differently or show any sign of already knowing. But they all stare dumbfounded. However, I did learn one thing: Raelyn didn't tell Claire.

"You extracted data from an Enlightenment member's domain?" Ayster says.

"No freaking way," Mason follows.

"Show me," Claire says.

"May I show only you?" I say, unable to trust anyone else.

"No fair," Astraea whines.

"Very well," Claire says. "Thank you for the debrief everyone."

She rises from her seat like a queen, slow and precise, every movement dramatic. Elegant gray drapes her shoulders in a well-fitted cape. It clasps at the center of her chest with a dazzling piece of silver. The same smokey color surrounds the length of her legs in well-fitted, pleated pants.

"I will reach out to you when your next assignments are ready."

The web nods in unison.

"Dismissed."

Ayster exits first, with a grimace on his face. Zane bumps my shoulder as he rushes past me.

"See ya later, badass," Astraea strolls out with a soft wink.

Mason and Raelyn are the last to leave, and they both look down, actively avoiding eye contact. It makes me shudder as I may have made a mistake in trusting Raelyn.

Claire approaches me with outstretched arms, and I almost flinch, remembering Astraea's embrace moments ago.

"It's so good seeing you," she says in a sweet tone.

"You too."

"We need your help," Eliza says, not wasting any time, which I appreciate.

Claire steps back and watches us intently.

"With?"

"I need assistance decrypting the information I managed to take from Ezra's estate."

"I don't know what I was expecting, but definitely not that."

"It's an encryption I've never seen," I say.

"Can you show me?"

I remove Iris, placing it on her table. The encrypted hologram glows as Claire looks into it.

"Iris was never implemented with this technology," she says. "This is incredible."

She twirls the locked file, surveying it with a keen eye.

"I haven't seen an encryption this intricate since Adalina."

My mother's name drags the air out of my lungs, leaving them dry. The blood in my veins feels like liquefied metal, slowly moving with sharpness, piercing my insides.

Claire recognizes my shift in posture, her motherly nature shining through apologetic eyes.

"*The* Adalina?" Eliza says, stealing more air.

Hearing it again provokes tears, and I don't know why. They hang on my eyelids like weights, ready to fall. Her face lights up in my mind, calming the horrors of the days without anyone. The days I thought I'd never survive.

Claire nods in Eliza's direction, confirming what I already knew.

Mom.

"A legend," Eliza says. "The stories of her efforts and abilities to go against the Enlightenment. I would have loved to have met her."

Eliza turns her gaze to me and smiles.

"She was incredible," I say with a full heart.

"Wait, you knew her?"

"Like no other."

"How?"

"She's my mother."

Eliza's mouth opens wide, eyes bulging like an animated character. All the questions in her mind reflect in her eyes, trying to find their way out.

"It'll have to wait." I refocus on the task at hand and look at Claire. "Can you decrypt it?"

"I cannot. These kinds of encryptions aren't easy to decode." She paces back and forth, hand tucked under her chin, contemplating. "But..." She stops, facing Eliza and me.

"What?" Eliza asks before me.

"I think it's time to meet another silk."

45

"We're here," Claire announces.

"This way," Eliza adds.

Like the Encryption classroom, this one is a sphere, but it's bathed in black. It's invisible until the main door reveals a broken lock. It slides open, prompting us to walk through. The space mimics the room, with the layout of seats and tables angled toward the center.

"Is it okay that I'm with you?" Eliza asks.

"Yes. I know she has you all trying to decrypt her identity as an assignment, but this is more important. Given the circumstances, it'll be fine," Claire says.

We file down the steps onto the platform and where a gray broken lock is displayed on the wall. Claire guides us through.

A much smaller area, filled with holographic screens and systems, appears with a woman sitting peacefully in front. Eliza and I are practically touching as Claire steps forward, providing a few inches of breathing room. The woman in the chair sits comfortably with her hands intertwined in front of her. With the only light coming from the screens, I can hardly distinguish any of her features.

"Sorry to disturb you," Claire says gently, "we have a guest who could use your assistance."

The woman rises, slow and precise, summoning the light with each motion. My eyes struggle to adjust with the drastic change from dark to light.

"And who is the guest?" the woman asks plainly.

Claire steps aside, revealing the woman clearly.

Fine hair, the color of storm clouds, falls like rain, flooding down her shoulders to wispy ends. Hard lines paint her face, showing age and wisdom. Silver hangs around her neck, a multitude of symbols that match the intensity in her stare. Her eyes squint, creating a piercing effect that cuts through me.

"My, my," she says softly. "You are the spitting image of her."

Every line forming her face is sharp and profound, giving her an edge—one daring to be messed with. My eyes trace her long, thin nose to the edge of her mouth, which is curved upward in a sinister smirk.

"Now, why would a Young need my assistance?" She tilts her head, looking me up and down with hard judgment. Her gaze sharpens, homing in on something inside of me that I can't pinpoint. Her slow movements make me question if she can actually help me.

"Speak, child."

"I... I need help decrypting sensitive files I took from the Enlightenment."

"Show me," she says.

I reveal the contents, and unlike everyone else, there is no awe, no surprise at the technology. However, there is a small wince in her eye when she sees the protected files. She turns away as her purple skirt flows around her in a whimsical motion. The skirt rises high, tucking in the shirt, creating an illusion of a one piece attire.

"Can you decrypt it?" I ask.

A low chuckle fills the air, gradually forming into a deep laugh. Why is she laughing? Nothing about my question was funny. Maybe Claire was wrong to ask her to help me.

"Child," she says, interrupting my thoughts. "I can decrypt anything I want, when I want, and however I want."

Her laughter fades, and she turns her head toward Claire, unleashing a hard stare.

"Ariadne," Claire says, grabbing my attention. "This is Dahlia Rune, the silk of decryption."

Eliza gasps, forcing Claire to pause. Eliza's eyes are wide with one hand covering her mouth. "The Black Dahlia," she remarks.

Dahlia spins to face us and the silver hanging from her neck and wrapped around her waist glistens in the soft light above. An onyx sphere attached to the silver chain on her waist reminds me of the device my father used to decrypt sensitive files when I was younger. My eyes return to the silver daggers in her eyes and my muscles tighten.

"I'm sure you know about the Zero Day attacks," Claire says.

"Of course," I say.

"Something you may not know: Zero Day was used as a way for your parents and many others to escape the grasp of the Enlightenment."

She completely turns to face me as she formulates her thoughts.

"For years, there have been people working for the Enlightenment that wanted a way out. The silks, Thaddeus, Xena, Dahlia, and I, were among some of those people. We worked out a solution. But, without Dahlia, it wouldn't have been possible."

Her sight returns to the frail woman, who continues to look away. Her hands, slim and bony, dressed in silver rings, connect behind her back.

"I initiated the Zero Day," Dahlia says over her shoulder, "which earned me the title your friend mentioned."

The Black Dahlia.

Eliza's eyes remain wide, in a daze. I return my gaze to Dahlia. The silver in her eye shines, reflecting the white light as her voice continues to pierce the air.

"The Enlightenment, as proficient as they are, were not prepared for the events that took place. A nationwide black out that I managed to achieve gave rise to many possibilities. During that short moment of vulnerability, Zero Day commenced, and we took everything from them. Everything that could end this forsaken nation, but..." She inhales sharply, closing her eyes as she appears to reminisce. The solemnity of her face makes it seem like she's living the moment again, traveling to the time she did what no one else couldn't. "After, we all split up due to the Enlightenment hunting us down and the decree to eradicate the hacktivist movement. All we had was lost. The day your parents died was the final act to end our fight. What we accomplished during Zero Day was for nothing."

"It wasn't for nothing," Claire interjects.

Dahlia's eyes quickly open, her trance clearly broken as the daggers in her eyes target Claire.

"Don't you dare say we have a chance," Dahlia snaps, her voice an octave lower than before.

"We have Black Web."

"And what else?"

Claire takes a step back, offended by the words. It's the first time I've ever seen her back down.

"This place where you house hundreds of script kiddies and low lifes has nothing on what Adalina, Dexter, and Octavio had," Dahlia spits. "I, for one, am only still involved to protect the legacy that was once promised."

Claire's head falls, and her shoulders slouch. She remains quiet, but the way her lips are pressed, I know she wants to speak. Hearing my parents' names spoken with disdain makes me do it for her.

"You blame them," I say.

"What of it, child?"

Her scorn focuses on me, and I almost flinch, but when it comes to my mother and father, I never back down.

"Why?"

"Not that I have to tell you anything. They cost the nation more than your mind can fathom."

"That doesn't answer the question," I push.

Dahlia's back straightens, making her appear taller as her eyes bear down on me. She takes a step forward.

"Child, your parents knew what we had and the risks of having it. Instead of lying low like the rest of us, they managed to go out of their way and provoke the tyrants that control this so-called utopia even more."

She takes another step forward, and with the small space surrounding us, it seems like a mile. I try to step back, but her glare pins me down with invisible restraints.

"Adalina and Dexter"—she forces a breath out—"as much as I loved them, like my own children in fact, they were in over their heads . Instead of sharing that information with the people that helped obtain it, they died."

Her voice softens and her original posture returns. Softer and frail again, she slowly backs away, and her eyes finally release their hold on me.

"I don't blame them for dying. They died for what they believed in, and for that, I admire them," she says, turning away. "What I blame them for is not releasing the truth beforehand, knowing they were primary targets of the Enlightenment."

As much as I hate the way she speaks about them, I can't deny the fact that she's right. Whatever information they had was clearly enough to change our world, but no one knows it. If only they'd told me before they were taken.

"So, I take it you won't help me?" I ask. "Even though this information I gathered could equate to what my parents found?"

"I never said I wouldn't help you, child. I only provided you with my personal take on our current and past situations."

I didn't expect that. From her talk about my parents, I was certain she'd pass on assisting me.

"I admire your fight, child. The same way I once admired your parents. And I'm not a fool. Your success at taking important information from the Enlightenment is enough for me to respect your skill. Maybe you'll make up for your parents' mistakes. Maybe there is a reason you came here in search of help."

I want to thank her, but she doesn't seem like the type who responds well to it. She holds out her slim hand. Pale and wrinkled. Symbols and drawings cover her forearms in black ink as her fingers gesture for me to approach.

"Give me the device."

I hand over Iris, and she connects it to a hologram, displaying the encrypted files.

"Intricate indeed," Dahlia whispers to herself.

Unlatching the sphere at her side, she raises it next to the hologram and it begins to glow. It radiates an array of colors before stopping and pulsing a vivid blue. I marvel at the ease with which she uses the sphere, recalling my own struggles when I used it.

"If you had that device, you could have done it yourself," Eliza whispers.

"Not necessarily," I say.

The sphere is designed to mimic whatever technology it's next to. When activated, it opens the files it's connected to, and each color symbolizes a task or objective. If I remember correctly, the blue she stops it on indicates the successful copy of the encrypted files, meaning she's able to get inside. Now, the hard part.

The sphere unlocks, opening with an encrypted holo-board.

"This will only take a minute."

A minute. I don't know if she means it literally, but if so, I'm in complete awe. The way her long fingers pound the board with perfection, correctly hitting every sequence as it trails down the hologram is nothing short of exceptional.

"An encrypted decryption." Dahlia's wicked smirk returns.

A technique my father once called impossible. One I could never accomplish but certainly wish were a part of my arsenal.

"This will stop the files from breaching our network, unlocking the encryption indefinitely—making it ours for the taking."

She flips the holoboard and unveils an embedded algorithm of mesmerizing sequences I've never seen.

"A new sequence here," she says, tapping the encrypted file. "And a new algorithm here."

The files glitch and transform into a new one. Made from her creation, Dahlia has formed a completely different sequence, effortlessly making the former encryption useless.

"She does it again," Claire says, reminding me of her presence beside me.

Eliza, on the opposite side, stares in disbelief of Dahlia's display of mastery.

"Annnd," Dahlia says, punching a few more symbols, stretching a wide smile, "done."

The files crack open and reveal a playback symbol for a video recording.

This is it.

My chance to enact my revenge, to see the Enlightenment crumble, tremble to nothing but a blank memory. Time for my wrath to rain on those who have wronged me.

"Ready when you are," Dahlia says, finger on the button.

"Amity, record everything," I say.

"Copy."

I nod at Dahlia as Eliza's hand tightens around mine. Claire smiles with a spark in her eye, reminding me of my mother.

The glitch of the playback system hums, taking my attention away as we prepare for the truth.

EXFILTRATION

46

"Testing. Testing."

The playback begins with an unfamiliar face in the focus of the lens. A young man, dressed in black with an oversized lab coat looks directly into the recording device.

"This is our first display of true autonomous robots. Location: Cybourne. Time: 1400 hours. Date: January 2085."

He moves out of view and an android stands idle. Coated silver covers the machine, black lines tracing the edges of it. The metal shines, glistening with an effect of newness. It's taller than the man in the coat by at least a few inches as he presses something at the neck of the android. A moment passes and its eyes flash open. Black with no other color in its sockets makes me want to turn away. It turns its head slowly, examining its surroundings. Then it begins to move. At first, it's robotic, animated and controlled. But as the seconds tick by, the robot flexes its hands, moving each finger, getting a sense of its own control. The connected wires in its long slender arms flex like the muscle in a human being, moving as the robot changes motions.

Everything about it becomes real. The way it blinks, motor functions—it all comes in a natural way.

"Jericho," another voice says, "how's it coming along?"

The young man returns in the view of the camera, examining the robot. Footsteps colliding with the floor can be heard as they approach the field of view. A different man with the same youth displayed on his face as the other arrives.

"So far," the man in the lab coat says, "perfect."

They step back from the robot in unison and watch it move, taking notes on holodevices.

"Can it speak?" the new arrival asks.

"I can," the robot says plainly.

Both men stop, wide eyed by the voice.

"Jericho, did it just say 'I'?"

Jericho. I take a mental note of the man in the lab coat.

"Yes, Octavio."

Octavio.

Claire mentioned that name before. The architect of Black Web. Dahlia also referred to him when she spoke about what he and my parents had.

"Child," Dahlia pauses the playback. "this may be it. The thing your parents knew."

"Maybe," I say. "Let's continue."

"I am," the machine says as the playback resumes.

"It recognizes itself. We did it, Octavio."

"This doesn't seem right," Octavio says. "Without control, this can become disastrous."

"What are you saying?" Jericho asks. He walks away from Octavio and as the camera pans from his face, his brow furrows.

"We have to be careful."

The playback glitches, turning off and then back on. This time, the view is inside of what appears to be some kind of storage hangar. Pods fill the space, and with the wider angle of the footage, more are attached to the ceiling, all connected through wires and rods, similar to the connectors in Black Web. I examine the pods closer and see they contain robots. Energy and light travel through the connectors and it appears to be an incubation of some sort. Metal thuds echo with machinery releasing air through the dense area.

Jericho's voice reverberates through the chamber. "Location: Cybourne. Time: 1800 hours. Date: November 2100."

A time jump of fifteen years.

Before I can process, a robot walks into frame, scanning the area of pods.

"We've done it," Jericho says. His age shows through the rough lines on his face.

"We have indeed," the robot responds.

"I am a god," Jericho announces. "Now we can conquer anything. The rebuild of this nation is in view. With you serving as my agents, we will be the center of the world and everyone will have no choice but to follow."

"What is your plan, Jericho?"

"To bring Enlightenment to the world."

As if his voice were a method of activation, the pods flicker, blue light emerging through the glass cylinders, creating a light show through the shadows. In unison, they all hiss open. Inside, the robots awaken, exiting and forming an army in front of Jericho. At his side, the first robot from the previous recording joins the congregation of thousands. They all step forward at attention, ready for instructions.

A door slams from afar, with running steps following quickly after.

"What have you done?" Octavio screams.

He arrives next to Jericho with panic in his breath.

"You haven't seen anything yet," Jericho says, snapping his fingers.

The first robot steps forward and the metal begins to sizzle. It bubbles and boils as it falls in a liquefied state. From the top, as it melts, organs begin to form. A brain and heart, beating softly. Lungs rise and fall as the liquid forms the creation of the entire digestive system in a metallic tornado. It reaches the bottom in a silver pool, resembling mercury. The silver reattaches to the feet but starts to change to a nude color. It rises swiftly, flowing through the legs, around its waist, up to the stomach and chest, over its shoulders, and covering the head. Finally, the eyes turn a vivid blue, with a red ring outlining the iris.

What remains is a human being.

"I call him Adam," Jericho says, "my first Enlightenment Agent."

The playback abruptly ends, changing to a blacked-out screen.

"We just witnessed the creation of Enlightenment Agents," Eliza says. "Holy shit."

So the archives did leave out an important detail: Red rings signify androids, which means every Enlightenment Agent is one. Carmen from the train to Millennia. It still doesn't explain the aspect of cloning I previously thought would play a role.

"There's more," Dahlia says.

The playback flashes to a lab with a man strapped to a vertical table. He wears a white gown and has dark shallow eyes. He doesn't struggle, showing he's been there for a long time. Next to him is a device I've never seen. Tubes extend from it, trailing into the man's arms and out the other side, where they attach to a silver pod. The same type from the incubation room with the androids.

Jericho steps into the frame. Blonde hair is neatly pressed, with dark eyes staring at us. With a grin across his wide face, he fidgets with a holodevice, proceeding to take notes. His eyes return to the camera as he speaks.

"Location: Cybourne. Time: 0100 hours. Date: October 2102."

He steps to the device splitting the man and pod, then spins on his heel as if he's presenting to a group of people.

"We used clones to help end the war before, without sacrificing casualties. Now, I am prepared to push the bounds further. I will be attempting to clone this man in an effort to replace the weaker version."

His head snaps toward the frail man.

"As you can see, he's weak, tired, and practically dying. Cloning him will create a stronger, more durable and effective human being."

He smiles as he presses the device. A hologram floats above it, turning into holo-imaging. DNA strands appear. He splits the bonds and creates a copy, coding it into the device. It transfers into the pod. Blood drains from the man and feeds the pod.

"Please," Jericho says, ushering an android into the pod.

Moments pass as Jericho watches, typing unknown notes onto his device. The pod hisses and slides open. The frail man turns his head toward it as a healthy version of himself steps out. Jericho holds his hands out wide and the clone walks toward him. The clone turns to the camera with a blank stare, its eye containing a red ring.

"And this is only the beginning," Jericho says.

I was right. Red rings are connected to cloning. But this is more. Clones are also androids, not human at all. It explains the stiffness in Carmen. How rigid she was when talking to me. My heart breaks at the thought that a real version of her exists somewhere but in a much worse condition.

"This connects to the intel Raelyn and Mason found weeks ago that you shared with me," Claire says.

"The early information in these files was strong enough, but this is the dagger," Dahlia says.

"This is insane," Eliza says. "We've been living with cloned people all this time."

My thoughts rage, causing my stomach to lurch. Blood thrashes beneath my skin at the idea of replacing human beings with technology. To use them alongside humans was far enough, but to replace us... I don't know if I can live with knowing that.

"There are a few more files," Dahlia says. "Would you like to take a break?"

"No," I say. "The sooner we unravel it all, the sooner we can decide what to do about it."

Dahlia nods and resumes the playback.

The new recording glitches, flashing to another location.

It opens with Octavio.

He sits at a desk with tools and holoboards shining with algorithms and pictures. The images are human skulls with drawings outlined around it. Octavio looks rugged and disheveled, like he hasn't slept in weeks. A lab coat messily drapes his shoulders as he looks into the camera.

"Location: Cybourne. Time: 0400 hours. Date: December 2105," he says shakily.

He moves out of focus as two robots step behind him, staring and waiting, clearly expecting something. Pulse rifles hang on their hips as they remain still, breathing like humans.

"How's it coming Octavio?" Jericho says, taking a seat next to him.

"Almost complete."

"Almost?"

Jericho, who no longer wears a lab coat, snaps his fingers, making the robots move. Without the coat, he looks slimmer than the previous recordings. His hair is shorter, but a beard covers his face with blonde strands.

"I've given you more than enough time," Jericho spits.

The robots stalk forward and grab Octavio by his neck and shoulders. "It's there. It's there," Octavio struggles. "I have a prototype."

"Ahhh."

Jericho stands, and his entire demeanor changes to that of a completely different person. He follows the path Octavio pointed to, leading to an adjacent table.

"I need help with the specifics and biometrics. To enable the camera to work inside the human eye without affecting them, we need to test it."

"What do you call it?" Jericho asks.

"The node system."

"Node?"

"It's a neural optical debilitation engagement system," Octavio chokes. "Implanted in the eye, it will record and watch everything a person does. It will attach to the brain and focus through the wearer's iris, making it impossible to remove. It's the system you wanted me to create, so you could monitor citizens."

"It's meant for more than that," Jericho says, marveling over the small device. "With it, we'll display control, forcing obedience, so we will remain the gods we are. Until the protocol for nationwide cloning can be done without people going against it, this will be our surveillance, and maybe we won't need the act of cloning."

"You have power," Octavio says, "What more could you want?"

"It was never really about power, you see. I honestly do believe in a world of better living. Aren't you tired of seeing people fight about money and skin color—belief systems that all preach the same thing? I want a world where none of that matters, where we live to live. If the only way to create that vision is through these methods, then it shall be. Enlightenment is the key to thriving, not just going by day to day, suffering among other people. With my agents and this device, we'll create the world I dream of. I will usher in a new age of Enlightenment."

The playback ends, and after a moment, it resumes, with Octavio alone in the lab.

"I've recorded this session in the hopes that someone will find it. If you do, I hope you make the right choice."

Dahlia pauses it and drops her head.

"Oh, Octavio," she whispers. "This isn't what you wanted. This is how they made you."

The recording continues and it again skips time.

There's no voice telling the camera where it is or the time frame. It displays a group of people, huddled together in what appears to be a briefing room.

"I wanted to honor you all," Jericho's voice announces.

He now wears a tailored suit. A man in charge. His face is clean, as if it's been surgically refreshed.

The group changes their focus from one another to him. Surrounding them are hundreds of people, dressed in Enlightenment Agent attire. Through the shades they wear, a red glow shines.

"Esmeray Knox, for your expertise in medicine and ability to perfect the node and provide us with a way to achieve what we wanted. Ezra Coleman, your funding and active regeneration of money through the citizens will always be remembered. Joyce Coleman, I thank you, for your leadership and worldly knowledge, which have pushed the bounds and made us who we are. Lastly, Lucian Castor, your military prowess and drive to complete my agents has enabled our perfect world."

Jericho raises his arms and smiles.

"The Areas of Enlightenment, our sustainable creation. There will be no more poverty, no more strife, no more crime. All of it, wiped away clean. We will thrive in a Utopia centered around the hope for a better day, with no aggression from citizen to citizen. The old days from before are over. Through democracy, we changed nothing, established only animosity and segregation among each other. We will change that. We will blaze a path of Enlightenment to all that serve. Welcome to the future."

He pauses and releases a deep breath.

"The future is the Enlightenment."

The video fades to black, leaving us speechless.

"Woah." Eliza finally breaks the silence.

I step back and dive into my mind. The amount of information presented makes it hard to determine where I should start processing. Jericho, the mastermind and creator of the AOE. Octavio, first partner and creator of the node. Cloning and the reasons behind it. The creation of EAs. And we now also have the names of the other members...

"What will you do, Ms. Young?" Amity asks the question steaming at the forefront of my mind, the one I desperately want to avoid.

The truth is, I don't know.

I've waited years for the chance to take down the Enlightenment. Two days ago, I had the opportunity to kill Ezra where he stood, and I didn't pull the trigger because of an active conscience.

Now this.

The information my parents died with before they could reveal it... They must have been trying to figure out a way to expose all of this without the negative repercussions from the Enlightenment. This is enough to shatter the nation. This isn't a theory anymore, we have the facts and evidence.

"Ms. Young?" Amity says.

"We strike now," I say for everyone to hear.

"How?" Eliza asks.

"The citizens," Claire says. "They need to know. This will lead people to the understanding that this is not the utopia the Enlightenment promised."

"But remember the bigger picture," I say. Claire's eyes find mine. "What will happen after we share this with the nation? The same question my parents most likely asked themselves..."

"I don't know," Claire says. "But we can't stand idly and wait for them to realize what we found. And with their address to the nation still hanging over our heads, we need to act."

"I'm all for it," Eliza says, "but again, how?"

We have no way to reach the masses. It'll take too long if we try word of mouth, and how many people would actually believe us. They'd think we're crazier than the times of religious fanatics.

"Any suggestions, Amity?" I ask.

"Cross running systems?" Amity says.

"It's too open. We run the risks of exposure."

"Did you say something?" Dahlia asks.

I shake my head no.

"Hmmm," she says, then clears her throat, conspicuously grabbing our attention.

"What do you suggest?" Claire asks.

"First, we'll need access to Black Web's core. With it, we attack the Enlightenment's central system, allowing entry to the nation's core. We'll be connected to every device, and from there, we expose the truth through an encrypted broadcast. Our code names will ensure indefinite disguise as we explain what we found. An effective method for doxxing."

"What's the catch?" I ask.

"Smart girl," she says. "We'll have one minute, maybe less. If I hold the intrusion too long, they'll find the source, pointing them to Black Web."

"Well, whoever is talking will have to be fast," Eliza says.

"Me," I say. "I'll do it."

This is what I've trained for. Lived for. It has to be me.

"Okay then," Claire says. "It's settled. I'll gather the remainder of the web, and we'll meet at the lower apex."

The mention of the web reminds me of my other problem.

The plant.

"Amity, any updates on the mask?"

"Nothing yet, Ms. Young."

We're going to do this, so we have to do it right. Claire needs to know there is someone who isn't who they say they are.

"Before you do that," I say, "can I speak with you in your office?"

"Of course." Claire gestures us out of Dahlia's space. "After you."

47

Iris shines, illuminating the snapshot of the pyro wielder. The three of us examine the display.

"What is this?" Claire asks from across her desk.

Her brows curl, deepening the age in her face.

"When I was at the estate, I came across this person. This was taken in Ezra's office," I say.

"And, as you can see," Eliza adds, "they're wearing a Black Web mask."

Claire begins to pace. Back and forth, all the questions plaguing my mind appear to do the same to her. She walks over to her side table and pours herself a drink, downing it in a few gulps. The amber liquid is gone, quicker than it came.

"Do you have any leads or people of interest?" she asks.

"Not yet. I am curr—"

"Ms. Young, systems have found a match with the mask," Amity interrupts.

"Who?"

"It appears Mason is the owner of the mask, Ms. Young."

My eyes grow wide and a hollow pit forms in my chest. Mason. How is that possible? He never showed any kind of animosity toward me. Raelyn would have known. Or maybe she did and didn't tell me..

"What is it?" Claire asks.

"I believe I have a person of interest."

Claire and Eliza both stare at me with blank expressions, ready to hear the worst.

"This is going to be hard to believe, but I think it may be Mason or Raelyn."

Claire's glass shatters on the table, sending tiny shards across the room.

"What?" Eliza shouts in my ear. She grabs me and turns my body to face her. "I thought you said Raelyn was an ally."

"She was."

"Until?"

"Until I saw the web members in the debrief before visiting Dahlia. Since then, Amity has been working on finding a match to the person at the estate. Mason's mask is a positive match. Not only that, but Raelyn was supposed to inform Claire about the threat after I spoke with her before the debrief, but she obviously didn't."

"I think she was going to tell me," Claire says, "She said she had important news to share, but I told her it would have to wait because of the debrief."

"It doesn't explain Mason's mask," I say.

Silence floats between us as we all dive into our minds.

"Ms. Young, this doesn't prove it is him," Amity says. "The mask seems to have been tampered with."

"How can you tell?"

"There's a scrambled code embedded inside. Forced to override the owner and hide the intrusion. Body scans of the individual at the estate don't match any of the Black Web members either."

What does this mean? If it's not them or any of the other members, who else could it be?

"It's neither of them," Claire mumbles.

"I do believe you, but how can you be sure?" I ask.

"She's my daughter," she snaps. "Don't you think I wouldn't know?"

I take a moment and step back. Seeing her frustrations, I let it go. I don't want to push further, with what's currently at stake for us. It is her daughter after all; she would know her better than anyone.

"Whomever this person turns out to be has thoroughly planned this out, Ms. Young."

"Okay," I say to Claire. "I just wanted you to be aware before this operation."

"Thank you. Anything else I should know before I go?"

Eliza and I shake our heads.

"I'll see you both at the core. Eliza, I trust you'll show her where that is."

"Will do."

"We'll find the plant." Claire walks toward the door. "They'll make a mistake, but right now, we have more urgent matters to attend to."

She exits the office with a soft smile, and I think about all the things possibly going through her head. The pressures of running Black Web. Fighting against the Enlightenment, virtually an unknown enemy. Learning the truth and history of the node system, it's a lot and I wish there was a way I could help.

I inhale, holding my breath and releasing, trying to calm myself the way Eliza does.

"Are you nervous?" she asks.

"Not in the slightest."

"I expect no less from the best."

She smiles and I can't control the emotions she stirs inside me. The way she looks at me and sees me. It's something I haven't felt in a long time, increasing the desires of want and need. I grab her hand, pull her close, and plant a kiss on her lips. The soft fullness makes me melt into her, and we hold each other in the moment.

"Thank you," I say, resting my forehead against hers.

"For?"

"Being here."

Our lips intertwine again, and I smile.

We leave Claire's office, heading toward the core of Black Web and the biggest mission I've ever faced.

48

The power of the core is intense.

Its planet-sized aura releases warmth like I'm close to the sun. The prism rotates slowly, its light like soft waves twisting and turning through the air, providing an immense amount of illumination. Even though it's encased in glass, it doesn't stop the strength of the massive shape.

"Something, isn't it?" Eliza says from ahead of me.

The narrow passage we cross is the last physical structure of Black Web. Air flow is tighter, making my lungs work harder. My eyes trail upward as I take in the full view of the facility. It's simply breathtaking, as if I'm witnessing it for the first time again. Reaching a large, framed door, Eliza ushers me inside, and the warmth provided by the core sheds off my skin, replaced by frigid air.

Black Web's theme continues to show as the spherical shape of the new space becomes clear. Hologram after hologram ignites like stars in a dense black sky. All around, as I spin and examine the walls, some reveal camera footage of Black Web. Others show data and sequences of some kind.

As we walk, our heels click on the shiny black surface, echoing through the quiet, creating a rhythmic sound. Computer systems come into view when we trail deeper inside.

Our steps become overshadowed by the entire web, huddled in front of an entourage of holograms. Claire resides in the center of them, talking and gesturing like the director she is. Dahlia sits in a holochair, dashing hands hovering effortlessly over holoboards. It still surprises me how quick she can be, given her age. Thaddeus stands behind her, conjuring memories of the panic attack in Encryption. I immediately push the thought away and focus my sight elsewhere.

Claire finally notices us, and she stops mid-sentence, gesturing for us to join the circle. When we do, I'm surprised no one gives me an odd look. I've grown accustomed to the gazes and disdain; this normalcy makes me feel more out of place.

"Perfect timing," Claire says. "I was just letting the web know what's going on and why we're all here."

"We hear you've managed to steal some pretty valuable information," Raelyn says cheerfully.

I smile, remembering Claire's words to trust her. Mason stands at Raelyn's side, giving a nonchalant head nod.

"Maybe Astraea was right," Ayster says, confusing everyone in the circle.

"Maybe?" Astraea scuffs.

"Right about what?" I ask.

"You being a badass."

My lips part and I stifle a laugh.

"That's definitely not a maybe," Astraea says. "I mean, none of us would have had the balls to infiltrate a facility owned by an Enlightenment member, alone I might add."

"I'm just saying…" Ayster smiles. "It's pretty badass."

"Thanks," I manage to say. "I did have some help."

Eliza's eyes light up with deep blue.

"It was nothing." She blushes.

"And Dahlia, of course. Without—"

"No need to flatter, child, " she interrupts me. "I'm already helping."

She's facing away from me, but judging by her soft spoken voice, she could be smiling.

"I knew you were capable of a lot, but definitely not this," Thaddeus says, his suit crisp as ever.

"Okay," Claire says. "Here's the plan."

Everyone gives her their attention, waiting and intentionally listening to each word she says.

"From here on, everyone will use codenames, just like with any other operation. This mission is extremely time sensitive. When Dark gives the word, that's when we'll begin."

"Almost done," Dahlia says.

Claire turns, eyeing each one of us as she continues.

"Viro?" she says to Zane.

I didn't notice him until now. Like a shadow, he stands next to Ayster.

"If anything goes against the plan, I shut it down indefinitely," he says.

"Kasper,"—Claire turns to Mason—"you assist him with any blackout that's needed."

"Got it," he says.

"Lumina, you will work with Lock and watch for errors that threaten our systems during the broadcast."

"Heard," Raelyn responds swiftly.

"Loud and clear," Thaddeus says.

Claire finds Eliza and says, "Echo, you'll amplify the broadcast to ensure it comes across clear as day."

"You know it." Eliza smiles.

"Phoenix and Illusia,"—Claire eyes the twins—"You have the second most important job."

"No pressure," Ayster says.

"We got this," Astraea follows, elbowing his arm.

"Phoenix, if the network fails, revive it. And Illusia, you will have to disguise Nexia throughout the entire broadcast."

"Understood," they respond in unison.

"Nexia," Claire begins. All heads turn to me, and my heart lurches, creating a hollow space within my chest. "The most important job is yours," Claire continues proudly. "No need to tell you what to do."

"I'm ready," I say.

"You'd better be," Zane says, stepping forward in the light.

His shadow-colored hair is all tucked back in a low ponytail. The amber tones of his skin highlight beneath the deep brown, giving a natural shine.

"You'll need one of these," he says, tossing me a Black Web mask.

I hold it in my hands, turning it, examining the hard surface. Tracing my fingers along the edges, I can almost feel the tech inside, a subtle vibration of connection, similar to Iris. My reflection glows in the black mirror, and for a brief moment, I think of all the time before this, of who I used to be. The mask flashes, quickly stopping my thoughts from progressing. Its neon facial features glow and copy my own. The black mirror is a digital code, giving it the power to display the wearer's expression.

"It's like looking at yourself through a hololens," Eliza says.

"Now it's official," Ayster says.

"Welcome to the web," Zane adds with a soft wink.

This new person he's showing surprises me. I didn't think he could be genuine or show any kind of acceptance toward me. Both he and Ayster have changed so drastically that paranoia starts to dig its fangs into me. The what ifs and constant worry of something terrible happening reveal themselves, dulling this moment.

"Try it on," Raelyn says, saving me from my inner thoughts.

I slowly lift it to my face, and I get a strong whiff of fresh metal. The silver lines of the black edges are the culprit. The mask seals around my face like a second skin. It's no longer hard or cold as I run my hands across my face. My vision is clearer and everyone in front of me highlights green, the aura glowing around them.

"It takes a moment to get used to," Mason says, "but it's incredible."

"Thanks, everyone," I say.

As the words come out, I no longer hear my voice. It's distorted and unrecognizable, like white noise and static recorded underneath.

"Oh, one more thing," Zane says. "I heard about your altercation at the estate and what you lost. Another gift from us."

He tosses a drone toward me, and I can't believe my eyes. It looks exactly like the one my parents left me, except for the color. Instead, it's white, absent of any color. Blue light flickers across it, creating a connection to Amity and

Iris. It hovers out of my hands and my reflection stares back. I smile uncontrollably beneath the mask as tears begin to form.

Before I can be awed by anymore specs, Dahlia spins in her holochair, a devilish smirk written across her face.

"It's time," she says.

Everyone disperses and finds a seat with a hologram, holoboards loading in front of them.

"Nexia," Claire says, "stand here."

She guides me to a circular device embedded into the black stone floor. It's barely visible, with only the low blinking light along its edge.

"When it glows completely blue, you'll be broadcasting, and the entire Area will see you on every monitor or screen."

"Okay." I nod.

"Remember," Dahlia says, "one minute, not a second longer."

My heart rate starts to increase its pace as the moment draws nearer. I thought I wouldn't be nervous, but now, the bile in my stomach rises.

"You got this." Claire smiles, stepping away and finding her own device.

"Amity, this is it," I say.

"Indeed, Ms. Young."

"You got my back?"

"Always."

I take in deep breaths, slow and steady to get my anxious nerves in order. Since I can't stop them, I refocus the energy into my speech. With it, my words will have the conviction I need them to have if our point is going to be taken seriously.

As my breathing becomes calm, I think about my parents and what they died for.

The truth.

Today, everyone will know it.

"Five," Dahlia says, making everyone move to their positions.

"Four."

The light flickers multiple colors beneath my feet, loading the software.

"Three."

This is for you. I think of my mother's soft eyes and my dad's unforgettable smile.

"Two."

One minute to change the world.

"One."

49

A bright light flashes from Dahlia's hologram into my mask. An aura surrounds me, and I emerge on every hologram in the room. Beneath my feet, the pad glows blue, giving me my cue.

"Good Afternoon citizens of Area 1," I say, still not used to my distorted voice.

"This is an emergency broadcast to inform you of the truth. The Enlightenment is not who they say they are."

I pause momentarily to let the statement sink in.

"They are murderers and thieves. People who claimed to protect the nation have done nothing but control you."

"Forty-five seconds," Dahlia updates.

"This is footage found from their archives."

Dahlia displays a clip of the lab playback showing Octavio's node creation.

"They created this device—the node, as you know it—to control you. To make you nothing but a pawn for them to use."

"Fifteen seconds."

As I prepare the last line to complete my speech, the power shuts off. Leaving the entire room in black.

"I thought you said fifteen seconds!" Claire shouts.

"I didn't end it," Dahlia says.

Dammit. The one video won't be enough to change anything. We needed those last few seconds to show more, to give the citizens a reason to believe us. As my chest swells, the power returns and where my face was displayed on every hologram, another takes its place.

Ezra Coleman.

His face makes me want to explode. The arrogant arc of his brows and lips makes my blood boil.

"Excuse that broadcast, dear citizens. Something is going on that we will take care of momentarily. Rest assured, everything is fine. Have an enlightened day."

We all watch in disbelief. Trading silent glances with one another.

"Systems detect an activated node," Amity says.

My heart sinks.

"You're in danger, Ms. Young."

MALWARE

50

Red flashes through the dark room. Light and power finally return as everyone looks around for an answer to what's happening. An active node in Black Web? When I first got here there were none, everyone appeared as node-free to Amity and me.

"What's going on?" Thaddeus says frantically.

"No idea," replies Dahlia.

"Phoenix," Claire calls, "have you tried bringing the network back online?"

"I have, but I can't get in," Ayster says.

"Amity, where is the node located?" I ask.

"Moving toward the main level."

The holograms and boards glow with red lines falling like rain, indicating a system failure.

"Encryptions remain steady," Raelyn announces.

Which means...

"It's an internal malfunction," Mason reads my mind.

"Ms. Young, more nodes have registered as hostile, and they've been updated to Iris."

His voice instantly stops my forward movement. Viro, Zane's code name. I think back to his introduction the day at the apex.

'I specialize in viruses, new girl.'

'Specifically, hidden viruses people never see coming.'

As my mind quickly rolls over the thoughts, I'm stunned I didn't see it sooner.

"Where's Zane!?" I ask urgently.

Everyone looks around as they realize he isn't in the room.

He must have found a way to exit while we were all distracted, similar to what he did in Encryption. Vanishing in the dark without saying a word. His obsession with me being in Eliza's room. The vagueness in Claire's debrief a week ago. And the way he smirked after I helped decode their findings. He must have supplied the information to Ezra back in Millennia, which means he's the one who can emit fire from nothing.

It all begins to make sense.

"Ms. Young," Amity interrupts my thoughts, "the agents are moving. This is indeed a raid."

"There's been a breach," Dahlia says.

"It's the Enlightenment," I say.

"How do you—" Ayster starts.

"Never mind that," Claire interjects. "We must defend Black Web. Everyone, in groups of two, defend each thread and make sure we take care of every intruder. Protect any younger members you find in their rooms or wandering the halls. I don't want them to panic."

Claire rapidly assigns the threads to the web, making them move.

Eliza and I break away and head to our thread: the main entrance of Black Web. As we head upward, I think to myself about how I want to end Zane's life. The traitor asshole has been working against us. Working with those who caused my pain.

This time, I will not hesitate.

51

"Zane!" Eliza snaps. "Should have fucking known."

We storm away from the center, where the elevator docks. At the entrance, two EAs stand at his shoulder. The mask sends all but pleasant memories of my extraction mission. The fiery trail from a simple hand gesture.

Behind Zane, there's no forced entry, implying he's been able to go in and out whenever he wanted too, allowing anyone to invade Black Web at will. There could be EAs everywhere in the facility by now. The thought seeps poison into me and makes me think about all the people here who don't fight or aren't ready. They'll be slaughtered if the rest of the web and silks don't reach them in time.

I draw my staff, not willing to exchange words or waste any precious time. The tungsten vibrates in my hand, the energy matching my raging blood; I desperately want to unleash. A wispy sound of air escapes through the space and breaks the silence. My eyes follow the trajectory of the sound to the main door. It slowly opens, daylight rushing inside like it needs a place to hide.

"Well, well," a voice says.

We're quickly outnumbered as four more figures stalk inside. I ignore the stall in my breath.

One of them is an EA, joining the others at Zane's side. The mask remains on his face but reveals no expressions. I try to make out who the other three are, but the sun's vengeful glare conceals them as heels clamp against the floor. The pace is slow, exact and eerie, with the shade of the sun dimmed by the dark atmosphere of Black Web. The main door closes, suffocating the light, finally revealing them.

Ezra Coleman claps as he takes a relaxed stance with Zane by his side. My eyes turn to the mask wearer from the estate, with the ability to produce fire. I thought it was Zane, but clearly it isn't.

Eliza looks at me with the same question in her eyes. The last person by Ezra's side stands idle. A hood conceals their full identity. Silver hair falls beneath the hood, highlighted against the black they wear.

"It is a pleasure to finally meet you," Ezra says in a smooth cadence.

He looks between Eliza and me with a stare both calm and dangerous. Blonde hair lying flat magnifies the sharp edges of his face. He's younger than I imagined as I glance past his smug smile. The insignia—a golden eye with the globe behind it glistens and against the deep blue of his suit, reminds me of the Central Square incident. It winks from Black Web's glow, making me tense.

"I bet you're wondering who this is." He gestures to the fire maker and person we thought was Zane.

Their mask retracts into a device on their head, unlike how we take ours off. As it disappears, my blood freezes.

Trace.

"What. The. Hell," Eliza whispers.

"What?" Zane says, the sarcasm seeping through his venomous voice. "You act like you've never seen a clone before."

He chuckles beneath his breath.

"Why?" Eliza asks bitterly.

"Oh, you can do better than that," he taunts. "Why not is the better question. Black Web has always limited our potential and forward movement. The Enlightenment doesn't."

The Enlightenment cloned Trace. But why? How? As my thoughts roar inside my head, I remember the recent debrief from Zane's mission. They found Trace's blood at the Panoramic Diner, and it was swabbed.

His death replays in my head, and my heart aches.

Everything about him is the same. His dark locs fall to his shoulders. My eyes follow the lines of the guy who saved my life, and I remember the times I had with him, but the warmth his eyes and smile once gave is gone. Now he stands and barely looks like he's breathing. But of course, he isn't. The video showed us clones are androids beneath the skin of their copies. Tears threaten to rise, but I hold them back, channeling hate and forcing myself to remember it's not the Trace I knew.

Ezra steps forward, making Zane and the silver-haired person go back.

"There's been a lot of mistakes in the past few weeks, threatening my hold over Area 1. The Enlightenment has made it apparent this must be fixed because everything we've worked to achieve hangs in the balance."

He paces and rolls his head, looking at the facility, but I can't stop staring at Trace. He doesn't move a muscle, and I tense when I meet his gaze. It finally forces me to look away.

"Don't worry about him," Ezra's gaze lands on me. "He hasn't been perfected yet, so he can't speak."

I inhale a sharp breath as his eyes narrow. He examines me and smiles.

"I don't believe we've met, but you do share a lot of similarities with a former colleague of mine. Hmmm."

A former colleague? When my mother was alive and we'd go places together, I'd always get people saying we looked exactly alike. If he means my mother, it would mean she worked with him. I can't bring myself to believe she was involved with them in any way.

"Got it!" He snaps. "Adalina was her name. Gentle and kind, yet tenacious and unyielding. What a love—"

"Don't ever mention her name again," I snarl.

It can't be.

His eyes light up with intensity.

"Are you related to her? How? Given the resemblance, I'm inclined to guess daughter, perhaps. But we captured her daughter, and she was imprisoned years ago. Unless..." His pacing stops and his eyes dip as the corners of his mouth arch. "You were the escapee from the Mirror's Edge."

The Mirror's Edge? The name of the place we found earlier, where they clone humans. I never knew the name of the prison I was in. Having a name doesn't make the memories of my time there any better—in fact, now there's a heavy weight placed on my chest. What if they cloned me?

There's no way. I would know.

Ezra's gaze sharpens as he formulates his thoughts. Eliza and I are severely outnumbered, but it doesn't stop the want to end his life. The way he speaks so calmly when he took everything...

"Another mistake I made... Nonetheless, Jericho will prevail. So will the Enlightenment."

Eliza draws her spheres with a swift rotation of her wrist. They fall in between her fingers and the look on her face says what her voice doesn't need to.

"Done talking already? Eliza, your parents will be very disappointed in you."

He snaps his fingers, mimicking Jericho from the playback, signaling the EAs. The four of them raise their rifles and aim. Instead of red beams streaming from the ends like I'm used to seeing, they burn a bright purple.

"Well, looks like duty calls. I'll be addressing the nation about this barbaric act. That'll keep their trust from wavering," Ezra says, backtracking to the exit. "It certainly was a pleasure meeting the daughter of such a lovely woman." He finds Zane and Trace. "Finish it. And remember what we talked about."

"The Enlightenment is the future," Zane says.

He leaves with the mystery person, and Eliza doesn't hesitate.

She sends two orbs at Ezra, but they knock two EAs to the ground instead.

Ezra's eyes bulge as he scurries through the front door, looking over his shoulder for another orb.

"Amity," I say, triggering the new drone.

It darts in the air as Eliza and I dodge an incoming pulse wave from a rifle. Another piece of technology I have never seen, only heard about. Heat engulfs the square base, intensifying as the purple beam trails along the ground toward me. It melts the marble, disengaging the protective layer, signaling an alarm. It blares and screams, echoing through the facility.

The familiar sound of the drone's weapons stops the death ray. Two EAs fall to the ground, their guns clattering beside them. Eliza rises and sprints toward Zane and Trace. Trace's mask falls down his face as fire flashes in his hands.

"Liz!" I shout.

She dashes to the side as a blazing streak of fire passes her. I get to my feet and dash toward Zane. He turns, not fazed by my approach. With a quick move of his hand, he aims a pulse hand cannon. That weapon I know. Slow to fire but causes severe damage to anything it manages to hit. However, to shoot, it requires biotechnology—a finger-print or eye scan.

I move fast and from a side pocket on my thigh, I'm able to quickly find an EMP pad. I throw it toward him as the wind-up of his shot echoes. The EMP ignites, and the shot doesn't register. Frustration grows in his eyes as he continuously pulls the trigger. A sound of clicks gives me the urgency to pursue him.

"Ms. Young, to your right," Amity warns.

Fire comes from the clone. A ball of heat, the size of a burning wheel, barrels its way toward me with immense speed. I spin, trying to get around it as it rushes past me, but the flame is too fast. It catches my arm and melts the sleeve. The explosion knocks me off my feet as I roll to the ground. It takes a moment for my nerves to acknowledge the agonizing pain. Excruciating heat travels through my arm as I hold my screams, fighting the urge, so I don't give these assholes any satisfaction.

Through my teary eyes, Zane fires a smaller version of the hand cannon at the drone. Instead of a pulse wave or bullet, it's a streak of red flashing when it hits it. Iris vibrates like the time Amity was affected, sending an unwanted chill through my body. At the center of my being, I sense something is severely wrong.

"Ms...Young..." Amity says through interference.

Iris frantically glows on my wrist with warning signals. "Virus...detected..."

The same thing from my extraction. A virus feeds through my systems. But when I rebooted Amity, I was prepared.

Expect nothing, prepare for anything.

The anti-virus triggers and makes the virus vanish.

"I see you've learned your lesson," Zane says with a smirk.

I ignore him as relief starts to settle, but it's instantly stripped away. A static surge shoots through the drone, and it moves away from me to hover above Zane's shoulder.

"Now what are you going to do?" he asks with a devilish grin.

"Amity," I say, "disengage."

"Ms. Young, all functions have been restored by the anti-virus. However, there is no longer a connection to the drone."

"That doesn't make sense. It's connected to you and Iris. How could—"

My voice trails as a thought reveals itself. It's not mine. My mind quickly plays back to the moment Zane gave it to me.

I heard about your altercation at the estate and what you lost. Another gift from us.

He destroyed my drone, a gift from my parents, and tried to use his own to infect my systems again.

I struggle and get to my feet. The burning in my arm strengthens alongside my inner turmoil over losing my drone.

The alarms continue to blare with a menacing shriek as the red lights flicker.

"Don't worry," Zane says, "I won't use it against you."

He toggles a device from his pocket and connects it to the drone.

"Seek and destroy," he says. "Find and kill Claire Hart."

Dozens of red dots paint the screen on my wrist, making me shudder. This many nodes are active in a matter of seconds. How?

"Can you determine who they belong to?" I ask.

"It appears they are agents, Ms. Young."

Bile rises in my throat, forcing me to choke it back. How did they get here? This facility doesn't reveal itself to people who are not among it. I turn my gaze and try to calm myself, but I only see the red lines again. My eyes move from one hologram to the next, and it finally comes to me.

"It's a virus," I say.

Dahlia's silver gaze finds me. I quickly remember a lesson from my father. The sudden crash of a network. Signaling of red going through a system and displayed as we see here always meant there was a virus present. Feeding on the internetwork. Once triggered, it has the potential to bring down entire frameworks from the inside. Undetectable until it's too late.

A Trojan horse.

"How could a virus have been placed without anyone knowing?" Eliza asks.

I don't have an answer as I scan the area. This type of virus would have had to have been placed a while ago. With an encryption disguising it, making it hidden. It would have to be someone who has access.

The plant.

Mason and Raelyn are together at a hologram when I start my approach.

"If it's a virus," Mason says, "Viro can reverse it."

52

The drone soars beneath the surface of Black Web, disappearing through the burning crevasse created by the EA's pulse rifle. Now, no longer in my control, it targets Claire, my aunt—the woman who saved my life and showed me a new one.

An electric current rips through my veins, making my mind go blank with rage, and everything in front of me becomes a target.

"Ms. Young," Amity says.

I ignore the call, already on my way to Zane. His smile lingers from taking control of the drone, but not for long. From my peripheral vision, another ball of flame travels toward me. It spirals, with orange at its center and reddish-yellow waves flowing around it like a chaotic dance.

Ignoring the ache in my arm, I roll as the flame travels above me and crashes into one of the pillars. An explosion of black pollutes the air as Black Web trembles beneath my feet. Lifting to a crouch, several feet away from Zane, I throw my staff. The silver reverberates as it tracks toward him.

He dodges and it collides with the main door, releasing a sharp clang. The energy from the staff forms a crater in the door as Zane's gaze returns to me. His jaw parts and eyes bulge. As he tries to regain his composure, my fist crashes into his jaw, sending his head sideways. He storms backward, hand to his mouth, blood dripping from the corners of his lips.

"Bitch!" he screams, charging me.

He throws a punch, and I sway. Using his momentum from the missed punch I push, forcing him off balance. Behind me, Eliza and Trace engage in hand to hand combat. With each strike the clone throws, an ember releases. Eliza flows through each, using speed and form to avoid them. It gives my mind freedom from the fire distraction.

Rumbling throughout the building continues. This building may not be made to withstand internal destruction.

With no time to ponder, I unsheathe a dagger hidden along my belt line. Remembering my failed accuracy of throwing my staff, I rush Zane. I slash once, testing his agility. I can tell he's used to ranged combat. I pursue him, quick jabs targeting his chest, forcing backward movement. In the dark orbs of his eyes, terror forms as my dagger slices his forearm.

A clean strip of blood seeps through his sleeve, and I use the advantage to continue swinging the dagger in different motions. I flip the dagger to my opposite hand in a fluid motion, making his pupils dilate. I'm better. Faster and smarter. With my empty fist, his head rolls sideways. He stumbles, and I go for the kill, aiming the dagger toward his throat.

He somehow gets enough balance to stop me. We both hold the blade in place as we struggle for leverage. He gains enough strength to strike my ribcage with a blow from his knee. I stagger back, wincing at the pain. A punch lands to the side of my head, momentarily altering my vision. The taste of metal builds at the back of my mouth, making me queasy. In my moment of weakness, he recognizes it and continues striking.

Wild punches, landing against my body and face. I find myself falling to the ground from the onslaught. His boot slams into the exact spot his knee found my midsection. A snapping sound in my ribs shakes the entirety of my body. Blood spills from my mouth as I roll to the ground from the impact.

I reach for my dagger, now inches away as Zane's boot comes down on my hand. A crunch in my wrist forces the screams I've been holding to escape. He kicks me onto my back and kneels, eyes glaring when he smiles.

"You're lucky they want you alive," he taunts. "Otherwise, you'd be dead."

Slowly, with my free hand, I reach for another dagger.

"My mission is not you. It's to kill Claire and annihilate this facility."

I find a hilt and secure it in my hand, holding it tight.

"Your friends however..."

He looks away, toward Eliza. His brow furrows and takes over his face like a shadow, giving me an opportunity.

With all my strength, fueled by rage, I plunge the serrated blade into his boot. He bellows, screaming wildly as blood spits and spews from his foot. I push harder, forcing the blade to pierce the ground. Trapping him in place.

Alarms continue to sound like a haunting echo, increasing the ache in my head. I rise slowly, the severe pain at my side and jagged breath confirming broken ribs. I tower over Zane, peering into the black pools of his eyes. The eyes I want to drain of life.

"You fucking—"

My fist makes blood shoot out of his mouth. It causes me just as much pain from the movement. The agony in my ribs escalates and I find it harder to breathe. I ignore it and pick up my loose dagger. The weight is heavier from the fatigue I've endured during his assault on my body. I place the pointed tip at his neck. The tension in his throat makes me press harder, pricking the skin. Drawing blood.

"Recall..." I struggle through my breath. "The drone..."

He spits at my feet, and I immediately drive the blade into his shoulder. A scream, louder than the alarms surrounding us, rips through the air from the back of his throat. As he fights and screams to be released, I head toward the main door. I know he won't recall the drone, which means Claire will die. But part of me believes that if he bleeds out, it'll give him incentive to do so. If he doesn't get medical treatment, he will also die. I retrieve my staff as his bellow continues. The familiar vibration rattles in my hand, new stored energy replacing what was lost earlier.

When I turn to walk back, I get a glimpse of the aftermath between Eliza and Trace's clone. She lies face down, the clone doing the same a few feet away from her. Scorch marks litter the space as I scan. The silver which once shed light is now tainted with black ash. Seeing Eliza on the ground forms a pit in my stomach; I hope she isn't dead. I want to help her, but my focus returns to Zane, and as the flame of anger flickers inside me, it prevents me from checking on her.

Stepping in front of him, I raise his chin with the edge of my staff. He flinches, half passed out from the blood loss. The weakness in his eyes reflects the damage of the two daggers as blood continues to spill out of him.

"I won't...ask again," I say.

"Fuck...you..."

I was wrong. He may be too far gone with the Enlightenment to care about living. I draw my staff back, the tungsten igniting the energy inside. And as I prepare to swing with all my might, the central elevator halts my forward movement.

"Wait!" Claire yells.

My eyes find hers, and I hold my breath when she says:

"We need him alive."

53

Claire walks over to me and places a hand on my shoulder, instantly cooling the heat under my skin.

"It's okay," she says. "We need him to find where the Enlightenment resides."

Beyond her, Eliza stirs.

Claire releases me, and I limp to her aid. Seeing Claire means the drone is having a hard time finding her. Given the size of Black Web, it makes sense. I fall to my knees next to Eliza and caress her body. The welted burns along her arms and legs make me wish it were me who'd fought the clone. Her eyes blink open softly, and I smile at the simple fact she is alive. She tries to sit up, wincing with every movement.

"Shhh. You're okay," I whisper, moving my hand through her ash-filled hair.

Trace's clone lies across from us and I can't tell if it's dead or not. Hopefully the former. Seeing Trace without it being *him* stabs a knife in me I desperately want to go away.

Claire kneels and looks Zane in the eyes. His head swivels sideways toward me with a blood-stained grin. My mind races to find an answer to the sinister gesture as Eliza rises to a seated position, also staring at me.

"What's wrong?" she asks softly.

I don't answer as Claire's gaze also finds me.

"You should have killed me, new girl," Zane announces.

He quickly flicks the device he used to control the drone.

"No," I whisper.

I move as fast as I can, but my ribs hold me back, slowing my movement. A familiar buzzing sound reaches my ears.

Oh no.

My heart stammers and my breathing stalls.

"What's going on?" Claire asks, standing straight.

Through the crevasse it vanished through, the drone hovers behind Claire.

"Amity!" I shout. "Shut it down!"

"There's no control of the drone, Ms. Young."

I panic and frantically check my suit for another EMP, but I find nothing to help. Claire doesn't see the drone as she looks me in the eyes. The whirling of the gun attached to the drone ignites, and bullets pierce her back. Blood stains the front of her white-collared shirt, red spilling from her mouth as she falls to her knees. She lingers for a moment before hitting the ground with a thud.

Then, the drone aims at me. As the guns charge, a snap of wind shoots past me, and the drone shatters. It rains down in pieces, and I turn to see Eliza. An orb returns to her hand as Claire coughs.

Adrenaline evaporates my pain, and I sprint to her side.

"No, no, no," I say. "Please...stay with me..."

Tears rush out of me as I sob. Claire wheezes. Blood streams down her face, staining the pure pale. I lift her head and gently rest it on my thigh. Visions of my mother flash in place of her. My chest grows tight. It's as if I'm witnessing the death of them both.

Another broken promise.

Memories play in my mind. From the first meeting at the diner, the video she shared of me as a child, her gift—Iris—the love and care she displayed from the very beginning. It all makes me suffocate under the longing in my heart for family.

She takes my hand, and my gut wrenches at the faintness of her heartbeat.

"Cy...bourne..." She coughs. "You...have to...find it." Her hand grips mine harder. "Thank...you." More blood, thicker and darker spurts out as she shakes.

"For staying alive...until I could find you... Your parents...would be proud... I'm proud."

Eliza falls next to me, and Claire looks at her with a smile. "Take...care...of...Rae..." A final breath escapes when she tries to finish, and her hand slips out of mine. The blank stare in her mossy-colored eyes releases the sobs I've been choking back.

From behind me, Zane stirs. He grips the hilt of the dagger I buried in his boot and yanks with all his might. The dagger flies free as he screams. Eliza tries to rise, but a bullet from his hand cannon pierces her and she falls.

Blood and bile rise within me, splattering across the floor as my body convulses from internal pain.

"Ms. Young," Amity says, "your vitals are failing."

My broken ribs must be the cause. With my adrenaline gone, the pain in my core erupts. Sharp, burning aches cause me to fold.

Then the main door of Black Web opens, stopping Zane's movement toward me.

"Why are you here?" Zane says, "I thought—"

My eyes blur.

Fixing my gaze, the silver-haired figure holds Ezra by his collar with an iron grip. They toss him to the floor as the doors shut behind them.

Zane turns back to me and aims the hand cannon as the convulsions continue. My mind goes in and out of blackness as I quiver beneath the pain in my gut. The memories of my parents flood inside me with everyone I ever cared for.

Zane's weapon fires, and my eyes close.

I reopen them, and his face grows pale as he looks to his chest. A blade extends through it, blood dripping off the tip.

It retracts, and he falls dead beside me.

Through my fading gaze, I find silver eyes peering down at me. The internal throbbing intensifies, and I lose consciousness.

"Ms. Young." Amity's voice breaks the fog.

My coherence comes back but quickly dips, and through my hazy vision, the person is gone, and my mother appears.

"Ariadne," a voice says.

I lie on the cold marble floor. Eliza is unconscious next to me, beside Zane's and Claire's bodies.

Everything else around me is blurred, as if I've been drugged. My movements are slow and groggy.

"Aria." My nickname travels through the haze.

The voice becomes clearer. Delicate and smooth, a voice I could never forget.

"Mom?" I ask.

Footsteps echo and through the short distance my vision can travel, my mother stands.

"Mom?" I repeat shakily.

"Hi sweetheart," she says.

Her dark wavy hair frames her slender face. Her eyes slant from the smile stretched across it.

"What's happening?" I ask. "Where am I?"

"Ms. Young," Amity says. "Ms. Young."

My mother tilts her head and kneels to lift my chin.

"Remember," she says, "everything is connected."

Iris glows, taking away my attention, and sends an electric shock through my veins. I scream as my body vibrates and the shock returns. I fall limp to the ground, unaware of what's happening.

"Ms. Young," Amity calls again.

I try to respond but can't.

Iris charges again, and I shut my eyes, tensing to endure the incoming shock.

I jolt awake with a deep inhale, causing me to choke. The pains from my ribs ignite but are dulled. Metal lingers on my tongue as I cough, spewing blood.

"Breathe, Ms. Young," Amity says. "Breathe."

My vision comes into focus, and I find I'm inside a pod. My heart thuds from not knowing where I am.

"What's happening?" I ask.

"You're going to the recovery ward, Ms. Young."

"Why?"

"An emergency embedded in my system was triggered to keep you alive, the same one that activated when you were in captivity. Combined with the emergency update that Zoe applied to Iris, you're stable. You're being taken to see her now."

The beats of my heart subside at the knowledge I haven't been captured, but the pain from fractured ribs returns with greater force, blocking my thinking. I shake from the sharpness erupting through my nerves.

Through the pain, my mother flashes in my head. I saw her. Or did I? It's hard to tell if I was dreaming, hallucinating, or if it really happened. Maybe the agony I'm in triggered my deepest wants.

"Amity, I saw her," I say.

"I know, Ms. Young."

So I'm not crazy.

"Dexter created a kickback, or essentially, a way for you to return from death."

"I died..." I can't bring myself to believe it.

"Almost, Ms. Young. But you may have seen Adalina during the small window when your brain signal was failing. She indeed was there, but only mentally. The voice you heard was mine. Your distress caused you to see your mother."

"She—you said everything is connected," I struggle to say.

"Yes, a coded message from Adalina."

"What does it mean?"

"Do you remember the data chip from the pen Adalina left with Claire?"

"Yes."

"The data transfer in your home also implanted my purpose for you, Ms. Young. Did you ever consider why I'm called Amity?"

"I never had a reason to ask."

"In its plainest form, it means peace, friendship, and understanding. However, your parents' creation means A Mind Interconnected Through the Years. I was originally a prototype, created to connect them to others in different Areas and sectors. A beacon that channeled hidden connections. It's how they remained under the radar for so long. Working against the Enlightenment."

"Everything is connected," I whisper.

"Precisely."

Amity has been the connection from the beginning. Originally serving as a communication outlet, it now serves me with the same power to guide me in my quest to avenge my parents.

My pod continues as the revelations play in my head. All white above glares through the glass encasing. Water splashes and creates a mist, letting me know we have entered Zoe's lab.

"But Amity, why tell me this now?"

"I suppose the connection I have with you only allowed me access to this once it was activated. This information was inside me, but inaccessible and unknown. Yet another encryption left behind by Adalina. However, this wasn't something for you to decrypt. It was all a cause and effect. The data chip giving my system the update, and the moment of you almost dying, gave the equation to unlock what she wanted to say."

"So it only appeared because I was dying..."

"Yes, and no. At this moment, it is that way. However, what was needed was a major shift in our connection on both ends. Perhaps it was the catalytic effect of the virus in my system in combination with your near-death experience."

I knew Amity was important to me, but I never knew how it affected the nation. I wish my parents were alive to make this all sensible.

"Furthermore, the central point of the node system was registered through the unlocked data. Your parents named it the Enlightenment Tower, where they monitor and connect every person's node—a connection they wanted to break."

I don't know what to think or feel after listening to Amity. My head feels heavy, as if it has received massive bytes of data. I thought what we found at the estate was everything my parents knew. I was wrong. They were a wealth of information, it seems, for intel on the Enlightenment. Connection to people throughout the nation, and the main place where all nodes are. Vengeance is all I ever wanted, but my path seems to connect with the dream my parents and Claire wanted.

The dream of freedom.

As I try to process, a fog creeps through the pod, and as I breathe it in, my muscles relax, making me sleepy. My mind quickly fades from thoughts of my mother, Amity, and the pain.

"You'll be okay, Ms. Young," Amity says.

My eyes close, and I drift away into my subconscious.

54

My eyes slowly open to find Eliza at my side. A gold holodevice tightly wraps her shoulder.

The lights hovering above let me know I'm on the recovery thread, the same place I was a week ago when I had a panic attack. My eyes trail back to Eliza, and bright blue eyes twinkle in the white light, making me smile.

"I thought you—"

"I'm fine," she cuts me off. "I was more worried about you. You've been out for three days."

Three days... It barely feels like a few hours. How could it have been days?

"Zoe induced a coma to repair the damage you received Ms. Young," Amity says reading my mind.

Through my mixed emotions about lost time, I smile at Amity's voice.

"How are you feeling?"

"I've seen better days."

"Apologies for the system malfunction. The virus... There was nothing that could be done."

"It's not your fault."

"Also, apologies for the amount of information I relayed to you during your duress."

My mind is foggy from the moments before this. I guess three days of unconsciousness are to blame.

Claire's blood-stained clothes haunt my thoughts, and my heart aches for her. I can't help but think it's my fault for hesitating again. My breathing shudders at the want to cry. I should have killed Zane before he had the chance to kill her.

I slowly sit up, and, like a meeting in the briefing room, the silks and the web stand at my bedside, battered and beaten.

Raelyn stands at the foot of the bed, the same way Claire did after my panic attack. Tears stain her face, yet she holds her head high. Everyone looks like they've been through hell and back, except for Zoe, who fiddles with some liquids on a side table.

"Welcome back," Raelyn says.

"Thanks." My voice cracks.

I want to mention Claire and what happened. The want to apologize for allowing her mother to die eats away at me, releasing the tears I've been holding.

Raelyn's hand lands on my feet as her eyes confirm what I can't bring myself to say. Our stares linger and end with soft smiles for each other.

"So… Three days, huh," I say. "What did I miss?"

"For starters," Dahlia says from beside Raelyn, "we have both Ezra and Trace's clone in a chamber. The clone hasn't spoken a word but is awake. Ezra, however, has yet to recover from the wounds he sustained. We're still not sure how or when he got them."

Ezra. The last thing I saw was the person with silver hair, and they threw him to the ground. Were they not working with him? If Ezra is our prisoner, the unknown person must have betrayed him.

"Ezra mentioned the clone isn't perfected," Eliza says. "So it most likely won't speak."

"Hmmm, perhaps we'll have to shut it down," Thaddeus says. He stands behind Ayster on the opposite side of Raelyn.

"That would probably be best," I say.

The idea of seeing Trace the way he is stings my heart. I still can't believe they cloned him.

"What about Ezra?" Ayster asks.

"Yeah, who caused his wounds?" Astraea adds. Her hands cross her chest as she shifts next to Eliza.

"Someone else was with him when he arrived with Zane," I say.

"Who?" Dahlia asks.

"I couldn't see their face, but they killed Zane as well."

"Ha!" Astraea shouts. "Good for them."

"Where is this person now, I wonder?" Mason, who has been quiet in the corner, asks. His sunken eyes show he's been crying for a while.

Closing my eyes, I try to think, still unsure if this person existed. I know I saw someone, but then again, I thought I saw my mother. In the moments of dying, I could have imagined other things.

"Either way, Ezra is still unconscious. Whatever they did to him has completely made him useless," Dahlia says. "However, we have news."

Everyone remains quiet, patiently waiting for her to speak. We put everything into this mission and lost Claire to it. Nothing played out how we planned, but in the back of my mind, I can't help but scratch an Enlightenment member off my list.

"Cybourne has made contact," she says. "An encrypted message was left with Ezra's body."

Cybourne, I repeat to myself.

The most unknown sector in the Area. Before Claire died, she mentioned it. With her last words, she told me and Eliza to find it.

"We need to act—" Dahlia starts.

"That'll have to wait," Zoe quickly interrupts. My eyes find her as she continues to explain. "You may not feel it right now because of the medicine I have given you, but you suffered severe internal bleeding. Your rib cage punctured your liver. Causing internal bleeding. I stemmed the flow, and you're stable now; however, you need rest." She takes a deep breath and attaches a liquid device to a cord feeding into my vein. "You'll live, but it'll take time before you're back in the field."

"How long?" Dahlia asks.

"It'll mostly depend on her, but I'd say at least two weeks."

"We need her much sooner."

"No," Raelyn says. "We need to regroup."

Everyone stares at her with wide eyes.

"She's right," Thaddeus says.

"With no director..." Eliza pauses, forming her thoughts. "We need a new plan of action for our next steps."

There's a moment of silence. It's something we've all been hovering around, too afraid to speak about what has happened: Claire, the director of Black Web. A mother and aunt. She should be here. Raelyn watches me as if she knows what I'm thinking. She smiles, and a feeling of forgiveness seeps inside. My thoughts settle, and I remember I have valuable information that they don't.

"I may have a start," I say.

Eliza's eyes move to me, and the others' follow.

"My A.I. has revealed something my parents had during their quest to end the Enlightenment."

"What is it?" Dahlia asks.

"The central point of the node system."

"Your A.I. has this information?" Thaddeus asks.

I nod as they all watch me intently.

"I believe my parents didn't rush to reveal their findings because they were looking for another way to help citizens see the truth. This is the other way. They wanted to break the node's connection to everyone."

"If it's true, that could be how we beat the Enlightenment. Your A.I. may have the key to it all," Dahlia says.

Hope erases the despair that once filled everyone's eyes. Their heads slightly raise, and strength fills the room at my words.

"I think we may have a new director," Eliza says.

"Who?" I ask.

"We follow you," Raelyn says.

"What?" I ask. "Where?"

"Everywhere." Mason steps forward.

"Those assholes will pay," Ayster says.

"Little badass in charge," Astraea says. "Hell yeah!"

"It's what Claire would have wanted," Raelyn adds.

"No," I say. "I can't. I don't know how."

"You can, Ms. Young," Amity says. "This is how you'll end the Enlightenment."

Eliza smiles and nods her approval. My head surveys the web, and they all smile, waiting for my answer.

My heart rattles inside my chest, thumping from the anxiety and pressure. The ache in my ribs returns as I try to gain strength. Everyone looks hopeful, and I don't know what to say.

"As we take time to regroup and fully form a plan," Dahlia says, "I think it's important to know I found who left the encrypted message with Ezra."

"Who was it?" I ask, using this as a distraction.

"I traced the message back to the unknown sector; someone transmitted it under the code name Glitch."

Glitch.

The name triggers a memory, one buried deep inside of me.

'If I ever become a hacker, my code name will be Glitch.'
It can't be.

A knock on the door breaks the silence in the room.

"I've invited them here," Dahlia says, stepping aside.

The door glides open as the unknown person walks in. They remove their hood, and my eyes can't believe it. Silver hair, different from the black I remember, falls down her shoulders as she steps inside. Smokey eyes force me to stare as the memories thrash in my head.

"Nexia?" Eliza asks, seeing the shock in my eyes.

"Nexia isn't your real name, is it?" the girl says quickly.

"Wren?" I gasp.

She winks and reveals that same smile I will never forget—the smile I thought was gone forever.

As she tilts her head to examine me, she says,

"We need to talk."

ACKNOWLEDGMENTS

Ahhhh! It's finally complete! My debut novel which has been in the works for years! What started as a project to heal from a very tough time in life, turned into a dream I could have never imagined. I am in awe and beyond excited for what's to come from this journey. Before I get into the people who have made this book happen, I wanted to share why I wrote this type of book: a dystopian novel. Ariadne Young came to me after I read laws about a world where the government would watch everything people did on the internet and then I thought, what would happen if they went beyond the internet. One of my favorite books is 1984 by George Orwell, so you can definitely see the influence there! But, to put it simply, I wrote this to shed light on the world and what could possibly happen with technology if not held in check and of course power. Okay okay, without further ado, the people who made it all possible!

Coded wouldn't have made it out of the notebook I started back in 2018 if it weren't for the love of my life, Madisyn, who listened and nurtured my strength when I thought this book was nothing. Without your love, support, and wonderfully cooked meals, this book would still be a draft. All my love and appreciation. Madisyn keeps me grounded when I'm too far gone in my writing, but she's also the one that inspires most of my ideas! P.S. Eliza is inspired by her.

My mother and sister were the first to hear the idea I crafted years ago. Thank you for your love and support from the beginning, when I thought I was alone. You both helped me through some dark times, and I couldn't be more grateful to have you both by my side.

To the college friends who made sure I wouldn't give up on my dreams, I thank you. You have no idea how much your words have pushed me to keep going. I won't forget them.

My colleagues at work, you are not forgotten. Your words of aspiration have helped me learn so much about life and myself every day. Thank you all for your wisdom and support.

And to my readers, thank you for taking the chance to read a debut novel from someone unknown. This book—I hope—is the start of a journey I will cherish to my core, and with you all supporting me and reading the wild stories I plucked from my mind, I'm sure it'll be a hell of a ride.

ABOUT THE AUTHOR

Born and raised in Miami, Florida. David always had a creative mindset. He has a Bachelor's degree in Fine Arts, where he found his love for writing. With a newfound passion for storytelling, *'Coded'* came to life. When he's not buried in a journal, taking notes, he watches and reads anything Sci-Fi/Fantasy related. David lives in Nashville, Tennessee with his fiancé and Cosima—a cat afraid of the world, just like some characters he reads and writes about.

https://www.authordaviddmyers.com

https://dashboard.mailerlite.com/for
ms/1144420/147412393195996354/share